SPACEBORN

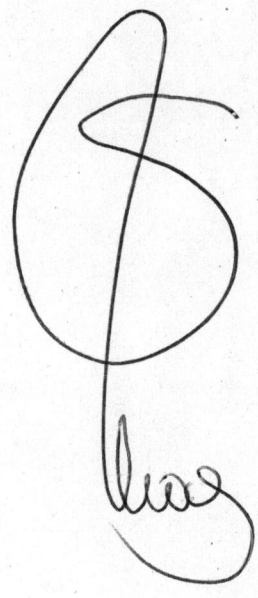

SPACEBORN

SPACEBORN

ILIAS SIAMETIS

Copyright © 2024 by Ilias Siametis

All rights reserved.

ISBN: 978-1-3999-6596-5

No part of this publication may be reproduced, distributed, or transmitted in any form or by any means, including photocopying, recording, or other electronic or mechanical methods, without the prior written permission of the author, except in the case of brief quotations embodied in reviews and other non-commercial uses permitted by copyright law.

This is a work of fiction. All of the characters, names, incidents and dialogue are either a product of the author's imagination or used fictitiously.

To Neil, who ignited my love for science.

The Sagan

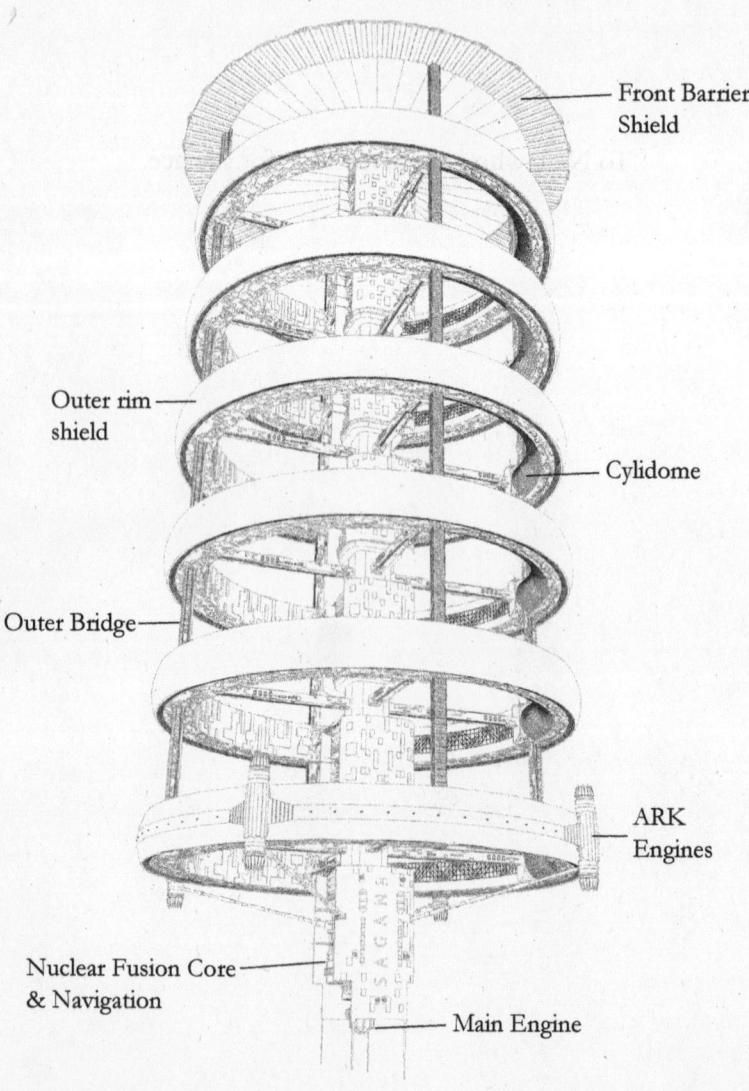

Ring Section

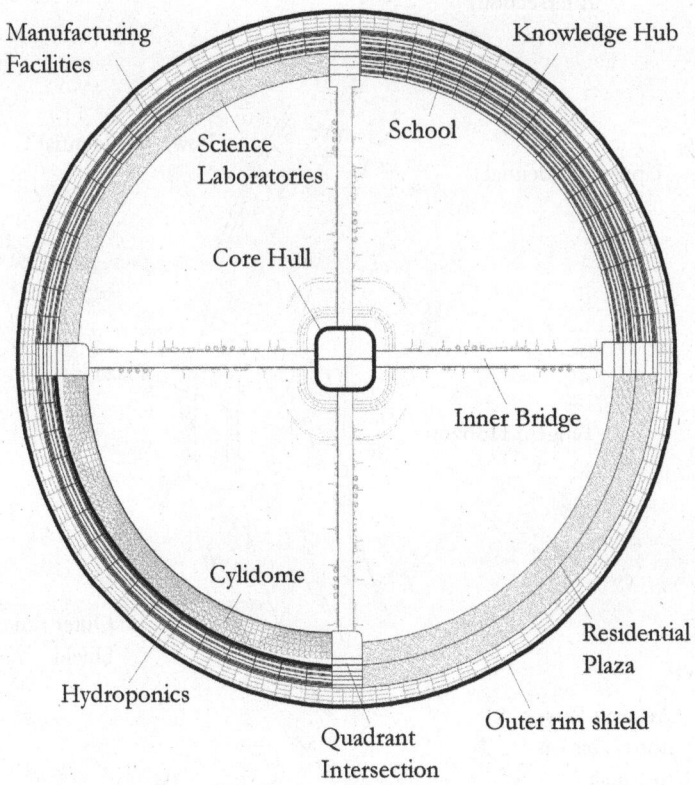

Residential Quadrant Section

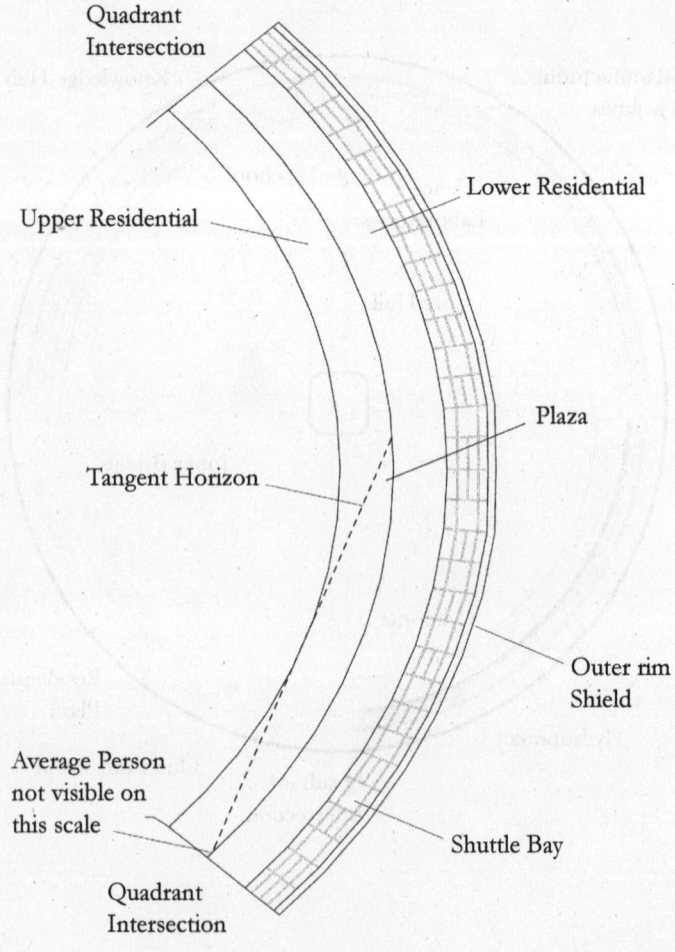

PART 1

RINGS OF SECRETS

CHAPTER 1
— Julian —

KNOWLEDGE HUB – RING 4

The structure at the rear of the ship was almost complete, although Julian couldn't keep his eyes on it for more than a few seconds before feeling his breakfast coming up his throat. A dozen builder-bots were floating around the outer rim of Ring Six, the blue plume of their tiny thrusters barely distinguishable against the black abyss they were leaving behind. He squeezed his eyes shut and pressed his temple with his fingers. That was surprisingly more than he could usually handle of the endless spinning of the *Sagan*'s Rings—the synchronous dance of trailing lights against the menacing tapestry of the black void.

Two bright green irises came into focus in front of him, their yellow streaks around the pupils perfectly resembling the golden, stellar dust of an emerald nebula.

"Do you need a bucket?" Rachel said while trying to stifle a smirk. She didn't succeed, her mockery plastered all over her round face.

"Shut up." He swallowed with difficulty and sat back in his chair. "What do you think they're building out there?" He tried to steal another glance at the peculiar structure that followed the shape of the last Ring.

"Don't know, don't care. I have more important things to worry about right now."

Like what? He stopped himself before blurting the arrogant sneer. There was nothing important going on aboard the *Sagan*, even their very existence was born out of necessity instead of a natural consequence of people falling in love and starting a family.

"Alex didn't show up for class this morning," she whispered as if the teacher hadn't already noticed her brother's absence.

"He's not here?" Julian turned around and scanned his classmates. Alex was younger but his aptitude for physics was so evident that they shared the class. He usually sat with his girlfriend towards the back of the room but she was alone this time, resting her head inside her palms as her black hair covered her half closed eyes. "Priya is back there," he shrugged. The girl looked defeated—or maybe just tired. She had slumped over the desk, her black eyes vacant under heavy eyelids.

"At least he's not with her, wherever he is. That's good news."

Julian pressed his lips together and cocked his head, trying to convey as little judgement as possible. "She's not that bad." He raised his chin over his shoulder to the direction of the brunette girl. "She seems... sad," he felt his brows furrowing at the tiny spasm of Priya's back. Was she crying?

"Mr Walker, would you like to offer an answer?" He jolted at the teacher's interruption.

To what question? He didn't dare say it out loud and tried to deduce it from the colourful hologram in front of the transparent board. What did Sol, Terra and Luna have in common and where were the rest of the Sol system planets? The sun looked tiny but he knew it was actually massive—able to fit a million Earths inside it, producing radiation that would disintegrate anything that came close. No, the question must have been about something that affected all three celestial bodies. *Gravity? Orbits?* He noticed the Earth's oceans coming out of the planet significantly on opposite sides, an intentional exaggeration rather than the reality. *TIDES!*

"Uhm, the Earth is rotating inside that bulge of water caused by the sun and the moon," he started, pointing at the planet he had never seen with his own eyes, biting his lip to buy himself more time to remember the rest. "The sun's gravity is pulling Earth's water on one side, the moon is pulling another way and the Earth is rotating in between these bulges." He almost cheered despite Ms Carter's unimpressed expression.

"That's correct but quite simple," the teacher rolled her eyes sideways and moved past her pedestal. Her worn heels clanked on the acrylic floor, every step exposing the torn fabric underneath. Probably second or even third generation shoes. "Anyone else?" She gave him a disapproving look but at least she hadn't figured out he wasn't actually paying attention. "Lydia, how about you?"

The girl who sat diagonally behind him tossed a strand of her thick, caramel hair over her shoulder and sat straight. "Even though the force exerted by the sun is somewhat two hundred times stronger than that of the moon, Luna produces almost twice as strong tidal forces on Earth because of its close proximity…"

The rest was just noise as Julian couldn't take his eyes off the series of freckles that painted her smooth light brown skin. Hues of orange stretched from one cheek to the other, leaving little blotches of red over her small, upward nose.

She met his eyes for a split second but didn't stop her intricate explanation.

Julian turned back to his desk, an uncomfortable warmth emanating from his face as he raised a hand to cover himself. *Good job, no one can see you now.* He brought the other hand to his mouth, biting the skin around his thumbnail.

"Wonderful, Lydia," Ms Carter exclaimed, returning to the raised platform behind the hologram. "You can find everything you need for the assignment in the Knowledge Hub. I don't want to see any plagiarism or AI work," she warned, her eyes darting across the room. "Also, it's due next Tuesday."

Ms Carter's words brought a unanimous dissatisfaction to the class while she allowed a smirk to appear on her face, clearly enjoying their misery.

Julian tapped his finger on the plastic surface of his desk and with a quick stroke logged himself out of the panel. The blue rectangle shrank into a thin horizontal line before disappearing into a single spot, leaving the desk white and boring.

"Please, do not forget your attendance to the Core Hull tomorrow is mandatory." The teacher raised her voice to make sure she was heard over the commotion of everyone getting ready to leave. "Most of you won't get another chance to see the main drive after the Halfway event."

"Unless we become scientists, right Julian?" Lydia softly grazed his arm as she passed in front of him, her fingers warm against his skin. The corners of his lips were raised out of reflex to her smile but he couldn't formulate a sentence in time. Lydia had already reached the door.

"Rachel, can I talk to you for a second?" Ms Carter approached their shared desk. She hadn't addressed him but her presence above him made him uneasy, like he was in trouble too. "You know I am forced to report Alex's absence, right?" She leant over them, brows raised and eyes misshapen from worry.

"I've got no idea where he is but Alex doesn't miss classes," Rachel said, locking her jaw and hiding her lips inside her mouth.

"I know, that's why I'll give him the benefit of the doubt for now, but if he's not there for the field trip, he's looking at a minimum twenty points deduction."

"He'll be there," Rachel said sharply and Julian turned his attention back to Priya's desk where Lucas had now joined her.

The overly muscular boy was almost twice Priya's size, looming over her like a statue of the old world. Her long nails were ticking on the desk in a steady melody and she was now sitting straight, her head slightly bowed and facing away from the notorious bully. Julian wondered if he had ever seen them together before when Lucas turned to him with a scowl. "What are you looking at, little monkey? Ooh Ooh Aah Aah!"

Julian hated his mother for calling him by that nickname in front of everyone a few years ago. Most of his classmates had forgotten about it but not Lucas, never Lucas.

"No clever comeback this time?" Lucas pressed when Julian looked away.

The words never came to him, only insults. He gritted his teeth, pretending to clear his side of the desk even though only his stylus was there.

"Come on, we have more important stuff to do than arguing with Lucas." Rachel nudged his arm. She was right but the urge to utter his comeback was burning his insides. *Cyber freak*. The words almost slipped his mouth as he made his way to the entrance.

"That's right, take a walk," Lucas raised his chin up in a motion to shoo him out of the class. His arm was around Priya's shoulders, his fat fingers clutched around her forearm, completely covering her birth control mark. The way her lips had curled and her shoulders had slumped inwards gave away her discomfort. But then her dark, brown eyes shot up to meet his and her expression morphed into one of fear.

Rachel dragged him forward and out of the class. Would he have stayed to help the girl if she hadn't? That would require standing up to Lucas. He couldn't stop thinking about it all the way out of the recreation quadrant, an uneasy sense of guilt creeping into his subconscious to become a relentless voice of contempt.

Rachel was walking beside him but her focus was solely on the roller in her hand.

"Hey, don't go too fast," she finally broke the silence when they reached the outer bridge connecting the two Rings.

"You know I don't like these bridges," he complained.

"Your grandfather's story again? Isn't it at least another fifty years or so until the next—what was it—*out* cloud?"

"*Oort* cloud... Still, there may be other objects out there, you don't know. All it took was a tiny speck of asteroid to kill those four people back then."

"I'm sure we'll be fine, no need to be scared."

"I'm not scared... just well informed," he countered but it came out as a whine.

"A little bit scared." She chuckled and softly punched his arm twice.

"Whatever gets you off that roller."

"I'm trying to find where Alex is, Julian. It's not like I'm trying to finish the last stage of fucking Dragon Quest!"

"Oh..." he muttered, regretting his choice of words. "What about your parents?"

"Both at work."

"You know, he's probably still in his room, sleeping or..." He trailed off, not knowing what else to suggest.

"That's the thing," she thankfully cut him off. "I didn't tell you earlier but he wasn't in his room this morning. I went to yell at him for being late but he wasn't there. I'm starting to think he spent the night somewhere else."

"He'll show up, don't worry." He waved a dismissive hand. "It's not like he can leave this place," he added and his lips curled as if he had stuffed a lemon in his mouth. No, there was no escape from the *Sagan*, no exotic lands to visit, no new places to see, just the almost identical ring structures that revolved around the main axis of the ship.

When she didn't say anything, he glanced at her out of the corner of his eye to see where his argument had landed. Her cheeks were inflated like a balloon, air seeping out in small puffs through her gritted teeth. "Let's go to the Hub," he suggested, "You said you wanted to get some painting done."

"Oh! That reminds me, let's pass by your residential first. I think Bolek's latest artwork's there." She suddenly perked up. "He does this amazing thing after he finishes a piece where he sends out a riddle to his followers with the location and I'm pretty sure it's around there somewhere."

There was a comforting peace in the residential quadrant around that time of the light cycle, with only a few kids running around—chasing each other giggling. The long strip of windows on either side of the ground floor provided a clear view of the ship and the blackness that surrounded it, steadily pressuring and bending the hull as it patiently waited for the inevitable first crack. They stayed by the left pilotis where the residential blocks were above them and the path to the end of the quadrant wasn't obstructed.

"So where is your councilman's painting?" Julian asked, his eyes studying the worn metal tiles and broken plastic covers of the soffit above them for signs of colour.

"He's not... I mean he *is* a councilman but he's not defined by it. He was a successful painter way before he joined the council." Rachel revolved around herself with every step until she came to a stop and gasped.

Julian tried to figure out what exactly she was looking at but all he could see were splashes of different colours on the floor and wall.

He moved closer to her as the colours started blending and uniting into a shape, until he stood behind her and the mural revealed itself—an arm leading into a fist, apparently levitating on air. There were six bracelets wrapped around it, all in different colours and linked together like chains. Thick black letters formed the vertical caption that read 'United we stand' that somehow seemed to be hovering in front of the painting. He took a few steps to the left and the mural disappeared into seemingly random brushes of colour.

"This is so weird," he exclaimed, scratching his head.

"It's amazing, isn't it? I knew even you would appreciate it." She crossed her arms and shifted her weight to one leg. "He calls these *spatial explorations*." She waved both hands in opposite directions. "The mural comes alive from a specific perspective. And did you notice the caption and the six bracelets? I think he means that people from all *Sagan*'s Rings need the same perspective, as in the same mentality in order to be united. I totally get his art," she chuckled triumphantly and squeezed her hands together at her chest.

Julian let out a strong puff of air from his nose with a smile. It was always so funny when she got so over-excited, either clasping her hands, clapping or even jumping around like a kid.

When she finally calmed down, they moved towards the end of the residential quadrant and into the recreation one.

The main corridor here was way narrower than the residential district, with countless doors on each side and a ceiling that would only go a few metres high, hiding the true height of the Ring. The walls were filled with holo-signs and arrows that supposedly made it easier to navigate through this labyrinth of architectural complexity. It had definitely seen better days, likely before Julian was born. Now, there were missing tiles on the fake ceiling where cables snaked their way out of their containment to hang naked from the opening. The smell of rusted metal and burnt bioplastic made his nose twitch. He tried to remember the last time repairs were done around his Ring—around any Ring. All of the ship's resources were dedicated to the renovations of Ring Six and the structure around its outer rim. His dad was involved in the project—or at least he'd heard him talking about it. He was the archivist after all, which meant he had to maintain and log all the activities that happened throughout the ship, filtering through the mundane, unimportant ones in order to keep a comprehensive record of life on their journey to Aquanis. He wouldn't tell him what it was though. No one knew.

The doors slid open to present the grandeur of the interior of the seemingly rectangular double height space. It stretched the whole width of the Ring with window strips along each side of the stencil decorated white walls. The *Sagan* was already more than a hundred Earth years old but this particular section seemed to be very well preserved in comparison to other parts that even lacked painting. There were no visible pipes running the length of the walls or random indentations with protruding air ducts.

He took in the beauty with a deep inhale, the sound of shoes on white acrylic floor panels putting an end to the monotonous clanging of loose metal tiles across the rest of the Ring. The ceiling was the same material as the floor—white, glossy, and reflective. The elliptical glass pods met at the top with a series of spotlights that followed the shape of the pods and arced in the direction of others, almost connecting with their neighbouring lights. A magnificent architectural dance of curves that got frozen in time, bound to perform that same move forever.

Julian peered through the glass rooms to the other side, focusing between the anatomic VR armchairs at the back and the two sets of eyes that were studying him from inside one of the pods. Two men in their forties, sharply dressed in the *Sagan*'s formalwear—the blue tracksuit and the white blazer.

He walked towards the semi-circular counter at the lobby area, stealing curious glances at them until the bold letters on the news screen caught his attention.

"Another person was reported missing earlier this morning. Authorities are not ready to release any further information at this point. If you see something that doesn't look right, please report it to the Administration server."

A pulse thumped inside his chest. He instinctively turned to Rachel, her unblinking eyes fixed on the announcement, her lower lip between her teeth as she leant forward. She was thinking the same thing.

"We didn't report him missing, Julian," she snapped when she caught him staring. "It's not Alex, ok?"

"I didn't say…" he fumbled for the right words to defend his hypothesis.

She clicked her tongue and sucked her cheek. "Come on, let's do something."

Julian pressed on the surface of the counter to reveal the booking options and touched the one that read 'VRA'.

"Seriously? The chair again?" Rachel complained with a soft punch at his arm.

"Well, I like the chair, you can book one as well and we can go in together."

"I want to do something myself, not sit my ass in VR all day." She complained with a distinct eye roll as the console chimed with a single tone, signalling her defeat.

"I thought you were going to paint something. Especially after all that inspiration from Bolek's artwork."

"Pfft, go enjoy your little virtual world," she muttered and stomped her way behind the glass pods.

He made his way to the VRAs, feeling the piercing eyes of the two gentlemen still locked on him. Relying only on his peripheral vision for verification, he suppressed the notion to look, uncomfortable to make contact again. When he caught a glimpse of them getting ready to leave, he finally snuck inside the armchair.

He sometimes wished this was his bed as it anatomically embraced his whole body, arching downwards at his knees while creating a comfortable curve for his lower back continuing upwards to support his head. He grabbed the headpiece and everything went dark.

"Welcome Julian." The soft feminine voice clearly lacked emotion but he didn't expect anything more from a VI.

The virtual curtains parted and he spawned at the beach of his home page, watching the waves lapping back and forth, listening to their exhales as they rhythmically came crashing down on the wet sand.

The sea extended as far as his eyes could see, merging with a sky of a lighter blue on the horizon and glistening like stars in the presence of the midday sun. He wondered if Aquanis had beaches similar to the ones on Earth. Maybe its oceans were greener or the sky had deeper hues of blue—there was more oxygen in its atmosphere than Earth so it wasn't too far-fetched to imagine a navy sky even during the day.

What a pointless thought. He wouldn't see it. He wouldn't even see the gas giants of the solar system, he wouldn't be part of the exploration and colonisation. He wouldn't feel the thrill of discovery or the sense of achievement. He was doomed in this unfair fate where he served only as a vessel for the next generation to be able to carry on the human species on the first planet outside the home solar system. He never knew Earth like his great grandfather did and he would never know Aquanis as his grandkids would. It was a cruel destiny that he should bear the rest of his life on that ship.

He had taken his small boat to the open waters when his headset was violently removed and the virtual world ceased to exist. He blinked a few times to adjust to the brightness of reality and rubbed his eyes before the fuzzy silhouette next to him took the shape of his ginger friend.

"It *is* Alex!" Rachel didn't even give him a chance to complain. Her eyes were restless, wide and unblinking while her brows were pushed together like tectonic plates forming mountains that wrinkled her forehead. He suspected as much already but didn't want to believe it. The sandy beach and the deep, blue ocean had only provided a brief distraction.

"The missing person from the headline?" He groaned as he slid out of the armchair and sat at its edge.

"Yeah, my mum didn't tell me because she said she didn't want me to worry. Fuck, it's on every screen of the ship, of course I would find out."

"Are you serious?"

"YES!" Her green eyes almost bulged out. "His roller is unavailable and my mum said they're going through the cameras to find him. I fucking knew it..." She paced in a circle in front of him, finally coming to a stop, her hands on her waist and her gaze fixed on the spotlights above them. "I fucking knew it the second I saw that headline."

"Rach, I'm so sorry. What are you going to do?" He managed to say, a hollow statement but the only one that would come to mind.

"I need to run to Administration. They need to talk to me."

"I'll come with you then." He stood up, only to be met with Rachel's palm facing him.

"Thanks but it's only family members at this point. They wouldn't even let you in."

"I'm sure everything will be ok. You know Alex, he's probably laying on the grass somewhere in the Cylidome."

"Since yesterday?" Her foot was twitching, her whole body restless, her chest heaving deep breaths as her nostrils flared for more air. "Sorry… I'll talk to you later," she sighed and rushed to the exit.

Julian pulled himself off the chair and realised the Hub wasn't as bright as when he had gone in his virtual world. The pale, orange hues of the early evening light cycle scattered on every reflective surface, drenching the Hub in a calming ambience—it did little to calm him.

The way home seemed longer as he pondered what might have happened to Alex. There had been over a hundred recorded disappearances in the last few years but no one was ever found. It always started with a big headline and community engagement that would eventually die out after months of fruitless efforts.

He suddenly felt naked and exposed, walking alone during the evening light cycle. The hooded figure sitting at the benches behind the plaza kiosks didn't help with the eerie premonition and he contemplated on a detour through the stair core. Where was everyone else? Even the robotic waiters at the food stalls were inert. Passing Kieran Bolek's mural, he couldn't shake the feeling that he was being watched—eyes stuck on his back, making every new step quicker than the last.

He placed his hand on the rectangular pad next to the door handle and pressed against it until it was filled with green light, followed by a short buzz. The living room was completely dark and Julian tried to blindly navigate around the furniture by memory in case his parents were already in bed. It did seem odd that the house was empty. His father wouldn't usually retire until a few hours after red lights. He'd stay in his study, reading a book in original paper form, despite everyone else mocking him for holding on to so much *waste of space*. His family was one of the lucky ones to have a special apartment, equipped with an extra room for his father's studies and he always made good use of it, keeping it tidy and clean—apart from his desk which was always covered with piles of thick, heavy books and pads for his notes.

He climbed on his bed, kneeling to look out the window occupying the whole length of the wall above his pillow. He gazed at the immense size of the *Sagan*, barely lit with flickering lights along its structure. The three Rings ahead were spinning at the same speed as his in a synchronised dance around the ship's main cylindrical hull while the stars seemed to rotate in the opposite direction. And that wasn't even all of it, there were two more Rings on the other side behind him.

No more than a few seconds had passed when he started feeling the usual excruciating pain inside his forehead that made his eyes feel heavy, compelling him to look away and fall head first into his pillow. He extended his hand behind him to blindly touch a button that brought the grey shutter down, cladding the room in total darkness.

Was Rachel still at the Administration? He couldn't possibly relate to what she was going through. He was an only child. He'd always wanted a little brother when he was younger but his parents had been removed from the birth queue after his mum had passed thirty. Rachel had felt like a sister sometimes but it wasn't the same.

His thoughts were interrupted by a distorted clanking from the living room, followed by footsteps and distant whispers. He brought his torso up and bent his neck to listen. The whispers quickly turned into a loud, heated dialogue between his parents, barely audible through the walls.

"What were you thinking, hanging out with those people?" His dad almost shouted.

"We were just having some drinks, what's your problem?"

"Do you take me for a fool, Freddie? I know everything that happens on this ship. These crazies are not to be trusted."

"They are people just like you and me Scott."

"People whose ideas can ruin everything so many generations have been trying to preserve."

"How can you not see that they have a point?"

"What point, Freddie? You know what, I can't deal with this again."

"Fine!" His mum yelled, followed by the loud thud of a door shutting.

Julian waited for a few minutes of silence to pass before falling back to his bed with a sigh. He grabbed his roller and reeled the transparent screen out from its cylindrical encasement until it was flat on his lap, tapping on Rachel's portrait to craft a message before turning to the side and closing his eyes.

CHAPTER 2
— RACHEL —
ADMINISTRATION - RING 3

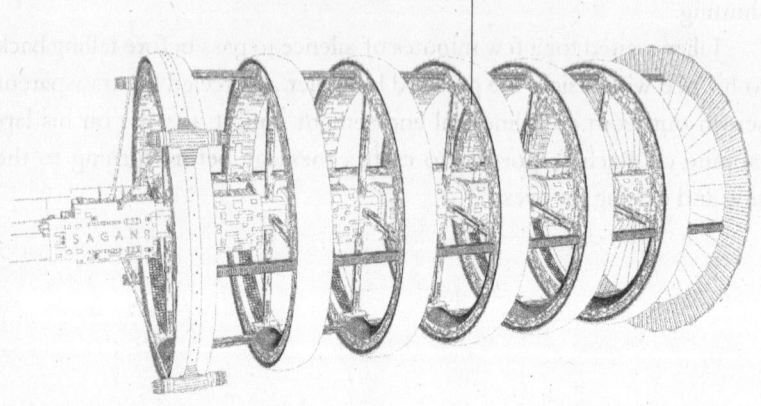

"Any news? Let me know if you hear something, ok? My parents are fighting again so I probably won't sleep any time soon."

Julian's message couldn't have come at a worse time. Right in the middle of a screaming match between her own parents, the administration officers, the receptionist and even some passers-by. Her mother had leant over the front desk sputtering insults to the pale, blonde man while her father was seconds away from starting a fight with the fat, uniformed officer with the bushy, black beard.

"Ma'am, it's too early to know for sure," the receptionist said, cowering behind his monitors.

"My son is somewhere out there, scared and alone." Her voice cracked and the lump inside Rachel's throat grew heavier. "How can your cameras not find him, they're everywhere!"

"Trust me, we're doing everything we can. We're trying…"

"Try harder!"

"Grace, calm down," her father said as he approached the desk, placing a hand at her mum's back that was immediately shrugged away. He frowned and twisted his mouth, his nostrils flaring with annoyance. "They'll take us in for some questions and we'll take it from there." He touched her again—harder this time—pulling her away from the reception and enclosing her in his arms. "One step at a time."

"My boy, Ollie. Where is my boy?"

"We'll find him... I promise," her dad said, caressing her mum's hair but Rachel knew it was bullshit—hollow words from a hollow man.

"What if we don't? They never found any of the others." Her mum couldn't help it any longer and broke down, sobbing.

Rachel was suddenly aware of her own breathing. Each shaky inhale was a struggle on its own as her lungs tried their best to reach their capacity. Her stomach was contracted and her back spasmed. The more she tried to understand what was happening to her, the more she felt her body trembling. She forcefully blinked to wash away the cold droplets that had gathered at the corner of her eyes and joined her parents in the middle of the atrium.

"Mum... we'll find him." She nodded a few times and stole her away from her father, wrapping her inside her own arms instead.

"He didn't say anything to you this morning?"

Rachel bit the inside of her bottom lip and shook her head. She could have easily told the truth but the words wouldn't come out. Her mum wasn't in a mental state that could handle her lying. Was it even lying if she was just omitting the truth? She had been in Alex's room that morning and he wasn't there, that was all. Maybe she was just scared of being screamed at like that poor receptionist.

"Mr and Missus Watson?" A well presented man in his thirties stood next to them. His hands were locked behind his back, wrinkling his spotless blue suit around the shoulders. His sharp jawline was sparkling from a clean shave, making the bruise under his eye more prominent. His sleek, black hair seemed to have taken ages to brush, still wet and stroked backwards. "I'm deputy director Rendall but you can call me Javier. I'll be personally taking over this investigation."

"Mr Rend... Javier." Her mother offered him an uncomfortable smile, wiping the tears and snot with her sleeve. "Is there any new information?"

"I'm afraid not yet but we're..."

"Look then!" Her mum threw her arms in the air. "Check every damned camera there is, every log. Swab the whole ship for DNA traces, I don't care."

"Unfortunately, it's not that simple," the deputy director said with a downward curl of his lip. "The cameras contain sensitive information that would jeopardise privacy laws. It's up to the AI to shift through the data. No human can have access to those feeds."

"Are you telling me you can't look for my son because of a technicality?" Her mum raised her voice again.

"Grace, please. Yelling won't help Alex." Her dad placed a hand on her mum's shoulder but she shook it off again, her whole body shaking. She seemed moments away from losing it completely.

"I understand this is a difficult time for you," Javier paused for a sympathetic nod and a tired sigh. "Trust me, we'll do everything in our power to find your son."

"Mum, please!" Rachel finally spoke up but her voice came out cracked and shaky. "We're wasting time talking about it here. How can we help, Javier?" She asked, turning to the dapper man.

"I'll need to interview all of you as well as any close friends or romantic partners."

"Priya... I knew it," she muttered under her breath. If you're looking for a suspect, Alex's girlfriend, Priya should be number one. She always got him in trouble, I'm sure it's no different this time."

"I'll keep this under consideration." Javier forced a smile which probably meant he wouldn't. "Now if you follow me, I'd like to take your statements."

Her mother went in first and Rachel sat in the lobby with her father. If he had anything to say, he was keeping it to himself. What was there to say anyway? He had opened his mouth a couple of times but hesitated to speak to her. At least he was there for once. It had only taken the disappearance of his son to get him off his lazy armchair.

She drew a deep breath and steadily let it out from her mouth.

Where are you Alex? The last thing she had told him was to fuck off when he had gotten in her room the previous night. Maybe he had wanted to tell her where he was going or something else important but she never gave him a chance. What a shitty sister. In her defence, he hadn't even knocked though.

An officer came out of the gate and gestured to her dad to follow him. He didn't even glance at Rachel, just stood up and went in with the admin.

She was alone in the atrium now. Maybe having Julian keep her company wasn't such a bad idea after all, she could have really used a hug. It was too late now. The administration might have been brightly lit but the rest of the ship outside the glass curtain-wall was bathed in the dim red of the night cycle. Her eyes felt cold and dry—it was either the exhaustion or the crying. She squeezed them shut and pressed with her thumb. When she opened them, two more silhouettes had joined the atrium.

"Rachel?" Lucas asked as he stepped back to study her. The fair, blonde girl next to him did the same. She was around her age but Rachel didn't recognise her which was weird. She was definitely from Ring One or Two.

"What happened to *little dragon*? I preferred it," Rachel scoffed, focusing back on the burly boy.

"I just didn't expect to see you here." Lucas' voice was somehow different, softer than his usual growling.

"Same goes for you. Did you run out of people to torment?" She snickered, shaking her head and raising her eyebrows.

"Never," he gloated.

"What are you doing here at this hour?"

"None of your business." Came the answer, sharp as a knife.

"Did you come to help with Alex's investigation?" She snorted a laugh and waved her hand, crossing her legs. "What am I saying, you don't give a fuck about anyone but yourself."

"Who are you to talk about Luke like that?" The blonde girl got in front of him and pointed a finger at Rachel. "You don't even know him!"

"You mean there's more to know than… this?" She traced a circle in the air with her finger while pointing at him and the girl almost lunged forward.

"Katey, chill babe," Lucas said, digging his fingers on the girl's shoulder, his hand almost bigger than her entire face.

Lucas was no threat to her, for all his bullying and cursing he would never touch a woman. That Katey girl however was clearly unpredictable.

The deputy director came out of the gate and beckoned Rachel over. His eyes widened for a second when he took notice of the couple and he mouthed something to them.

"Do you know these people?" Rachel asked as she approached him.

"Lucas is a regular here. Let me guess…" he turned to him, "Another assault?"

Lucas hesitated but eventually agreed, bobbing his head around while Katey was still fixated on Rachel. Katey—that was too cute a name for such an angry girl.

"You know the drill, talk to reception and I'll see you later," Javier said and softly guided Rachel towards the glass door.

"Where are my parents?" she asked as they walked through the transparent partitions that divided the offices.

"Your father is still being interviewed and your mother…" He pointed at the kitchen area at the far end. "She refuses to leave the office until we find your brother."

"Is she ok? Can I talk to her?"

"There's going to be plenty of time later. Try to focus on your interview for now." He opened the metal door for her and gestured inside the dark room.

"Thanks, Javier," she said before going through the threshold.

The four spotlights on the ceiling came to life, preset to a warmer white than the rest of Administration. The one directly above her flickered annoyingly but she didn't pay too much attention to it as she sat on the brown, curved chair. She crossed her arms and allowed her eyes to dart around the monotonous metallic tiles that comprised the floor and walls. There were no cameras, no monitors, no panels, the entire room was empty other than the small table and the two chairs.

The door creaked open and Katey sat opposite to her, grinding the chair closer and closer to the table. She was wearing the admin's uniform, the blue pants, the white shirt, the cyan vest, the navy jacket with her name embroidered above her chest, the whole attire. She rolled up the sleeves and fixed the collar of her jacket. Her skin was smoother than Rachel had previously observed, it wasn't just her face; she didn't even have hairs on her arms or freckles or the random mole, it almost seemed unnatural.

"So... Miss Watson," Katey started, "When was the last time you saw or spoke to Alex?"

"Nu-uh, I'm not doing this with you. Where is Javier?"

"I understand we started on the wrong foot. Had I known you're the sister of the missing kid I wouldn't have behaved so... poorly." She leant over the table and met her eyes, slightly tilting her head. That was a huge understatement but Rachel blew past it, letting the girl continue. "I'm sorry for that," she said sitting back in her chair, "But I really am a senior administration officer. I suggest we forget about all that for the sake of your brother." She narrowed her piercing blue eyes with the tiniest hint of a smile as if she was mocking her.

"I can't trust anyone who associates themselves with Lucas Bjorgen."

"Never judge a book by its cover, Miss Watson."

"Drop the *miss*. You're what, four-five years older than me?"

"More like twenty." She smiled broadly but her face didn't wrinkle. *How is her face so tight? Does she even have muscles in there?*

"Can we start talking about Alex now? Time is not on our side." Katey suggested.

She was right about that last part and no matter how much she already hated her, finding Alex was more important.

"I last saw him last night."

"So he was in the house for the night cycle?"

"I think so. Although he had left in the morning when I went to wake him up for school. I don't know if he left during the night or very very early."

"Good, good. You see? That wasn't so hard now, was it?"

Rachel took a long inhale and held the breath inside. Every part of her body screamed to launch forward, climb on the table and tear her stupid golden hair off. *That patronising bitch!*

"Did your brother mention any plans to you?"

"No." She finally exhaled.

"Have you noticed anything unusual in your brother's behaviour lately?"

"No."

"Does your brother have any medical problems or mental health conditions?"

"No."

"Has your brother ever been involved in any criminal activity?"

"No."

"Does your brother have a history with drug abuse?"

"No."

The spotlight above her flickered again and she almost jumped from her seat.

"It's ok, don't be scared. It does this sometimes." Katey glanced at the ceiling. "Do you need some water maybe?" She offered, her soft, sympathetic voice carrying a distinct tone of sarcasm.

"No," she said louder than before and continued to tear apart little pieces of skin from inside her mouth.

"Does your brother…"

"Oh, shut up! Just… shut up," She finally snapped, banging both her fists on the table. "Instead of focusing on what may be wrong with him, how about we talk about where he might actually be now?"

"This is standard procedure, Rachel. I understand you're emotional at the moment but you need to trust that we know what we're doing."

"Like you knew what you were doing with all the other missing people?" She blurted what her mum had feared. What she had thought already but didn't dare utter it up until now.

"They are still open investigations. No one has given up on them."

"This is a waste of time." She stood up and leant with both hands on the table. "Alex used to hang around the Cylidome in Ring Four. There's a clearing around the 87th long and 452nd wide beams."

"That's some very… interesting information." She paused to write something on her roller. "We'll investigate as soon as possible." Her sentence was positive but her fake smile betrayed her lie.

"You're not going to check any of that, are you?"

"We will… after we follow up on any actual leads."

"Fuck this!" She pushed the table but it didn't budge, barely producing a screeching groan against the floor. "And fuck you!" She pointed at the blonde woman before storming out, banging the metal door as hard as she could on its frame.

Her mum wasn't in the kitchen anymore but Lucas was still at the reception, talking to a brunette girl this time instead of the clerk.

"You still here?" Rachel spat, still fuming from the encounter with his girlfriend. Were they together? She wasn't really sure what the nature of their relationship was.

Lucas only offered a brief glance but the girl turned around with widened eyes.

"You?" Rachel came to an abrupt halt. "How dare you show your face here?"

Priya tried to mutter something but it was drowned in a squeaky cry. Her dark eyes bore a red glow and her wet cheeks sparkled in the bright light of the lobby. She must have been crying—fake tears, Rachel was sure. Every time Alex was in trouble, it was because she had convinced him to do some weird shit. Even when coming back from their regular dates, Rachel could see the life sucked out of him.

"So, you've come to turn yourself in then?" She stared at the snivelling girl.

"What have I ever done to you?" Priya sniffed.

"It's not about me. It's what you've done to Alex. You've turned him into this apathetic, sad husk of his former self."

"I... only thing I ever did was love him for who he is." She took something out of her pocket and crumpled it inside her fist, next to her thigh—it looked like a piece of paper. "No matter what you may think, I love you too, you know?" She opened her trembling arms, her whole body shaking as she took a feeble step forward.

Was she seriously trying to hug her? How stupid was she?

Lucas grabbed Priya's wrist and lowered her hand down, pulling her back to the reception desk.

"Yeah, no thanks," Rachel scoffed. She didn't know why she did it but she also gave Lucas a nod—a 'thank you' gesture for keeping the girl away from her.

"Priya, we're ready for you." The voice came from the gate behind her. Javier had extended a hand but Priya hesitated, eyes darting around the lobby in panic. It was after Lucas' nudge that she finally moved, hunched with her head down.

"Rachel, why don't you go get some rest?" Javier suggested with a reassuring nod. "I will call you the moment we have any news. Besides, your parents are still here, don't worry."

CHAPTER 3

— Julian —

Core Hull – Engines Section

The cold blue light of the morning cycle was as annoying as always. It didn't help that the thin rectangular lamp occupied half the ceiling of the living room. He dragged his half-awake body to his spot at the dinner table and welcomed the earthy aromas of coffee. The mug, filled to the top, was still exuding a wavy, vertical steam and next to it, a chunky, orange power bar. There was music coming from his father's study, adagio as always, the kind of piano and violin mix that should put someone to sleep instead of waking them up. His mother's loud banging of cupboards and drawers in the kitchen almost added the much needed drums like one of those concerts Rachel had dragged him to.

"Clean up your mess before you leave," his mum ordered as she entered the living room and pointed at the scattered clothes on the couch and floor.

He took a cautious sip of coffee, careful not to spill anything on the splintered, mahogany table and placed the mug back on its coaster. *Better eat the bar over the sink too.* His mum wasn't in the best mood—her long blonde hair was all messy and curled up in different spots with strands flying off in different directions.

The chair in the other room squeaked, a sound of rusty swivelling and his dad joined him in the living room. He ran a hand through his curly black hair and raised his thick, rectangular glasses back to the level of his nose bridge. "Core Hull today, huh? Excited?"

"I'm a bit worried about the zero g but yeah."

"You'll be fine, monkey," his mum chimed in, "Your father and I went through it too back in the day. It's a shame you can't visit again unless you're an engineer or a scientist."

"There's a good reason for that, Freddie," his dad said as he sat on the opposite side of the table, "We're talking about the nuclear reactor that powers everything on the *Sagan*, the ARK controls, the main engine drive, the navigational controls, basically everything that makes this ship go," he explained.

"Thanks Dad, I'm not stressed at all now." Julian saved his breakfast in his pocket for later and grabbed his shoes from the shining, metal rack near the entrance.

"Julian." The chair ground on the floor and his dad stood up. "I didn't want to start with this but if you're leaving already…" He approached the main entrance, giving a cautious glance at his mum. Surprisingly, she did the same but with a softer expression—more like a roll of the eyes but without actually doing it. "Have you heard anything from Rachel? I was thinking of giving her dad a call but I'm sure he has his hands full right now."

"Uhmm, last I heard, the whole family was at the Administration. I'm supposed to meet her now at the intersection."

His dad nodded, his lips pressed tightly together and Julian closed the door behind him with a shaky exhale.

The plaza appeared in his tangent horizon, one kiosk at a time as the curvature of the Ring concealed the rest of the quadrant. He pondered if he'd ever get used to how weird this place was. It was the only home he had ever known but it definitely didn't seem right. The lift was taking him downwards to the ground floor of a ring shaped structure that was spinning around its main cylindrical axis, which was also propelling itself forward in space. It appeared to be such a complicated series of motions and somehow, they all seemed to be in harmony with each other.

Rachel was waiting at the quadrant intersection, leaning against the wall with the sole of her left foot pressed against it. Her dark, ginger hair was not tied in a ponytail this time—it instead fell unevenly to her shoulders, uncombed and frizzy. She was wearing the same black t-shirt from yesterday, the one with the red crown logo that matched the colour of her skirt. Focused on the roller in her hands, she seemed disengaged from the world around her until she saw him and cracked the glass screen at the edge of her roller, reeling it back to its plastic cylinder.

"Have you slept at all?" He placed his hand on her forearm.

"A little bit," she replied but the black circles under her eyes indicated otherwise.

"How did it go? Any news about Alex?"

She shook her head.

"What about the cameras?" He asked, feeling stupid after having uttered the words. Of course they'd have checked the cameras.

"They..." she sighed and finally met his eyes. "Let's not talk about it now, ok? I'm just too..."

"Yeah, of course. Sorry, I didn't mean to..."

"I just need to clear my head. Let's just get to Ring Six."

The two guards before the outer bridge of Ring Five scanned their wrists and showed them in. Only build-bots lived in Ring Six for the last few years—the renovations were in abeyance as resources were diverted to the mysterious structure around the outer rim.

There were no guards on the other side of the bridge, their physical presence replaced by that of drones hovering in a circle around his classmates, red dots blinking—monitoring.

Liam was the first to ask about Alex, his dark blue eyes shifting between him and Rachel, desperate for answers. Then James came running, the twisted locks on top of his taper fade haircut wobbling. They were both trying to force a smile but their locked jaws and raised eyebrows meant they were in the same awkward situation he was, wanting to help but unaware how.

Rachel snapped when others started forming a circle around her but thankfully Ms Carter's loud voice drowned the overlapping chatter that had blended into white noise.

"We will soon start our ascent to the Core Hull and I need everyone's undivided attention. That includes you Lucas," the teacher called out the *hunk of muscles* who kept whispering to his similarly fit friend, Ares next to him. On his other side, Priya stood idly like a statue. "I expect you all to behave and listen to everything I say as people can easily get injured up there. This is not like any other part of the ship and for most of you it will be the first time in zero gravity. Form a queue behind Lydia and follow me," she ordered as she stopped in front of the mysterious white door at the end of the intersection. The orange holocircle rotated until it turned green, revealing a bleak grey shaft that housed the spiralling stairwell.

By the time Julian made it through, the line of students had come to a halt and Ms Carter's voice echoed from the top of the vertical tunnel—another set of orders for safety protocols.

"Do you think there's any chance Alex might still show up? Rachel whispered next to him.

"I wouldn't count on it," Lucas interjected as he passed them, "There's no waking him up now."

"Luke! What are you doing? Come on up," Ares shouted from the level above them.

"What does that mean? Do you know something?" Rachel rushed behind the bully who was cutting the queue, shoving their classmates aside. "If you know where my brother is, you need to tell me now!" Rachel tried to keep up with him climbing the stairs. "Lucas!" she growled and grabbed his arm before he had reached the half landing.

"Don't touch me." He slapped her hand away. "I don't know where your stupid brother is."

Rachel pressed on but Ms Carter scolded both of them for disrupting her instructions.

"Do you really think Lucas knows something about Alex?" Julian asked when he finally caught up with her.

"He was there yesterday, supposedly waiting to be processed for assault," Rachel said, her tiny frame rocked with every shallow breath. "And I think he's dating that admin, Katey."

"I don't know, I wouldn't put any hopes on *him* being helpful."

Julian couldn't hold back the scoff. Relying on Lucas for help was like being injured in the ancient Earth plains and asking a lion to lick your wounds.

The line started moving once again. By the time Julian reached the top, almost everyone was already inside the huge lift, fighting over seating arrangements. There were only single spots left, the least uncomfortable one being next to Hailey. She was stroking her blonde hair nervously, her feet barely reaching the ground as she stretched her toes to make contact like a ballerina. Rachel sat opposite to him next to Liam who weirdly enough wasn't sitting with James this time. After everyone was buckled in, Ms Carter traced her finger rhythmically above each of their heads, her lips parting with the whispers of numbers.

"Ok, right now, we are on one of the four inner bridges of Ring Six, connecting the internal rim to the core of the *Sagan*. Centrifugal force diminishes the closer we get to the centre of the spinning axis so I want to see everyone strapped in." She scanned each of them, her eyes falling at the buckle around the waist. "This lift is on rails and powered to go up and down regardless of gravity. The AI has to regulate how much power is required to move our collective weight in comparison to when we reach the other side and compensate."

"Is this lecture part of the trip?" Lucas interrupted the teacher's flow and she turned to him with a loud inhale, her chest heaved and her shoulders raised. "Everyone ready?" She asked, taking her place next to the threatening red button.

In the beginning, Julian didn't feel much different than any other lift; it was only after he saw a stylus floating that he realised what was going on. Hailey's feet had come up to the level of her seat, she had forgotten to engage her magboots. Even if she had, she was too short to place her feet fully on the floor. She gasped in excitement and giggled while lifting her arms above her head. Everyone followed her example, filling the loudly whirring elevator with echoes of laughter.

When it screeched to a stop and the doors slid open, Ms Carter gave the signal and everyone unbuckled their straps.

The lift had stopped in the middle of a catwalk that connected the Core Hulls of Rings Five and Six. Below—or above, he couldn't orient himself—was the mechanical infrastructure of Ring Six, machinery so colossal that had him questioning whether humans had actually built it. This was the heart of the Ring's spinning mechanism, its vibration resonating through the handrail he had clutched tightly. His eyes wandered around the enormous, open space until he spotted the other catwalk directly above him on the other side. Its perforated metal floor looked like ceiling from where he stood. Four internal bridges, four lifts and four catwalks, yet inside the main axis of the ship, there was no up or down, no left or right.

The interior of the Core Hull was even more disorienting. When the circular, bulkhead door released its interlocking panels back inside the wall, the first thing Julian could notice was the top of a scientist's head. He was still standing upright on the catwalk but in front of him was the top floor of the Core Hull like a wall to his orientation.

There were multiple levels of decking with connecting ladders and they all looped around a thick cylinder suspended in the middle like an ancient tree house. The lower decks started where the main engine would be, ending at the entrance they had come through. The structure reminded him of the skyscrapers of old Earth, albeit sideways and without cladding.

It was fortunate he hadn't had breakfast after all.

The scientists all wore the same long, white robes he had seen before in the science quadrants and didn't seem to bother with the group's presence until a tall, bald man came to greet them. Judging from the amount of wrinkles and moles on his face, he was quite old but the way he effortlessly hopped along the deck was contradicting.

"Yolanda, always so nice to see you," the scientist said.

"Dr Richter, thank you for having us."

"When will you learn to call me Albert?" His accent had a deep elegant tone and it sounded like he was dragging certain vowels on purpose. "I am sure you're all very excited to be here." He scanned the students from left to right, stopping for a double take on Julian and their eyes met for a second. Julian looked over his shoulders to make sure there was no one behind him and the scientist continued. "This is the most important and fun part of the ship. Shall we start, Yolanda?"

Ms Carter agreed with a slight bow and Dr Albert Richter cleared his throat.

"Your basic education comes to an end in the coming days and you will need to find your role within this ship and how you contribute to its journey. Is there anyone here already interested in physics or engineering?"

Julian wanted to raise his hand but no one else did, not even Lydia—her gaze was fixed at Lucas' face, which shifted through a dozen grimaces as if he was trying to have an inaudible conversation with someone.

"Boring subjects indeed," Dr Richter exclaimed and Julian turned his attention back to the scientist. "I personally prefer the life sciences, the study of living organisms, for without them there wouldn't be a need for all these technologies. BUT..." He raised a finger clad in blue latex. "In their defence, the cosmic scientists have given us something magnificent, the ability to harness the power of a star and through it, interstellar travel. Follow me to the lower level and you'll witness it first-hand."

Julian winced after climbing down the last rung as the bright light seeped out of the enormous window strip around the oval shaped chamber. He forced his way through his classmates, squeezing in for a better view, his interest peaked and his manners gone in the presence of the magic of science. The interior wasn't as big as it seemed from the outside. It was covered with rectangular panels in shades of grey circling around a column in the middle in a toroid fashion. The edges on the top and bottom of the column were illuminated so intensely he couldn't make out the material underneath. What had gotten his attention more than anything else was the levitating plasma in the middle. It gave off a bright pink light, forming a thick elongated ring around the column that appeared violent and threatening. It was so stable in shape that he could argue it was solid but for the small, almost indistinguishable fluctuations around its edges.

An unexpected touch on his hand startled him and he turned to Rachel, only to find Priya standing next to him instead. She was focused on the nuclear fusion but her fingers intertwined with his, sliding a thin piece of paper in his palm.

"Pocket," she whispered, her tone so faint Julian thought she had mouthed the words.

He put the note in his jacket and gave her a curious glance. She was still staring at Dr Richter as if nothing had happened.

"Not here," she said when he tried to have a peek. He reluctantly crumpled it into a ball of folds and wrinkles and shoved it in his pocket with a soft rustling.

Rachel was, of course, not paying attention to any of the science, she had even turned her back to the reactor. Julian traced her unblinking eyes to Lucas and waved a hand in front of her. "You won't let it go, will you?" he whispered.

"Why is he talking to our James? And where is Ares?"

He scanned the whole deck—Ares was gone and Lucas had stayed at the railing with James, away from the rest of the group.

Dr Richter drowned their small chat when he started explaining the process of nuclear fusion in detail, mentioning words Julian hadn't heard before like superconductors, magnetic field lines and so many different types of coils and particles that made no sense to him. He felt shame; all this was so interesting to him, but he didn't have the brain capacity to comprehend how it all worked. He wished he did. For as long as he could remember, it had been his dream to become a scientist. All this time he had spent in his virtual world learning about different things seemed in vain now. This was actual science in front of him, scary and complicated and more importantly, real.

Dr Richter seemed so knowledgeable, so educated. The way he was explaining the process resembled that of an AI, spitting out information from its infinite database. The even more impressive part was that he was a life scientist—or at least that's what he'd labelled himself. Describing the fusion of deuterium with helium-3 was not something the average life scientist would know. He kept going on about electrolysis and the trillions of litres of water stored in Core Hulls One through Four, barely even stopping for a breath. "Now if you follow me to the lower decks, I can show you how the heat from the nuclear fusion is transformed into electricity, a pairing between the nineteenth and twenty-first centuries."

Julian followed the direction of the group but a hand locked on his wrist, holding him in place. Rachel beckoned towards Lucas and James who were still at the edge of the deck.

"Rach, you don't have to talk to him now."

"I won't talk to him... I'll follow him," she said as the two boys headed for the ladder on the other side of the fusion chamber.

She climbed the railing at the edge of the deck instead of following them directly and his stomach formed a knot at the realisation of what she was about to do. He wasn't going to jump from one deck to the other from outside the frame, that much he knew.

He huffed and made his way to the ladder as fast as the magboots would allow him, staying close to the reactor's wall.

There was no window to the plasma at this level, only scattered stations and monitors. He grabbed a lab coat that was coming out from a half opened cabinet like a ghost finally free of captivity and hastily buttoned it to hide his casual clothes. It was a good idea to blend in but the only other scientist he had seen with a buttoned coat was Dr Richter. He patted it down and smiled with how good it looked on him—a shame he was only wearing it as a disguise.

There weren't many scientists around these upper levels; he had seen two so far who hadn't bothered looking away from their graphs since the group had first walked in.

Rachel smiled when she saw him but didn't join him at the consoles, only pointed at the series of extrusions and thick pipes above them. He'd been climbing up all this time but in reality he was moving from the back of the ship to the front.

Lucas and James were in front of an old console with buttons and levers. It must have been them, although they were both wearing lab coats. Lucas' size was unmistakable, his coat more like a low cut dress on him. They knew what they were doing, pressing buttons in a specific sequence and flicking switches like it was their job. Julian didn't even know what the console was for, only that it connected with a series of cable trays and pipes to the other side of the wall, the Core Hull Five.

A scientist approached him and Julian had to look busy. Tapping at random icons on the monitor in front of him, he felt the cold sweat trickling down his forehead.

"Are you new here?" The man asked, rubbing his wrinkly forehead with the edge of his sleeve. He looked more like an engineer than a scientist—weren't engineers scientists as well? His hair was oily and a shiny fringe was slipping in front of his left eye like a half-open curtain, covering the brown smudge that was brushed across his cheek.

Lying would probably get him in bigger trouble, and he wasn't that good a liar anyway.

"I'm here for the field trip." He managed to say without stuttering. "I just wanted to see how it would feel to be a scientist."

The engineer studied him with a cautious look before his brown eyes widened. "Wait, you're Scott's son! He mentioned you'd be here today. I'm Toz, mechanical systems engineering."

Julian forced a smile and shook the hand Toz had offered. "How do you know my dad?"

Now it was the man's turn to appear blindsided. "Just old friends," he replied, his eyes wandering awkwardly behind Julian. "You can't be here though, let me escort you back to your group."

He stole a look at the console and the edge of the deck but neither Rachel nor the two boys were there anymore.

⚛

Julian felt all his weight pulling him down on the metal floor once again. The group had dispersed after exiting the lift except for Rachel who was staring at her open roller.

"What happened back there?" He asked in a sharper tone than he'd intended.

"I had to find out what he's up to. You saw it yourself, there's no reasonable explanation for what they were doing."

"Sure but it's no excuse for the acrobatics you did. You could have gotten hurt, Rach."

"Relax, Julian. I can handle myself." Her riposte was fast but then she paused, biting her lower lip again as she always did when nervous. "I can't stop thinking about it, Julian. I keep hearing Lucas' words in my head... how he's not waking up now." Her voice cracked.

He averted his gaze without a reply. It pained him to see her like that, a vulnerable, hunched shadow of her former cheerful self.

"Do you think..." she started to snivel, "Do you think Alex is d..." She didn't finish with what had crossed Julian's mind already—the word that couldn't be uttered.

He grabbed her shoulders, ready for some optimistic comment but her eyes began to water. All he could do was to cover her into his arms, enveloping her whole body within his embrace. She let out a stifled whimper trying to hold back her tears, but Julian knew she was crying—he could feel the warmth of her breath on his chest as her tears soaked through his shirt. She locked her arms around his back and squeezed tightly as if it was the last time she would see him.

"We'll find him, Rach." He gently stroked her hair, zero inclination in his head for how he could deliver on his promise.

She finally freed him from her tight grasp and stood idly before him. "What if it's true? None of the others who disappeared ever came back."

Julian didn't have an answer to that either. It was the same train of thought that had guided him to the terrifying scenario.

"I don't know what to do, Julian. Tell me what to do!" She cried, wiping her nose with her arm.

Julian drew a long breath, stuffing his hands in his pockets and pressing inwards, his shoulders hunched and his jaw clenched.

"The note!" he exclaimed when his fingers made contact with the sharp edges of the paper.

Rachel stared at him quizzically, her gaze falling on his hands as he unfolded it.

"I'm being watched. Ring One, recreation, -3, F146, Wednesday, 1700 relative. Say Alex invited you," he read it out loud. It was written in a short, cryptic way but not hard to figure out.

"Who gave you this?" Rachel stood next to him and took the note in her own hands.

"Priya... during Albert Richter's speech."

"Priya..." she repeated, a frown forming on her forehead as she opened her roller. "Says here multipurpose room twenty-eight." She held her finger on the screen.

"Should we tell the admins?"

"Admins are useless, Julian," she remarked in a sour tone. "No, first we'll go to the clearing like I told them. We have two days until Priya's *thing* anyway."

CHAPTER 4
— Rachel —
The Cylidome – Ring 4

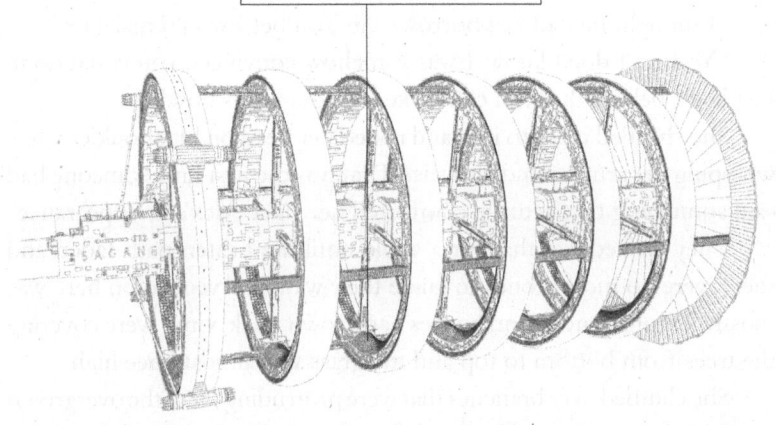

Her nostrils flared wide open filling her lungs with the powerful, intoxicating aroma that lingered here. A combination of floral, earthy, and fruity fragrances filled the open space of the agriculture quadrant. The trees had grown taller over the years, some of them even reached the ceiling—a glass curtain-wall spanning the whole length and width of the quadrant. Only colourful flowers and bushes lived near the entrance, spread around an unevenly spaced stone path. There was no tangent horizon, not with all these tall pine trees towering above the smaller evergreens like a gold medallist standing on the winner's pedestal.

She felt the scaly bark of a lonely holm oak and glanced back at Julian who was following a few feet behind. For a brief, precious moment she was a child again playing hide and seek in the forest. Alex was always so annoyed that Julian would find her first. She had never told him of course that she was revealing herself on purpose to see the smile on his face.

Julian quickened his pace, stomping on the crunchy, brown leaves that laid lifeless on the mossy dirt path. "What were you smiling about?"

Was she smiling? She hadn't realised. "I was remembering how we used to play here all the time... all three of us."

"Remember when you bet us you could reach the steel lattice by climbing to the top of a pine tree?"

"I didn't even make it halfway." She chuckled.

"Yeah and you made me lose my S-drone to Alex."

"I thought he had just borrowed it. You bet I would make it?"

"Yeah... I don't know, I was somehow convinced you could do it. Just like I believe that you can make it through this now."

She shuffled close to him and rested her head on his shoulder while wrapping her arm around his waist. That was the first time someone had said something that actually comforted her since Alex's disappearance.

They walked like that for a while until the beaten path faded and there were no more stones to guide their way. The vegetation here was mostly left unattended and bushes had grown thick, vines were covering the trees from bottom to top and the grass was almost knee high.

She climbed over branches that were protruding from the overgrown green bushes and hopped behind the oak tree that was marked with the three slashes on its bark, a reminder of the time she had thought they could build a treehouse. The small opening beyond was surrounded by tall, red pine trees as far as the eye could see and in the middle, a small jungle of wildflowers in the palettes of blue and yellow.

"So, are we looking for something specific?" Julian revolved around himself.

"I don't know Julian. I don't know what I am doing here," she cried and threw her bag on the grass. "Anything that could be linked to Alex I guess."

"Ok let's look around then," he suggested and headed for the edge of the clearing.

She stared into the bushes for a while not knowing what to do. Even if she found nothing, she had to keep looking, even if that meant she had to examine every single blade of grass and turn all the twigs and stones around.

"Rach! Come check this out," Julian shouted from the edge of the clearing. He was on his knees, tilting his head quizzically in front of a tree.

"I don't think this was here before, I would've noticed it." She studied the crescent moon shape that was carved on the bark—faint enough to get missed by the random passer-by. "Look how clean the cut is, it must be fresh."

Had Alex ever mentioned anything about a crescent moon? Rachel crossed her arms and peered into the trees, the world around her blurring out of focus. She had seen the image before but then again who hadn't? It was the lunar cycle. "I think Alex may have drawn something like it." She looked away, a faint memory materialising in pieces around her. She'd gotten into his room to ask something—or maybe yell at him? The memory of barging in without knocking kept repeating itself in her head—the rest was hazy.

"We're doing tides in Physics class, maybe that's why?" Julian offered the logical explanation as always. "Still, why would he carve it here?"

She barely heard the question, trying her best to focus on that drawing she'd seen Alex working on. It wasn't just the moon—there was a sun on the other side. Yes—a crescent moon opposite a yellow sun. Was he really doing homework for tides? Why was there no Earth though?

Her gaze returned to Julian—his mouth curled on the side and his lips clicked as they parted. "Still, there's very little to go on."

"We should keep looking around then." She stood up to study her surroundings.

"Or we can take a break? When was the last time you ate?"

"I'm fine," she lied. Her stomach gurgled just at the thought of food, even if it was only a power bar. She had survived on coffees and water since the previous night.

"Rach…" Julian trailed off, tilting his head, the rest of his sentence conveyed through his peering blue eyes that had called her bluff.

"OK." She let out a long exhale that relaxed her muscles. "But just for a few minutes and then we're back on Alex's trail." Maybe it wasn't the worst idea ever if she sat down for two minutes. "What do you have with you?"

Julian dug in his backpack and revealed a red cloth with white stripes which he then threw on a patch of flattened grass in front of him. He sat down on his crossed legs and tapped twice on the ground next to him.

"Is this why we stopped by your place first? I knew there was something weird about you carrying a backpack. You hate carrying stuff," she exclaimed with a soft punch on his arm. "You had this planned." Her anger was mixed with hunger, a deadly combination. If it was someone else and not Julian, she would have probably carried on with the punches.

"Look, you've got to eat and let your mind drift for a minute. I'm as worried about Alex as you, you know that, right?" He met her eyes with furrowed brows and a slight purse on his lips—it was his apologetic look. "You're no good to him if you're barely awake." He softly held her hand and pulled her down on the cloth beside him. "Just ten minutes, ok?"

"OK," she agreed in a whisper and licked her lips. "So… what do you have?"

He put the bag on his lap and produced two sandwiches covered in airtight bags.

"Mmm, what is this?" she asked as she frantically tore the packaging apart.

"This is what the people of Earth used to call a picnic." He made a gesture stretching out his hands.

"Does it have meat?"

Julian snorted a laugh that made him spit his bite right out. "This is just a veggie roll," he explained as he wiped his mouth, still laughing, "What we're doing here inside the forest, sitting on a piece of rug and eating is called a picnic."

"People used to do that? Like just go to the forest and eat on the ground?" She scoffed.

"Yeah, not just the forest. Parks, beaches, anywhere really. They would stay there for hours to escape the city noise and enjoy nature." Julian's eyes were filled with excitement. "I've done it a few times in the VR but always alone and without any food."

"So, how does it work, we just sit here and eat? And then what?"

"We can lie down on the ground, talk… I don't know."

She took another bite before even swallowing the last one, rubbing her stomach with satisfaction. Her head felt light and her eyelids were heavy, like she had taken one of these euphoric drugs James had told her about. Her body was shutting down, the pain from her overtired muscles finally catching up with her and she stretched her legs, balancing on her elbows behind her back.

"Uhm, what are you doing?" Julian asked when she kicked off her shoes and threw them aside.

"Come on, take them off too." She tried to untie his shoes, but he quickly pulled them back.

"You're not serious. I am not taking them off, there are so many bugs hidden in the ground. What if they go in my shoes or even worse climb on my bare feet?" he cringed.

"You said you wanted to take my mind off things. Now you have to keep your word."

He sighed, having lost the argument so quickly and placed his trainers next to him.

The rug was small, and they could barely fit on it as they laid there side by side looking at the opening above them. Julian kept scanning left and right for signs of worms or other insects, but eventually gave in, his fidgeting and wiggling finally coming to an end. The dead silence was comforting in a way as she peered into the treetops. From this spot she could see the top of the trees from farther down the forest, sprouting from the ground almost horizontally to her position as the quadrant curved to form the rest of the ring structure. The trees around her grew straight up, but the ones in the distance curved as if they were attached to the walls like spokes of a bicycle.

Her muscles were numb, vibrating like a constant current coursing through them and she dared close her eyes for a second. Memories of Alex flashed in her mind—the times he was running around the clearing, guiding his little drone through the trees, almost always taking some branches with it.

"Rach, you promised me ten minutes." Julian placed a hand on her shoulder when she sat up.

"I can't shake it off, Julian," she let out a tired exhale, her eyes starting to well up again.

"Okay, I know!" He softly guided her upper body back on the rug. His hands were cold on her skin but his delicate touch made the tiny hairs on her arms rise. "If you could choose to live anywhere on Earth," he started, moving back to his side, "Where would it be?"

Rachel glanced at him with the corner of her eye and turned on her side. The guilt was creeping up inside her but maybe he was right. Maybe she needed to distract herself and clear her mind for just a bit.

"Uhm... I don't know, Julian," she let out a puff of air, images of earth succeeding one another in her head. It was such a big place compared to their ship. She pondered what the chances of finding Alex would be if he'd disappeared on Earth instead. Possibly zero.

"Didn't you visit any place in the VR more than once?" He pressed on.

"Uhm, let's see..." She forced herself to conjure an image from memory. "Probably one of these huge vertical cities but definitely not in the city centre, somewhere away in the suburbs, maybe near a river. Oh, and it would have to be someplace warm and sunny." She could almost picture it now. She didn't know what metropolis she was imagining but she had seen it somewhere, maybe during history class. The view in her mind was aerial, an endless white with patches of green sporadically cutting off the wacky road grid. There was a river passing through the city, bending it to its shape and tall skyscrapers towered along its length like a surreal colonnade.

"Any city in particular?"

"Come on, what is this a geography quiz? I don't remember the names."

"Fine. For me it would be a cabin by the coast somewhere in the Mediterranean Sea where there were no flood barriers. Or better yet..." His eyes glistened wistfully in the few rays that penetrated the thick foliage above them. "There's a lighthouse in the Adriatic sea that is only accessible by boat. Maybe a little boat of my own that could handle waves and I'd be set to explore the world." He shook his head, staring blankly at the treetops.

She didn't know where any of that was so she didn't bother commenting on his choice. She never really cared about Earth. "That's all very nice, I don't remember asking you though," she said, waiting for him to turn around all surprised and offended. And he did.

"I... I thought.... we... we were exchanging...."

"You... what... I... we," she snickered at his loss of words.

"You're the worst," he sulked, frowning with all his face and deforming his smooth skin, his hands folded on top of his chest.

Rachel gasped as if she was offended and climbed on top of him locking his wrists on the ground. "I'm the worst, huh? Say you're sorry!"

"Never," he grunted as he tried to slip away from her tight grasp, "I can very easily get out of this."

"I want to see you try. Go on, try. There's no one around to see you pinned down by a little girl."

"You're quite strong for a little girl." He grunted louder and finally flipped her on her back. "How about that?" he smiled triumphantly.

"I don't really mind," she blurted without thinking. Her stomach contracted with every rushed breath as she tried her best not to shy away from his eyes. Her cheeks burned but his smile turned into a puzzled grimace and he swallowed with difficulty as he pulled away, releasing her wrists.

"Uhm... maybe we should get back to looking for Alex now?" he said while clearing his throat.

She only nodded and hid her lips inside her mouth. What was she thinking? She had allowed herself to be distracted by his dreamy eyes and inviting lips when her brother was lost somewhere. She fought the urge to slap herself and paced around the clearing while Julian sat on his knees, his hair askew, hastily folding the rug.

"It's actually getting orangey," he said, prompting her to take notice of the wall of blackness that had encircled the clearing. "We really need to leave if we want to make it back before red lights."

They passed the wrinkled oak and headed for the tall grass as the darkness slowly enveloped them. It grew as a hungering shadow, eating away trees and bushes from her horizon. The evening lights of the steel lattice fought a losing battle to reach the ground, their orange hues barely reflective enough to shine through the treetops.

She stomped on the grass, crunching and flattening it with every step, thinking what else she could do to find Alex. She went back to their conversations, brief as they may have been and tried to remember a clue, something that would give her a hint to what had happened to him. Her eyes wandered around the shadowy barks of the trees and that's when she noticed it with the corner of her eye, another marked tree, away from the curved path.

She kneeled in front of the spotted bark of the curvy birch and Julian followed. It was the same shape she had seen at the clearing, although it seemed bigger this time. "This can't be a coincidence. Do you think they're connected?" She asked, hoping she was on to something.

"Hmmm." Julian crouched next to her, stoic and sceptical, running his fingers through the lines of the carving. "It seems to be the same pattern."

"What if these trees are not randomly marked?" She turned to him to see if his expression would validate her suspicion. He raised an eyebrow and his lips tightened inside his mouth. "What if they lead somewhere?" She suggested as the sudden rush of adrenaline made her heart flutter. The thought was unsettling but thrilling at the same time.

"You mean like directions? How would you follow them though? You would have to search the whole forest."

"I don't know Julian... I am trying to hang on to any possible clue here."

"Rach, we don't have time for this," he looked up as the bright red lights declared the start of night hours.

"You can go if you want. I don't want to get you in trouble. Just head straight this way and you'll reach the quadrant intersection." She vaguely pointed behind her.

Julian followed the faded path with his eyes but didn't move. Was he thinking of actually leaving her? She studied the carving again, keeping an ear out for his reaction.

"Wait! Take a look at this." She ran her fingers across the indentation on the tree. A red arrow accompanied by a number had appeared in the middle of the crescent moon shape. "This wasn't here before, was it?"

"No it wasn't," he agreed and leant over her shoulder to touch the red numbers himself. They disappeared under his finger but came back when he removed it as though they were etched in the bark itself. "It seems to be only visible in red light." His brows furrowed as he tilted his head. His brilliant mind was at work. "It must be written in white marker or something so it's hidden during the day... that's why whoever did this, chose birch trees. To hide the white marking on the white trunk!" He exclaimed his epiphany that made no sense to her.

"What do you mean hide it in the white trunk?"

"If something is white, it reflects all colours of daylight so we see it white as well, right? If you only shine a specific colour, it will only reflect that colour instead of the full rainbow. You only give it red and it will reflect red back to us."

"Why not orange or blue during the other light cycles?"

He rested his chin between his thumb and his index finger, his eyes fixed somewhere above her. "Because the other daylights are actually white but in different temperatures." He snapped his fingers. "Night light is literally only red."

"It's times like this that your obsession with science finally comes in handy." She threw her arms around his neck but he pulled back. *Yeah, too much physical interaction for Julian.* It was an instinct to hug him, a natural consequence of hope being kept alive inside her. She pulled away and knelt in front of the carving again.

"Are you sure about this?" she asked, glancing sideways to get a glimpse of his reaction. "Would that mean that someone definitely did this intentionally?"

"I'm sure about the science. No idea who did it or why. Do you think it means something?"

"If I am right and these markings actually lead somewhere, I'd say it's the direction and number of steps until the next tree." She stood up and positioned her body to where the arrow was pointing.

She was right! Exactly ninety-eight steps later, another marked birch kept her hope alive. The next two trees were easier to find as they delved further into the overgrown flora of the Cylidome. She could feel the adrenaline coursing through her body, a seemingly unlimited energy boost keeping her eyes wide open and her limbs alert.

They both stopped and turned to different directions at the sound of a twig snapping that echoed in the empty forest.

She pointed at the big rock that was enveloped with overgrown ivy, letting her eyes do the talking.

Leaves rustled behind it, masking the faint incomprehensible dialogue that was taking place on the other side. If someone was there, they weren't aware of their presence yet.

She watched her step and made her way around the edge of the boulder, slipping through the hand Julian had extended to prevent her. The gasp came before she could cover her mouth.

"Who's there?" James asked from the other side.

It wasn't what she was expecting to see but the familiar faces were more comforting than a threat.

She exposed herself completely in a swift movement. "Hi... guys..." She tried not to sound too awkward but it definitely came out wrong.

Liam's exposed, pale chest was like a spotlight in the darkness surrounding them. Next to him the dark, fit figure of James was indistinguishable from the shadows as he hastily put a shirt back on before turning around to show his face. "Rachel?" he whispered with a confused look.

"Hi James." She couldn't help but smile at the awkward sight. "What are you guys doing here?" She wiggled her body with an insinuating tone. It was a rhetorical question.

"Noth... nothing," he stuttered.

"Are you guys...?" She finished her sentence with a gesture of her hands joining together in a weird shape.

"No! Are you crazy?"

"I saw you with my own eyes. You were on top of him," she insisted while Julian nudged her and passed in front of her.

"No, we were just talking but it was so hot we took our shirts off, that's all," James defended himself.

"Such a lame excuse. It's never hot *or* cold on this ship."

"James, she saw us," Liam interjected. "It's fine, it's Rachel and Julian, we can trust them."

"So are you guys... like a couple? I've known you for years, how come you never told me?"

"We're not a couple, ok?" James refused to let it go.

Liam sighed in frustration. His chin dropped to the bottom of his neck as his lips pressed tightly together, "Yeah we're definitely not a couple," he assured her and swiftly passed between Julian and her, disappearing in the darkness behind her.

"Shouldn't you go after him?" Julian turned back towards James.

"He'll be fine... what are you two even doing here at this time?" His tone made it sound more like a threat than a question.

"We're trying to find any clue about Alex." She sighed and took a step closer to him. "You were with Lucas at the Core Hull. You did something there. Do you know anything about Alex? Has Lucas mentioned anything?"

"What makes you think I was with Lucas? Why would I hang out with Lucas in the first place?"

He was lying to her face. She needed a longer inhale to not lose her shit. "You're not good at lying, James. I saw you. Top deck after boring bald guy finally shut up about his pink light."

"Hey, that's Dr Albert Richter. You can't talk like that about him."

"Why, you know him?"

"I... he's just a very well known, respected scientist."

"I had never heard of him until today," Julian interjected, "And I know most scientists on the ship."

Rachel's gaze shifted between Julian and James. "Who cares about some scientist? What were you doing with Lucas? James, if you or Lucas know something I swear..."

"Easy, Rach." Julian grabbed her shaking arm until it relaxed again.

James twitched his mouth and clicked his tongue. He was about to say something but changed his mind with a sigh. "I wish I could help, Rachel. I really do. I'm sorry for what happened to Alex but I don't know anything." His tone was apologetic but definitely fake.

She bit her lip and sucked in her cheek. James was on the defensive already after having his relationship exposed. He wouldn't say anything even if he knew.

"Pffft. You've changed James. Be careful with Lucas, don't let him influence you any more than he already has." She shook her head with disappointment. "Let's go Julian."

"Rachel, what you guys saw here tonight... let's keep it between ourselves?"

"Don't worry about us spilling your secret. We're still your friends," Julian said.

"For now," Rachel muttered, almost mouthing the words.

She looked up to the steel lattice at the engraved numbers on each of the beams and cross beams to orient herself. They were still on the 270th wide which meant there was still a long way to go.

"What about the marked trees?" Julian asked when they were out of James' earshot.

"It's too late now," she huffed, still pissed that no one could give her the answers she needed. "We should go home."

As they walked to the quadrant's exit, the events of the last couple of days played in her head. Lucas' words, his fiddling with the controls in the Core Hull, Alex's drawing of the crescent moon next to a sun—and then there was Priya's note. It sounded like a secret meeting but she still wasn't convinced Alex's girlfriend was being helpful. Part of her wanted to confront her but the carved trees sounded promising—she only had to wait for Julian to leave.

He hugged her tightly and told her to get some rest before disappearing into the quadrant intersection—of course she wouldn't. She had to turn every stone, every slim chance of a lead, anything that could give her a sliver of hope. The forest looked like something out of a nightmare from far away, bathed in the dim scarlet light that barely penetrated the thick, grey foliage. Maybe she could have used Julian's company but he would already be in trouble for staying out past the night cycle. On the other hand, her own points meant very little to her. She already had two warnings that month, what was another week with shitty food and first generation clothes.

The deeper she delved into the forest the harder it was to see, even though her eyes had adjusted to the darkness. The previously colourful tapestry had transformed into a black and grey monochrome. Only the tulips maintained their bright red petals; she had never noticed how many there were before. *Because red is the only colour reflected during night lights.* Julian was so smart for knowing stuff like that.

She made it to the clearing and started tracking the marked trees all over again. They were similarly spaced, every hundred steps or so there was another carved birch tree. She picked up the pace and even started running until she found herself back in the clearing.

Well, Fuck!

She must have been doing something wrong. They had to lead somewhere, otherwise it would have been the most pointless prank anyone had ever done. She started over but this time with her roller in hand, tracing the position of each marked tree against the long and wide beams coordinates. It took longer but by the time she reached the clearing again, she had mapped the entire system. It was a weird polygon after all, kind of like an ellipse along the length of the quadrant. She sat on the grass and stared at her roller. All this walking had taken its toll and there was nothing else edible in her bag. She had barely slept an hour since Alex's news and from the looks of it, this was going to be a long night as well. She studied the shape while biting her lips. Sixteen edges with irregular angles. Maybe the vertices were pointing at something or there was something at the centre of it, but how would she calculate it? If only she had paid more attention in maths class or if Julian was still there with her, he would have figured out the pattern for sure.

Fuck it, she drew a new ellipse over the shape on her roller using the two x vertices instead of the centre like the software had recommended. It took a few tries but she had an approximate position.

There was no clear path to the centre, the vegetation outside the clearing was full of towering bushes and thorny vines. She had to make her way around while glancing at her roller to not lose track of where she was going.

"Fuck's sake," she mumbled when she verified she was at the right place. It felt like someone was playing a sadistic trick on her as she leant against the big rock where she had found James and Liam. There were no red markings before, she would've noticed—nothing now either. Did the boys know about this place? She needed a better vantage point but the boulder was steep. She wedged her foot in the only sharp edge it could fit and hoisted herself to the top. And there it was—an actual sentence this time, shining in the bright red reflection of the lattice lights and making no sense at all.

"We were sent back but our voices still live here," she repeated a few times. "What the fuck do you mean?" She stared at it and covered her face in her palms, defeated.

"It's *Tyson-7*." A weak, croaky voice made her head jolt and her spine tingle.

Rachel stared at the woman who was standing at the bottom of the rock, still as a statue and dressed in a long, black overcoat that matched her straight, frizzy hair. She looked like an apparition in the already eerie ambiance of the scarlet forest, her gaze fixated upon her.

"Who are *you*?" Rachel asked, glancing briefly behind her to evaluate any possible escape from the other side of the rock.

"I am you... but with a lot more years and desperation on my back."

"Huh?" Rachel scooted further back to the edge of the steep slope.

"Do you know who Lester Yau was?"

"The first kid to go missing?" she replied, noticing the past tense the woman had used.

"I'm his... mother," the woman said and Rachel let out the breath she was holding inside her chest. Why had she expected her to say killer instead of mother?

"I've been where you are, we all were at some point." The woman continued, "Your parents rely on the admins but you... you're out there looking for him like I was, all these years ago." The woman spoke in a slow tempo as if uttering the words exhausted her.

"We—you mean the other relatives? Can you get me in touch with them?"

"There is... a support group. They meet on Wednesdays in Ring Two, level five... no, four. Section E, room... thirt—no, fourteen." She seemed to be drifting in and out of thought as she tried to enunciate the correct location. At least she was talking, the scary aura of her sudden appearance dissipated into dialogue. "They do not take me seriously, though. They think I've gone mad."

Rachel bit her lip to prevent herself from saying something stupid. That woman was the only credible help she had so far despite her ominous look and posture. "What were you doing here?"

"I come here from time to time, looking for anything I've missed over the years."

"So you know what this means? *Tyson-7* you said? The shuttle?" She knew the small spaceships under the ring structure were called *Tysons* but the number meant nothing to her.

"We were sent back but our voices still live here," she repeated the phrase from the rock as if she knew it by heart. "It can only refer to the shuttle that left in year three to return to Earth."

Year three? That was ancient history, more than a hundred and twenty years ago. Humans had gone from riding horses to smartphones in that kind of span. Pity Julian wasn't there, he would've appreciated her knowing that.

"Does it have something to do with your son? Or my brother?" She asked, not sure how any of that could help her.

"I never found a link. Lester used to come here a lot though. It must have meant something to him." Her voice trembled but she didn't cry.

"Have you checked the archives about it? My friend Julian, his father is the archivist, maybe he knows."

"Be careful who you trust, Rachel. The cosmic scientists are as bad as the evolutionists."

Rachel pulled her head back and pushed her brows together. She knew cosmic scientists were engineers, astronomers, physicists and the likes but she had never heard of evolutionists before. Had she meant life scientists? That was her closest guess. Her eyes darted across the forest and the thorny shadows cast on the grey soil. If she couldn't trust Julian, then there was no point in trusting anyone and she would bet his father was the same. Was he willing to help though and wouldn't he have done so already if he could? That was an entirely different question.

She turned back to Miss Yau but only found grey blades of grass flickering ever so slightly against the tiny bit of ventilation draft. The woman had disappeared as suddenly as she had appeared.

CHAPTER 5
— JULIAN —
ENGINEERING QUADRANT – RING 3

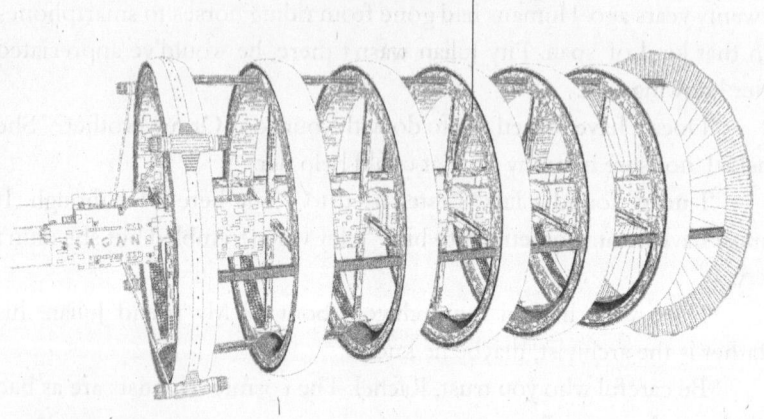

The smell of freshly cooked food that permeated around the plaza kiosks made him regret his choice to leave so early and without breakfast. The alternative was to endure the awkward silence of his parents. They hadn't exchanged a single word and his mother hadn't even greeted him. His parents' fight had apparently carried on from the previous night when he found them screaming at each other. It had worked in his favour though, since neither of them had bothered with how late he had come back.

He hadn't made more than a few steps in the outer bridge before he stopped and moved to the side of the suspended tunnel that connected Rings Four and Three. A group of people were coming in the opposite direction, walking behind flat trolleys filled with a tower of chamfered, semi-transparent boxes.

"Lydia," he exclaimed, blocking their way and raising a hand to greet her.

His body had acted on its own and now he found himself awkwardly standing in front of the whole family who had stopped for Lydia to come out behind the hovering, superconducting trolleys. "Are you not coming to class?" Julian asked, stealing a glance at the cautious looks of her parents.

"I don't think I'll make it today. We are moving to Ring Six."

"Is it done already? I thought they were still working on renovations and that big structure around its edge."

"They still are but we were chosen…"

"Lydia!" Her mum cut her off. "We're only moving some things over, not a big deal. We're not officially moved in yet," she said in a serious flat tone. She had the same thick brown hair and strong facial features as Lydia, but instead of freckles, it was wrinkles that decorated the otherwise smooth skin of her face.

"Hello Mrs Garcia," Julian said, his cheeks burning.

"You are Freddie's son, no?"

"Yes, how do you know my mother?"

"We work together."

"But you live in different Rings."

"All horticulturists talk to each other. Listen, we really have to keep going though. Lydia." She beckoned her daughter to start walking.

"Bye, Julian." The young girl smiled shyly.

"You want to maybe get together later and talk about what you've missed today?" He blurted, not believing it himself that he had asked her out.

"Sure, I'd love that," she nodded and turned around to follow the rest of her family, taking the hand of her younger brother—Matteo if he remembered correctly.

Their conversation was shorter than he had hoped but longer than he had ever gone without saying something stupid. He was getting closer and closer to her. This time she had even tucked her hair behind her ears, a clear sign of attraction—or maybe nervousness. A good sign regardless.

A woman had stayed behind from the family's trolleys—she didn't look familiar and Julian wasn't sure she was with the Garcia's before. She looked a little bit older than him but he knew Lydia didn't have a sister. He smiled uncomfortably under her gaze and moved on, glancing back to the peering black eyes that followed him like cameras.

Julian often thought Mr Vaun's class to be the most boring one even for him. He didn't understand what use anyone would have for biology in space. His dream of becoming a cosmic scientist came with an inherent arrogance towards the life sciences. The two scientific fields were at an intellectual war since before the *Sagan* was even built—or so he was told—kind of like architects and engineers. The only interesting part of biology class was the thick moustache that decorated the professor's upper lip, which drew his attention every time he looked up from his desk. He had seen him comb it a few times at the edges, turning the wavy black hairs into a curled shield for his big brown mole to hide under. He always spoke so slowly that time slowed down as if the ship was passing next to a black hole.

The professor started talking about the biological differences between Terrans, Martians and Spaceborn and it wasn't long after he had finished explaining the variances in the eyes and spinal growth that Julian felt his eyelids closing. He was sure he was still paying attention until he felt an elbow on his ribs.

"You're falling over to my side," Rachel whispered under her breath.

The class was over and he found himself blindly following Rachel, rubbing his eyes as he tried to keep track of her swaying, ginger ponytail.

"I'm doing it. I'm going to talk to Lucas before PT."

"You still want to poke the biggest, baddest wolf, huh?" He said, hoping they would somehow find Alex before having to confront Lucas. "How sure are you that he actually knows something?"

"A hundred percent!" She held him in place and pointed at the huge boy who almost occupied the entire hallway with his overly massive body.

"I don't think Lucas has ever missed Physical Training." Julian squinted to peer through the end of the bulkhead. "Where do you think he's going?"

"That's what we'll find out."

"But we have class!"

"Exactly! So does he. Julian, I can't wait for useless Admins or put my hopes on Priya's little note. I need to talk to him myself."

Priya hadn't been in class that day. He had wanted to talk to her about her mysterious note since she wouldn't even reply to his messages.

He bit his thumb and stared at the end of the hallway where Lucas' shadow had just disappeared. "What would we even say to Ms Williams?" he asked.

"Cramps, idiot. Works every time," she answered faster than he'd expected.

Julian rolled his eyes and took the anticipated feeble punch on the arm.

"Stop thinking what you're thinking. We've been over this a million times." She hissed, her widened eyes half buried under her curved brows.

"I am sorry, ok? You're right, it's a great excuse. What do we do if she realises we lied though?"

"Relax, you didn't even have a warning this semester. You'll be fine."

"I wish I had a warning for that punch," he muttered.

"You deserved it," she said with a shrug and a mocking smile. "Now come on, let's go before we lose him."

Rachel hurried forward but he remained perfectly still, staring at the word 'Gymnasium' that was engraved in the middle of the white door in front of him. If he took another step, it would slide open and everything would be fine. Rachel needed him though. What kind of friend would he be if he didn't help her find her brother—his own friend.

He glanced at both ends of the corridor and jolted to the shadowy figure behind him—a silhouette that had vanished inside the intersection. He squinted, leaning slightly forward but there was no one there.

Feeling a cold tingle on his spine, he briskly walked to the opposite side of the corridor where Rachel was.

"Were you really thinking of bailing on me?" She gave him a tilted glance, her brows twisted inwards in an expression of shock and betrayal.

"Just had to recover from the punches," he lied, trying to hide his fear behind a forced smile.

"I think I saw him going through the exit, it will be harder to find him in the crowd."

"He's huge. There!" He pointed at the other side as they entered the quadrant intersection.

"It's one thing for Lucas to skip PT, but to even enter the science quadrant, now that's a *whole* other level." she said quite dramatically, flailing her arms around.

They followed him in and came to a disappointing halt once again. The ground floor area was oddly overcrowded despite its architectural openness. Julian stood on his toes and looked around the science district with frustration. It appeared as if the architects who had designed it were so lazy that they stole the blueprints of the residential and agricultural quadrants and mixed them together. The reality was not so different according to his father after all. The strip of greenery along the middle of its length as well as the opposing blocks on either side presented a striking resemblance to the way the flats were built to face each other, leaving a void in between for the plaza. Instead of food kiosks though, it was tall pine trees that rose all the way to the top, almost touching the glass lattice that prevented them from escaping to the blackness of space.

Rachel tapped on his shoulder and yelled next to his ear. "At the park!"

Lucas had made his way through the stone paved path and was standing in front of the glass lifts on the left side of the quadrant.

She grabbed Julian's arm and pulled him behind an overgrown bush holding her index finger in front of her mouth.

"What?" Julian protested.

"We can't get in the same lift, but if he goes down instead of up, we'll lose him for sure."

"What do you suggest then?"

"I'll go check where he stops and text you the number. You take the lift on the opposite side and I'll wait for *his* to come back."

Julian nodded and rushed through the grass to the other side of the strip. The roller chimed just as he stood in front of the lift, panting, and Rachel's face appeared on the screen along with a single number, -8.

Once inside, he felt his stomach jumping to his chest as the park was swiftly replaced by his reflection on the glass against a pitch black shaft. When the doors slid open again, it was to a barely lit hallway, painted with a monotonous white. Two silhouettes were walking in the opposite direction in the far distance, becoming clearer and bigger as they moved towards him. They hadn't noticed him yet, giving him the time to hide in the nearest intersection. Running his hand through his hair as the sweat had started to trickle down his forehead, he leant out of the wall for a peek.

James had joined Lucas—they were talking like old friends who were just catching up.

Julian hid behind the wall with a thud. They were getting closer, their conversation still hard to make out even though it echoed throughout the empty hallway. All he could hear was his pulse drumming inside his ear and he suddenly became aware of his own breathing—the rhythm was steady but fast, like coordinated pistons pumping air throughout his body.

The old metallic tiles clanged louder and louder under two sets of footsteps that approached and came to a halt only a few metres short of the intersection.

"We walked so much more because of your stupid suggestions. We could've taken the other lift." Lucas growled.

"That's where they told me to wait for you, alright? I didn't know where the room was either" James complained.

A familiar electronic device beeped and a door slid open, the vibrations coursing to Julian's back through the hollow wall.

When the door clanked shut, he finally came out into the main hallway, standing in front of the door the boys had gone through to study it. There was no engraving, no number or any other possible form of indication for its purpose.

The squeaky sound of Rachel's shoes echoed from the other side of the corridor, rubber slamming on loose metal tiles with force as her pace quickened.

"Did you lose him?" she asked out of breath.

"They went in there," he answered reluctantly, knowing what was coming.

"Who's they? And why didn't you follow?"

"'Because they would see me?" He shrugged. It was one thing to follow Lucas, a whole other thing to confront him—in a tight space—alone.

"Just open the damned door Julian," Rachel snapped, filling her cheeks with air like balloons—*I didn't mean it*, her eyes meant to say.

He placed his palm on the panel and tilted his head quizzically when the reader buzzed with the red screen. "That can't be right," he muttered and tried again, this time pushing all his fingers on the surface.

"Let me try," Rachel suggested, stubborn as always and shoved him aside after the second failed attempt.

"It's probably biometric," Julian remarked, "Why would James have access to it though?"

"James? Our James? Oh, he's in a world of pain." She took her roller out of her bag, unfolding the glass into a flat display. Licking her lips, she tapped on the screen a few times and revolved around her position to orient herself. "It shows here that there should be another entrance from the back, so maybe if we follow that hallway?" She pointed at the corner Julian had used to hide. "Apparently this is a huge lab or something, maybe some sort of manufacturing facility that occupies the whole block? It only says here, Annex 5E."

The back door presented them with the same problem. The panel kept blinking red despite the repeated attempts and the different hand placements.

Rachel let out a sigh and forced her shoulder on the door.

"Well, first of all, that's a sliding door, not a push. And secondly, we've tried everything, nothing works. Let's get out of here," Julian suggested.

It felt like talking to a wall as she approached the door and placed her ear on the surface.

"Thirdly, all doors are also soundproof."

Rachel stuck her tongue out to mock him before placing a finger in front of her lips. "I think there are more people in there," she said after a few seconds.

"Do you think this is where Lucas and his friends meet?" Julian whispered, realising at the same moment no one could hear him either from the other side of the door.

"And what is James doing here? There's no way he's hanging out with Lucas' friends. He's smarter than this."

"You never know. Up until yesterday we didn't even know he was seeing Liam."

"There's only one option left then," she said, her lips pressed tightly together, her eyes wide and filled with determination and Julian knew the next thing she'd say was going to push their luck. "I'll stay here in one of these intersections and wait for someone to come out. You go to the other entrance and do the same," she said casually as if they were talking about seats in the theatre.

Julian didn't pose any objection this time. He had spent too much time and energy already to let it go all to waste. He just nodded and returned to his previous hiding spot at the intersection. He sat on the floor against the wall and pulled his roller out of his pocket.

His head jolted when the wall behind him vibrated and the door slid open scraping across the threshold. He unwillingly held his breath at the sight of two men walking past him on their way to the lift and tried to remain completely still. Thankfully, they didn't notice him and went about their way, allowing him to finally fill his lungs with air. A woman's voice stood out in the racket, it was shrill and nasal, the kind of voice that only dogs would normally hear.

"It's finally our time," she said, her annoying voice becoming clearer as the short woman appeared at the intersection next to an older man. She had her arm wrapped around his and leant on his shoulder, the top of her head no more than a few inches above it. "I only hope everything goes according to..." she trailed off when she caught a glimpse of Julian, studying him from top to bottom with an arrogant frown before nudging her friend to walk away faster. He didn't even know the woman, yet she acted like she hated him. He took out his roller and started composing a message to Rachel before a throaty cough grabbed his attention.

"What are you doing here, you cosmic fuck?"

He slowly looked up from his screen feeling a strain at the back of his neck from having to stretch it so high like watching the peak of a mountain from its foothills. The insult didn't even make sense to him but Lucas' threatening tone made it sound worse than it probably was.

He had to answer fast to not look suspicious but the words slipped his mind, his heart pounding inside his ribs and his feet trembling under his weight. He was somehow managing to stand still however, albeit voiceless in his terror. He opened his mouth to speak, but no words came out. He used all his focus to will his jaw in action and finally stuttered a sentence.

"Hey... Lucas. I am here for research," he blurted without thinking, feeling his eyes widening from the mistake.

"Bullshit," Lucas growled, moving closer and forcing Julian to grind his back against the indentation of the corridor. "You can find everything on the server, I am not stupid. Now tell me the truth before you have to do some research on how to put broken ribs back together."

Julian gulped, trying to wet his dry throat. "I am here with Rachel... we were looking for a quiet place, for you know..."

Lucas lifted one eyebrow, his whole face moments away from bursting in laughter. He finally let out a snort that sounded like gravel being ground inside his nostrils and placed his heavy hand on Julian's shoulder.

"Nah, little dragon is way out of your league. I mean look at you." He waved a hand in front of him with a cringe. "And then look at Rachel. She's becoming a fine woman." He leant over him by using Julian's shoulder as a prop to support his massive weight and whispered, "You know what happens to cosmic shits like you who hide things from me?"

Julian could feel the warmth and stench of his breath, a mixture of rotten eggs, raw protein, and whatever extra synthetics he was eating to overgrow those muscles. He wrinkled his nose in an attempt to seal it but the bile had already reached the bottom of his throat.

"I was just passing through." His third excuse was the worst.

"And then you dropped your roller." Lucas exposed a sinister smile before knocking the roller off Julian's hands. The glass shattered as it hit the floor and its segments went flying to the other end of the corridor.

"What the hell are you doing?" He protested, unable to process what had just happened. "There are cameras everywhere, they'll deduct so many points from you for this."

Lucas looked over his shoulder at the black sphere on the ceiling of the intersection and asked with a provocative smirk, "What cameras?"

Julian had to examine the camera with his own eyes to verify that there was indeed no red light blinking on the glass surface.

"Luke, you coming?" A girl shouted behind him.

"Coming babe," he backpedalled, his eyes still locked on Julian. "I did you a favour. Now they can't track you." He wrapped his arm around the beautiful blonde girl who was waiting for him in the middle of the intersection with her legs crossed. She was so short—or maybe Lucas was that big—that someone could easily mistake her for his daughter.

"Sorry Katey, had to teach that boy a lesson." His obnoxious voice echoed from the end of the corridor.

Julian took a deep breath and looked around for the fragments that were scattered around the floor. Anyone who was in that room was already gone, leaving him alone to pick up the shattered pieces of his roller, struggling to understand what Lucas meant. The more he thought about it, the more it validated his theory that he was being watched—followed even.

His heart jumped to his throat when he heard footsteps behind him and he immediately turned, jitters running throughout his body.

It was Rachel, a puzzled look on her face as she approached. "What happened?" she asked, placing a hand at his back.

"Lucas happened. He smashed my roller."

"What, really? Oh, we are definitely reporting him. That camera over there, what's its number?"

She stood on her toes to get a closer look at the thin metal plate the camera was attached to and wrote down the number on her roller.

Julian sighed, "Don't bother, it's not recording."

"What are you talking about? It's working fine."

He stood up and studied the black sphere above him, flummoxed by the blinking red light that had just appeared again. "I swear it wasn't working before."

"What do you mean it wasn't working? It's a camera, it's always on."

"No, it wasn't," he insisted. He hadn't imagined it, had he?

"Where was James in all that?"

"I didn't see him come out. There were actually a bunch of people in there, I don't think I know any of them though."

"Fuck, we shouldn't have split up."

"We shouldn't have been here in the first place!" He shouted.

"I'm sorry for dragging you in this but you're the only person I can trust, Julian."

He drew a long breath, knowing she had quite a big part of the blame but not wanting to upset her. "It's not your fault."

The problem was not the shattered roller itself but the fact that it was virtually irreplaceable. *Glass film is not easily recyclable, Julian,* his dad had told him when he'd first given it to him. *You need to take good care of it. Think of it as an extension of your hand.* It did feel like that actually. Without a roller he was cut off from the ship's network and kicked back to ancient times.

"Maybe your dad can give you one of his? He always has three or four laying around at your place," Rachel tried to smile but her expression came off more creepy than comforting.

"They're all for his work." He scooped up the last piece of glass and as he put it on his open palm with the rest, he twisted his wrist, letting them fall on the metal tiles with a clanging bombardment. "What am I going to do, glue them together? There's no point."

"What about Mark?" Rachel suggested.

What did Mark have to do with anything? He stared at her with what must have looked a very perplexed grimace because he could tell she was stifling a laugh.

"Didn't you say he took a job in maintenance?" She asked, giving Julian no hints for where she was going with it.

"Yeah, fixing pipes and hull plates, not rollers."

"I'm not saying he'll fuse your roller back together but he can probably get us in the control room. Maybe the camera wasn't recording but it was definitely still…"

"Streaming!" He finished her sentence.

She smiled at him and softly punched him in the arm. "You see? Together, we're unstoppable."

"Maybe we can also find out what they were doing in there. Hopefully something that will lead us closer to Alex."

"My thoughts exactly! The only question is… Will Mark help? We've got twenty-four hours before the stream is overwritten."

Julian squeezed his eyes to adjust to the shift in light cycles as the bright, reflective white faded into a warm, welcoming, yellow hue. It had been a long day already and all he really wanted was to go back to his virtual beach at the Hub. He needed to hear the calm waves frolicking on the wet sand and dip his toes in the crunchy earth and water mixture—even though it was all just a lie. There was still something burning inside him however, a feeling he wasn't particularly fond of. A scorching tingle that started on his chest and exploded through his veins across his whole body with every beat of his heart.

"OK, let's do this. Yellow light means he should be back home in a bit. We should hit his flat."

CHAPTER 6
— Rachel —
The Control Room – Ring 3

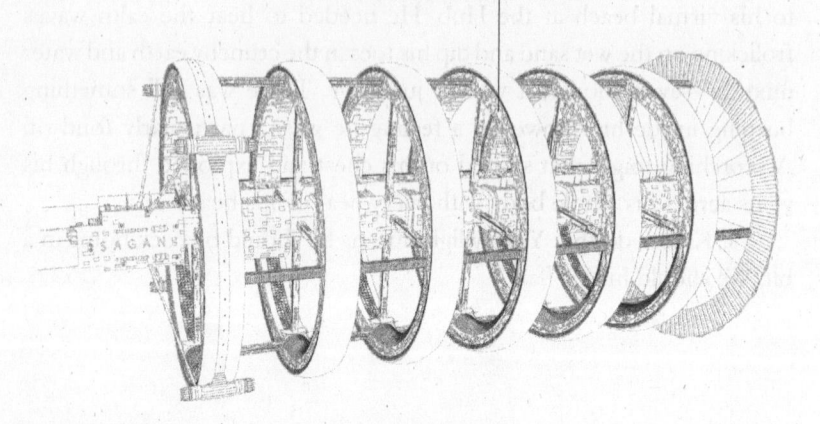

The residential area as was busy as it usually was around this time. The overcrowding due to the renovations at Ring Six meant there were always queues at the kiosks. It had been four years already but it still pissed her off, having to wait for a simple sandwich. Her stomach gurgled but there was no time to wait in line, even though the peppery, smoky and spicy scent of her favourite soup tormented her nostrils.

"I didn't know he lived in my own Ring. Weird I've never seen him around," she said when they got in the lift. "And if I remember him right, he's a very noticeable guy." She glanced at him for his reaction.

"We're here to ask a favour, Rach."

"Yeah, a date," she lied, eliciting a scoff and an eye roll from him.

"He's older than you anyway." He slapped the button on the panel.

"And just two floors above me? Have you been hiding him from me?"

"We were going to the Knowledge Hub all the time together. Not my fault you rarely joined. Come on, it's that door over there." He pointed along the balustrade.

The teasing was over but it had offered a pleasing distraction in her misery.

Julian knocked on the door and a blonde woman greeted him with a hearty smile. Her figure contradicted the wrinkles under her eyes making her look younger than she probably was.

"What a pleasant surprise. I haven't seen you in a while," the woman exclaimed, welcoming them inside.

"Eh, I've been quite busy lately." Julian shrugged with the answer. "I'm trying to figure out what specialisation to choose for next year."

"It can be a difficult choice, but you know you can always change it afterwards. And who is your friend here? My my, aren't you a cutie?" She eyed Rachel from top to bottom, a sparkling look of widened eyes and raised eyebrows that made her a little uncomfortable.

"That's my friend, Rachel." Julian's wording hurt a little but how else would he have introduced her? "Ms Spoles, is Mark here by any chance?"

"Yeah, he just got back actually. Mark? Julian is here," she shouted, summoning the tall boy from his room.

His long black hair was wet and stuck on his shoulders, the weight of the water pulling the fused strands down. His eyes were as narrow and long apart as she remembered but seemed very symmetrical under his thick eyebrows. He fiercely shook Julian's hand, leaning in for a shoulder bump, "Where you've been, J?"

"Busy, can we talk?"

"Straight to the point as always. Sure, let's go to my…" he trailed off when he noticed her, "Is this Rachel? Wow, good job growing up."

"Hah thanks, you look great too," she offered him a smile. She had to be on her best behaviour to get his help.

"Yeah, ok. As I said, can we talk?" Julian interrupted with another eye roll.

"Hold on a sec." Mark gently nudged him aside to get to her. "I heard about Alex… as we all have. How are you holding up?"

She hated that phrase and the pity that came with it but she needed him. "I'm trying to keep it together." She used the sympathetic nod that usually followed that question, feeling the pressure of her teeth grinding behind her sealed lips. "It's mainly why we're here actually. We were hoping you could help us with something."

"Yeah, of course. Anything I can do." He cupped her hand with his.

"Thanks, you're sweet."

"Don't worry J, I'm not going to steal your girlfriend." Mark said when Julian faked a dry cough.

"She's not... anyway. Let's talk in your room?" Julian whispered, glancing at the kitchen where Mark's mum was.

"What can I do for you?" Mark sat in the swivelling chair while grabbing a bowl of peeled carrots from his desk and placing it on his lap.

"So, Lucas broke my roller earlier and the camera there wasn't recording for some reason. Is there a way to access the feed regardless?"

Mark scoffed, "Lucas. Fucking hate that guy. Wait, so many questions. Why did he break it, where was that camera and how do you know it wasn't recording?"

"Julian is leaving out the whole story as always. Let me tell you what happened," Rachel chimed in.

She started from the beginning and explained everything that had transpired. Julian tried to comment on her story with his own perspective, but she shushed him every time. He eventually climbed on the bed with his back to the window and waited for her to finish.

"So, what do you think?" Julian pulled himself to the edge of the bed when she was done.

Mark flicked his hair behind his shoulder and reached for the last carrot in his bowl. He chewed for a few seconds and turned to Julian after swallowing, "I think you should definitely let this go. Take it from me, you don't want to mess with Lucas Bjorgen."

"It's not just about Lucas. Our friend James is somehow involved as well and Rachel thinks it has something to do with her brother. Did you not hear the story?"

"I... I don't know what to tell you, J. It's very unlikely that a camera would stop recording just like that. You have the backup chip that kicks in immediately and if that fails as well, the hardware pings the error to the control room."

"So there's a possibility for the camera to fail completely?"

"Technically yeah, but then I would have heard about it in maintenance. They send me out for all the grunt work like that."

"What about the stream?" Rachel crouched in front of him. "Can you get us in the control room before it's erased?"

"Wow, that's a big ask, I'll tell you that. I only started this job a few weeks ago, I can't really go poking around secure networks for a camera."

"Please, Mark? No one will tell me anything, the admins are useless and Lucas is the only lead I have left." she begged, a new low for her.

Mark stood from his chair and looked outside the window, both hands on his waist. He let out a long exhale and his lips shook. Then his eyes bounced around the room and finally returned to her.. "Ok I'll do it. For Alex, not to get back at Lucas, although that boy needs to be taught a lesson at some point."

"Yay! You're the best," Rachel cheered.

"Hold on, it's not going to be easy." He gave her a wary look. "I can get us into the control room, but it needs to happen after red lights. Meet me at the quadrant intersection between recreation and science." He tied his hair above his head and picked up his jacket from behind the chair.

She followed him through the flat and glanced at Julian behind her. "I thought it'd be harder," she mouthed the words to him.

"Are we really going to the control room right now? Isn't someone always there?" Julian's eyes were fixed on his friend, the icy blue of his irises pushed to the brink by the expanding darkness of his dilated pupils.

"No, control is handed over to the AI after the last shift," Mark explained.

"And that won't be a problem?" Julian pressed on with his endless questions.

"It'll be fine," Mark assured him but Rachel could tell it did little to comfort him. "Don't be an air-locked."

The term stirred a distant memory, the one where they had gone out of the ship for the first time. She had stayed behind with him while the rest of their classmates were goofing around on the outer rim shield.

He'd managed to lock one magboot outside the hatch but never went further than that. Supporting him through the comms was out of the question, no one could know he was about to throw up from standing on the spinning Ring.

The memory carried her all the way to the empty science quadrant and the lifts in the centre. They exited a few levels below and Mark cautiously checked every direction before finally leading them to a double door.

He exchanged a few serious looks between them and declared in a low voice, "Now if this works, I will also have to delete any footage of us having ever been here, meaning that if I get caught, you get caught as well. Are you sure you still want to do this?"

She turned to Julian hoping he wasn't having second thoughts but thankfully he nodded in agreement. She needed him to feel safe, to maintain what little sanity she had left. He was definitely out of his comfort zone, biting his nail again and his eyes danced around like he was being chased by someone.

Mark kneeled and placed his finger under the plastic encasement of the door's panel and tapped twice. The chamfered box opened in four pieces, one for each side, and pushed the hand reader out of the wall. He pulled it out and let it hang from the multi coloured cables that were attached to its back. He took a long thin case out of his pocket and revealed a slim needle no thicker than a few hairs together. He leant in closer to the panel and carefully placed its tip inside a miniscule opening. A blue spark zapped his hand and he jumped back, shaking it frantically.

"I thought you had access here. Are you breaking in?" Julian asked his rhetorical question.

"I only said I can get us in, didn't say how."

"This is surely illegal though. We might get in a lot of trouble if someone finds out."

"That's why I'll wipe the footage after we're done. Relax, I know what I am doing." Mark assured him but Julian was in stress mode already.

"What exactly are you doing?" Rachel asked, curious and with nothing else to do other than wait for Mark to do his thing.

"All Maintenance crews have one of these special needles to restore failed systems. It has a magnetic tip interrupting the circuit in the panel," he explained and carefully tried once again. "The problem is that if you hit the walls of the hole with the metal surface you get shocked."

"What if you wear gloves?" Julian asked, leaning on the wall.

Mark pulled away from the panel and looked at Julian with a sneer, his eyes droopy and vacant. "I didn't really have all the time in the world to prepare, did I?"

"I mean, they could have even made it out of rubber or something and prevented this whole issue altogether."

"How about you put in the recommendation to the engineering lab tomorrow and let me finish this?"

Rachel lightly slapped Julian on the arm and pulled him close to her. "Will you shut up?" She whispered. "Do you have to always do this everywhere you go? Let science have a break for a day."

"It's ok Rachel, I've grown used to it over the years. It's just that I need to be very focused to... get this... right!" Mark cheered as the door slid open with a buzz.

The ceiling lights turned on automatically one by one in succession and illuminated the space with a bright white glow, so blinding that she had to cover her face with both hands. Once her eyes got adjusted to the difference in brightness between the red of the hallway and the white radiance of the control room, she stepped inside the area of the ship she had never seen before. It was a boxed space no bigger than her flat, but without any internal divisions. The walls were made of stacked thin monitors, covering the surfaces of all three sides, each telling their own story about the ship. The only furniture in the room was a polished white, elliptic island counter in the middle, which was inhabited by empty chairs and dirty mugs.

"Warning, unauthorised personnel detected."

The female, humanlike voice of the AI repeated her threat three times in a row.

"Fuck, this isn't good. I need to hurry up," Mark said and ran to the desk in the middle.

"But you're going to erase everything after you're done, right? Like we were never here?" Julian asked, his gaze fixed on his friend.

"Yeah, yeah. The problem is that this bitch has probably already notified Mr Kaplan. Just… don't touch anything and let me do my thing. Kaplan will be too lazy to get off his ass and come here anyway."

Julian let out a loud exhale from his nose and cracked his fingers one by one, stopping at his thumb and manically biting the skin around it.

She looked around the room and moved towards the nearest wall to inspect the monitors—Julian was far gone into stress mode, there was nothing she could do to calm him down now. Each video feed exposed a different part of the *Sagan*, showing empty hallways, rooms, plazas, and labs, all with the same blinking message in the middle of the screen 'AI Systems Online'. They all looked very different from a close examination, but very much the same from a few steps back. "Do you know what monitors show my Ring?" She turned to Mark.

"There should be a description on each feed at the bottom. I haven't been here that much so I don't really know either," Mark replied without even looking at her. He was tapping his fingers on the flat surface inside the counter where the alphabet had appeared, illuminated in a blue light that encircled every letter.

"Manual control override."

"I got in," Mark exclaimed, almost surprised by his own achievement.

She sat in the chair next to him while a vertical plane sprouted from the counter's surface—a continuous screen that displayed various graphics and data, stretching all the way around them, following the shape of the furniture.

"What was the camera's number?" Mark asked, sitting back with an exhale.

"Here." She passed her roller to him and leant with both elbows on the desk, resting her face on her open palms. "Do you think you can find out what happened to it?"

"Guess we'll see," he said with a brief shrug.

She silently observed several numbers moving horizontally

through the screens, windows opening and an enormous amount of incomprehensible data and lists appearing within them. Mark was frantically tapping his fingers on the virtual keyboard making them disappear while at the same time splitting his attention among the surrounding displays. He brought his hands back to his lap and slumped in his chair.

"Well, that can't be right."

"What is it?" She asked, lifting herself from the chair.

"It shows here that there was nothing wrong with the camera."

"So, was it actually recording?" Julian asked, stopping his pacing around the front of the room to stare at his friend.

"No, it wasn't. But it had nothing to do with the camera being faulty or anything. You see, every year or so, the cameras back up all the data back to the servers. They stream live as you can see around us, but only a series of images is saved on the repository. That is supposedly backed up once a year. Are you with me so far?"

She exchanged a vacant look with Julian and waited for Mark to continue.

"Every camera has its own backing up schedule when it goes completely offline for an hour or so to copy the data over. The engineers have scheduled most of the cameras to do that overnight when nothing happens anyway. Now for the interesting bit. If what's shown here is correct, that camera was listed to do its yearly backup a few hours ago."

"So, it was just an unlucky coincidence?" She frowned and sat back in her chair.

Julian grabbed her from the shoulder and turned her around along with the swivelling chair, raising his question to both of them, "That doesn't explain how Lucas knew about it."

"Maybe he had access to sensitive information from someone who works here?" Mark suggested.

"That's even more worrying. What else can you find out?"

Mark bounced on his chair to make himself comfortable again, crossing his legs to sit on them. He didn't fit but apparently that's how he liked it. "Come check this out. I did a check for yearly backups on all cameras and look what I got." He pointed at a series of highlighted lines on a data sheet. "There are cameras that are scheduled to do their backup tomorrow but look. They're not even full yet."

"Relative year 128. 1500 relative time. Camera R1RCQC334," she muttered.

"And see that one down here? Same date, same time, right in the middle of the day," Julian added.

She squinted to follow the correct line and read it out loud, "Relative year 128, 1500 relative time and the camera's number." She pulled back and turned to Julian. "What is relative time?"

"Do you really want me to explain *now* how time passes differently for us than it does to those living on Earth?"

"Not if you're going to use that tone. I don't know, I found it weird," she shrugged apologetically.

"I'm sorry, I didn't mean to snap, It's only that…"

"I know, it's okay," she cut him off. Julian was already doing a lot more than he was comfortable with in order to help. "So… all these cameras do their back up tomorrow, how does that help us?"

"Because my unobservant friends, you haven't paid attention to the weirdest thing of all. Look at the cameras that go offline at the same time tomorrow. R1RCQC334, 346, 378, 379."

She stared blankly at Julian who mirrored her confusion.

"Guys, all the cameras are in the same place. R1RCQC334, aka Ring One, recreation quadrant, camera 34 of the third floor. The number marks the corridor they are located in and guess what? All these cameras highlighted here are forming a rectangle on level three of the recreation quadrant."

Julian rolled his eyes. "How were we supposed to know that?"

Rachel nodded in agreement but didn't linger on it. "So, do you think they intentionally go offline around a particular room?" she asked, her brows hurting from how long she was maintaining that confused frown.

"I'm sure, let's see which one." Mark swiped his fingers on the keyboard and produced a plan of the area on the other screen showing all the cameras with a blinking green dot.

Julian leant over her shoulder to read the tiny letters out loud that described the function of each room and hallway. The blinking spots were encircling a wide area around the gym and the theatre, cutting off intersections and corridors that led to them.

"What was the room in Priya's note again?" Rachel asked, filled with anticipation of a new lead.

"It was Ring One as well…" Julian turned to her, his eyes widened with the same realisation. "No, same Ring, same quadrant but different level and time." He shook his head, putting the piece of paper back in his pocket.

"Can't we stop them from doing the backup and catch them in action?" Rachel suggested.

"That's actually a good idea. Can you do it Mark?" Julian backed her up.

"I don't think so. Something like that would need high authorisation but let me try."

He sat on his foot and cracked his fingers one by one, "This might take a while," he declared and started tapping again, his hands moving faster than a professional pianist playing at high tempo.

When she looked up from the screens, Julian had already moved to the open door to give a brief glance in both directions of the hallway. He lingered for a few seconds, hunching his shoulders and lowering his head, probably making sure the bulkhead was quiet and safe before joining her at the wall of monitors. She approached every screen individually to read their description, until she came upon one that read 'R3RSQC025'. The code made sense now, it was showing the ground floor plaza of the residential quadrant in her home Ring. The image of the deserted kiosks drenched in long, scarlet rays seemed very familiar as she tried to remember the last time she had gone home before curfew. Her parents didn't care anyway. Her mother was too self-absorbed with Alex's case and her father—well her father never cared even before Alex's disappearance.

A loud thud made her jump and turn to Mark who groaned and used his hand to massage the bottom of his fist. He stretched his hands, cracking his elbows and placing both hands behind his neck. "I can't do it," he growled, standing up defeated. "It needs Mr Kaplan's authorization. I can't crack coding like this."

"At least we know where Lucas is going to be tomorrow." She settled for the small victory. "Did you manage to get the feed from earlier today? Isn't that why we came here in the first place?" She asked.

"No, when the cameras do their backup, they are completely offline. We would've had better chances if it was a faulty one. What I did find however is this." He tapped on the keyboard and the schematic of a Ring took over the whole screen.

"What are we looking at?" Julian leant in, squinting.

"Spit it out, Mark!" Rachel snapped, annoyed by Mark's natural flair for drama.

"There are more cameras that go offline tomorrow but way later in the night cycle."

"Where?" She peered at the blueprint to find a pattern in the overlapping layers of architecture drawings.

"All of lower engineering at Ring Six."

"What do you mean… all?" Julian stepped back.

"Yeah, not for the same reason as the others though. They are scheduled for a restart which would take them offline for a whole cycle. They switch on and off to calibrate to the light cycles."

"Don't you think that's probably part of the renovation works?" Julian suggested.

"All I'm saying is I went hunting for shady cameras and that's what I got." Mark said and replaced the schematic with the previous database screen.

"Ok but no one goes in Six, not until they open it to the public anyway," Rachel added.

"Wait, no. I saw Lydia with her family today, they were moving to Ring Six."

"Did you see them going in? The outer bridges are all sealed."

"I only passed them on the way to class, I didn't follow them. They were carrying stuff though, maybe it's open for a select few? She did say something about being chosen." Julian scratched the stubble on his cheek and looked away, lost in thought.

"I think Ring One-recreation sounds like a more promising lead," she said softly, almost in a whisper, her eyelids heavy, exhaustion starting to take its toll on her.

"Let's do that then," Julian exclaimed, still peppy. "We know where Lucas and his group is going to be, let's notify administration and catch them red handed whatever they're doing."

"And say what?" Mark sneered. "We broke in the control room and found out a group of shady people is meeting on level three?"

Rachel exchanged a few looks between the two boys and finally pointed at Mark. "Mark's right. No one will believe us anyway. No, we have to do this ourselves."

Julian took a deep breath and looked away but eventually nodded with a long exhale. "We should get going then. We've stayed here long enough."

"Let me just interrupt the feed from the cameras around here and we're good to go," Mark said and got back to work.

"I'll be outside," she said to both of them and stepped out of the bright room into the dim, crimson hallway.

Another defeat but the fire inside her was still burning strong. There was no way she would ever quit looking for him, not when there were still leads to follow. In reality, they were more like tiny breadcrumbs but leads nonetheless.

"Is this going to take long?" Julian asked from inside. He was probably still nervous about their sneaking there but had managed to keep it together so far.

"Almost finished. I am gonna put them in a loop for a couple of minutes after we leave just to be sure," Mark reassured him.

She rubbed her eyes and leant against the wall. Her legs trembled and with a swoop she was down on the floor, the pain of the fall barely registered compared to her aching muscles. It felt like her whole body was pulsating, stiff and sore from the lack of sleep.

Julian rushed to the door and knelt next to her, wrapping his arm around her. "What happened? Are you ok?"

"Just… tired." She drifted to the side and caught a glimpse of the white light at the end of the bulkhead. "Fuck, the lift is stopping at this level," she groaned trying to get back on her feet.

"Mark, come on we've got to go," Julian pleaded.

A chunky silhouette emerged from the lift, enveloped in a shadow against the bright glow of the shaft. Mark rushed out and slid in front of the panel he had deconstructed earlier.

"Hey you. Stop right there!" An elderly yell echoed through the corridor.

"Hurry up Mark!" She implored him, waving her hands back and forth.

His fingers slipped and the reader fell off the wall, only hanging by the cables attached to it. He hastily jumbled the cables inside and forced it to its original position.

The man was briskly walking towards them, becoming clearer and louder with every step, but not running. The reflection of the white light emanating from the control room gave form to an oddly shaped, old man; his gait was unsteady, favouring his right leg and limping on it like a boat drifting away between waves.

"Go, go, go!" Mark urged them when the panel finally clicked in place.

She ran with whatever energy was still left inside her as Mark passed her and called the lift on the other side of the hallway. Julian was in front of her but pacing his steps to match her speed.

"I'll find you. You're not getting away with this," the man yelled from the control room.

CHAPTER 7
— Julian —

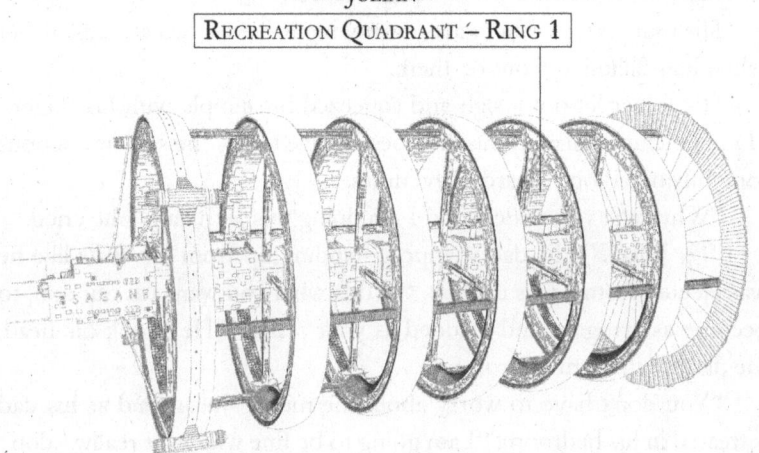

Recreation Quadrant – Ring 1

His parents were fighting again. It had become their morning routine. His mother kept endlessly pacing in a circle around the coffee table and his father was sitting at the dining area, his chair facing towards the living room. The apartment fell silent when he entered and he crossed through them, his eyes half open, desperate for the bitter stimulant.

"Why can't you realise that this is the best choice for us?" His mum started in a softer tone. "I am doing this for *us*."

Julian took a sip of coffee and stood under the kitchen's threshold, the warm steam wafting over his face. "Do you maybe want to include me in all this at some point?" He asked, his patience depleted.

His parents exchanged a look between them in an inaudible conversation with their eyes.

"We're moving to Ring Six." His mum finally broke the silence.

"We're moving? Why?" Julian asked, as shocked as his dad who threw his hands in the air in exasperation. He would have never guessed that's what their fight was about.

"That's what I've been saying all this time," his dad shook his head, letting sharp puffs of air through his barely parted lips.

"Julian, it's going to be better for us in Six." His mum stopped her pacing for a second to address him. "They're making me head of Hydroponics over there and the refurbishments are so…"

His dad scoffed and she trailed off. "Where did they find the materials to refurbish a whole Ring, Freddie?"

His mum lowered her gaze, narrowing her eyes, two strands of her ashen hair falling in front of them.

His father let out a sigh and squeezed his temple with his fingers. "Don't include Julian in this, he doesn't have to go," he said in a serious tone Julian had only heard a few times.

"Why can't you understand I am doing this *for* Julian," she cried.

"*For* Julian?" His dad snapped, standing up from his chair like he was ejected from a jet's cockpit. "Is this what you want for our son, to become as arrogant and deluded as your *friends*?" He shook his head, the disappointment clear in face.

"You don't have to worry about me mum," Julian said as his dad retreated in his bedroom. "I am going to be fine wherever really. I don't get why you're fighting over something as trivial as that."

"It's not just that, little monkey." She threw a cautious look to the closed door of the bedroom before continuing, "Can you start packing your stuff? We need to move in a couple of days."

"Couple of days? Julian huffed but didn't press on. He had endured enough confrontation for one morning.

⚛

Rachel wasn't at their shared desk when he sat in class but Liam quickly filled her spot, balancing his pale cheek on his palm, his elbow propped against the flat surface.

"Have you seen James," his friend asked the question he didn't want to answer.

There was no easy way to tell him James was involved in some shady dealings with Lucas. "James is acting a bit weird lately," he deflected.

"I know, right?" Liam took the bait. "Look, I'm sorry you had to find out like that but you saw how he reacted. I couldn't tell anyone." He let out a cathartic exhale. "Feels good that someone knows though… like a heavy load has been lifted from my shoulders, you know what I mean?" He lowered his head, his eyes still fixed on him.

He didn't but agreed anyway. "Have you two talked since the

Cylidome?"

"No, I wanted to talk to him after PT but he wasn't there. Now that I think about it, neither were you." His head cocked with the realisation.

Julian averted his gaze and stretched his arms to give himself some time to think of an excuse. "Rachel convinced me to skip class. You know how stubborn she can get sometimes."

"Wow, Julian Walker going against the rules and skipping class. I haven't seen that for a while now. What did you guys do?"

Julian felt cornered. How had Liam managed to turn the conversation around? Thankfully, Rachel walked in to his rescue, shooing Liam from her spot next to him.

"Hey, Rach. Julian was just telling me how you got him to skip class yesterday. Got to say, very impressed." he winked at him with a smile before returning to his desk a few rows behind.

"You told him about yesterday?" Rachel snapped in a contained whisper.

"Of course not. If we can't trust James anymore, the same goes for Liam."

"Duh, I'm glad to see you know that."

"Ahem." Lydia ran her fingers through her long, straight hair. It seemed shinier and slimmer than usual, almost reaching her waist where her short t-shirt allowed her skin to be exposed. Julian followed her hair with his eyes from top to bottom stopping at her hip bones that stuck out under her shirt.

"I can't believe you forgot about me yesterday," she complained with a cute frown.

"Oh yeah, sorry. In my defence, I had a really bad day. My roller broke and I had to take care of some other stuff too," he blurted, unable to form proper sentences when talking to the girl of his dreams.

"Oh, in that case, I forgive you." She smiled again, both hands now playing with her hair. She gave a brief glance at Rachel and leant on the desk in front of him, licking her pink lips. "Listen, I wanted to ask you, I know it's not a thing or anything, but I was thinking, how would you feel if we went to the Halfway together?"

Julian choked on his own saliva from the excitement. "T-The

Halfway event? As in... a date?"

"Yeah, exactly like a date." She formed that smile again. Even her teeth were symmetrical and perfect.

Her body fell off balance as the desk was pushed forward with a grinding thud and Julian jerked to find Rachel rummaging through her bag, her face almost entirely inside.

"Okaaay..." Lydia rolled her eyes and continued, "How about you come pick me up like half an hour before the event then?"

"Yeah sure. I'll be around anyway now that I am moving to Six too."

"Really?" she pulled away from the desk and replaced her smile with a confused frown. "Who told you?"

"My mum... this morning actually." *You don't seem very excited*, he wanted to add but refrained from uttering the assumption.

"What else did she tell you? No, you know what? Don't tell me here." She rushed to her desk as their teacher entered the class.

Julian turned to Rachel. "Are you ok?" he asked almost in a whisper.

"Yeah everything is fine," she replied with a slight nod.

Julian had to turn on his terminal when Mr. Kodolski greeted everyone and started his course. Maths was his absolute worst; he wished he could understand it, but he couldn't even remember what the squiggly symbols and Greek letters meant. He would often accuse himself of not trying hard enough, but the excuse of him not having the brain capacity for it was such an easier thought. He glanced at Rachel again. Her nose was runny and the green in her eyes was imbued with a red glare.

⚛

His eyes darted across the empty hallway and his mind drifted while waiting for Rachel to come out of the women's lockers. Most of his energy these past couple of days was dedicated to distracting her and keeping her safe and sane. The picnic had been somewhat successful, although it may have backfired. He still wasn't sure what she had meant when he pinned her down. Was she suddenly interested in him or was it the emotional vulnerability of the moment? He didn't know how he felt about either scenario. Whatever it was, his priority was to keep her from doing something truly stupid in her reckless search for Alex.

There was an annoying, rhythmic tapping somewhere above him—more like the precise clinking of tiny footsteps that resonated with metallic echoes on the pipework. The yellow hues of the afternoon cycle could barely penetrate the horizontal forest of rust-encrusted tubes, the stacked cable containment trays and above them all, the network of discoloured ductwork that remained obscured in the shadows. Standing on his toes and squinting, he focused on the tiny red light lurking in the darkness.

He jolted to the hiss of the door opening and Rachel finally walked out, wrapping her hair around her roller to keep her ponytail in place.

He heard that clinking again but when he looked the mysterious light had been swallowed by the shadows.

"Where have you been?" he asked, the eerie feeling of something crawling on his back altering the pitch of his voice.

"I haven't had a shower in two days, what did you expect?"

"It's still five minutes maximum, no? Do girls get more water allowance?"

"No, Hailey gave me her time. Jen offered too. Those girls keep treating me like a wounded, little bird, it pisses me off." Her sharp tone matched the erratic movements of her hands. "But I really needed that long shower so I went along with it."

"That's nice of them. Did you talk to Mark?"

"Yeah, he should be at the intersection already."

Mark was wearing his usual grey tracksuit, occupied with his roller at hand. Julian stood in front of him and waved over his screen to get his attention.

"About time you guys made it. You know I am missing work for this, right?" he complained.

"Yeah, thanks Mark." he apologised.

They made their way through the maze that was the recreation quadrant climbing staircases and walking in empty corridors turning left and right, always allowing Mark to lead—or rather the database he'd stolen from the control room to lead. They reached the third level and stopped in the middle of a bulkhead, much like the others they had passed already. Mark revolved around himself and looked at the ceiling.

"Okay, that's the centre of the rectangle. All cameras in three intersections radius are about to go offline in five minutes."

"It looks awfully quiet." Julian observed.

"Look around, see what you can find." Rachel shooed them away.

Julian walked to the nearest door, realising it was the gym. He figured it was unlikely that some clandestine group would want to meet in such a high profile place but he studied the frame and controls for any sign of abnormality or tampering. He followed Mark's line of sight to the opposite door further down. "The theatre?" His muscles instinctively formed a grimace of disbelief.

"Are you sure this is the right place?" Rachel shouted from the other end of the hallway.

"Of course I am," Mark scoffed. "There are other rooms inside the theatre," he added, "Maybe they..."

"Shush!" Julian placed a finger in front of his mouth. "Do you hear that?"

Mark and Rachel both nodded simultaneously. A faint conversation between two men echoed through the empty halls reaching them as a warning.

"We should hide," he suggested.

"It's still daytime, we have every right to be here you know," Mark countered, "I say we just play it cool."

Rachel looked at both of them, her eyes swooping left and right like a pendulum, "Julian is right," she declared, "If there is nothing going on, we're just three people talking to each other outside the theatre. If there's something shady happening though, we are three people waiting for them in front of their secret meeting."

The voices of the two men became louder and clearer as their footsteps produced an irregular rhythm on the metal tiles of the stair core.

"Try the door," Rachel whispered manically.

"What if that's where they're going?" Mark protested.

Rachel huffed and shoved him aside. She pressed her hand on the door panel and cursed when it turned red. "That's the fucking theatre, why is it red?"

"The gym. Quickly," Julian suggested and they all ran towards the opposite direction, almost stumbling on each other. The door of the gymnasium chimed successfully, offering them a chance to escape in time.

"Now what?" Mark asked.

"I don't know," Rachel shrugged and stood against the empty reception desk in the gym's lobby.

Julian put his right hand through the holocircle in the middle of the door and waved it counter clockwise to lock it. Then placing his ear against the cold metallic surface, he waited for any indication of what was going on in the hallway. He was sure both men had come to a stop just outside but their conversation didn't make any sense, distorted as it was through the solid metal.

"Fucking finally, only a couple of days left and we're free," one of them said.

Julian couldn't make out the reply as Mark and Rachel were yapping behind him.

"Shut up, I am trying to listen," he hissed, pressing his cheek harder against the door, cursing its near perfect soundproof quality.

"Can we trust the mid-gens got the job done at the Core Hull?" The other man asked. He had a deeper voice, a baritone of authority. Were they talking about Lucas and James? Mid-gens was what his generation was called, the one to suffer the middle part of the trip to Epsilon Centauri.

"You can never be sure with those teenagers. The real problem is the water. The tanks took longer to get built than expected."

"It was the doctor's idea to mask it as renovations. Are you questioning him?"

There was no answer to that question, the voices died out and only the faint vibrations of the ship's mechanical systems remained.

"Three, two, one…told you," Mark exclaimed and Julian turned back to find the others staring at the camera on the ceiling, its glass surface black—inactive.

"I think they went into the theatre," Julian said, uncomfortable and naked in the absence of safety the cameras provided. "That was the centre of your exclusion zone, right?"

Mark nodded after a brief glance at his roller.

"Can you get us in like you did in the control room?" Rachel rushed in front of his taller friend, grabbing his arm and shaking it with both hands.

"You want to go inside the wolf's den?" Mark sneered but her determined glare must have changed his mind because his head bobbed about and he finally unveiled the maintenance pin from his tracksuit's front pocket.

They couldn't go barging through the front door; Mark led them through a hatch on the hallway's indentation and into the cramped service corridors underneath the floor. Light was split in individual rays as it passed through the evenly spaced grates above them, birthing dust particles into existence.

They climbed down a ladder to the level below and Mark had to turn on his roller's torch function as the mechanical plants had denied natural light entry to their leaky, damp domain. Natural light was a compliment—the nearest star was light years away.

Julian had lost track of where they were but at least the plant room was big enough for them to stand on their feet.

"Up there." Mark pointed at the ladder that was tied to the huge, perforated unit. Its blue, metal frame was discoloured with yellow streaks like an enormous zebra and the label, painted in white, made no sense—HVAC.

The rungs clanked with each step and once at the top, they were met with another ladder, one that brought them back to the crispy, odourless air of the recreation quadrant.

"I always wanted to see what the backstage looks like," Mark chuckled, running his fingers through the various costumes at the air hanger.

There was commotion on the other side. Julian snuck a peek through the circular window on the door that led to the stage to find the theatre full of people—people who had gone to extreme lengths to ensure their secrecy.

What am I doing here? His pulse was throbbing inside his ear again and his heart must have stopped when he saw Lucas dragging a girl backstage.

"Hide!" he almost shouted, clenching his jaw for his stupid mistake.

Mark rushed to take cover behind coats and curtains while Julian barely made it in time behind the props of an ancient play where Rachel was. He squeezed in the cavity of the thick, wooden boards, their bodies pressed together so tightly that he had to lean his head over her shoulder to avoid an uncomfortable close contact.

"You need to put her under," Lucas barked when the door hissed shut.

"It's not that simple, Luke." The girl's voice was familiar but Julian couldn't place her in his head. "Do you realise how many contribution points are required to get the materials for a new pod?"

Rachel let out a soft, throaty growl, eyes filled with anger under twisted brows. "Katey," she mouthed the name to him, so close he could feel the warmth of her breath on his neck.

"I can't protect her forever," Lucas pressed, his tone slightly whinier than usual. He was annoyed, but not in a threatening 'I'll break your bones' way.

Rachel shifted her body, trying to wiggle her way out of the cavity. She was going to confront them.

He held her wrist and shook his head, widening his eyes on purpose to convey the negation.

"Whose side are you on, Luke?" Katey asked from behind the partition.

"That shouldn't be questionable after everything I've done. It's just two days, all I'm saying…"

"You know what's at stake," Katey cut him off. It was the first time Julian had heard anyone interrupting Lucas Bjorgen without getting beaten to a pulp. She had authority over him, like a dog on a leash. "I've waited almost forty years for this, you can wait two more days."

"Tell him to lock her in Nightfall then. She doesn't deserve to die, Kate."

Die? Had he actually uttered this word?

The door hissed again but Julian wasn't sure if they had left the backstage area or if someone else had entered. It was only after hearing Ares' voice that he held onto Rachel's wrist even harder. "They're giving out final assignments, come on."

"This isn't over," Lucas snarled, switching back to his usual intimidating tone.

"Julian, for your sake, let go of my hand," Rachel commanded when the footsteps retreated and the door slammed shut. She squirmed, trying to wriggle between the wooden board and his chest, growling until he let her go.

She was still fuming when he slid out of the cavity of the prop, her nostrils flaring with every annoyed breath and her big, green eyes locked on him.

"I'll keep you safe at all costs, even if that means protecting you from your stupid self," he stated.

"Look what you did." She brought her hand right in front of his eyes and twisted it so he could get a good look of the purple bruise.

Mark jumped out from under the costume racks, sharing a wary look between them, his lips pressed in a look that matched his words. "We shouldn't be here."

"This is exactly where I should be," Rachel countered, "The answers I need are here." She swung her arms about, on the verge of a mental breakdown.

"Did you not hear them saying they're going to kill someone?" Julian snapped.

"I agree," Mark chimed in, "Have you seen how many people are out there?" He peeked through the window on the door and ran back to them. "No... we're leaving. I'm responsible for both of you. Don't make me force you." He lowered his head for extra convincing points until Rachel nodded—thankfully.

Taking the same route back through the service corridors, they talked about what they had witnessed, always coming back to the same question.

"Do you think that *this* is related to Alex?" Julian repeated it, extending his arm towards the general direction of the theatre.

No one had an answer until they had climbed out of the hatch and Rachel clicked her fingers, her features morphing with an epiphany, "You know who would definitely know what's going on? Your dad!"

"No no no. No, Rach, I am not bringing my dad into this. For starters, I can't tell him what we know without revealing *how* we know. And he has way too much on his plate already with my mum and all, I can't have him worrying about all this as well."

"I am not saying you tell him directly. I am saying you could snoop around his computer, see if you can find something."

"S-Snoop... are you crazy? You know who my dad is right?" The suggestion was preposterous despite being the only realistic option left.

"Come on Julian, you know your dad will definitely have something in his files—something about the people Lucas is meeting. Or maybe unreleased information or profiles on the people who went missing. Anything that can help us find Alex," her voice cracked.

"Rach, you know I want to find Alex as much as you but we have no idea what we may be getting ourselves into. These people clearly want to remain hidden."

"I agree," Mark nodded, his jaw tight and askew. "You should report all this to the admins as an anonymous tip and let them escalate it."

"The admins are part of it!" She yelled. "That girl, Katey, she's a senior admin. Who knows how deep this goes. Maybe that's why they haven't found anyone, because the system is corrupted from within. And killing people? On the most peaceful ship ever made? I can't stop thinking that I... I-I'll probably never... I'll never see Alex again," she hunched forward and covered her face in her palms.

"OK, OK. Come here," Julian threw his arm around her and pulled her in. "I'll see what I can find out," he said softly, his chin nestled inside the ginger jungle of her unattended hair. A mixture of aromas filled his every inhale, earthy and intoxicating like freshly watered flowers after an irrigation cycle.

"Can't believe she convinced you so easily J," Mark laughed.

"Yeah, that's her talent," Julian admitted. "First we need to check Priya's note and maybe then I'll check my dad's files. Only as a last resort," he remarked in a scolding tone, raising a finger to enhance the seriousness of his statement.

"Yeah about that..." Rachel started, her mouth twitching left and right as she chewed on her lip. "There's something I haven't told you."

Julian studied her. What kind of secrets was she keeping from him?

"That night at the Cylidome... I went back."

"You went back?" He said in a high pitched voice. It was exactly this kind of stupid, reckless thing he was trying to prevent her from doing all this time.

"Can you let me explain?" She huffed, reaching for his hand. "I followed the trees with the crescent moon and ended up at the rock we found James and Liam. There was a sentence. We were sent back but our voices still live here. Then a woman came, Lester Yau's mother, she said it was referring to the *Tyson-7* shuttle and now I'm going to a support group for the relatives of the missing people."

This was a lot of information to process but it only meant one thing; he would have to go to Priya's location alone. He turned to Mark who must have gathered as much from his look because he wrapped his arm around his shoulders and shook him in the overly excited way he used to since he'd met him.

"There's no way you're going there alone, J." He exclaimed and Rachel heaved a deep breath.

"Thanks," she said, bowing her head graciously, "I'll let you know if I find something."

"Don't go anywhere alone after red lights again," Julian shouted as she jogged towards the outer bridge.

"I can't promise anything." She gave him a brief, nervous smile and disappeared into the bulkhead.

Julian pulled out Priya's note and showed it to Mark again. It wasn't far from where they were. All he had to do was follow the holo-annotations on the walls.

One... two... three... he counted in his head to the rhythm of his breathing, trying to cancel out the asynchronous pulse of his pounding heart.

CHAPTER 8
— Rachel —

Recreation Quadrant – Ring 2

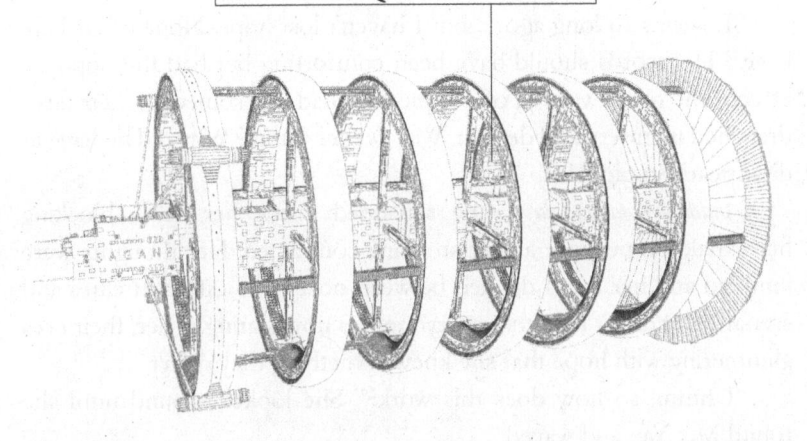

The bright, white light seeped through the half opened door and blended with the warm hues of the hallway to create a welcoming threshold. She hadn't been to Ring Two that many times but Mrs Yau's directions seemed correct. She softly pressed the door open and peeked inside, wondering if she had the right place after all. The unfamiliar faces didn't take notice of her apart from a woman who approached her with open arms. The hug was uncomfortable and unsolicited but even worse, it felt good.

"Welcome, dear. I had expected to see your parents but they never replied to my messages. Any family member is good though." The woman grinned, the wrinkles on her cheeks and under her eyes stretching wider.

If her parents had been invited to the support group, they hadn't told Rachel about it. Her mum spent most of her time in the Admins lobby and her father… she hadn't seen him since that first night of interviews.

"And you are?" She asked in a bitter tone. The woman didn't deserve her rudeness but the mental image of her incompetent father sitting in his armchair like everything was fine had instinctively contorted her face to a cringe.

"Oh, yes of course. I'm Francesca Venali, I'm the mother of…

Matthew Venali but you can call me Fran." She tried to maintain her smile but it was clear she was forcing it this time.

"The seventh disappearance, back in early twenty-one ninety-eight."

"It seems so long ago... but I haven't lost hope. None of us here have." Her words should have been comforting but had the opposite effect. The room was full of people who had lost someone, their faces drenched in misery and despair. Was *this* her future? Why did he have to disappear? Stupid Alex.

Aaaaaaaaaaaaaaaaargh, she screamed inside her head, blocking her exhale on purpose as her stomach contracted. Her thoughts were jumbled and her focus divided between dozens of different clues and scenarios. It didn't help that everyone was now staring at her, their eyes glimmering with hope that she knew something they didn't.

"Uhmm, so how does this work?" She looked around until she found Mrs Yau and waved.

"Don't bother, she's far gone," the man next to her whispered as he leant closer to her chair. The rest of the group pursed their lips and shook their heads in silent agreement.

"I'm sure you don't want to hear about how sorry we are for your loss blah blah blah," Francesca said and paused for a sip of wine from the bland, white mug she was holding. It must have been wine because the bitter aroma of pressed fruits and old wood tormented Rachel's nose. "You're here because you're sick of the sympathetic nods and pitiful glares."

Rachel agreed. It was refreshing to finally be with people who understood how she felt.

"I don't mean to be rude but..." A blonde girl a little bit older than her started, "We're all hanging by your lips here. Please tell us everything. Any clue, report, rumour, anything that will help us find the killer."

"Killer?" Rachel jumped from her chair as a pulse coursed throughout her body, originating in her chest and spreading to her limbs like a wave of electricity. "You don't really believe someone... k-killed him?" The last word was hard to even utter. The first time was by surprise but the second, she knew exactly what she was saying. The thought had forced its way into her mind once or twice but it was quite different coming from someone else. Especially a group of people who had lost their loved ones years ago. Lucas had also said it—Julian and Mark had reminded her. No, there was no way Alex was dead. He was somewhere on the ship, doing who knew what. Worst case scenario someone was keeping him against his will but he wasn't dead. She felt a sudden chill creeping up her spine and jittered. People were talking to her but it all sounded as an overlapping, inconsistent ringing.

"I don't really know anything, I was hoping you did," she finally said as the strangers came back into focus.

"The admins must know something, last location from the cameras or a suspicious message on his roller?" The man opposite to her leant forward at the edge of his seat, his round eyes wide open behind his black, loose fringe.

"The admins are useless, Jack. We've all been there, you know how they operate." The blonde girl spoke again. "Didn't we even have a theory that the killer is an admin?"

There it was again, the word that pierced her heart like a broad sword and twisted it all the way to her back, depriving her of breath.

"Still, they must have told her *something!*" Jack threw his hands in the air.

"I'm sorry, no. Not yet at least," She replied, taking notice of the unanimous, disappointed sighs. They were supposed to help *her*, not the other way around.

"Have you forgotten how it felt when you first lost your loved ones?" Francesca chastised them. "It's still all fresh for her, don't push her."

"You'll find out very soon that it's only up to us," the blonde girl retorted, her words sharp as knives. "No one else cares, a person disappears, a family is bumped up on the birth list."

"I-I'm sorry, Rachel," Jack started, sliding back in his chair. "Cassie is right, unfortunately. I hope you don't reach the point I am. It's been a long time since my *boy* was taken from me." His voice carried a deep sorrow, especially how he enunciated the word *boy*. No, it wouldn't come to that. She would either find Alex or his... his kil—no, she couldn't even think about it. She replaced the thought with the first thing that came to mind. Maybe Julian and Mark had more luck with Priya's note.

Maybe they had even solved it by now. Wouldn't they have messaged her if they had?

"Cassie has a point though." Francesca interrupted her train of thought. "Don't expect people to help. It's only up to us here. That's why we're desperate for some new leads."

"Uhmm, there is a person in my class," Rachel started, putting her only clue on the table, "Lucas, who I think knows what happened but he's avoiding me."

"Who is that *Lucas*?" Cassie leant in.

"Bjorgen." The answer came from the corner of the room in a low, croaky voice.

"Mrs Yau, you know Lucas?" Rachel stood up and approached the old woman who remained silent. She was staring at the wall as if she hadn't said anything. "Mrs Yau?" Rachel repeated and knelt in front of her.

"It is at their lowest when a person can be easily manipulated." The woman said without making eye contact.

"What does that mean?" She turned to the others, mouthing her question again but they all shook their heads apart from Cassie who twirled her finger next to her head like drilling a hole in her temple.

"The lowest, dear, rock bottom." Mrs Yau continued. "Questioning your very own existence. That's when you become easy prey for the ruthless predator." She finally glanced at her before finishing her sentence, her grey eyes hiding behind the split hairs that fell in front of them, unattended and uncombed for who-knew-how-long.

"Leave her be, it's ok." A woman with dark red hair motioned Rachel back to her seat.

"Why are you people so fast to dismiss her? She may be on to something." She looked back at the old woman to find her lost in thought once again. Crazy or not, she had to turn every stone, every tiny hint of a clue before disregarding it.

"It's the depression theory," Francesca explained. "We tried it, it didn't pan out."

"Depression?" Rachel asked, confused as to what that would have to do with anything.

"We were looking for anything our lost ones had in common;

personalities, hobbies, interests, circle of friends…"

"We found out that twenty-five of the victims were attending a therapy group," Jack interjected.

"Yeah, out of how many disappearances?" Cass added in a sarcastic tone, "The dates didn't even align, it was different sessions for my sister, Francesca's and Jack's boys and Marie's and Kim's daughters."

"Maybe the rest hid it better from their families… from *you*." Rachel waved a hand towards the centre of the circle of chairs. "I definitely wouldn't be broadcasting it if I was seeing a psychologist."

"No, it must be something else." Cassie shook her head. "Something all hundred and thirty-five victims had in common."

The constant use of past tense pissed her off. They had accepted their fate, filled with vengeance and bitterness.

"Wait, so what was the theory?"

"We thought maybe… maybe they had committed suicide," Francesca said in soft voice, a little louder than a whisper.

"Or isolated themselves somewhere no one could find them," Jack added.

"But no bodies were ever found. Have you searched the whole ship then?" She knew the answer to her rhetorical question but she preferred Jack's scenario. Maybe they were hiding away somewhere, detached from the rest of the ship. Why would Alex want to do that though?

"We've searched every single room on every Ring multiple times, trust me…" Jack said.

"Not all Rings," Mrs Yau cut him off.

"OK, apart from Ring Six but no one can get in there, let alone some teenagers."

"Oh believe me, if there's a way in, it's teenagers that would have found out about it," the young boy on her left exclaimed, glancing at her with the corner of his dark, blue eyes. He was around her age, probably there for a missing brother or sister. Rachel hadn't seen him before, he must have been from Ring One or Two.

Cassie scoffed. "There's no way into Six, Kaiden. It's a robot town. We've all seen it on the news, it's full of bots for the damned renovation works."

"And all outer bridges are sealed on Five," Francesca added.

"So no one has actually checked Six?" Rachel asked, wanting more than anything to believe there was hope but Ring Six was dead. She had seen the feeds in the control room herself.

"How?" Jack asked, his voice still loud. "To even suggest the killer operates from Six would mean they are either council members or someone with extremely high authorisation."

"Why killer? What happened to them choosing to be isolated?"

"They won't believe their kids are alive" Mrs Yau interjected, "For all their words of hope, they have actually none left."

The group fell silent. Mrs Yau had struck a chord apparently.

"I'm absolutely sure Liz is still out there," Kaiden stood up, giving her another brief glance.

"Liz as in Elizabeth Correy? The last missing person? I mean the last one is Alex, but…"

"Yeah, Liz is my younger sister."

"She disappeared around a year ago, right?" Rachel tried to remember the latest headline. She hadn't paid much attention back then—she didn't care. She didn't know Elizabeth, she was just another person on the ever growing list. The disappearances had started even before Rachel was born, it was part of her life. Cassie and Jack were right, no one would care for Alex now. It was up to her.

"Eleven months, nine days and… thirteen hours." Kaiden slipped his roller out of his slim, khaki pants to check the time. His eyes were sharp and focused while his chiselled jawline was set in a resolute expression, a relentless resolve that radiated from his entire posture. "Look, this is pointless. No offence, Rachel, I know exactly how you're feeling right now but if you have no new information we don't already know, then we should just call it a day. No point going in circles around old theories and dead clues."

"Do you all agree with this?" Francesca asked, revolving around herself. "Okay, let's not keep Rachel any more. I'm sure you're tired, dear," she said when no one objected.

It was relieving to see that no one gave her the usual sympathetic nod or the annoying pat on the shoulder. Mrs Yau was still sitting in her chair gazing at the opposite wall, seemingly unaffected by the sudden commotion.

"Wait, don't leave yet." Kaiden softly grabbed her arm as everyone else made their way out.

"What is it?" Rachel asked when they were alone in the room with Mrs Yau. Francesca was still there but on the other side, arranging some cutlery in the wall cabinet.

"How far are you willing to go to get your brother back?" Kaiden asked, creases forming on his forehead as his fair, symmetrical face morphed into a scowl. It surely wasn't intended for her—more of an outcome of his undying determination that conveyed there was only one right answer.

"As far as I need to." The words came out quicker than the time it took to formulate them in her head.

"That's what I like to hear." He grinned. "Mrs Yau and I have narrowed it down to the science quadrant of Ring Six."

"The science quadrant? How are you planning on getting in?"

"You didn't object to the Ring Six bit, that's good. I've been mapping the maintenance tunnels under the outer bridge for months now."

"And you found a way in?"

"I sure did." He flashed his white teeth with a grin.

"Why haven't you gone yourself then?"

"It's not that easy," he paused for a deep inhale. "There are people living there, guards, alarms, defence bots."

"Seriously?" Rachel snorted a laugh. She had meant to scoff but the claim was preposterous.

"Yes, SeRiOuSly," he mocked her in the tone of a child and she fought the urge to punch his arm or his pretty face. "Mrs Yau has seen them going in through the maintenance tunnels too."

"But... but how? Six is supposed to be under renovations, it's not pressurised, no oxygen flowing." She tried to rebuke him with what Julian had explained a while ago.

"Oh they're renovating alright. They're also building that massive ring structure under the outer rim shield."

"Ok, let's say I believe you, what does it have to do with the missing people?"

"I don't know what their goal is but we know they're connected to the disappearances. Mrs Yau says the therapy groups are where they choose their victims."

"The bright sun is shining for all of us, it is the nightfall you need to worry about." Mrs Yau hummed.

Rachel peered at Mrs Yau, still sitting in her chair and wondered if the rest of the group had affected her perception of the old woman. Was she as crazy as they made her to be? A secret cult abducting kids was not the sanest conspiracy she had heard. Her cryptic words didn't help her case either. Then again, the last days had proved that a lot of shady activities were taking place on the ship. Lucas' group was secretive too, whoever they were and whatever they were doing in their gatherings. Was there a chance they were even connected to the cult Kaiden was talking about? It was worth a try. "Mrs Yau, you said you knew Lucas Bjorgen. What do you know about him?"

"The boy is the harbinger of our doom." She said in her croaky voice and fell silent again.

"You know, I've seen Lucas going into the maintenance tunnels," Kaiden said. His face was a hard one to read but why would he be lying? He wanted to find his sister too. If he was telling the truth, that was the only argument she needed to investigate Ring Six herself.

"One last thing. Why haven't you shared this with the others? Or with the admins?"

"We have. The administration claimed there was no suspicious activity in Ring Six. I even recorded them once for proof but when they investigated, they found no one. These people are very careful."

Rachel bit the inside of her bottom lip. A lead was a lead, however crazy it sounded. She wanted to believe that Julian had found something but she couldn't rely on that alone.

"Ok, lead the way then." She motioned him towards the door.

"What, now?"

"Yes, now! I'm not going to wait eleven months like you."

CHAPTER 9
— Julian —
Recreation Quadrant – Ring 1

The door was old and rusty around the edges, but that was definitely the right number. It might have seemed like nothing more than a supply closet from the outside, but the room inside was large and bright. Chairs were set up in a circle, occupied already by people he didn't know.

A man not much older than himself stood up and gestured to him to come closer. "Welcome." He smiled and extended his arm for a handshake. "I'm William."

Mark introduced them both—a good initiative because Julian was stuttering even for his own name. He didn't know what they were walking into and after what he had overheard in the backstage of the theatre, the *Sagan* didn't seem as safe as he once believed.

"The first session is usually a bit intimidating for everyone, *believe me I know...* but you'll get used to it." William waved a hand towards the centre of the room.

Julian glanced at Mark who gave him a sharp, reassuring nod. He sat in the uncomfortable steel chair and looked around with hunched shoulders. Most of them were around his age, probably students like him but from other Rings. He felt a poke on his arm and turned to face the only familiar face around him.

"Priya? What's going on here?" He whispered, his eyes still studying the room around him.

"It's a therapy group." The brunette girl leant over his shoulder, her voice barely audible.

"Why couldn't you just tell me about it? Why the note?"

Her eyes widened and swung from left to right like she was deliberately bulging them to point at something.

"Was Alex part of this too?" he asked and she pursed her lips to shush him without making a sound—barely a hiss.

Her lips parted, ready to say something but she quickly jumped back to her seat.

"Everywhere I fucking go!" The voice behind him made him turn but this time the familiar face was not welcoming. "What is Walker doing here?" Lucas revolved around himself, the question intended for the rest of the group.

"We were invited," Mark answered first, standing up in front of him. Mark was almost a full head taller than Julian but Lucas still towered over him. He had dealt with the Lucases of the world in the past, able to hold his ground albeit for the twitching of his right leg.

"Yeah, Alex invited us," Julian added before Lucas had a chance to challenge him.

Lucas' gaze snapped to Priya, his expression difficult to read. It was hard to tell just by his curled brows and hung mouth—half of his face was angry and the other half was shocked.

"Our Alex?" Another familiar voice asked.

Julian turned towards the entrance to find Katey next to a tall man in a blue suit. His chiselled jaw was sharply shaved and his black hair was combed backwards like a cow had licked it.

This is fucked up. That was the only thought he could produce. Lucas and Katey were both there and suddenly he wished he hadn't spied on them earlier—hadn't heard about the murder that was bound to occur. He glanced at Mark for some sort of comfort but his clenched jaw and pressed lips meant he had come up to the same realisation.

"Have a seat, Julian." The man that had greeted them motioned him to the chair. "Everyone is welcomed here."

Julian did as he was told, exchanging a few looks between Lucas, Katey and the man in the fancy suit.

When everyone sat down in the circle, William stood in the centre with a resting smile on his face that did little to diminish the tension that hung heavy in the air. His uniform was the same design and fabric as the standard issue but completely different and new—a faded blue instead of grey and a yellow sun embroidered where the *Sagan*'s logo should've been.

"Hi everyone," William exclaimed, "As you may have noticed we have new people with us today, maybe you had a chance to introduce yourselves already, make them feel welcomed in our little therapy group?" He gestured to Julian and Mark like he was presenting them on stage.

For all the scenarios he had produced in his head regarding Priya's note, a therapy group was not one of them. He had thought about trying it himself a few times in the past but always hesitated to actually show up even for a single session. The real question was what Lucas was doing there? Maybe it was an endless supply of troubled victims to torment.

"Julian, do you want to tell us a little bit about yourself?" William asked and everyone turned to stare at him.

Julian bit his thumb and tried to formulate a sentence in his head. "Uhm... I- I am... Julian is my name..."

"You don't have to say anything more than what you're comfortable with. No one will judge," William said, gesturing to everyone around him.

"What am I supposed to say, like what my hobbies are?"

"It doesn't have to be anything too specific. Lucas, maybe you can get us started?"

"Seriously?" Lucas huffed, adjusting his massive body in the tiny chair. "Fine..." He cleared his throat and clicked his tongue. "Still no progress with my anger. Especially when *people* keep pissing me off." He gave Julian an ugly scowl.

"Have you tried the breathing exercises we talked about?" William sat in his chair in the middle of the circle and crossed his legs.

"They don't work. It's like I phase out and someone else takes over my body. I have no control of what happens next."

"What about a Hormony?" A young, brunette girl suggested. She was sitting opposite to him, her dark, brown eyes devoid of expression, lost in the darkness of the tired black circles under them.

"Hormone regulator? No thanks," Lucas spat.

Julian leant in his chair and balanced on his knees. Were they openly discussing cybertech like that?

"Lucas, it's all that testosterone. Try it," the girl insisted.

"I already have a Kerzi...I'm sorry, has someone explained the rules to Walker?" He glanced at him with narrowed eyes.

"Yes, it goes without saying," William started, "This is an anonymous group, anything discussed here doesn't leave the room."

Julian nodded hesitantly and checked on Mark next to him who did the same.

"You better keep your mouth shut or I'll break it," Lucas spat.

"Easy, Lucas. It's taking over you again," the man in the blue suit intervened.

"You see? That's what I'm talking about. It drives me crazy sometimes."

"Julian, maybe you're ready now?" William suggested.

"I don't have any problems like that to share," Julian tried to evade the question.

"How about you tell us what troubles you in your life on the ship then?"

"Uhm... I don't know... I guess I'd have to say the pointlessness of it all. There's nothing to look forward to."

"Good! That's good," Will exclaimed. "Does anyone want to add anything to Julian's thoughts?"

The thin boy opposite to him leant forward, stuttering before starting his sentence. "The other day, I took the advice you guys gave me and talked to an actual person. I mean I just asked for directions to the Hub but still... so I'm looking forward to having more conversations." He grinned as his eyes narrowed even more than their original elliptical shape.

"That's amazing. Andy here hadn't said a word in his first six months in this group and look at him now. I'm proud of you, buddy." William had gotten up from his chair and patted him on the back.

Julian softly clapped to join the unanimous applause of the group. There were people with bigger problems than him, it seemed. He wasn't exactly social but at least he could talk to strangers if he had to.

"That is very good Andy, but I have to agree with Julian," Katey crossed her legs and sat back in her chair. The blue shorts she was wearing exposed her smooth, shiny skin—so sleek that it glistened as if covered with oil. "I would rather go to Nightfall than spend another minute talking to anyone on this ship," she said with a certain bitterness in her voice, giving Julian a side glance.

Nightfall... Lucas had also mentioned it in the theatre. Julian felt more eyes on him, pressing him with an uncomfortable expectation to respond.

Thankfully Katey continued after her brief pause. "I don't get it, how no one is bothered by this. How can they go about their lives fully content and unaffected by the reality we're born in? The other day my mum celebrated finally beating a stage at Dragon Quest like that was the pinnacle of her life. I mean seriously, every other person I talk to tells me about that useless and uninspiring thing they achieved to distract themselves from the fact that we're nothing more than idle reproductive marionettes!" She glanced at Julian again as if she was waiting for his approval.

Julian averted his gaze and tried to look occupied with his fidgeting fingers. He couldn't have said it better himself though. There was something about this girl that spoke to him. Maybe it was the way she talked or the complete lack of facial expressions or even those cold, blue eyes that looked like the underwater part of an iceberg, refracting light into brighter shades of blue. She was right. People didn't care about any of the real issues as long as they had some pathetic entertainment to distract them. These were his thoughts as well but he was always laughed at when he would share them out loud. He was digressing in his head. Contemplating his existence wasn't what he was there for—that could wait.

"There's no need to get upset Katey. I think everyone here agrees with your worldview." William gestured with open palms.

"What world, William? Look around you. Do four walls inside a spinning bicycle wheel look like a world to you?" She kept looking at Julian after every sentence, waiting for his reaction.

"Can anyone with a more positive view challenge Katey on this?"

William revolved around the room.

One by one, almost everyone shared a story or a little achievement as Julian just sat there and listened. It was comforting to hear that other people were struggling with the same issues he was. He finally didn't feel completely alone in his nihilistic perspective of life. Mark had been silent the whole time—he wasn't the type to be nuanced by existential crises although they had talked about subjects like that in the past.

When the session ended and everyone stood up, Julian grabbed Priya by the hand and led her out of earshot.

"Why did you want me to come here?" he whispered, glancing over his shoulder. Mark had caught up with his plan, he was standing between Julian and everyone else at a safe distance.

"I'm being watched. You are too," Priya said in a somewhat threatening tone. "Alex wanted to tell us something," she continued when he couldn't think of anything to say. He wasn't crazy after all—he had felt it anywhere he went on the ship, a watchful eye tracking him, listening.

"What was it?" he asked, stupidly. If she knew, they wouldn't be in this situation now.

She kept tapping her foot on the floor, her arms crossed over her chest and her shoulders slumped. "It has something to do with that sun William is wearing on his uniform." She beckoned towards the other end of the spacious room where the session's facilitator was talking to the man in the blue suit. On the other corner, Lucas was in a silent but heated conversation with Katey, wildly gesturing with his meaty arms. They were probably picking up from where they'd left off at the theatre—not a good sign.

"Who's that next to him in the suit?" Julian tried to point as subtly as possible.

"That's Javier Rendall, he's working with Katey in administration. He's interviewed everyone here for Alex despite it being an anonymous group and all."

"Priya, that girl is dangerous. We heard her talking to Lucas about killing someone and I'm sure that's what they're saying right now." He tilted his head towards the couple but after a glance, Lucas wasn't there.

"I know. She was with Alex all the time before he disappeared. I'm scared, Julian." Her voice quavered and her widened eyes locked with his before darting nervously behind him.

A loud groan made him jolt to find Mark on the floor. Lucas was marching right at him like an unstoppable bull that no matador could evade. His legs froze and he instinctively placed a hand in front of Priya for whatever little protection it would offer.

"Didn't I tell you not to talk to anyone?" Lucas spat, enraged, his face as red as an open wound. He stopped in front of him and Julian couldn't help but wince, shying away, his body ready to receive the slam. "Especially Walker!" Lucas exclaimed, offering a hand to the girl Julian was protecting.

"I did nothing wrong," Priya cried, a soft whimper of agony.

"Walker has his *daddy* to save him," Lucas sneered, "Who do *you* have?"

"What are you talking about?" Julian asked, unable to control the trembling of his voice.

"Come with me, both of you!" Lucas ordered, grabbing them by the hand.

It was futile to fight him—Julian tried to resist but his body almost floated from how hard Lucas was dragging them out in the corridor.

"GO! Run!" He pushed Julian with such force that he stumbled and fell on the metal tiles, rolling over like a cut down log.

When he got back to his feet, Lucas was carrying Priya on his shoulder. Her sobbing echoed in the bulkhead as her hair swayed wildly on Lucas' back.

A sharp, visceral sound sliced through the air with a bright flash, a jarring concussion that demanded silence.

"NO! What have you done?" Lucas cried. Julian had never heard that frequency in his tone before.

Before he even had a chance to find out what had happened, Lucas was on his knees and Mark was limping out the door, bloodied.

Then Lucas turned back towards him, Priya lying motionless on the floor behind him in a pool that glistened in the same red as the night cycle. "GO!" His growl was deafening, reverberating across the metallic surfaces of the hallway, making every single hair on his body jitter and his spine to shiver.

What just happened? His throat closed and his heart fluttered. Was he breathing? The inhale was short and sharp, the exhale shaking his whole body.

Mark ran to him, limping and staining the floor with blotches of red.

"Go Walker!" Lucas repeated and Julian finally blinked, awakened from the shock of the realisation. They had killed her.

Mark nudged him as he passed and Julian's legs started working again.

He ran.

CHAPTER 10
— Rachel —

Engineering Quadrant – Ring 6

The pistons and tubes around her whirred with a persistent grinding as she tried to squeeze through the narrow corridor between the massive pipes. The intricate maze underneath the outer bridge was warm and for the first time in her life she felt beads of sweat forming on her forehead without having to do cardio. The long, thin path between the utilities was dark, the blue dotted lines along the metal floor glistening on the small pools of water that smelt of old metal. She glanced back at the pitch blackness and wondered if she should have come with Julian instead. It was already red lights whenshe and Kaiden had gone in from the science quadrant of Ring Five.

"Have you done this before?" She asked, still unsure whether she could trust the boy that was leading her further inside the mechanical plants.

"Don't worry, I know how to get us there." His answer would've been reassuring if it wasn't for his hesitant pacing and cautious movements.

A bright, red light was emanating from the end of the service corridor, pulsing steadily and drenching the brushed metal of the end of the pipework in a reflective purple. Inside, there was a circular shaft with a series of vertical pipes, ducts, cables and panels that disappeared into the abyss below.

Kaiden grabbed one of the smaller pipes that wasn't attached to the riser and wrapped his legs around it like a monkey. "See you down there," he said and disappeared into the darkness that swallowed him.

She wasn't going to let him think she would hesitate and extended her arm over the void, allowing gravity to take her.

The plant room at the bottom of the well was illuminated in white despite the late hour cycle. Colossal, mechanical units occupied the corners, corroded metal trays filled with cables ran above her head and pipes of all sizes connected everything together, thin layers of metal sheets coming out like the bark of a tree.

Kaiden was standing in front of a valve half his size, grunting to turn it clockwise.

"Here, let me help," she offered but he pushed her hand away.

"I've got it," he claimed but for all his grunting the valve only creaked with a screeching groan.

"Are you afraid I'll hurt your manly pride?" She mocked and held a tight grip around the circular handle.

The valve unlocked and the thick door opened to a dimly lit bulkhead. They were in Ring Six now.

"Where do we go from here?"

"I don't know, that's the farthest I've ever gotten."

"Are you fucking kidding me? You said you knew where you were going."

"No, I said I could get us in. We should be in the right quadrant, I just don't know where to start looking."

"Are you completely sure about the quadrant at least?"

"Yes, I heard them talking about keeping something in science and engineering. We think they were talking about our missing people."

"The cameras!" She exclaimed as she remembered Mark's finding in the control room. She had dismissed it back then but what if it was all connected? Had they disabled the cameras in engineering so that no one would see people walking about? But who were *they*?

"What cameras?" Kaiden asked, his confidence dissipated and his face plastered with confusion.

"No time to explain, follow me." She briskly stomped her way to the end of the bulkhead.

There was nothing to suggest the engineering section had been renovated. On the contrary, it looked worse than her own Ring. The walls were cracked and the paint was either faded or smudged with second hand colour. The stair core wasn't in a better condition, the yellow strips at the edge of the steps were loose or missing completely. The annotations on the walls weren't holographic like the rest of the ship—they were painted and barely legible as the black paint was either missing parts of some letters or filling others with a different layer of stencil.

Her eye caught a fat 'C' that must have had a lot of repairs done to it as it was almost filled with layers of half circles on top of each other.

Wait, that's not an ordinary 'C'. That's a crescent moon! She squealed inside her head as she felt her eyes bulging out of their sockets. She picked up the pace, climbing down the stairs two steps at a time, holding the rail to pivot at the landing to the other side of the spiral.

"Hey, why the sudden rush?" Kaiden tried to keep up behind her.

"I know where we're going." She felt her cheekbones stretching from her wide smile. She was close now, so close she could somehow feel it.

The door to the minus eighth level clearly stated it was an emergency exit but she shoved it open to reveal a corridor drenched in darkness and foul smell. She covered her nose from the musty and stale stench and tried to peer into the intersection. There were no lights anywhere, not even on the exit signs. Only the light from the circular window on the door behind her reached the intersection walls and faded out as it was eaten away by the darkness that laid beyond.

"Power must be out," she expressed her thoughts out loud and pressed her roller at the bottom of its cylindrical casing.

The light from the torch was quite bright but very narrow, little more than a few rays of light banding together into a thin beam and revealing the hidden particles of dust that danced inside it before twinkling out of existence in the surrounding darkness. The sounds of her own footsteps echoed through the empty halls, bouncing off the walls like the whisper of ghosts. Every step produced a different crunching sound from the debris that laid on the floor—tiles, metal rods and shattered pieces of glass that were left to decay, probably for years.

There was a distant rustling and then a silhouette moved across the intersection at the end as if the shadows themselves were alive, shifting and writhing in the dim light of her roller.

She grabbed Kaiden by the arm and pulled him close to her behind the indentation of the bulkhead, snatching the roller from his hands and turning the torch off.

The light from the lift illuminated the intersection at the end as it slowly reached their floor. A figure loomed tall in front of it, waiting motionless while casting a sharp, elongated shadow behind it. As the silhouette walked inside, the contrast between light and dark intensified, obscuring its features and shrouding its movements in a deep, inky darkness. Kaiden was right, there were people here. The thought brought a chill at the nape of her neck and her whole body jerked.

"So it's true." She managed to utter after the initial shock.

"Told you so," Kaiden gloated.

"It doesn't matter, we can't go back now. We're too close."

"You know what Rachel, I knew I'd like you."

"Keep it in your pants, Kaiden. There! Another 'C' that looks like half a moon."

"I...I-I didn't mean it like that," he muttered as he followed closely behind her into the perpendicular hallway.

They stayed close to the walls until she spotted another distorted annotation. This one read 'C2' and had a small arrow coming out of the tail of the number. It meant a right turn.

She followed two more annotations and stopped in front of the third one, 'C44'. It was right outside a big double door and had two arrows coming out of the bottom of both numbers. No one would have noticed if they weren't looking for it. The crescent moon looked like overlapped stencils and the arrows were nothing more than a few blotches of paint around a dry brush stroke.

"This must be it." She panted and kneeled in front of the weird looking panel. It felt metallic on touch—not the usual smooth bioplastic like the one Mark had fiddled with at the control room. There were actual buttons sticking out of it like some ancient contraption and all the light from her roller was eaten away by its matte, black surface.

This was the place. She was about to get the answers she so desperately needed. The only problem was the rectangular device that didn't even seem to have a screen display, let alone any holo-interface.

"Old world tech," Kaiden said. For a moment she had forgotten he was there as she examined every sharp corner and crevice of the panel.

The only person who might have been able to understand what it was and how to unlock it was Mark. He was handy with panels, maybe he could help her if only she could get a hold of him. Her roller beeped in a steady tune but there was no answer. Maybe they were still at Priya's thing—whatever it was.

"Who are you calling?" Kaiden leant over her.

"A friend. He might be able to help us with the door but he's not picking up." She growled.

"I know it may sound stupid but what if..." Kaiden trailed off to shove his shoulder at the middle of the double door with force but it only clanged as the metal scraped against the tiny opening between the two frames.

"It also looked stupid." She chuckled but the laugh didn't last long as she caught a glimpse of a blue light with the corner of her eye.

It was moving, hovering in the middle of the hallway, approaching. It gave shape to a spherical object underneath it, full of external armour plating and crevices that hid its systems in the deep shadows. Rachel froze and her heart raced. It wasn't the drone itself that threatened her or the fact that she was caught, but the two small cannons attached on either side of it. As she stared at the blackness of the long, menacing barrels, the drone emitted a high pitch whine followed by the sound of gears turning like a mechanical snarling. Why weren't her legs working? She should have been two intersections away by now but she was so close to her answers.

"Uhm, Rachel?" Kaiden whispered as the drone started whirring and beeping.

Suddenly, all noise came to a stop and the drone started a continuous humming that intensified as it approached them.

"RUN!"

CHAPTER 11
— Julian —

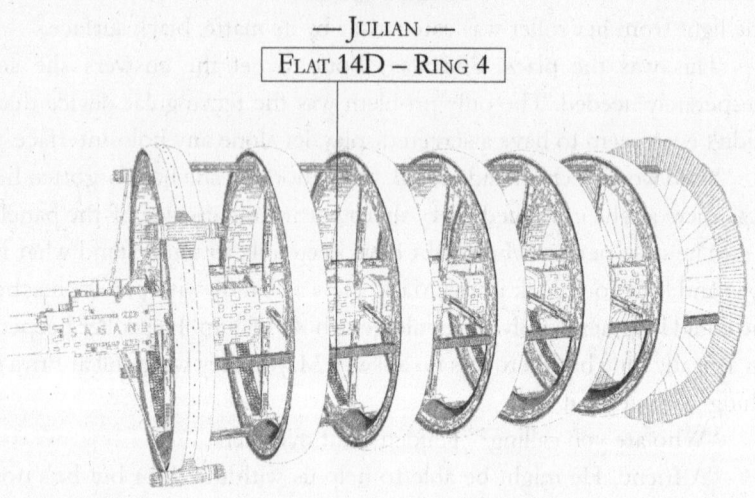

FLAT 14D – RING 4

The intense luminosity of the living room made him flinch and squint as he opened the door to his flat. At least it wasn't as bright as the infirmary where he'd left Mark. He had only sustained minor injuries after all, the most serious one being the blunt head trauma from Lucas' head-butt. Javier Rendall had also visited later—he was apparently moonlighting as a medical professional other than his day job at the Administration. If it wasn't for him, Katey would have probably had her way with Mark. She had apparently picked up from where Lucas had left when he dragged Julian and Priya out. The whole night was a haze, coming back to him in fragments, the image of Priya laying lifeless on the floor imprinted in his head forever. He tried to lock it away somewhere at the back of his head where he could never find it again but it kept flashing back right in front his eyes.

The rhythmic splashing of water drizzled on the bathroom tiles while a smoky, bitter aroma lingered in the living room.

Who drinks coffee just before red lights? He thought when he noticed the cup of coffee on the dining table.

The swivelling chair in his dad's study squeaked and he cautiously approached the doorless frame. His father was manically shoving papers on his desk aside and glancing at his roller. He opened a few drawers only to forcefully close them again with a loud thud and finally sat on his chair with a huff.

"How long do you need, boss?" A woman's voice came from his dad's roller on the desk.

Did she call him boss?

"I'll be there in five. Do not engage, Nyx."

He hadn't noticed him yet. "Are you going somewhere? It's red lights out." Julian pointed out and his dad slammed his finger on the roller, reeling it back to its default tube configuration.

"I wouldn't be your father if I didn't bend the rules a little." He forced a chuckle but he was clearly disturbed. His glasses had slipped just above his nostrils, black curls flying freely on his head from his erratic motions and his brows firmly pressed above his nose. "There's been an incident and they need me," he said while zipping his standard-issue *Sagan* tracksuit.

"An incident?" Julian repeated. Was he talking about Priya?

"Just go to bed, Julian. Don't answer the door for anyone," his father instructed, grabbing his coffee from the dining table and slurping a careful sip.

Seeing his dad twisting the lid on his cup and walking out into the red cycle, a terrible idea formed—one that Rachel had suggested.

Sitting in his father's chair didn't feel right. The stitches and patched repairs that were protruding from its brown leather skin didn't allow him any comfort either. He waved a hand in front of him and the transparent screen filled with a blue gradient. The last time he had been in this seat was a few years ago and his father had been next to him all the time, showing him pictures of the Earth they had left behind. He'd forgotten most of the names, but vividly remembered the sandy beaches, the crystal waters of a waterfall, the endless greenery of a forest and the long stretches of a desert dune. A city popped in his mind as well but all the architecture was blurry. He could only see tall boxes towering over smaller ones. The sky on the other hand was clear in his mind, smooth blue brushes painted on an endless canvas in different hues and interrupted by blotches of white here and there.

"Show me recent reports," he commanded with clear enunciation but the results were related mostly to maintenance, inventory and energy outputs.

He scratched the few hairs on his chin and changed his wording to 'recent incidents'. Minor accidents and complaints. He stacked the papers and pads his father had left in front of the monitor aside and double tapped the plastic surface with the stylus. A thin blue line expanded into a rectangle that covered the middle portion of the desk's surface. He stretched his hands above it where the English alphabet had appeared, every letter encircled in a blue light. His toes smacked the floor, setting the rhythm for the stirring of his fingers above the keyboard.

His involuntary dance came to an end at the sound of the bathroom door opening. His mother was dragging her feet across the living room until she finally appeared in the study, wearing her fluffy, red towel and grey flippers.

"What are you doing at your dad's terminal? She asked after scanning the room.

"He said it's okay," he blurted the lie, staring at the careful way his mum tied her wet, blonde hair on top of her head without spilling any water on the floor. "Mum, is everything alright with you and dad? You guys are fighting *a lot* lately."

Her lips parted—she had the answer ready but only sighed instead. She sat in the armchair in front of the bookcase and hunched forward, her features softening under those neatly shaped eyebrows. "Julian, there's a lot going on between your father and me, things I can't really explain to you... or maybe I can, I don't know. You're old enough to understand a few things and judge for yourself."

"So tell me then."

"I can't, monkey. I'm sorry."

"Why not?" He pushed in an unintended high pitch tone.

"I told you, it's complicated, Julian. I don't want to put you in danger. You'll find out soon enough, I promise."

Danger? What was she talking about? He pressed on but all his attempts to find out were met with the same negative head shake and lame excuses.

"Once we settle in Ring Six, everything's going to be fine." His mum extended her arm to grab the edge of the desk, reaching for the hand he'd placed on top of his father's stacked papers. She slumped back in her seat when he didn't reciprocate the gesture, lips pursed and brows bent. "Do you want me to make you some tea or something?" she finally said as she stood up to leave.

"Mum? Will you and Dad be ok?" He asked just before she was about to retreat to her bedroom.

She turned around with a faint smile, then approached the desk once again, tousling his hair, "Of course, monkey. We both love you so much, don't forget that no matter what. But also, don't forget to pack your things tomorrow for the move, alright? I have a surprise for you when you get there." She kissed him on the forehead and left him alone with his questions.

Julian stared at the long list of reports on the monitor and typed in a new search word, 'Divorces'. He was curious to see how many couples had split up since the beginning of the ship's journey and was surprised to see such a small number. He assumed that it didn't include all the open marriages he had heard about as this was an official report on divorces but found solace in the fact that the numbers were in his favour for once.

He squeezed his temple with his fingers, racking his brain to guess where his father would archive all the important events of the ship. His inner monologue provided him with the search word itself as he typed it on the keyboard. The archive list seemed endless but he had to be thorough. It contained everything from the human integrated technologies and eugenics ban to the birth queue list. He was tempted to have a peek, to find out who would proudly remove their stamp of contraception from their arm but a more interesting folder caught his attention.

Ship Critical Events

The new list seemed to be sorted by date, starting with Sol year one when the engines turned on and ending at the Halfway event at the bottom. He knew he wouldn't find what he was looking for in the first generation's records but wasn't sure if he would ever get another chance to go through the archives alone. He tapped on every available date trying to read as fast as possible, only paying attention to titles and picture descriptions.

It was at Sol year three that he bounced in his chair and brought himself closer to the desk. It detailed the expulsion of the shuttle *Tyson-7* from Ring One. That was what Rachel had found out in the Cylidome from Mrs Yau but the information on the event was minimal. When the *Sagan* had reached Neptune's orbit, some of the first residents had decided to go back to Earth—that was it. There was a document containing the list of the passengers but the names were blacked out.

Weird. Did they want to remain unnamed or had someone redacted the information?

"We were sent back but our voices still live here," he repeated the inscription. If they were sent back, why was it logged in the archive as their own decision?

He ground his teeth and sat back, crossing his arms in front of his chest. It almost felt like homework, searching for the right pieces of information and stitching them together into something coherent. There was nothing else on *Tyson-7* but something was off about it.

He couldn't linger on that for too long, his time was limited on his dad's terminal. He opened the admin registry even though he wasn't sure if classified reports was something his father would have access to. The administration office operated separately from council's authority almost as an independent function. He didn't waste time going through the numerous folders this time. He instead voiced his search and there they were, an array of folders about the missing persons, each bearing a name and a date. He tapped on the document named 'Investigation' instead and opened the latest data report.

135 missing persons in total — Likely more but not reported.
Average age 19. Indicates trend in younger population.
Possible hack of control room. Further investigation required.
Inside job?
Last known witnesses appear innocent.
Kidnapping? Murder? Where are the bodies?
No evident link between the missing persons.
Signed — Deputy director Javier Rendall.

Julian took a deep breath and went back to Alex's folder. There was a lot of information on Alex himself but very little on his whereabouts. The only thing he made sure not to forget was his last appearance on camera. "Science & engineering quadrant, outer bridge of Ring Five," he enunciated under his breath.

Why couldn't the other cameras follow him any further though? He couldn't have vanished in thin air.

He returned to the main archive tab and went through the rest of the list from where he had stopped until he found a rectangle about ongoing projects. This directory looked different from the others—every name had its own icon instead of the usual rectangle and they were spaced further apart from each other without any order. On the top left, there was an icon of a corn seed named 'Hydroponics genetics'. Below it, a human silhouette about AI & Robotics development and next to it a symbol of a microchip for Nano-quantum technologies. A drawing of a crescent moon was on the other side of the screen placed at the same height as the drawing of the yellow sun next to it.

"Project Nightfall and project Icarus," he meant to whisper but almost shouted in excitement as he touched the centre of the half-moon with his finger. That was the same icon he had seen in the Cylidome, carved in trees and the sun next to it was quite similar to the one on William's uniform. Katey had mentioned Nightfall during therapy, were the two related? His father seemed to have figured this out already, matching the name under the logo of the crescent moon.

A small black window appeared warning him that this item was password protected followed by an input prompt. He pressed on the folder with the sun but the computer only gave him the same error. He decided to try a few combinations of his father's birthday, wedding date and their names but with no success. He was able to access the other icons, although he didn't bother reading any of the articles inside and leant back to his chair, letting a strong puff of air from his tightly shut lips.

He looked around the desk for any loose paper or note that might have contained the password even though he knew his father wouldn't be so stupid as to leave it out there in the open. He stood up, stretching his legs until he could feel a burn on his quadriceps and rushed to his dad's favourite furniture—the bookcase that stretched the whole length and height of the wall.

Tracing his finger along the chipped edges of the shelves, he studied the titles while tilting his head to read the worn spines. *There's nothing sadder than a damaged spine*, his dad had told him once.

Most of the books in the 'Not digitised' section were torn, discoloured with hues of yellow and mistreated with dog-ear marks. He winced.

"Psyche and the collapse of the world economy," He read out loud. One of his dad's favourites but empty on the page-turn. What was he expecting, a note with the password handed to him?

He stood on his toes and slid the only perfectly preserved book out. The title stretched along the cover in a big, yellow font and behind it, a brownish, orange planet.

This 'Pale blue dot' as it was called was probably one of his earliest memories. He had later found out it was non-fiction but somehow his dad was always able to create a story out of it. He wasn't a normal dad, singing fairy tales about princes and dragons. No, the dragon in his stories was Jupiter, eating all the comets and asteroids that would dare oppose Earth. Instead of knights, he heard about the moons of Jupiter and Saturn, the gas giants of the solar system he would never see. His father always called it home, despite never having seen it either, the birthplace of our species that we would ultimately have to leave in search for a new home.

He sat back in front of the terminal and tried different variations of the book's title and the author's name. *Carl Sagan*. He must've been quite an important figure in his time if the ship was named after him. Nonetheless, all his tries were incorrect.

He searched around the room for anything he had missed, opening drawers and looking behind the furniture until he fell in the brown armchair by the bookcase, defeated. He pushed himself further back in it and felt an uncomfortable object against his lower back. Arching forward, he pulled an open roller from where it was lodged between the cushions. He flattened the glass screen and tapped on it a few times to make sure he hadn't accidentally broken it. It was one thing to snoop around his computer for historical and current events that would be considered common knowledge but going through his personal messages and notes was something he wasn't ready to do. What if the password was somewhere in there though? Was that enough of an excuse to justify his disrespecting his own dad?

He argued with himself in a loop, always ending on the same thought somehow as he hovered his finger above the picture of a man, roughly the same age as his father. His big smile and the grey hat on his head produced a symmetrical contrast with his dark skin that was uniquely beautiful to Julian. Was it called a fedora? He was sure he had seen that hat before, it wasn't something one could easily miss as it seemed to be something that belonged in a museum rather than someone's head. Was he friends with Julian's father? Julian had seen him around a few times but couldn't place him. Stretching his back, he heard the roller chiming as he had unknowingly touched its surface. Had his finger moved on its own or had he meant to do it? The smiling man had disappeared and was replaced by the message he had sent to his dad.

"The girl had no family to report her missing. Bolek is on top of it. This was the last straw, Scott. We need to..."

Julian jolted to the sound of the apartment's door opening, pushing the roller back where he'd found it and running back to the terminal to close down the tabs he'd left open.

The unknown footsteps were quick and decisive, reaching the study room before the main door had even closed.

His father locked eyes with him, panting. He leant with his back against the frame, letting out a tired exhale. "What are you doing here, Julian?"

Julian held his breath inside his trembling jaw. There was no lie good enough to absolve him. He scratched under his nails with his other hand while searching the room with his eyes, stealing a few quick glances at his father in between.

"Where is your roller?" His dad demanded when the answer to his first question wasn't answered. "I've tried calling you ten times already."

"I... I broke it." Julian said softly. Whatever his dad was mad about, this wouldn't help his case.

"You *broke* it? Julian you do realise we don't have Earth's resources lying around here, don't you?"

"I'm sorry… It was an accident. There was…" he couldn't finish his excuse. What would he have said anyway—he was following Lucas Bjorgen to a secret gathering while the cameras were offline and got caught?

Thankfully, his dad cut him off, "It doesn't matter, we'll come back to the roller once you finish explaining what you were doing on my terminal."

"Research?" His lie was so bad he said it like a question. His dad cocked his head to the side, hands crossed on his chest, unimpressed. Part of his unblinking eyes were hiding under his lowered brows, two semi circles of ice cold blue that pierced through Julian's lie as easily as he had uttered it.

"And what kind of research were you doing in my classified archive?" His dad took a sudden step forward, straightening his posture and pushing his glasses up his nose bridge.

How he knew was a mystery but mattered little now. He was caught—this was his chance to go on the offensive. "About projects Nightfall and Icarus." He answered in a softer tone than he had intended, unable to believe the words had actually come out.

His father jumped in front of the desk and stood above him, eyes bulging out. "Listen to me, Julian! Don't ever say these words out loud," he snapped, his eyes twitching and his jaw trembling like he was about to have a seizure. "To *a-ny-one*!" He enunciated each syllable. "Not Rachel, not even your mother."

"Then tell me," Julian cried. "I think both projects might be related to Alex's disappearance. If you do know something you owe it to Rachel to help."

His father inhaled with such force that his nostrils flared like trumpets. His face was all red and the wrinkles on his forehead had joined the ones that deformed his nose. He took another deep breath through his mouth and exhaled in small continuous puffs.

"Julian," he huffed, his voice still shaky, the tone abated. "This is important stuff that affects the whole *Sagan*. People who have come too close have disappeared as you said. I honestly don't know as much as you think I do, but I do know that you're my son and I can't allow you to be involved in any of this. Promise me you will not tell anyone, not Rachel, not your friends, not even your mother."

"Why n…"

"Promise me!" His dad smacked the desk with the bottom of his fist, sending the stylus flying off its edge.

Julian flinched and exchanged a few looks between the monitor and his father. Aggression—his dad must have reached a new level of desperation.

His chest burnt with the desire to growl—a wild animal caged within his ribs. He was so close to the truth but denied its disclosure. Eventually, he only bobbed his head about in an unwilling agreement.

"OK, now get off my desk before you *accidentally* access any more confidential information."

Julian slid out and traded places with his father, slowly stepping towards the exit and coming to a halt before the threshold. The message he'd seen on his dad's roller was eating him from the inside, urging his lips to part, the words at the tip of his tongue. "I was there when they killed her," he said, the memory still fresh and hauntingly disturbing.

The pregnant silence lasted for what felt an eternity but he remained perfectly still, his eyes bouncing around the living room furniture, blurry and out of focus. The footsteps behind him took forever to reach him until his dad enveloped him in his arms, his quivering breath carrying a noticeable tremor, betraying his diminished mental state. He flipped Julian around and grabbed his shoulders, lowering his head to meet his eyes. "You understand then why I'm so worried about you?" His question was rhetorical but Julian nodded. Seeing his dad on the verge of breaking down in tears formed a lump at the bottom of his throat, wedged so deep that he could barely swallow his own saliva.

"They won't dare touch a single hair on you as long as I'm still breathing," his dad continued with an unyielding resolve in his ice, blue eyes and Julian felt his own eyelids watering and his nose getting warm and stuffy. He sharply pulled him in again and patted him on the back a few times, probably to mask both their sniffling.

They both pretended none of that had happened when they parted—an unspoken rule between a father and a son.

His dad cleared his throat and returned to his desk. "Have you seen my spare roller?" he asked and Julian sucked in a sharp breath as if someone had punched him in the stomach. He stood there frozen in place as his father searched around the room until he finally found it lodged where Julian had left it.

He tapped on it a few times and handed it over to Julian with a wary look, "Here, use this and make sure you take good care of it this time. I did a factory reset."

Julian glanced at the roller and turned to leave, only to stop at the threshold again at his father's request.

"I won't ask how you found yourself in that therapy group but you need to promise me you'll stay away from these people." He said in a scolding tone.

Julian had so many follow up questions but he couldn't push any more than he already had. "OK, dad," he muttered and retreated to his bedroom.

CHAPTER 12
— Rachel —
Nightfall – Ring 6

Rachel sat at the bench near the Spicy Foods kiosk staring at her roller, the once intoxicating aroma of the earthy soups not doing anything for her anymore. When was the last time she had eaten something? Her stomach had curled into a tight ball, rejecting any notion of solid food.

"Would you like to place an order?" The robotic waiter raised its humanlike, fake eyebrows.

"Shut up," she said sharply and moved away from its sensor range.

Where the fuck is he? She growled inside her head but then she saw him, his blue eyes glimmering in the even lighter cyan hues of the morning cycle. He hadn't fixed his hair, it was all scruffy and short strands were falling in front of his face. A flat trolley was following him, loaded with a tower of boxes and further back, Mark blindly walking while tapping on his roller. They hadn't really talked much about his move to Ring Six and she hadn't had a chance to process the fact that he was moving three Rings away from her. There were more pressing matters—matters she needed answers to.

She snapped at them before even exchanging pleasantries—neither of them had sent her anything apart from the rendezvous details for that morning. They both seemed unfazed by her loud questioning and she took a moment to study them. Mark's nose was bruised, his eyes droopy and a thin strip of med-tape stretched above his eyebrow. Julian on the other hand looked fine—handsome as ever despite his grumpiness. She knew that look, he was deep in his own world of thoughts, detached from reality.

"What happened?" She asked in a softer tone this time, regretting her previous outburst, blaming it on hunger.

Julian gulped and the corner of his mouth twitched, formulating the sentence in his head most likely as he always did. He unfolded his roller and swiped towards her.

Her hair vibrated and she took her own roller out from where it was keeping her ponytail together. "The outer bridge between Five and Six?" It couldn't be a coincidence after what she'd found out the previous night.

"Yeah, but nothing on *Tyson-7*. The passenger list was redacted," he added, his eyes darting around the plaza like he was looking for someone.

"What about Priya's note? Did anything come out of it after all?" She asked and the boys shared a look, a clear struggle in their deep inhales.

"I need to get my stuff to Six," Julian deflected. "I'll tell you on the way." He tapped on the trolley's panel to get it moving again.

Julian stopped at a cliff-hanger when they reached the outer bridge to Ring Six, just when Lucas was about to drag Priya and him out of the therapy session. Her mind went to her support group—the abandoned theory they had about the killer preying on therapy groups. She didn't want to believe it either but Julian's information had her heart racing.

The two guards at the sealed bulkhead door raised their palms to halt them. Their uniforms were the same as the grey ones they all had but instead of the *Sagan*'s logo, it was a yellow sun that decorated the upper left part of the torso.

She glanced back at Julian who had stopped next to his trolley, frozen in place and gaze fixed on the guards.

"The bridge is off limits." The thinner guard on the left waved a hand to shoo them away.

"Uhm, it-it's ok... I-I... I'm allowed to go in." Julian said in a shaky voice, rolling up his sleeve and revealing his wrist to them.

She narrowed her eyes and studied him. He was acting weird and not in the cute, quirky way that she loved—his eyes were constantly searching for something, a ghost only he was able to see. What wasn't he telling her?

The man had to grab his wrist to keep it steady enough for the scan and it beeped in a single tone. "Mr Walker, you can go in but they can't." The guard exchanged a look between Mark and her. "There will be someone to receive you on the other end of the bridge."

"Wait, what? How am I supposed to unload all this stuff?" Julian extended both arms towards the hovering trailer behind him.

She'd almost expected him to go with it but something seemed off—he was nervous, scared even.

The guards mumbled something, the slimmer one holding a finger to his ear. "Okay you can all go through but there will be an escort waiting to take you to your new flat."

"That's alright, thanks." Julian agreed, biting his nails again.

She didn't like the idea of having someone watching over her every move but Julian was too fucking polite to say anything.

The door hissed and gears whirred inside it. The circular disk in the middle did a full rotation, locking in the mechanism and splitting the door in two halves. A warm, stale wind blew on her face, flicking her hair behind her shoulders. She stood there staring at the two boys as they went in the long, empty tunnel. Was she ready to face that drone again? She hadn't shared her plan with the boys yet but counted on their help. More importantly, was she ready to face the answers it was guarding?

The residential quadrant of Ring Six seemed like it was built only a couple of months ago. Most of the floor and wall panels were shining, the lights were all working and the freshly cut grass filled the air with an earthy mixture of oxygenated hydrocarbons.

They walked under the apartments and towards the lifts in the middle where Julian stopped, looking puzzled.

"Did you know Ring Six looked like this?" Julian said looking around the stone paved plaza and its colourful kiosks. "It seems like they used all their resources to refurbish just this quadrant."

"I don't even remember the last time I was here, but it definitely didn't look like this," Mark added.

The two guards accompanying them had been silent all the way there but their presence was irritating. Even Julian must have felt uncomfortable, stealing brief glances at both of them, probably studying them in that statistical brain of his.

They made their way to the second floor and stood in front of a recently polished white door. Julian touched the panel with an open palm and the apartment came to life, acknowledging their presence and highlighting the edges of the ceiling with a bright, yet calming, white light.

The guards turned around and stood firm against each side of the door until all three of them had gone in.

The layout was distinguishably different from the home she had grown up in. It featured one huge room where the kitchen counters were at the far end, a black leather sofa was in the middle accompanied by a long, brown coffee table and a metallic dinner table at the back wall. No corrosion, no dents, no scratches. Everything was... new.

"This must be my parent's bedroom," Julian said after opening one of the two doors at the end of the living room. "But.... I must have the wrong flat," he continued when he stood under the threshold of the second door.

"So are you going to be sleeping on the couch or in the tub?" She remarked when she followed him to the bathroom.

"My mum did mention something about a surprise. Did she mean I get my own place now? I can't live alone, I haven't even finished school." Julian flopped on the couch, releasing some of the trapped air in the cushions and causing the whole thing to scrape an inch along the floor.

She should've been happy for him but what was he whining about? A whole flat to himself, his own home.

"You're lucky, J. Even I don't have my own place yet," Mark said with a grin, swiping the dust off the kitchen counter with his finger.

"You can both stay here sometimes if you want. This couch seems quite comfy actually," Julian said and leant back stretching out his legs along the sofa.

"Let's concentrate on finding my brother first and we can have all the parties you want afterwards."

"I didn't say parties. I was only talking about you two," he corrected her with a shrug.

"Well if I'm here, there's going to be a party, J," Mark chuckled, taking a seat by the dining table to closely inspect the grooves of the wooden texture.

"Ok, let's try to blow past that." Rachel rolled her eyes as subtly as she could. She still needed him. "Mark, what do you know about drones?"

"Huh? Drones? What kind are we talking about? Repair, maintenance, surveillance? I've worked with different kinds." He raised his head from the surface of the table.

"I don't know, Mark, big ball with a blue siren," she replied sharply. Why did she have to blurt everything out, why couldn't she think about her answer for two whole minutes before opening her mouth like Julian did?

Mark huffed and for a moment she thought he'd snap at her. "Yeah, you're describing pretty much every drone."

"I may know where the crescent moon leads." She bit her lip to check their reactions—they were both more puzzled than shocked. "The problem is there might be a drone guarding it."

"I can probably deal with the drone, Rach," Mark exclaimed.

"Hey, no *Rach* for you yet. You have to earn it first." She pointed a finger with a raised eyebrow.

"Did you get that from your support group yesterday?" Julian chimed in.

"Something like that." She sat on the stool opposite to him and unfolded her roller on the coffee table. "I've been writing notes in a document all this time, you want to go over it with me? Maybe I've missed something?"

The boys nodded and she cleared her throat before tracing the first line on her roller with a finger.

"Alex disappeared on the sixteenth of seventh, twenty-two thirty-eight. He is the one hundred and thirty-fifth person to go missing. Lucas knows something. He and James did something in the Core Hull. Priya handed a note to Julian about a supposedly secret gathering. I followed crescent moon marks on trees. Trail stops at big carved stone that reads 'We were sent back but our voices still live here'. Lucas and James are part of a secret group. Cameras go offline just before they meet. Adults involved. Intercepted their next meeting in R1. Lucas and Katey were talking about killing someone. Julian and Mark to investigate Priya's note. Julian to look for info on the *Tyson* shuttle on his dad's computer." She finally took a breath. "Which brings us here." She enabled the keypad and typed the next sentence out loud. "Went with Kaiden Correy to Ring Six. Used maintenance tunnels under the outer bridge. Followed the crescent moon to engineering section. People live here already—secret cult? Drone armed with cannons chased us out of Ring Six. Plan in place with Kaiden to go again tomorrow."

She almost wanted to burst into laughter just by looking at their faces, their widened eyes and their gaping jaws that they both tried to cover with their hands.

"A-Are you... are you being serious?" Julian finally asked.

"I found it, Julian! It's on this Ring, the marked trees, the renovations, the guards, even that big thing they're building outside the Ring, it's all connected somehow. Something big is happening on the ship."

"This Kaiden... is he Elizabeth Correy's brother or dad or something? Did you meet him at your support group?" Julian gave her a troubled look of curled eyebrows and narrowed eyes.

"Yeah—brother. He should already be in here waiting for my signal."

"Let's go back to the drone with the cannons, please," Mark chimed in. "You never mentioned cannons. Actually what does that even mean?"

"You'll see for yourself when we go."

"We're going now?" Julian asked.

"Did you not hear what I just said? When else are we going to get this chance? This Ring is guarded apparently." She threw her hands towards the flat's entrance.

"No, I heard you say *cannons*," Mark interjected before Julian could answer.

"Look, I'm going with or without you. Kaiden is waiting for me. It's your call."

The boys exchanged a long stare between them, an inaudible discussion that she wasn't part of.

"Rach..." Julian started, sitting up on the sofa, his elbows balanced on his knees as he leant in. "Priya's dead."

"What do you mean dead?" She blurted, the words still being processed inside her head. She couldn't be dead—that would mean Alex was also possibly...

"They killed her, Rach. Right in front of me." He dug his face into his palms with a groan.

"Who?" She asked, realising she was pacing around the room—she didn't even remember standing up.

Her eyes turned to Mark who only shook his shoulders, wincing as he traced a finger over the med-tape above his black eyes. "Don't look at me," he said softly, "I got beat up by a forty year old girl-looking woman."

"He means Katey," Julian explained.

Rachel drew a shaky breath. The disappearances always carried a sense of hope due to their natural ambiguity. A murder however was finite, its finality embedded within the word itself. The clouds of blind optimism parted inside her head and the world around her turned dark and grim—the monochrome polarity of life and death.

"Was it Lucas?" She asked, the icy chill on her spine balanced by the fire that started burning inside her chest.

"No, but he knew the killer," Julian replied, falling back on the couch.

Her rage overtook her despair in that split second that Julian finished his sentence and she dug her nails inside her palm. It was all so fucked up. She couldn't linger on any of it though, her answers were behind that door in lower engineering. If there was a chance Alex was still alive, that door was her last shred of hope. She'd have to kill Lucas after that.

The problem was their escort outside the flat. They boys were hesitant at first but Mark eventually picked off the tiles in Julian's new bathroom to reveal the duct that led them to the stair core.

Leaning out of the door to the ground floor, she surveyed the plaza. There were two men on the balustrade of the second floor but they seemed too preoccupied in their conversation to pay them much attention. She gestured to the boys to follow her and jogged as silently as she could to the quadrant intersection. There was still the long, main corridor of the recreation grounds to traverse in order to get to engineering—a wide bulkhead with minimal cover, meaning were they to run into anyone, they would be completely exposed. But her worry eased as they approached the walkway's far end without meeting another soul and she thought perhaps luck was finally on her side.

Until she reached the final bend and had to take a sudden step back, knocking into Julian in her haste to avoid being seen. They squeezed on top of each other for cover behind the threshold of the main entrance as the science and engineering quadrant teemed with people.

"How can we reach the stair core now?" Mark whispered.

"A diversion," she replied, the plan in her head already in motion as she removed her roller from the loose bun on her head. Kaiden was supposed to be in the agricultural quadrant already, waiting for her signal.

"Are you in position?" She typed.
"Yes." The reply came immediately.
"Do it."

There was a sudden commotion on the ground floor giving them the chance to slip inside.

"How did you do that?" Julian asked, trying to catch up with her pacing.

"I had Kaiden burst a few pipes under the Cylidome," she exclaimed and beckoned towards the lifts at her tangent horizon. "Now come, it's down on minus eight."

The lift descended and the doors opened to the abandoned engineering section she had visited the previous night. She blinked and rubbed her eyes to adjust to the darkness, turning the torch on her roller to guide the way.

"The drone should be stationed after this next turn. Mark, are you ready?" She whispered.

"I would be if there were any frequencies to pick up." Mark replied, tapping wildly on his roller.

She took a feeble step into the intersection and dared to shine some light to the double door—the corridor was empty.

"We're here," she announced, tracing along the edges of the panel with her torch.

"Wow, I've only seen these in the course material." Mark got on his knees to study it. "Some Rings were built earlier than others. I'd have to presume that this being the first one because of the engine section, it has a lot of this old mechanical technology."

"Do you know how it works? Please tell me you do. What are the buttons for?"

"It needs a passcode. Even if I try to remove the panel, the mechanism is embedded in the cavity of the wall, it won't budge."

"Fuck... fuck!" She stomped on the cracked tiles, raising a cloud of dust. "Can we not force it open somehow?" She pleaded, pressing her palm against the cold, metal door panel.

"No way, we would have to cut a hole in the door," Mark explained.

"Maybe if we had some UV light we could see which buttons are pressed more than others," Julian suggested and joined him next to it.

"Good job science." Rachel sneered. "Now all we need to find is some UV light." She bit her lip, immediately regretting her tone towards Julian but the frustration was pushing every nerve inside her, pumping the blood through her veins so fast that it was bound to burst out any second now.

"My boy, J is not wrong. We may not have any source of UV but he did give me an idea. I can probably find out how many digits it is at least." He placed his ear next to the panel and slowly pressed random buttons, waiting for the faint clicking inside. "Damn, it's more than four. Shhh, don't talk," he ordered them even though no one had interrupted him. "Eight digits? That's a damned long passcode."

"Which means there is no chance to guess it," Julian sighed.

"Imagine how weird it would be if I had opened it on the first try?" Mark chuckled.

"Are you being funny right now?" She stopped her pacing to chastise him.

"Maybe a date? Day, month and year?" Julian suggested.

It could still be anything—from a random birthday to a specific day that everyone from Lucas' group knew. Maybe she'd missed or overlooked something in her notes.

"We were sent back but our voices still live here," Julian muttered and she looked up at him, her breath trapped inside her chest.

"Of course! *Tyson-7*," Rachel cheered, her voice echoing in the deserted bulkhead. "But do you know the date? Did you find it in your dad's archive? Did you? You did, didn't you?"

"Try 22-05-2113," he enunciated clearly.

Mark pressed the buttons in order and the panel buzzed as the door hissed and creaked open.

She cheered, throwing her arms around Julian and giving him a kiss on the cheek. He pulled slightly back but she didn't care. The door of the crescent moon was open.

Grabbing both door handles, she let out a tired exhale, an eerie premonition fusing her legs to the floor. Her lungs inflated with air, expanding to her ribs. Whatever was in there, she would face it nonetheless.

The space was so enormous that the curve of the ceiling concealed the edges of the room on the long side. The foul stench was potent as if the room hadn't been properly ventilated in months. There was a weird feeling on her skin that she hadn't felt before, a drop in temperature that made the hairs on her arms tingle and her body to shiver. More interestingly, there was electricity down here. The faint light from scattered monitors only illuminated the space around them, but enough to give shape to the metallic beds that were connected to the ceiling with a series of cables, tubes and wires.

The reek of the stale, salty air mixed with what could be animal excrement and urine was just too much. A cold liquid splashed on her forehead making her jitter in disgust and quickly dabbing herself before pointing her torch above her. Pipes extended all the way across, rusty and discoloured. Water was running along the bottom edge of the middle one accumulating into a big droplet at the bolted connection that was patiently waiting to detach and fall again on her face.

"What the fuck is this place?" she asked, following the pipes with her eyes.

"Yeah, I don't know what I am looking at either," Mark replied, flailing his light around the edges of the big room.

"It's Nightfall," Julian muttered—more like a whisper under his breath that was barely audible.

Did he know about this place? She would have followed up with more questions if she hadn't noticed the bulge under a dark cover on the bed closest to her. Her chest tightened. No, it couldn't be.

She ran to the monitor at the foot of the bed which portrayed the anatomy of a human male along with some live graphs and numbers coming out of various parts of the body. Her spine shivered. Most of the wires connected to where the head would be and the rest of them disappeared under the sheet. She suddenly became aware of her own breathing, every inhale short and raspy while the exhales were long and shaky.

"ALEX!" She shrieked, her voice echoing in the darkness that closed in around her. Her lungs screamed. There was not enough oxygen, a heavy rock inside her chest was blocking her airways. Her legs trembled, barely holding her weight.

She scampered to the top of the bed and removed the cover. There wasn't enough time to prepare herself for the sight before her but she was relieved it wasn't a dead body at least. She finally took a breath. The boy was around her age, pale with long blonde hair that escaped the device that was covering his face. Most of the wires were leading to its black encasement while the tubes were inserted into the boy's mouth and arms.

"He's alive!" Julian sparked a tiny flame of hope inside her. "It looks like some sort of prolonged virtual simulation."

"Alive yes... aware no," Mark added, studying the terminal above the boy's head. "It seems like a state of coma. His heart beats are normal from what I can tell." He lifted the boy's arm only to let it flop with a puff on the sheet beside him.

"I-I... I don't understand," Rachel stuttered as her voice cracked. Was this what Lucas meant when he'd said there's no waking Alex up now? "Why is there no one here? Where is Lucas' group?"

"This place feels more like a lab than a base of operations." Julian shone his light around the other beds.

She sprinted past him, flicking off the sheets, her heart fluttering with every whoosh that enveloped her in clouds of dust.

Her tremulous breath shook her jaw and ground her teeth as she reached for the edge of the last sheet. She winced and squinted in reflex but even in the darkness that surrounded her, she could recognise the soft features of her brother's face.

The shriek couldn't come out her throat—barely a whimper as she dug her head between his neck and the headpiece. Her back spasmed, contracting with every snivel as she squeezed her eyes shut, tears spilling out on the sheet. The lump in her throat grew heavier and she felt her heart stopping and restarting as if it had just endured a hundred stabs.

"A... Al?" She tried to speak but the words bounced back inside her chest. "Alex, I'm here... I'm here, little brother. I got you."

Julian and Mark's footsteps approached behind her but they stood there in silence.

"I've got to take him out of here. Help me get him up." Rachel grabbed some of the wires and tried pulling them out of the headpiece just as Julian held her hand back.

"No, Rach! We have no idea what's going on here. Who knows what will happen if you suddenly disconnect him."

"I need to get him out of this, Julian!" she sobbed, snot dripping on her upper lip while she squirmed to free herself from his grasp. "Mark, you know how to wake him up, don't you?"

"I'm sorry... I can barely understand how this works." Mark gestured to the life support system above her brother. "He seems alive and well, health-wise at least," he continued while going through the information on the terminal, "In a deep coma like the others though."

"I'll kill him. I'll fucking kill him," she cried as she wiped the mixture of tears and snot from her face.

"Who, Lucas?" Julian asked his stupid question.

"Yes, of course Lucas. He knew... all this time he knew where Alex was. What kind of a sick mother fucker does this?"

"Rach, let's not do anything rash that might hurt Alex even more, okay?" He softly let go of her hand. "Let me call my dad... please?"

"You... y-you want to call your dad and tell him about this? He'll kill you."

"There's no other way. We need help, we can't get these people out of here on our own," he said and raised his roller in front of him.

"Yes? Julian, where are you? Why is it so dark?" Mr Walker's voice came from Julian's roller.

"Hi dad, I... ummm... I found Nightfall."

There it was again. Nightfall. What did Julian know about this place? There was no way he knew where Alex was all this time. He would have told her sooner. What was going on?

"What? Julian, I thought I made myself very clear last night. You went on and did the exact opposite? What the hell were you thinking?"

"Dad, I can expl..."

"No dad, no nothing. Are you hurt? Just tell me where you are."

"I'm fine, Dad. Ring Six, engineering, level minus eight, section C44."

"I'll be there in a few minutes. DO NOT MOVE!"

"Dad, we found Rachel's brother... along with all the other missing people."

The long pause meant his father must have been as surprised as they were. "Stay where you are, we can't talk about this on an open channel," he said out of breath and the call dropped.

"Julian, I'm only going to ask this once," Rachel raised her shaky voice and pushed him back, tears running freely along her cheeks, blurring her vision. "Did you know about this place... this *Nightfall*?"

"Now listen, Rach. It's a long story..."

"Did you know this is what happened to Alex?"

"No, Rach I swear. Last night when I was going through my dad's files, I found two classified projects one of them being Nightfall. It had the same icon we saw in the Cylidome. I wanted to tell you but my dad made me swear to not even tell my mum about any of that."

"So your dad is involved in this? Are you *fucking* kidding me?" She pushed him further back. "And now he's on his way here?"

"Just because he knows of it, doesn't mean he's involved. You know my dad, he would never be part of anything like this. Rach, you can trust me."

She eyed him from top to bottom. His widened eyes and raised eyebrows usually meant he was offended. She did trust him, this was Julian after all.

"Rach, you understand why I couldn't tell you, right?" Julian reached for her shoulder but she twisted away from his touch.

The heavy, metal door at the entrance creaked loudly and a bright light reached them from the other side of the room, reflected on the metal beds and floor tiles. "Rachel?" Kaiden's whisper travelled through the lab like a snake's hiss.

"Over here, Kaiden," She said after coughing, her throat still heavy and sore.

"Who are they?" He pointed at the boys when he approached. "What is this place?" He revolved around himself, the light from his roller following his direction.

"This is Julian and Mark. They helped me get in. It's apparently called Nightfall, the place our loved ones were kept… or at least a few of them."

"I-Is… is this…"

"Yeah, that's Alex… and over there should be Elizabeth."

Kaiden rushed to the bed next to his sister, the sight of him sobbing bringing tears to her eyes again as she turned to look at her calm, motionless brother.

"Guys, I know you're having a big moment here but I have some bad news," Mark broke the series of cries.

"What is it?" Julian leant next to him for a peek at Mark's roller.

"I'm picking up a frequency… although I shouldn't be. This is combat drone frequency. The *Sagan* doesn't have combat drones."

"Oh trust me, the people here do," Rachel said as the moving sphere drifted into view at her tangent horizon.

"It's highly illegal to print weaponized drones," Julian exclaimed.

"It's also illegal to kidnap people and stick them in comas but here we are." *Fuck's sake, Julian is so dense sometimes.* "Mark, you said you could deal with it, right?"

"I thought you had already dealt with it," Kaiden complained, stepping firm in front of his sister.

"I don't know," Mark cried, "I haven't dealt with a combat one before."

There was no warning this time, no allowance for them to run away like last time. The drone started humming and a blue electrical current fluctuated inside its long barrels. It accumulated and intensified, releasing a jagged beam of blue-white light.

Kaiden fell on the floor with a thud before she realised what had happened. They all stood shocked in silence until the drone started its threatening song again.

"Behind the bed!" Julian suggested.

"I won't use Alex as a human shield," she cried and tried to get to the other side but a hand held her back, forcing her on her knees behind cover.

"How much time do you need?" Julian looked at Mark for an answer, his grip around her wrist tight as a blood pressure machine.

"Shouldn't take long, it's just different parameters of the same code."

"Julian, let go of me!" She squirmed but without success.

"The drone is protecting them, you said it yourself, it was guarding the door last time. These beds are made of aluminium, they're our best chance," Julian explained without making any sense.

"What does aluminium have to do with anything? Let me GO!"

"The only way that drone can see in this darkness is with TIR. Do you have time for me to explain how thermal infrared works?" He looked at her with raised eyebrows. "Didn't think so," he continued when she had no answer.

The drone whirred and beeped as it approached, its humming strengthening and dwindling as it tried to find its target. Was Julian right? Had his science saved them?

The shot splashed on the metal tiles next to her, scattering debris in all directions. A different munition this time, a physical one.

"Stay still," Julian whispered, his hand moving from her wrist to cup her hand.

The mechanical buzzing grew louder, the drone was almost above them... above Alex. It hissed, jets of air spewing in all directions as it rotated slightly, beeping like a time bomb ready to explode. Julian squeezed her hand and the drone chimed in a playful tune.

"I did it!" Mark yelled and stood up to face the inert mechanical sphere. "I got you, you little shit!" He poked it at its circular, glass dome in the middle.

"We're alive," She exclaimed, throwing herself in Julian's chest.

"Don't know if we can say the same for him." Mark beckoned towards Elizabeth's bed.

"Fuck, Kaiden!" She rushed to the boy who was laying on the floor, still like a piece of wood. She ripped his shirt at the collar but there was no wound, no blood, not even a bruise. "What was this drone firing?"

"The cannons are definitely ballistic!" Mark exclaimed with the excitement of a little boy receiving the gift he always wanted. "There are so many functions. I think I can repurpose it to fire different rounds, maybe even arcs of electrical currents which is possibly what got that guy."

"He has a name, Mark."

"Well when you introduced us, I had just discovered the drone, ok? Sorry for saving our lives."

"Is he... dead?" Julian asked, his face half covered in his palms.

Rachel placed her ear in front of Kaiden's mouth and remained still. "He's alive," she cheered when she felt the faint warmth of breath on her ear.

"Identify yourselves!" A loud, male voice echoed in the lab of nightmares as three flashlights beamed towards them.

I'll fucking sleep for three days straight if this day finally ends.

"Don't worry, I repurposed this guy to attack anyone other than us three," Mark said and the drone beeped in agreement.

"No, wait!" Julian stood in its line of sight. "That's my dad."

"Julian, are you alright?" Mr Walker asked as he approached, lowering his flashlight.

"Oh, I've been looking for this place for a long time," the man in the weird hat beside him said, his skin barely reflecting any light in the darkness.

"These two friendlies?" A woman came out from behind the two men, a rifle propped against her shoulder, its guiding laser moving from Rachel's chest to Mark's. Where had she found the rifle? There were no weapons on the *Sagan*.

"Dad, who are these people? I thought you were coming alone." Julian asked.

"Julian, you've done enough for one day. All of you go wait at the entrance." Mr Walker said with an authoritative voice but no one moved.

"I'm not going anywhere without my brother!" She stood at the edge of Alex's bed.

"It was not a request."

"You'll have to make me then," she stated, gripping the sheet and twisting it in her fist. There was no way she would let anyone come between her and Alex now that she had found him.

"We don't have time for this." Julian's dad waved a hand. "Andre, systems. Nyx, get Kaiden on a bed and prep the rest." Mr Walker spoke like he knew what he was doing, ordering the other two around with tasks she would have never thought of. "You two, back at the entrance." He pointed at the boys.

Julian gave her a soft nod before walking away, his eyes telling her what she needed to hear—that everything was going to be ok.

The woman with the wild, black hair picked up Kaiden like he weighed nothing to her and placed him on one of the empty beds at the back. She then came back, her eyes as dark and menacing as the lab itself. She glanced at Rachel and tapped on the terminal at the foot of Alex's bed. It chimed and folded its legs under it, hovering above the ground around the height of her knees. The sleek, angular rifle was strapped around her back, its thick, gold barrel reflecting the dim light of the monitors.

Then the lights came on, followed by the humming of various systems powering up. These people knew what they were doing. The lab looked less terrifying under the intense luminosity of the spotlights—more like an infirmary. Most of the beds were floating while the cables and tubes had been retracted back to the ceiling. They were moving them out—how was still to be seen.

"Patients are ready for transport," Andre informed them.

"And I'm ready for some payback," The woman swooped the rifle in front of her and gave it a kiss before propping it on her shoulder.

"Nyx!" Mr Walker tilted his head towards Rachel.

The woman gave her a side look with a raised eyebrow and shrugged. "They've got to learn at some point anyway."

"Not today," Mr Walker said sharply and twisted his finger in a spiral above his head. "Let's move out."

The beds followed him like train carriages until he stopped at the entrance to have words with the boys.

"We can fight too." She heard Mark saying as she joined the group. "I have this drone now."

"No you don't." Andre shook his head and with another playful tune the drone fleeted off beside him.

"You can't do that!" Mark complained.

"Andre, take the boys back to HQ," Julian's father ordered. "It's not safe here."

"What about the guards outside my flat?" Julian asked. "They'll be expecting us to come out at some point."

"You don't need to worry about that." Mr Walker waved a dismissive hand and pointed at the bulkhead's intersection. "Andre, now!"

Julian's worry was written across his face as the big man with the weird hat basically shoved them forward. There wasn't enough time to say goodbye or at least thank him for helping her find Alex as the boys disappeared into the intersection.

"Listen to me, girl." Nyx startled her, grabbing her by the jacket. "I need you focused on what's about to happen upstairs. It'd be a shame to die after having saved your brother."

Rachel nodded, chewing the inside of her bottom lip.

"Good." Nyx kept peering at her, her unblinking eyes as threatening as the rifle in her hands. "The mammoth is this way. Stay behind the drone, girl."

Nyx was leading at the front, then the drone, followed by a train of floating beds and Julian's dad at the end. As they entered a conspicuous manufacturing facility, a huge platform was waiting for them—was that the mammoth? Mr Walker started from the tail and came to the front, pressing a button on each bed as he walked by. A modular shutter rose from each of them, enveloping the patients in a metal covering. It all looked quite grim now, like they were carrying coffins with them.

The platform screeched to a halt and Nyx led the way out to the ground floor. She lowered a visor that was previously nested inside the jungle of tangled curves that was her hair and raised her rifle. "Behind the drone." She glanced back at her one last time before kicking the door.

Mr Walker rushed past her, ordering her to stay put.

Commotion followed on the other side, no weapon fire, just a faint incoherent dialogue. She glanced at the metalclad beds behind her and cautiously pushed the door open for a peek.

"I said drop it!" A snarl echoed in the open quadrant.

Nyx was revolving around herself, her rifle still at the ready, aiming at the balustrades above them.

"Easy, easy. No need for anyone to get hurt here," Julian's dad raised his hands.

"You sure? I can easily take these amateurs," Nyx said.

"Albert!" Mr Walker shouted like he was summoning someone to a duel, "You don't want to do this."

Who the fuck was Albert?

"Scott Walker." The croaky, familiar voice came from somewhere above them, arrogant and patronising. "Still fighting your misguided war I see. I respect your work too much to kill you. The woman on the other hand..."

"I found the missing kids here in your Ring, right under your nose. They're all in induced coma. I don't suppose it will look good for you when the news breaks out."

"What missing kids?" The elderly voice asked.

"Don't play dumb with me, Albert," Julian's father continued, "Let me take the kids away and…"

"I have no idea what you're talking about, Walker," The man said, finally appearing on the opposite side of the science blocks, his bald head barely coming out of the first floor balustrade, more than two hundred metres away. Rachel could only see his upper figure, features blurred and concealed from the trees of the middle strip.

Nyx repositioned herself towards the mysterious man.

"If you really don't know, then someone kept these kids alive against your orders, am I right?" Mr Walker took a few steps forward. "We gave you a whole Ring to yourselves and you've repaid us in nothing but schemes and secrecy," Julian's dad continued, "This was the last straw." He raised his voice with a threatening tone. "Let me have the kids and in return I'll buy you a couple of days before Administration storms this place."

"On what grounds? I don't even know who you have inside those med-beds," the man said and disappeared inside the first floor labs.

Mr Walker revolved around himself as the science quadrant suddenly cleared of people. He whispered something to Nyx and rushed back to where Rachel was peeking from all this time.

The beds started moving again, drone at the top of the column. What had just happened?

Rachel exchanged a few looks between Julian's dad and Nyx, desperate for some explanation. Finding Alex had created more questions than it had answered.

The convoy moved unhindered to the quadrant intersection but Nyx was still cautious, her rifle on her shoulder and her eyes behind the scope.

Alex's capsule was the last to enter the outer bridge to Ring Five. They were safe. Alex was safe.

CHAPTER 13

— Julian —

Residential Quadrant – Ring 6

Julian pressed the bell icon on the door panel and leant against the balustrade behind him. It felt weird that he was going to see his mum but didn't have access to her flat, almost like visiting a stranger. The plaza below was brimming with people in blue uniforms. Ring Six had apparently opened its doors to the public, although they were still building something in the middle of the food kiosks. The build-bots were transferring material in and out of the quadrant. Life seemed to be going on as usual despite last night's events. They had found Alex but there were still so many questions left unanswered. His dad knew— he'd probably always known. The crew he had brought with him meant he was prepared for a situation like this. *No matter what happens, I want you back in Ring Three for the Halfway event. Don't tell anyone what happened yesterday.* That was the only thing he had told him, cryptic as always.

His mum opened the door with a smile and welcomed him inside. His parents' new apartment wasn't that much different from his own. His mum had already decorated it in her own minimalist way as she used to describe it with only a few vases and wall panels that broke the monotonous grey colour of the furniture. The distinct scent of lilies filled the room; they must have been fresh from her garden as the stems hadn't fully blossomed yet and only partly exposed their grainy, red and purple petals.

"Do you want some tea? His mum offered. "We only grow this one here at Six."

"Sure." Julian sat on the couch that had way more than the required pillows, the formal black suit he was wearing making every little move feel like a gym exercise. The layers inside his jacket prevented him from bending his elbows and his pants were so tight that they wrinkled and compressed under his knee. He stretched his legs and adjusted the belt that was depriving him of full breaths.

"Does it not fit you? Come on, stand up, let me see you," his mum said as she carefully placed the two cups on the table.

"It's fine. Just a little uncomfortable." He patted himself down to straighten the creases on his blazer and pants.

"Now aren't you a handsome young man? You look so... dashing," she exclaimed and straightened his collar.

"I feel like an idiot. Stupid scanner took my measurements wrong."

"I think Lydia's going to love it. I've got to tell you, I am so happy you guys are finally going out."

"Mum, we're just going to the Halfway event together, it's not really a date or anything," he explained and took a sip of the bitter tea. After Priya's death and Nightfall, the last thing he wanted was the stress of a date.

"Just promise me you won't ditch her to go on your usual *Julian* adventures for once." She flailed her hands dramatically when saying his name.

"You should worry about not embarrassing us in front of everyone. Worrying about dad's speech is enough."

"Speaking of your father, have you seen him today?"

"Uhm... yeah, this morning," he lied under a fake cough. His father hadn't come home until white lights and wasn't in the mood for any conversation. Julian had waited at his old flat for the whole blue light cycle to talk to him but without any success. His father had been very clear about not mentioning anything to anyone, even his own mother. She didn't need to know anyway—it was bad enough that one parent had already found out about all his recent misdeeds. "You haven't talked to him at all today? When was the last time you guys actually saw each other?" He asked like he didn't care, fearing the rift between them had grown bigger.

"No, I was busy moving everything. He hasn't helped at all, you know."

He refrained from commenting on his mum's complaint.

"How is Rachel? Did you show her the new place?"

He barely had an answer to this for himself. He would have found out if his dad hadn't confined him inside the flat for the whole morning. Bouncing messages wasn't an optimal way to convey feelings. He had spent most of his morning on his roller with Rachel who was still in the infirmary. None of the people they had found had woken up but at least they were stable. The most frustrating part was that his dad hadn't answered any of their questions about their escape through Ring Six. *Better if you don't know, it's for your own safety*, he'd said. Alex was safe, that's all that mattered, right?

"Yeah, she liked it," he finally said reluctantly. Was there even anything else to say without divulging the horrors of Nightfall?

"How is she dealing with her brother's disappearance? It's so sad what happened to him," his mum pressed in her ignorance.

"Uhmm… she's handling it." His chest felt heavy as he bit his thumbnail. She must have been a wreck in reality. She had stayed all night next to her unresponsive brother like a sleepless guardian trying to figure out the mystery of the crescent moon. All the missing persons had it tattooed behind their necks, an icon that still posed more questions than it had answered.

He took one last big gulp and placed his cup back on the table. Kissing her goodbye, he went for the lift to Lydia's apartment.

Standing in front of the door, he straightened his suit, patting down his pants and shaking his hands to align the layers inside his blazer. Was this a date? He wasn't sure of the right etiquette if it was. He'd rather just pick her up and go to Ring Three—simple.

A shaky exhale first and then the doorbell. Elena Garcia opened the door and gestured to him to come inside. She looked a little different than usual; black lines highlighted her eyelashes and the skin of her face seemed lighter than it used to be.

"You look very nice Mrs Garcia," he blurted.

"Save it for my daughter, young man. She's down the hall to the right."

Julian nodded shyly and followed her directions. Their flat was much bigger than his family's house back in Ring Four but seemed quite cluttered and dark. If there were hidden lights at the edge of the ceiling, they weren't turned on, but for an oval spotlight in the middle of the living room. Clothes occupied the better half of the long couch as well as the backs of some chairs at the wooden dinner table. He walked towards the end of the room where a hallway led to the bedrooms, avoiding the scattered toys of Lydia's brother on the floor. The little spaceship drone reminded him of some of the toys he had to give away when he'd turned twelve. He wouldn't have minded taking it for a quick trip around the residential quadrant if he had more time.

Knocking on the door, he straightened his collar again, just in time before the brunette girl welcomed him with a smile. She was still in her pink nightgown and must have just come out of the shower as her hair was still dripping wet on her shoulders, flowing down twilight rivers in the valleys of her collarbone. She stepped on her toes and her soft lips touched his cheek. Her perfume enveloped him, numbing his senses—subtle hints of jasmine, vanilla and honey. Taking his hand, she pulled him in the room and hopped to the other side behind a black and white partition.

He blinked back to reality, as if he had dreamt the whole thing. His cheeks were burning and the prolonged smile hurt his face.

"You're not ready yet?" he finally managed to formulate a sentence.

"I won't be long. Just need to figure out what to wear, do my hair and makeup and we are good to go."

"That's at least half an hour. I am going to miss my dad's speech."

"You know, instead of complaining, you could help me," she said while extending her head out of the divider.

"How?" He shrugged. He knew nothing of how girls got ready.

"I have some dresses in the wardrobe to your left. Can you choose one for me?"

He tapped on the wardrobe's panel and the frame turned transparent, revealing a row of hanging dresses that varied in shape and length—all arranged according to the colour spectrum. Purple and blue on the left, green and yellow in the middle and different shades of orange and red on the right. This was one of the little things he liked about her—she wasn't just some pretty girl in his class, she was incredibly smart and methodical, probably even more than him.

"I love how you've arranged them. Although maybe you should find a cyan dress to complete the spectrum."

"Yeah, but did you see my beautiful infrared at the end?"

"No, where?" His eyes fell to the dark, red, frilly gown.

"You can't see it silly, it's infrared," she giggled behind the small wall.

"Ah, you got me," he said and his spine shivered. His last experience with infrared would have cost him his life if it wasn't for Mark. He tried to shake the eerie feeling away by taking out a couple of dresses to inspect them. The bright red one was simple enough. Straight lines, decent length, no tears or stitches—maybe even new. He didn't bother comparing it to the rest and held it out for her next to the divider.

"So, did I tell you I got my own place now?" He leant against the wall near the door and crossed his arms.

"All to yourself you mean? Your own?"

"Yeah... I don't know how my mum pulled it off but..."

"She must know the right people. I still have to live with Matteo across the hall," she huffed. Julian had always wanted a little brother but Lydia not so much apparently. "Is it in upper or lower resi?" She leant over the divider and studied him for a few seconds. Her shoulder was naked, red freckles accentuating the shape of her deltoid.

"Here, on the first floor." He tried not to stray too far from her eyes.

He was still unsure of his decision to live in Six after last night's events, especially with the Icarus logo embroidered in every officer's vest. If Nightfall had turned out to be a prison of comatose people, he wouldn't even dare imagine what Icarus was.

"So... does that mean they told you everything then?" she asked as she lost her balance and sidestepped out of the partition while trying to put on her dress.

Julian didn't know if he should look away or enjoy the moment. She was facing the other way but hadn't finished putting the dress over her upper body yet, revealing her toned muscles around her naked spine.

She pulled the straps around her shoulders and giggled.

"You know there was a better view if you were smart enough to look at the window instead of my back."

Julian jolted his head to the window above the bed and caught her reflection staring at him. He felt a fire starting to burn inside his cheeks as his eyes darted around the room.

"Oh, you're adorable," she choked a laugh and turned around with a big smile. "So how do I look?" She twirled her dress with a spin around herself.

"Wow," he blurted, fighting the urge to punch himself in the face for uttering something so stupid. Were there even words to describe someone so beautiful without falling into a cliche?

She sat in the chair in front of her desk and waved her hand in front of the wall panel. The frame that was previously portraying a colourful blotchy painting was replaced by her own reflection as a series of lights along its edges illuminated her face. She leant forward and widened her eyes to apply a layer of black lines over her eyelids.

"So... you didn't answer my question."

"What question?" Julian approached behind her and observed her careful strokes around her almond eyes. The contrast between the smoky brush strokes and the brightness of her light brown irises created a beautiful conflicting symmetry, like shining coronas on an inverse total eclipse.

"Stop staring," she smiled as their eyes met through the mirror.

"Uhm... yeah, sorry." He turned around and unfolded his roller, Rachel's portrait waiting for him. There was more than one message, the last one being quite worrisome.

"Where are you? Your dad was looking for you and now he's not here for his own speech."

His dad's speech wasn't supposed to happen for another twenty minutes or so. Had they called him on stage early? He started typing but then deleted everything. He couldn't tell her he was in Lydia's bedroom, he felt guilty for some reason like he had to be there supporting her instead. They had found Alex though, it was over. He started over, this time only saying he was still in Six and asking her if she was already at the Grand Hall. He switched to his dad's portrait and typed another question.

"Dad, Rachel said you blew off your speech? I'm still in Six so I'm glad I didn't miss it. Where are you?"

He exchanged a few looks between Lydia and his empty blue screen until the door opened and a tall man with groomed, black hair entered shouting, "Are you still not ready yet?"

"Just doing my makeup, Dad. I'll be out in a couple of minutes," Lydia replied.

"Just like your mother," the man sighed and eyed Julian from top to bottom, "Are you that Julian kid?"

"Uhm, yes sir. I take it you are Mr Garcia?" he said and extended his hand.

"He's smart, I like him," he laughed and reached for a handshake.

Julian felt his hand being crushed, but managed to stifle his whimper, "Nice to meet you sir."

"Lose the *sir*, just Victor will be fine. Would you like to join me in the living room while we wait for the ladies?"

Julian nodded uncomfortably and glanced over at Lydia who was now combing her hair. She smiled and sucked her teeth as an apology.

He followed her dad in the main space of the flat and sat on the only cushion of the couch that was free of clothes.

"Sorry about the mess, we haven't really had the time to sort everything after the move."

"That's ok, I only brought my stuff here yesterday so I'm in the same situation… boxes everywhere," he admitted nervously.

"So you were one of the last minute ones as well," he said and reached inside the small, white cabinet, "I've been saving this forever," He produced a bottle with a dark brown liquid, "My great grandfather brought it with him when they departed from Earth. I wanted to share this with my father on this special day, but he passed away last year; and since Matteo is too young, maybe you and I can share a glass."

"What is it exactly?"

"This, son, is the oldest whiskey on the *Sagan*. Fermented premium grains grown on Earth's soil and aged in unspoiled oak barrels of the Mediterranean. This right here is the taste of Earth." He clicked a mechanism on the neck of the bottle and poured only a few ounces in two glasses, "Now it's important to pressurise it again so it doesn't go bad when we open it again on Aquanis," he pressed the same spot again and held it close to his ear as the enclosure made a whistling sound. Handing the glass to Julian, he took a long sniff of his own drink like it was the most fragrant flower.

Julian took a sip and swished it inside his mouth for a moment before swallowing. It tasted like bitter caramel or vanilla, somehow mixed with the flavour of wood.

"How good is that?" Victor asked as he leant over the coffee table.

"Are you giving alcohol to the boy during yellow lights?" Mrs Garcia remarked when she came out of her bedroom.

"Relax, I only poured two, maybe three sips," he winked at Julian with a grin. "It's a big day today."

"And how do I look for such a big day?" She posed in front of her husband.

"Perfect as always," Victor exclaimed and Julian looked away from their kiss.

The awkwardness remained even after Elena went to fetch her daughter. Talking to the father of the girl he dreamt about kissing himself wasn't an easy task, despite how pleasant Victor was. Julian laughed at his jokes and nodded at his questions, although a lot of them were about Aquanis. He knew he wouldn't see their destination planet up close—pondering on his sad destiny was almost a routine.

Victor was talking about the distant planet like he'd already seen it, describing the possible life forms in detail and even the terrain of the expedition's planetfall site. Julian gathered he was a life scientist and his bias took over—the eternal feud between cosmic and life sciences. No one knew how it had started—not even his dad—but there was always this tension between the two groups.

Heels clanked in the hallway and he was saved from the

awkwardness—or so he thought because his expression when he saw Lydia must have been so inappropriate that Victor jokingly scolded him. In his defence, he'd never seen such a gorgeous girl. The red dress he'd picked up suited her perfectly albeit tightly, accentuating her figure and exposing her smooth, perfectly shaped legs. It must've been eugenics or something but he'd never ask.

"Ok, let's go finally!" Victor exclaimed and clapped a few times in excitement.

The plaza on the ground level was even more crowded than earlier and a continuous chatter echoed throughout the quadrant. Why were there so many people gathered here instead of the Grand Hall where the Halfway event was taking place?

When he asked about it, Lydia's answer was even weirder.

"That's our own event, silly," she said, wrapping her arms around his. Her perfume was intoxicating and no matter how hard he tried to appear casual, his whole body yearned to get closer to her—a force greater than gravity.

"What event?" He asked, feeling Victor's eyes peering at him.

"I asked you earlier. When you said you moved here, I thought they told you."

"Who is *they*?"

"If you really don't know, it means it was for your own good." Victor chimed in and motioned him to follow into the plaza.

They navigated through the kiosks and reached the middle courtyard. The overlapping conversations were hard to follow, but much easier to understand than from the fifth floor balustrade.

"I can't wait to explore the oceans," a girl who was a few years younger than him told her mum. "Do you think there will be huge fishes like sharks?"

"I don't know if I can live next to the engines though," a man in a grey suit complained to his friend.

Then one voice was clear in the haze of chatter, one he knew very well.

"You've got to be kidding me. What are *you* doing here?" Lucas shoved him, making him lose his balance and fall on his knees—thankfully after releasing Lydia's arm.

"Lucas, if you want to be able to use those metal hands of yours in the future, you should keep them to yourself," Victor rushed to Julian's defence.

"He should be on the other side with the rest of them," Lucas pointed towards the quadrant's exit, the end of his sentence full of bitterness.

"And you should have told us about Alex. Rachel will kill you on sight after what you did to her brother." He rebuked him, a sense of safety enveloping him with Victor around.

"So you found him, huh? Where was he hiding them?"

"Don't act like you don't know. Do you not have any shred of empathy?"

"Don't talk to me like you know me!" Lucas lunged forward, foot stomping the floor for extra intimidation points. "I tried many times to convince him to stay quiet. It was either dreamland or death."

"Is that the same option you gave Priya?" Julian blurted, adrenaline suddenly coursing throughout his body after seeing the fury in the bully's eyes.

Lucas' face went through rapid transformations, his anger bursting out from his flushed cheeks. He rolled up his sleeve and tapped on a blue holo under his tricep with his other hand.

Human integrated technology, Julian purposely blinked to make sure his eyes were working.

Whatever cybertech he was wearing, it had worked because Lucas closed his eyes and his chest heaved in rhythmic bursts, his anger swallowed by nano-injections of tranquilliser most likely. It must've worked too well as the massive boy was now snivelling. He tried to hide it but Julian saw the tears glistening in the bright spotlights of the plaza.

"I tried…" he quivered, fixing his posture. "I tried to fucking warn her," he growled, his voice returning to his usual barking. "You're lucky you're a Walker." He pointed a finger at him. "Priya didn't have that privilege." He turned his back on him and returned to Ares and the rest of his friends behind the Tasty Delights kiosk.

The interaction had Julian frozen in place. Lucas was a bigger mystery than Nightfall itself.

"Don't worry about Lucas, it's not his fault he's like that, it's all that cybertech he's wearing," Victor said like it was common knowledge, "You know it's messing with his brain, right?"

"I can tell." He patted himself down before facing the father of his date. "But I worry more about what's happening here." He revolved around himself with open arms.

Mr Garcia exchanged a look with his wife and she whispered something in his ear. Mumbling something in return, he grabbed Julian by the shoulder, pulling him in beside him.

"All these people around you have something in common. We all hate the fact that we were born on this ship for the only purpose of procreating, like animals. Breeding machines for the next generation to do the same, until ultimately our great, grand children have a chance to colonise Aquanis."

"Yeah, these are literally my thoughts every single day, so what?" Julian agreed.

"Or so they'd have you believe." Victor leant in front of him with a crooked smile.

"Who?"

"Cosmic scientists of course. Interstellar engineers, exo-physicists, planeticists, the whole lot."

Julian felt like he had unknowingly picked the wrong side. His dream was to go into cosmic sciences eventually, the field that pioneered the space revolution and even made this journey possible. "You mean to tell me that cosmitists are to blame for our misery?" He rushed to the defence of the people he regarded as role models.

"Precisely. You see, that was never the plan. Us life scientists had always argued that the trip could be made in one lifespan, prolonged lifespan of course but…"

"One lifespan?" he scoffed quite arrogantly, realising afterwards how rude that must've looked to Lydia's father.

"Yes… if the trip took a hundred and sixty years instead of two hundred and seventy."

"You'd have to be almost fully synthetic to make it to that age," Julian disputed. The absurdity of the statement had him fighting an eye roll.

"A lot of us here are," Victor whispered, his grasp around Julian's shoulder tightening.

"But that's illegal and highly unethical," Julian countered with what he knew on the subject from his dad's paper books. The quest for immortality had seen a boom in the twenty-second century, only to be quenched by a planet-wide uprising. It was never clear in the books if the cause had been a virtuous one that demanded an equal distribution of technology or if it was hatred for the undying caste that guided the lower classes to revolt. The *Sagan* had departed right in the middle of a civil war, the resolution of the conflict left unanswered. Colonising an exoplanet was a righteous goal but leaving the chaos of Earth behind was an equally valid incentive. "Isn't that why we left Earth?"

"Don't let the council's propaganda cloud your judgement, Julian. You're a smart kid, if there was an opportunity to step on Aquanis in the next thirty-seven years instead of a hundred and forty-two, wouldn't you take it?"

"Pffft, in a heartbeat. Wait, so this is actually true? We'll be on Aquanis in thirty seven years?" He asked, glancing at Lydia's nod—her smile was heart-warming and her eyes sparkled with excitement.

It felt like his body was suddenly awakened from a long slumber and didn't know how to function properly. His heart was vibrating in his chest harder than the spinning of the Rings as his lungs fought for just a little bit of oxygen in rhythmic inhales. Was his dream of sinking his feet in the sand and feeling the strong wind blow on his hair about to become real? The virtual world he had built in the Hub was a lot like that. He felt his limbs jolting as if they wanted to move on their own and he had the desire to clap for some reason or at least shift his legs in and out. His insides were ready to explode, like a pulsing bomb trapped within his chest that would only be disarmed if he could share the excitement with someone. He took out his roller and started typing to the first person that came to his mind. "I've got to tell Rachel! She'll go mad."

"No!" Victor's voice was loud and sharp as he swiftly took it from his hands, "At least not until we're finished here."

"You should forget about Rachel," Lydia added before he could protest and wrapped her arm around his waist, bringing him closer to her.

"I can't just forget about her, she's one of my best friends."

"And that's why he was a liability risk," Elena whispered next to Victor but Julian heard it.

There was a strange feeling building up inside his chest. Something didn't feel right. Why all the secrecy? Reaching Aquanis in their own lifetime was definitely good news.

The commotion on the first floor distracted the Garcia family but he couldn't just let it go. He had to ask. "If we can get to Aquanis in our lifetime, why can't I tell my friends about it? Actually... Why is this the first time I'm even hearing about this?"

"Because the people who came up with this plan were silenced, Julian," Victor explained, his sharp tone and the slight twitch of his mouth indicating his patience with him was running out. "It's up to us to see their dream fulfilled."

"Silenced? You don't mean... killed, do you?"

"We may never know for sure. One man persisted though. A brilliant one that would inspire us to reach out for what we deserve, who would lead us to our salvation." Victor pointed at the balcony on the first floor where a man in a black suit rose above the railings. He waved his gloved hand as the crowd applauded. Julian had seen him before. The wavy wrinkles between his eyebrows, his polished bald head, the way he smiled. This was the scientist who had guided his school's field trip to the Core Hull, the old man in the white coat who had beautifully explained the laws of thermodynamics and nuclear fusion. Yes, that was definitely him, Dr Albert Richter.

"So, we're not going to the halfway event then? I should really be in the Grand Hall by now."

No one gave him an answer—they were all too excited by the scientist's appearance.

There was still time, if they rushed after Richter's speech they could still make it for the engine cut-off. Would they still shut down the engines if the ship was supposed to keep accelerating? How else would it reach Aquanis in thirty seven-years? It was all so confusing. "Can I have my roller back though? I've already lost one in the past few days.

My dad will go nuts if I lose another."

Lydia and her father exchanged a quick look and hesitantly granted him his request. His dad had called him a few times already and had also left him a message.

"Julian, whatever you're doing, stop and get back here immediately. It's not safe there."

Short and to the point as always but with minimal context. There was something off about this gathering in Six's residential but he couldn't reply now, not with Victor lurking next to him and Lydia disabling his one arm with her grasp. There was a voice inside him that was telling him to run as fast as he could but his curiosity couldn't leave it alone. Setting foot on Aquanis—wasn't that his home screen in the VR? He felt bad for a moment, for ditching his dad, but how often was it that someone would come along and tell him his dreams were about to come true? He looked up to the man who was supposed to deliver that promise.

CHAPTER 14
— Rachel —

The Grand Hall – Ring 3

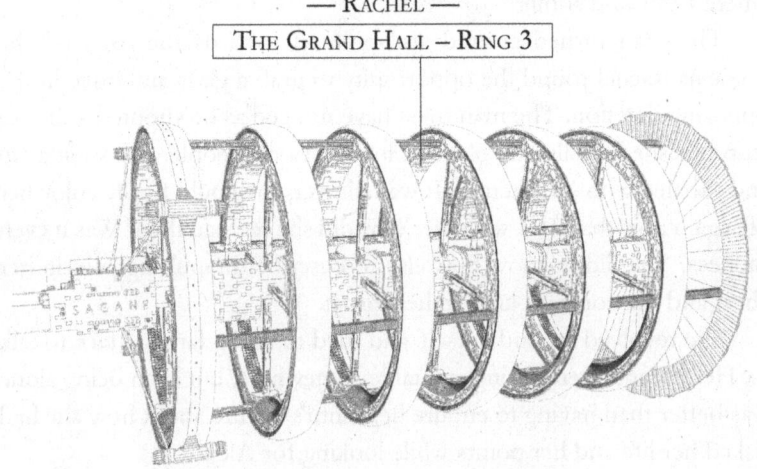

Rachel stood below the threshold before entering the enormous dome, wondering how all this structure could fit inside the quadrant. The whole room was made of geodesic panels that joined in triangles until the top, producing a gigantic, united screen around her. A hologram of a blue planet hovered just below the apex while curved lines in shades of blue and green cascaded downwards until they met the floor. *Julian must be loving this.*

Her long, violet dress was pissing her off, the strap kept slipping off her shoulder and she pulled it up for the hundredth time. Her grandmother must have been taller than her—there was a gap of at least two fingers between her skin and the inside of the strap when she pulled it.

She walked towards the centre where an elevated, circular stage was being prepared. It was surrounded by round tables that people had already occupied and long counters decorated with small flowers and resplendent buffets. She hadn't eaten anything since last night but she wasn't hungry. The tall glasses containing some yellowish liquid at the edge of a counter on the other hand seemed very enticing as she approached to grab one.

"Excuse me miss, these are alcoholic beverages and you don't seem to be over the legal age of consumption." The waiter in the black suit stopped her.

"Oh I am so sorry sir, I thought it was juice. Can you show me where I can find some?"

The man turned around and pointed towards the back of the dome as Rachel found the opportunity to grab a glass and leave in the opposite direction. The man must have noticed as he shouted at her to stop but she had already blended in the sea of people. She took a sip and exhaled with satisfaction. It was all over, she could finally enjoy her life again now that Alex was safe. Why did she feel sad then? Was it even sadness? She didn't know how else to describe the pulsing pain in her chest and the constant knot in her throat.

She revolved around herself and tried to find a familiar face to talk to. Her parents were sitting at a table somewhere, but even being alone was better than having to endure her mum's lecture about how she had risked her life and her points while looking for Alex.

She took another sip and shook her glass around, staring at how the remaining liquid formed a whirlpool towards the bottom. She had almost made it halfway to the other side of the centre stage, walking blindly all this time when she caught two girls waving at her. The short blonde girl, Hailey, was easy to talk to but the lanky brunette, Jennifer, required a lot of effort and energy most of the time. Hailey's charcoal dress seemed new, not the typical recycled fabric like the one she was wearing that belonged to her grandmother. Her pale skin and golden hair seemed like a light bulb on top of a black lamp—the thought made her chuckle but she tried to hide it behind another sip. Jennifer's beige, wavy dress was simple enough to not qualify for a second look.

"Hi Rachel, how come you're alone? Where is Julian?" Hailey asked in her soft, thin voice.

It was a question she didn't want to answer, even the thought made her cringe. "He's with Lydia."

"Oh, that's nice. They look cute together," Jennifer said as Rachel fought the urge to snap at her.

"Uhm…" Hailey started awkwardly, nudging her friend with her elbow, "I heard they found Alex, is it true?"

"Yeah, they'll officially announce it at some point tomorrow."

"That's great news, I'm so happy for you," Hailey cheered.

Rachel only nodded and swished the fruity beverage in her mouth.

The news was bittersweet at best. Yes, she had found him but he was in a coma, without any indication if he would ever come out of it. For all she knew, all her efforts had been in vain.

"Rachel. Hi, sorry to interrupt." Julian's dad came out of nowhere. "Can I talk to you for a minute in private?" he whispered the question.

"Mr Walker! Yeah sure," she exclaimed, glad to be leaving her conversation with the girls. "Did Alex wake up?" She asked when they were alone.

"No, but he's fine, this isn't about your brother unfortunately. Julian was supposed to meet me here but he's late. Have you talked to him in the last hour or so?"

"Uhmm, no, we haven't talked since morning. He's supposed to be with that girl, Lydia."

"Garcia? Do you by any chance know if he went to pick her up?"

"I think so, but that's all I know." She tried to end the discussion as fast as possible. Just the image of her holding his arm and smiling made her claw the inside of her palm.

"Can you give him a ring and find out where he is? He promised me he'd be here."

"Oh yeah, your speech thing. Aren't you supposed to be getting ready to go on stage?"

"Soon. That's why I need you to find him. You'd think he would use that damned roller I gave him. Maybe he'll answer if it's you," he patted her on the back and disappeared in the crowd.

Rachel chewed on the inside of her lower lip and typed a short message before the commotion on the centre stage grabbed her attention.

An oval table was placed in the middle, occupied by council members that had already taken their seat around it. She could recognize their faces but only knew two or three of them. The man in the formal blue suit was one of the few she knew by name, her own personal role model, Kieran Bolek. He was the latest addition to the council and despite being the youngest, he had risen through the ranks to one of the most influential council members. He tapped on his ear a few times and cleared his throat before his voice started echoing loudly in the dome.

"Hello everyone and welcome to the biggest event of this ship's history. I am sure you're all excited to be here tonight and we'll do our best to not bore you too much with our speeches. Mine is the first one and believe me it's not that long, maybe one or two hours only." He chuckled, pausing for the crowd to join in with inconsistent laughs. "All kidding aside, we have some very interesting speakers tonight. But first, let me tell you a little bit about the importance of this event. Our little community has lived together for a hundred and twenty-eight years and in this time, sure, we had our differences but more importantly we had a common goal to always bring us together. Keep the *Sagan* going and basically just stay alive together." He laughed again and the crowd followed.

Liam nudged her arm, suddenly beside her. "If this is how the whole night is going to be, I might need something stronger than juice to get me through it," he said jokingly.

"Shush, I love this guy. When did you get here?"

"I saw you standing here all alone and thought you could use the company." He gently rubbed her back and continued, "You can't be serious, you really like this guy? He's just a cute front for the council."

"If you must know, he's one of the main reasons I got interested in painting in the first place."

"What, the paintings on the walls around the ship?"

"Yeah he's amazing. And I love the little, grey hairs at the tip of his beard."

"This we can both agree on."

"This is the moment our children will thank us for," Kieran exclaimed and walked along the edge of the stage, "We did our part, we got halfway there and it's now up to the next generations to do theirs. To become the first ones in the history of our species to colonise a planet outside our home solar system."

"I heard they found your brother, that's amazing news," Liam put his arm around her shoulders and squeezed her in.

"Why do people keep saying this? *They?* It was Julian and myself who found him after chasing breadcrumbs and dead leads all over the ship for days now."

"Shut up. For real? Why didn't you tell me anything? I could have helped, you know I would've." He gave her a disapproving look.

"I didn't want to get you in trouble. Julian has his father who can get him out of anything really, you are not that lucky."

"True... so, where was he all this time? Is he alright?"

"His vitals are fine but he's comatose, all of them are."

"I heard they all have some weird moon tattoo on the back of their necks, what's that about?"

"Yeah, Alex has one too. It's a crescent moon actually but I don't know what it's for."

"Weird... do you think he was part of some cult or something?"

"I don't know Liam... can we talk about something else please?"

"Yeah of course. Sorry, I didn't mean to pry."

"It's ok, it's just that I haven't had much sleep since yesterday. I had to stay there with him all night until my parents came around white lights."

"How come you're not sitting with them?"

"I could ask you the same thing," She deflected. The only person she wanted to spend the evening with was probably somewhere in the crowd with his new girlfriend.

"Fair enough." Liam shrugged with a smirk as Kieran Bolek continued his inspiring speech. "James told me he loves me, you know?" He dropped the news bomb and Rachel could only squeal.

"Are you fucking with me? Talk! Details!" She demanded.

"Well, that's the thing, he told me he loves me and that he tried his best or something, I don't know..." He trailed off to press his lips together. "And then he kissed me... in front of everyone, right in the middle of the plaza, in his own resi district."

"Didn't you ask him what the hell that means?"

"Sounded like goodbye to be honest." He shrugged the sadness off his shoulders while staring at the stage again.

Rachel scoffed loudly. "A bit dramatic. It's not like he can avoid you forever. There's no escape from this floating prison."

"Wow, floating prison? You start to sound a bit like Julian there," Liam laughed.

"Oh shut up!" she said and resorted to a weak punch on Liam's arm when he didn't stop giggling. "That's always effective." She smiled as he groaned and rubbed the hurt spot.

"OK, I deserved that one. Knowing you though, I am sure there's more where that came from so I am out."

"No, stay with me. I can't possibly go through this alone."

"How about you go grab one of these delicious yellow drinks?" He pointed at the buffet with the tall glasses.

"Already had one. Very refreshing."

"Why am I not surprised?" He chuckled. Let me know if you want to catch up after all the speeches. If of course I am not asleep in some corner by that time," Liam yawned as a new speaker took to the stage.

Miss Okada's dress was something out of a fairytale, new and elegant as it was expected of someone of her status. The bodice was fitted around her thin figure, cascading into a pristine gown that fell gently on the floor, twirling behind her as she walked. The spotlight followed her as the clusters of diamonds that adorned her dress twinkled with every graceful step.

"I am councilwoman Dr Erin Okada, head of interstellar technologies for the *Sagan*." Her voice resonated with a commanding presence. "I couldn't be prouder to be on stage tonight to share with you the importance of this halfway event. I know what many of you are already thinking, she's going to talk about maths, but rest assured I will keep it short and simple." She smiled and cleared her throat. "None of us here were even born when the *Sagan* started its journey. We have the most important job of all though; to flip the engine burn and start the slowing down process towards Epsilon Centauri. This deceleration process needs to start now for three reasons. One, the *Sagan* cannot decelerate at Gs beyond its indicated structural specification. Two, we can only turn the ARK engines to burn in the opposite direction. The main drive is embedded within the hull of Ring Six and cannot change direction. And three, we need to reach a slow manoeuvrable speed to guide the ship through the rest of the celestial bodies in Epsilon Centauri. A lot of hard work has been done over the years to get everything right; the maths, the engineering, the physics. This event marks the culmination of all the efforts of the middle generations, the people who didn't ask to be on this ship but made it possible for the next generations to safely set foot on Aquanis. And to give us a bit of insight on our own history and how we got here, let's welcome our ship's archivist on stage, Mr Scott Walker!"

The crowd applauded as the councilwoman stood still on stage, peering through the sea of people as she called out his name once again. She tapped on her ear and whispered something to the council members sitting at the oval table.

Rachel mimicked the reaction of everyone around her, stretching her neck and surveying the room. The indistinct chatter among the crowd intensified to a continuous white noise until Erin Okada's voice drowned it with her assertive tone.

"Mr Walker doesn't seem to be present right now so we'll move on to our next speaker, councilman Opoku," she graciously bowed and took her seat.

Rachel walked to the edge of the dome where the crowd was thinning out and climbed on a chair for a better view. She squinted as she scoured the hall for Scott or even Julian, but nothing seemed out of the ordinary. There was only a man in a familiar hat that was walking briskly towards the exit shoving and pushing bystanders in his way. Rachel put her feet back on the ground and reached for the back of her head where her roller was holding her hair together in a bun. She rolled it out and hovered her finger above Julian's picture. She bit the inside of her upper lip while frantically tapping her fingers on the screen.

"Where are you? Your dad was looking for you and now he's not here for his own speech."

She blew a strong puff of air upwards to fling a twirl of her hair to the side and started making her way towards the exit. The man in the weird hat rushed out in a hurry just before Rachel could get a good look at him. It must have been Andre, no one else would wear that ridiculous fedora so proudly. There was something going on. Did it have anything to do with Alex? Scott had said he was safe but what if that was the reason he had to run from his speech? Her heart fluttered as if someone had pushed a long needle through it. When would it finally end? All she wanted was to go back to her normal life, was that too hard to ask?

When she stepped out, the man was turning at an intersection at the end of the corridor. Unable to run in her heels, she came to a halt after only a few steps when the pads on her toes cramped. She took off the clips on the side with a relieved sigh and walked the rest of the distance barefooted.

Leaning out of the door frame at the intersection, she saw him talking to Julian's dad and the woman from the previous night, Nyx. Her hair was still wild and unattended with curls flying in different directions.

This was Scott's cleanup crew. He hadn't introduced her properly to them but she had caught on while moving Alex to the infirmary. She jolted her head to snap out of the anger that was building up inside her for keeping her in the dark and quietly placed her heels in front of the sensor of the door to keep it open. She should have rushed in to confront them but a little voice inside her head told her she should hear what they had to say first. It sounded like Julian's voice—he had left her to do this alone this time. The three of them were the only people in the intersection, their conversation carried through the empty atrium as if she was next to them.

"It's happening now. Our intel must've been wrong," Andre sounded out of breath.

"Argh, the crazies are one step ahead of us as always," Nyx growled.

Julian's dad placed a finger under his ear and paced back and forth, his head facing down, huffing. "What do you mean they're siphoning our water?" he asked no one in particular. He must've been using a private comms device. "Stay out there and be on stand-by."

"I take it Richard was right all along?" Andre took his ridiculous hat off to wipe his shiny, bald head from sweat.

"I told Okada so many times not to trust them." Mr Walker rolled out his roller and tapped wildly on the blue screen.

"We all did," Andre agreed. "What do we do now though?"

Mr Walker drew a few sharp breaths and rubbed his temple with his free hand. "We still don't know exactly what their real plan is but if Richard was right about the water, we should assume their goal is to isolate the Ring."

The others only nodded and the ship's archivist continued. "Nyx, you go scout the bridges. Andre and I will go to the control room. We need Abeone."

"On it!" Nyx's rifle swung with her as she turned around towards the outer bridge, only to stop after a few steps, "Why is the door over there still open?"

"Where?" the two men asked at the same time in low voices.

Rachel drew a sharp inhale and hid behind the frame. She grabbed her heels and started running in the opposite direction as the double doors slid back and closed behind her. She had dashed on her bare feet as fast as she could before taking a quick glance over her shoulder to see if anyone was after her. The doors were still shut as she turned into an intersection to catch her breath.

Who the fuck were these crazies? None of the conversations she'd heard made sense. It was a good thing she had followed Julian's advice to not reveal herself—they would've made her go back to the Grand Hall.

She didn't know if she should feel happy or worried that no one cared enough to pursue her but didn't waste any time arguing with herself. If she was fast enough, she could reach the control room before the two men. She took a long inhale through her nose and steadily exhaled all the air through her mouth. The laps she used to run around the Ring with Julian had finally proved to be useful in some way. She divided the two heels between her hands for better balance and sprinted through the long hallway to the next quadrant.

One of the lifts at the science quadrant was almost at the top while the one on the opposite side must have been on the lower levels. She decided to take her chances with the latter and pressed the button on the panel repeatedly until the glass box arrived at her level. She took a guarded look around and entered the elevator to the engineering section below.

The doors opened to a dark hallway as if the lift had stopped between floors, the only source of light being the blue exit signs that blinked repetitively in unison along the walls of the long bulkhead. A beeping sound made her spine tingle, forcing her to hop out of the lift in reflex. The doors closed behind her and the lift disappeared, taking with it the bright white glow that was illuminating the intersection. The control room was straight ahead, but the complete darkness made her steps small and steady. Her bare feet didn't produce any sound on the cold, metallic floor but her loud breath echoed inside her ears.

The doors of the control room slid open, triggered by her proximity, and let out a blinding white light. A hooded, feminine figure dashed out—a similar size to Rachel but strong enough to shove her aside. Rachel flew against the wall; her back thundered with pain and she flopped on the floor, sucking her teeth with a groan. Her eyes were still closed but she could hear the strides of the mysterious person that had pushed her fading away in the distance. The doors closed and the darkness enveloped her as she slowly laid on her back. Who could possibly have that much strength to literally launch her all the way to the other side with such force? She rubbed the back of her head, groaning.

Stretching out her hands on the floor, she remained completely still for a few heartbeats until the elevator shaft was illuminated once again.

"For fuck's sake," she grunted as she crawled behind the nearest intersection.

CHAPTER 15

— Julian —

Residential Quadrant – Ring 6

Dr Richter softly gestured with gloved hands and turned the deafening overlapping shouts into a sea of tranquil silence. "My fellow travellers," he started in a steady voice that echoed throughout the quadrant, "It has been a long journey and of course I don't mean about the *Sagan*'s course. I am talking about our journey through difficult times and adversity. We held true to each other for years through cooperation and trust. Forced to live in the shadows, not able to speak up for what we believe in…. No more!" he shouted, "Today is the day we achieve what we have longed for since our coming to this travelling world. Today we find purpose again, we claim our lives back from a repressing regime; a system that has forced its own totalitarian ways onto all of us without question. They had us trapped in a prison of their own making but we will fly true. Years and years of human evolution and ingenuity out of reach because they were scared their precious *Sagan* wouldn't handle it, afraid *we* wouldn't handle it. Our species has achieved eugenics, re-genetics, human integrated technologies, nano-quantum technologies and many more that we were simply deprived of. Think of how many fathers, mothers, sisters, and brothers we have lost to their arrogant conservatism. But our time has come. Project Icarus will bring us closer to our destiny, to what we were meant to be. To finally be… FREE!" He exclaimed, raising his fist in the air, revealing a silver, metallic arm underneath.

The crowd cheered and applauded but Julian only gasped, his eyes bulging out of their sockets. His heart stopped, the information overwhelming him and sending his mind into overdrive. Icarus. He had seen it everywhere around Ring Six, he had seen it in his dad's classified folder and now he had heard it being spoken for the first time. What did his dad know about Icarus? Was he involved in it somehow? He wouldn't have it locked in his archive if he wasn't. Dr Richter kept going on with his monologue but his words were just noise. Julian's peripheral vision blurred and his focus narrowed.

"Are you okay?" Lydia asked in her soft voice.

Julian nodded and exhaled all the air that was trapped inside his chest. He couldn't believe he hadn't asked it yet, all the excitement from his dream possibly becoming real clouding his judgement. "Victor, how exactly is Dr Richter planning to get us there in such little time?"

"I don't think he will go over the details now but it's a solid plan." Lydia's father leant in, his gaze still fixed on Richter. "We just won't slow down and once there, we'll use the other planets for reverse gravity assists."

"That won't be enough at the speeds we're going. The ship won't be able to handle the stress." he countered. He had seen a few documentaries about this in his VR, he knew the science behind the importance of the Halfway event.

"That's why we have the shuttles." Victor shrugged and cocked his head to the side.

They were planning to evacuate the *Sagan*—the realisation hit him like a punch in the gut. All for the sake of making it to the planet in their lifetime. His whole body jittered, and he felt like the crowd had squeezed all around him, leaving him no space—no space to breathe.

"What are the rest of the people doing at the Halfway Event then?" He managed to ask through his trembling breath.

"I told you, Julian," Lydia leant on his shoulder, "This is our new life now, it's best if you let the past go."

"What does that mean?" He pushed her away and stared at her, her light brown eyes seemingly less attractive than before.

"The time has come to take our own path," Dr Richter raised his voice, drowning their conversation. "We've all worked hard for this but everything's in place. In a few minutes Ring Six will be detached from the *Sagan* and our freedom will begin."

"WHAT?" Julian yelled and everyone around turned to stare at him. Did all these people already know this?

"Pipe down." Victor pulled him closer as if he was trying to hide him. "It's a sacrifice we must be willing to make to fulfil our destiny."

"It's not *your* sacrifice, it's everyone else's. Are you really leaving thousands of people behind? They'll all die without the engines, without power." He tried to whisper but his anguish couldn't be contained.

"They made their own choices. They weren't worthy."

"Are you kidding me?" Julian couldn't believe what he was hearing.

"Listen, young man. You're very lucky to be a part of this, even in your obliviousness."

Julian gasped for air and exhaled shakily. He felt a pain on his cheekbones while pressing his teeth together and flared his nostrils once again for his next attempt to breathe as Dr Richter continued.

"My friends. Let's stand together as we reach for the impossible and the bright future that awaits us."

The quadrant fell silent as if everyone was holding their breaths. Julian turned to Lydia who had closed her eyes, her chin pointing up. She blindly extended her hand and locked it around his arm while he looked around and realised everyone was in the same state of trance as her. He wanted to run away but couldn't break free of her tight grasp this time. If the Ring was about to be detached, he had to at least let someone know about what was going on. His dad was right... he was always right, how could he have been so foolish as to think otherwise. He slowly slid his roller out and tried to crack the screen open against his leg. Rachel's face was there again to greet him next to a similar message like the one he had received earlier.

"Are you still in Six? Something bad is about to go down over there. Come back here. I just found Alex, I can't lose you now."

Typing an answer with his one free hand was harder than expected as he couldn't reach some of the letters on the edge of the screen. He kept his message as short as possible and put the roller back in his pocket as a female computer voice finally broke the silence.

"Five minutes to Ring isolation."

The crowd broke into cheers and laughter while clapping repeatedly.

"Are you really going to detach this Ring from the others? What about friends and family?" he asked aimlessly at everyone around him.

"That's the plan," Victor replied while clapping.

"What about my parents, Rachel, our friends? Are we not going to see them ever again? You're sentencing them to death!"

"Julian, I thought you wanted to see the new planet," Lydia said.

"Not if I have to sacrifice everyone I know and possibly the ship itself."

"What's wrong with the kid?" a deep male voice interjected from behind him.

"It's nothing, he was a last minute transfer and just found out everything," Victor chuckled.

"Maybe he shouldn't be here with us in the first place," the man replied.

"Well, it's true. I shouldn't be," Julian said and took out his roller again.

"Four minutes to Ring isolation."

"What did I tell you about the roller?" Victor shouted and took it from his hands with force, "I've been more than polite and patient with you so far but you're starting to get on my nerves."

"The rest of the population need to know as well. This decision can't be made for them."

"Julian calm down," Lydia pleaded, "Everything is going to be better here. We'll have something to look forward to… together," she said softly, her fingers sliding down his arm to cup his hand.

"What about everyone else? They will all die, adrift in the middle of nowhere!" He shook her hand off, her spell on him now broken.

"I want to see Aquanis, just like you. I want to build a life there, explore the new world. I am just not afraid to reach out and grab the opportunity no matter the cost." Her voice was thinner than usual—fake.

"The cost is cutting ties with everyone outside your precious circle and making them martyrs to your crazy plan."

"Three minutes to Ring isolation."

"It's not crazy. Scientists of the group have worked for years to perfect the simulations," Victor interjected.

"You're taking the ship apart!" Julian yelled.

"That's it young man," the man behind him said sharply and grabbed him by the arm.

"What are you doing?" Lydia cried.

"He doesn't belong here. I'll take him to the lower levels."

"Leave me alone," Julian screamed and twisted his body around to break free of the man's grasp and face him.

He was at least twice his size with veiny arms that could have been bigger than Julian's legs. Julian took a few steps back as his eyes scanned the area around him. Almost everyone was staring at him in a circle where he was the centre, whispering and grimacing at each other.

"Two minutes to Ring isolation."

"I've got to go," Julian said while revolving around himself to find the exit.

"No, Julian, please stay. You can't leave." Lydia extended her hand to him.

"I have to warn the others."

"You promised your mum you'd stay with me."

Where *was* his mum? She must have known about all this. But then again, she wouldn't have left him to find out from other people, would she? He gave a quick glance around in a hopeless attempt to find her among the crowd that encircled him.

"Yeah well, I promised my dad I'd hear his speech, yet here I am," he said and took a few quick steps towards the crowd.

He pushed through the bodies in his way and slipped through the ones that tried to grab him.

"Don't let him get away!" the big man shouted.

He shoved a girl with his shoulder, but this wasn't the time for apologies. He had to get out of there as fast as possible. He reached the long strip in the middle and ran through the grass to the end of the quadrant where the crowd was beginning to thin out.

"One minute to Ring isolation."

He had to make it to the outer bridge. He jumped over the flower pots and felt a lateral force pushing him down. A boy not a lot older than him had tackled him and tried to pin him down. His long black hair tasted like dry grass as he spit them out of his mouth. He pressed his knees on the boy's chest and pushed him aside, jumping back on his feet and glancing behind him at the horde chasing him. The doors were near now. He ran, careening to a stop in front of the panel, forced to wait for them to hiss open. He hammered on the door with his fists just managing to squeeze through as a hand almost touched his back.

"Thirty seconds to Ring isolation."

The intersection was empty. There was no one else in his way to stop him. He ran as fast as his legs could carry him in the uncomfortable suit he was wearing. Someone was right behind him. He could hear their breath as if it was right behind his neck. A strong vibration coursed through him from under the metal tiles and he dropped on his knees. The ship creaked as the new, polished wall panels cracked and fell on the floor with a deafening clanging. He glanced behind to his pursuer who had also fallen down, face first and covered in blonde hair as a loud alarm blared.

"Outer Hull Breach in auxiliary water storage."

Outer hull breach? Was it even safe to enter the outer bridge now? His grandfather's story popped in his head, the image of the four souls who had lost their lives in there flashing before his eyes.

"Ten seconds to Ring isolation."

The synthesised voice continued like nothing had happened. He scampered to the outer bridge door and hit it with his fists as if it would make it open faster. The long corridor was right there in front of him, its eerie emptiness foreshadowing something horrible was about to happen as debris flew outside the window strip. A set of hands locked around his waist and pulled him outside the threshold as the door slammed shut and locked next to him.

"Please don't go, monkey."

CHAPTER 16

— RACHEL —

OUTER BRIDGE – RING 5

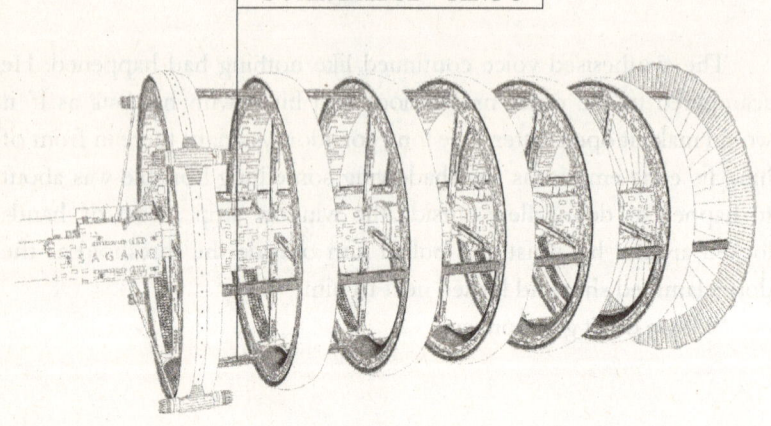

Two sets of cautious footsteps approached her position, stopping in front of the control room.

"Why is this already open?" Scott Walker's voice was a little throaty, a raspy tone of someone who hadn't exercised in a while, "Check the other corridors."

Rachel hugged her knees and curled against the extruded dent of the bulkhead as the tips of two brown shoes stopped next to her. The leather squeaked as the man leant forward and squinted in the pitch blackness, flailing his torch around the shadows of the hallway. He turned around and checked the other corridors of the intersection in the same way before heading back to the control room.

"Hey, whose shoes are that?" Andre asked and the beam from his torch bounced wildly around the bulkhead.

"Stay here and make sure we have no more surprises." Mr Walker's voice grew fainter as he finished his sentence.

Rachel finally let out the breath she was holding in and tried to stifle the groan while standing.

She reached for her roller and replied to Julian's message while chewing on her bottom lip. The thought of something happening to him made her lungs gasp for air. No matter how long the inhale, the air was just not enough. Her heart raced, the drumming pulse throbbing inside her left ear.

She poked her head around the indentation of the wall and adjusted her eyes to the white light emanating from the open door. The man in the old hat was busy on his roller, leaning against the door and glancing behind him every now and then. He extended his roller in front of him and the woman with the curly hair appeared on its transparent screen.

"Any luck your side?" Nyx whispered.

"We just got here. Where are you?"

"I am at the bridge, Six side. It seems they're in the resi quad so I came to the Cylidome intersection. Only four guards but I shut them up."

"Fucking piece of shit!" Scott shouted from inside the room.

"We might have to come to you so stay put," Andre whispered close to the screen.

"Fuck! I think it's starting soon, you need to get here asap," Nyx said and the screen went black.

"They disabled Abeone." Julian's dad must have come out because his voice was clear again.

"What?" Andre cried in disbelief. "Are you certain?"

"Yes." Came the answer in a sorrowful tone. "The ship has no AI anymore."

"Can you not get her back online?" Andre sounded desperate.

Mr Walker didn't give an answer. "Richard, are you still there?" he asked instead.

Was there a third person with them? No one replied but the ship's archivist—who apparently was a lot more than that—carried on as if he had gotten an answer. "You'll have to blow it up. There's no other way."

The two men ran back towards the lift as Rachel found the courage to come out of the intersection. *What the hell is going on?* None of the dialogues she had overheard made any sense to her. She checked her roller once again and tapped on Julian's face.

"Still here. They're locking down Six."

The knot in her stomach tightened as she started to realise what was happening. An unsettling thought tormented her—she couldn't be away from him, she needed him in her life even if it was just as a friend. She had to make it there in time despite the ringing in her head. She gulped and followed the light blue rectangles towards the end of the hallway to the lift on the other side and hunched over the panel. She could feel the muscles of her back pulsating with her every breath, pushing her lungs and shortening every single inhale.

She reached the ground floor and walked as fast as she could towards the Cylidome quadrant, running through the outer bridge to Ring Four and heading straight for the next one to Ring Five. The two men were almost at its end. Her feet were in excruciating pain—running around the whole ship barefooted had numbed her soles to the hard, metallic floors. Her strides were getting shorter and shorter as she finally reached the last bridge between Rings Five and Six.

She balanced her upper body on her knees and wheezed a few long breaths, gulping with difficulty as she tried to wet her dry throat with any saliva left. The pain at the back of her head was excruciating and she tried to massage it, touching strands of hair instead that were stuck on her neck, dripping beads of sweat down her spine, tickling her as they trickled down inside her dress.

The doors of the bridge slid open, revealing her presence to Scott's group who were standing at its end. She tried to jump behind the frame as Andre's deep voice echoed through the bulkhead, "Hey! Show yourself!"

Rachel remained silent. Andre repeated the question but his voice was dwarfed by a loud synthesised warning from the other side.

"Three minutes to Ring isolation."

Ring isolation? They were really planning to lock it down. A small part of her didn't want to believe Julian's message, but the announcement was surely real. Three minutes was barely enough time at her physically broken state for another five hundred metre sprint. Leaving Julian stranded on the other side wasn't an option though. No time to think, she strafed away from the frame and limped her way inside the bridge.

She had made it past the middle when the red laser blinded her. Nyx had propped the long, thin rifle on her shoulder, her finger hugging the trigger.

"Rachel? Nyx, no!" Julian's dad lowered her gun giving Rachel the opportunity to run again.

"I won't jeopardise the mission for anyone!" Nyx raised her weapon again.

"Thirty seconds to Ring isolation."

"Rachel? What are you doing here?" Scott Walker cried but she didn't give out any answer, "Rachel, stop!" he screamed as loud as he could.

Even if there was something to say, there weren't enough breaths inside her to utter the words. Her legs kept going on their own, dragging her pained body forward towards the exit.

Then a blinding light flashed from outside the windows and the whole bridge shook, knocking her off her feet and onto the cold tiles. Debris smashed on the bridge's outer layers, followed by a hailstorm of tiny, white needles that splashed on the hull and faded into the surrounding blackness.

She groaned to get back on her feet. It was the new structure they were building all this time—a geyser was spewing out a translucent liquid into the void, transforming it to icicles of frost.

She was almost there now, just a few more steps.

"Ten seconds to Ring isolation."

"Rachel NO!" Scott dashed towards her and tackled her to the ground inside the bridge as the doors shut down with force behind him.

"Why wouldn't you listen?" He cried.

"Julian is in there..." she said softly as her eyes grew heavy and everything around her turned black.

CHAPTER 17

— JULIAN —

THE CYLIDOME – RING 6

The spicy aroma of a flower tickled his nostrils. Lillies—he'd never mistake that honey-like smell. His living room seemed different; there was only a single tall vase filled with colourful flowers in the middle of the coffee table. He rubbed his eyes and inspected the pyjamas he couldn't remember putting on for the pain underneath—three distinct bruises on his chest had turned blue. Sensitive and tender at the touch, he sucked his teeth, groaning as he stood up.

The bitter smell of burnt coffee guided his body to the kitchen and he wondered if he'd put the machine on a timer as he bent his spine in pain. The realisation dawned on him after the first sip and he chugged it all, his brain almost like an engine craving a few drops of fuel to turn on. This wasn't his flat.

The memories from the previous night flooded his mind in a haze of screams and agony. He was surrounded by an angry mob threatening to vent him to space. His mum had spoken up for him, but the words were unclear. It was the least she could have done after denying him the opportunity to leave the Ring—especially after having forced him there in the first place.

He pushed his temple with his fingers and squeezed his eyes. The throbbing pain in his forehead was pounding inside his head like a monotonous repeating drum.

"I have some A-pills in the top left cupboard," his mother's voice startled him off the sofa. It was calm and steady like it was just another morning in their old flat, like last night had never happened.

A surge of warm fury emanated from his whole face but she had already gone into the bathroom. Swallowing one of the oblong shaped pills with what was left of his coffee, he circled around the living room, mentally preparing for his imminent outburst.

"I can't believe you lied to me! All this time... LIES!" he yelled when she came back, completely disregarding the sentences he had formulated in his head already.

"Easy there, monkey, there's no need to shout," she gestured to him to calm down and moved past him towards the kitchen.

"You are not even going to look at me?" he cried, his nails digging into his palms.

"How about you let me get some tea and we can have a chat like grownups?" she suggested as she placed a variety of dried leaves in her cup.

Julian let out a tremulous, loud exhale, thinking back to all the excuses and lies she had fed him. Even her presence was infuriating.

"I can see you're upset," she remarked in an annoying calmness as she sat in the black chair opposite the couch.

"You think?" He stopped his pacing but his whole body shook and twitched, unable to stand still. "Why am I here?"

"Well, the alternative was the temporary confinement area in lower residential."

"A prison? Seriously? Did we somehow time travel back to the twenty-first century while I was sleeping?"

"Only a temporary measure until we get back on track with the mission."

"The mission," he scoffed, more memories from the previous night coming to the surface, ones that involved genocide. "Did they... did they really detach Ring Six from the *Sagan*?"

"No, there was a... complication. "We did however manage a complete isolation. We shut the bridges and blocked all communications from that point onwards."

At least there was some good news in the series of messed up events. Isolation was better than detachment. There was still hope that the other side would find a way to break through—maybe his dad was already on it. "What about dad? Is he still on the other side?"

"Julian..." she trailed off with a sigh and her eyes darted around the room. "Your dad knew what we were doing and willingly chose to be on the other side."

"No... no. Dad warned me, he told me not to come but I didn't listen. So fucking stupid... I wanted to go out with Lydia, I wanted to make sure you were safe here after everything that happened with Nightfall."

"With what?"

"DON'T! No more pretending and no more lies!" He raised an accusing finger. "Y-you... you manipulated me M... Mum." His voice cracked no matter how hard he tried to control the trembling.

"I would never do such a thing to my son. Come on, monkey, you know how much I love you."

"No, you orchestrated everything so I would stay in Six by the time the isolation happened." A huffed breath slipped through his gritted teeth. "And to find out about Icarus from a random stranger."

"Julian, you're a very smart boy. Having this information would put you in huge danger and we didn't know which side you would choose. You saw..."

"So you chose *for* me then!" he threw his hands in the air.

"You saw yourself what happened to the people who wanted to turn on us. They had you marked as a liability, the only way to bring you here was to keep you in the dark. Do you know what I had to go through to convince Dr Richter to allow you on board?"

"Oh please, do tell me about all the sacrifices you made."

"Julian, I wanted to tell you about Icarus so many times, I really did, but...'

"But you knew I'd find it crazy so you took it upon yourself to decide for me, is that it?"

"No... all I wanted was for you to..."

"Answer my question! And try not to lie to me for once!"

"Julian you don't understand..."

"Yes or no, Mum?" he yelled but she looked away, fidgeting with her fingers on top of her crossed legs. "Yes or no, Mum?"

"Yes. I chose what was best for *my son*!" Her whole body jerked forward.

"No, you chose what was best for you. You wanted me with you on this side of the ship and you got me," Julian paced faster around the living room, his hands shaking and his heart pounding.

"Everything I did, I did because I love you so much." The last part was drowned in a squeal as her voice quavered.

"You only love yourself."

"Your father made his choice to stay on the other side, fully aware that he wouldn't see you ever again. Why are you not mad at him?"

"No, Dad tried to keep me in Ring Three, to keep me safe… And it doesn't really matter now, does it? Because thanks to you I'll never have the chance to even discuss it with him. I take it you assumed since he's not here I'd just believe you though?" He rushed to the door and banged his hand on the panel when it denied him access.

"What are you doing?" his mother whined with half opened eyes. She tried to wipe the tears forming on her eyelids but most of them had already escaped and splashed down on her red cheeks.

"Open the door!"

"You can't go out yet. They'll throw you in pris… in confinement."

"Open—the—door."

"Julian…"

"Open it, damn it!" His whole body shook. "I can't even look at you right now," he yelled as loud as he could.

"You're in your pyjamas, how will you walk outside?" his mother rubbed her nose with a loud snivel as she approached the door.

"I don't care. At least it's *my* choice," he squeezed out as the door slid inside the wall cavity.

He hid his shaking hands inside his pockets and fought the urge to look back as he walked away towards the lift. He could still hear her loud sobbing but at least she wasn't following him or trying to stop him this time. His heart was still racing and his legs could barely hold his weight.

The people at the plaza took notice of him the moment he came out of the lift. Was it his carefree attire or the fact that he had broken out of his imprisonment? He couldn't tell for sure as the worrying eyes pierced through him and kept his adrenaline rushing. A young man stood from his chair and looked at him with an aggressive scowl. His long bushy beard hid half his face but his red, scornful eyes were enough to convey his hatred. He almost lunged forward but was held back by the woman beside him. She grabbed his hand and whispered something that apparently calmed him down enough to sit back in his chair.

Julian picked up the pace and walked briskly through the rest of the residential district. He didn't know where he was going exactly, only that he had to keep walking. The quadrant junction was empty but for two men in blue Icarus uniforms and slim, orange visors. They stared at him and whispered something to each other while holding their fingers under their ears. Julian tried not to look directly but he could tell they were coming for him, trying to cut him off before the Cylidome entrance.

"Sir, could you hold on for one moment," the taller man waved his hand.

Julian put his head down and marched straight for the double doors.

"Sir, we need to verify your ID," the other man blocked his way. He was a little older than Julian and shorter than the other guy, but more muscular than both.

"Why do I have to show you my ID? What year is this?"

"It's not a request sir." The tall, blonde man put his fingers around the holster on his belt and revealed a small power weapon.

A gun? Seriously? It wasn't the first time he had seen one but it still surprised him. The woman his dad had come with at the Nightfall lab had an even bigger one but he hadn't dared ask about it. He felt his chest pulsing and hesitantly extended his arm.

The burly, young man grabbed Julian's wrist and forcefully lifted his sleeve up to his elbow. "Mr Walker... it shows here you should be detained in flat 7E. Any particular reason you have broken free of your confinement?"

'I just needed some air. Look, it's not like I can go anywhere anyway since you've locked us all in here," he beckoned towards the blast door of the outer bridge.

"Oh, he talks back. I like that, it gives me an excuse," the guard reached for the long black stick that was strapped around his leg.

Julian took a step back and winced as the man raised his weapon, ready to land a blow.

"Woah woah woah. What the hell are you doing, man?" a familiar voice made the guard halt his attack half way.

Julian turned around and narrowed his eyes as the man that had saved him approached from the residential quadrant entrance. He had shaved the sides of his head apart from an afro mohawk but that was still definitely James.

"And you are?" the guard pointed his baton at James.

"James Parker. I told Julian to meet me here so I could show him around," he extended his arm with confidence.

"Curfew is still in effect, Mr Parker. He needs to be back in his confinement before red lights." The guard sheathed his weapon after inspecting James' wrist.

"Give him a break, he's new here. We'll take a walk and I'll escort him back."

The men in the Icarus uniforms eyed James down and gave a cautious nod before walking past them towards the residential area.

"So it's true," James exclaimed, wrapping his arm around Julian's shoulder but he winced away. "I didn't know if I should believe Lucas when he said you're here," James said as though nothing had happened, like they were still back at school waiting for class to start.

"Yeah, here I am... unfortunately. How can you hang out with people like Lucas, James?"

"He's not as bad as you think. He's actually a decent guy trapped in a tight body."

"How could you keep all this a secret?" Julian flailed his hands about. "I thought we were friends."

"It wasn't up to me, Julian. There are psychological evaluations for each passenger. When your name came up, they said you were... unreliable, that you couldn't be trusted with our secret," James showed him inside the Cylidome.

"That might be true actually. I don't think I would've let it go if I knew beforehand. I would've either told everybody or run away. I tried to run away last night as well but they stopped me."

"Wait, so you're the guy everyone was chasing last night? Did they really shoot you with electric bullets and you peed yourself?" James sucked his teeth at the realisation of his babbling.

"My mum must've left that part out." It had to be true—it would explain the change of clothes. "How can you be on board with all this, James?" he snapped, the emotional whiplash caused by those he thought close to him draining the last bit of his patience.

"Come on man, don't be like that. Focus on the future. We get to see Aquanis."

"At what cost, James?" he cried, stopping to study his former friend. Who knew how many others had betrayed his trust. "What about Liam?"

"You think I don't feel like shit about that? You think I didn't try to bring him here?" James snapped back at him, his voice gaining momentum and intensity with every word, "I had to choose between him and my mum. You think it was an easy choice? You think I didn't cry for days knowing I had to leave him on the other side?"

"Leave him to *die*, you mean." Julian countered his hollow argument—there was no reason to believe anything anymore. "Along with all our friends and twenty thousand people?"

"Hey, we wouldn't be in this situation if they had stuck to the original plan."

"Are you really blaming innocent people for something they didn't even know was going on?"

"They're all responsible. They shoved us in the shadows, they forbade HITs and cyberware like we still live in the twent-first century, they…"

"Yeah, yeah, I heard the speech yesterday." He shook his head, too annoyed to even continue talking to him.

"It was the only way, Julian. There was no other choice."

"There's always a choice, James." Julian patted him on the back and turned away.

"Where are you going?"

"I need to be alone for a little bit, you know… process all this."

"OK, just don't get me in trouble as well, yeah? Back before red lights."

Julian only gave him the thumbs up and dragged his slippers through the dried leaves. He really wanted to keep the middle finger up instead but hesitated at the last second.

He reflected on their conversation as he walked through the tall pine trees. He definitely wanted to step on the new planet but not without his father, his friends, Rachel. His train of thought repeated in a cycle that always ended with the same question. Why couldn't there be a middle ground? Was the possible happiness from reaching Aquanis able to compensate for all the lives sacrificed? Of course not. Maybe the other side could be persuaded and there wouldn't be a reason for division. Was the science even true though? All his life he had learnt to trust in it, but it didn't feel right this time. *The only way to refute science is with better science.*

He stopped at a small clearing and sat on the grass to clean his slippers from the tiny pebbles that had found their way between his toes. He leant back and balanced himself on his arms wondering what to do next. He imagined spending day after day in that clearing looking up at the steel lattice that held the massive pieces of glass of the elongated dome. That was a boring thought, maybe even a miserable one. He checked his surroundings for any sign of bugs and laid on his back. Why couldn't they carry on with their plan with the whole *Sagan*, why detach the Ring? Maybe the mass would be too much. He felt ashamed again. Understanding how science worked was one thing but actually practising it was a completely different one.

He drew a long breath and turned his cheek to the soft grass. The itchy blades tickled his face as the smell of dry soil reminded him of the last time he was here. It was a different Cylidome but the scents carried around in the air were the same. Similar pine trees towered above him and thick bushes surrounded him; there was only one thing missing. He tried to imagine what she would be doing at that time and how she would have taken the news of the Ring's detachment. His imagination brought her to life above him, pinning him down like last time. He wondered if he would ever get a chance to see those piercing green eyes again that so symmetrically opposed her pixie nose. If she was there, she would've definitely given James the middle finger. He on the other hand was too reserved, too dejected to do it himself.

He sighed and hunched over his crossed legs looking around at the overgrown flora. He had always felt trapped inside the ship—'floating prison' he used to call it but he never thought there were worse prisons than that, ones that not only kept him away from oceans and beaches but also away from the people he cared about.

CHAPTER 18
— Rachel —

| Flat 14D – Ring 4 |

The voice of the AI rang inside her ears, vibrating her already pained temples. It wasn't the usual greeting; it had addressed her as a guest. The sheets had a familiar musky scent and she nuzzled her face in the pillow. She rubbed her eyes and scratched her fuzzy hair as she sat at the edge of the bed. All her stuff was gone from the bedroom apart from a set of folded clothes on the desk and a model of a black sailing boat underneath it. She was sure she had seen that boat before; it was one of the ancient ones that had a mast and an actual sail. This was Julian's room, the one before he had moved out. The pungent smell of her sweat made her nose twitch as she pulled the strap of her dress aside to take a whiff of her armpit. *Ugh...*

Julian's old flat was transformed into a base of operations. Monitors of all sizes were hung on the walls and Mr Walker's old study was now housing a few angular canisters in a row which emitted a faint blue light from the top. The apartment seemed rather busy, occupied by men that were yelling at each other until they took notice of her and eyed her from top to bottom. The tall, blonde man had wrinkles on his forehead and under his eyes, while the one next to him was younger, probably a little bit older than herself. Two middle aged men were occupied with the cabling in the study and a small group of young people around her age—two boys and a girl—were discussing in front of a large monitor.

Only the man sitting with his back to her seemed uninterested in her presence and kept tapping on his roller, "Scott, she's awake," he said without losing his focus.

Julian's dad popped out of the kitchen and smiled. "Aaah, you're up. Good, good, I see you found the clothes I left for you. Listen Rachel..."

"NO, *you* listen!" She interrupted him, her own voice giving her a headache. "Why did you stop me? And better yet, how did I end up here? I need to call Julian, make sure he's ok."

"You can't. Ring Six has disabled all communications beyond their bridge."

"No... no, don't tell me they actually detached it?"

"Not yet, thankfully. I'll answer all your questions, I am sure you have a lot. How about you go take a shower and we can talk about it over a fresh cup of coffee?"

She scowled but adhered to his advice. Dousing her skin and muscles under hot water was much more pressing than yelling at him.

The new shorts and t-shirt were quite big for her but at least they were clean and fresh. It felt weird wearing Julian's mum's clothes but it would have to do for now. She stepped into the living room, her hair still too wet to tie up and left dripping on her shoulders.

"Here you go, Miss Watson." The blonde man offered her a warm cup of coffee and she studied him again. It was probably the clean uniform he was wearing or his broad smile that made him look younger than he was despite the wrinkles below his icy blue eyes.

"Thanks." She felt forced to return the smile and sat on the couch, crossing her legs. "So, Mr Walker..." she started, feeling the peering gazes of the men around her.

"Come on, Rachel. How many times have I asked you to call me Scott?"

"Fine. So, Scott... What's with all the secrecy and knowing everything but sharing nothing? You knew about Nightfall and said nothing and now this whole shitshow with Six detaching and there you are yet again, one step ahead of everyone else."

"We were actually one step behind but go on, it seems like you're on a roll there," the man in the chair said without turning.

"Rachel, I told you when we brought your brother in, I had nothing to do with Nightfall. If I knew where all these people were, you think I would've let it happen?"

"I don't know what to believe anymore and the only person I can trust is apparently stuck in Six all by himself."

"Rachel, you can trust me. Did I not save your brother? I'm trying to do the right thing here."

"Then what about the classified folder with the crescent moon Julian found in your archive? You still haven't given me a clear answer."

"That was basically a compilation of all the evidence we had at that point."

"Yeah, I am sorry about your brother, Miss Watson, but we really didn't know what Nightfall was even about." The blonde man sat at the other end of the couch, one leg crossed under him and his chest bent so he could face her.

"Ok, seriously who are you?"

"I guess some pleasantries are overdue. I am Richard Lahtinen, head of interstellar engineering for the *Sagan*. The young man over there is Noel, my apprentice. The operations trainees are Lee, Christoff and Alina." His finger traced their heads from left to right. All three of them were in space uniforms instead of the standard *Sagan* tracksuit as if they had just come back from outside the ship. "Toz and Mo are working on the generators in the other room and behind me, you should already know your own councilman."

"Councilman?" She repeated. The hair did match the description and his voice had been strangely familiar. She rushed in front of the man who was still sitting unaffected by this conversation and squealed. "You're Kieran Bolek!" She cheered and clapped. "I am such a huge, *huge* fan. I've followed your work since... since I was born, basically."

"Always glad to meet a fan," he grinned, stretching his thin beard across his cheeks, the white hairs on his chin even cuter up close.

"As I was saying," Richard cut in, "We thought Nightfall was some sort of branch of Icarus up until yesterday, cutting out loose ends to maintain the secrecy of their operations."

"Exactly," Scott agreed, "We still don't know who's responsible for it or what happened to the rest of the disappearances. We only found fifteen people down there." He pushed his glasses up his nose. "Out of a hundred and thirty-five."

"You mean *I* found." She coughed on purpose.

"Yeah you, my oblivious son who would follow you anywhere and a guy who broke several laws by breaking into the control room. Quite the team."

Rachel gulped and lowered her eyes without an answer. So he had found out about that after all.

"The evolutionists have always been one step ahead of us." He took off his glasses completely to rub his eyes with a long inhale.

"Evol-evolutionists?" She looked away, her eyes unfocused. Mrs Yau had mentioned something about them that night at the cylidome.

"Or 'crazies' as we like to call them," Noel finally spoke. His voice was thin and betrayed his younger age.

"Actually, I don't know how you managed to uncover Nightfall while chasing around the wrong group," Scott said. He looked like a different person without glasses. "Lucas is an evolutionist, his parents are too."

"And what do these evolutionists want?" Rachel crossed her arms while raising an eyebrow.

"They believe that we should be able to use our full potential as humans with complete disregard to rules and ethics. They want to introduce gene editing once again, synthetic integration to human bodies, eugenics and pretty much everything our ancestors tried so hard to put an end to."

"And I assume you guys are against that?" She opened her arms to address the room. "Is that why they want to detach the Ring?"

"Yes and no," Richard replied with a head bob, "At first, we let them be because we thought they just wanted to be in their own Ring."

"*We?*" Julian's dad interrupted him. "No, *we* warned everyone multiple times that the evos had a hidden agenda."

"Scott, don't start," Kieran exasperated. "You know the council's decision was unanimous. They never listened to me."

"Yes and now we're all paying for it."

"You still haven't answered my question though," Rachel cut in through the sudden bitterness in the air. "Why detach the Ring?"

"We can't be sure yet but…" Scott started hesitantly.

"Yeah, we're sure," Richard dismissed him with a sharp gesture. "They believe they can reach Aquanis in the next forty years or so."

"Seriously? Wait, can they though?" She asked, tired of turning around to whoever was speaking. Her mind went straight to Julian. He had wished for this so many times, an unending desire to see and explore the new planet. Was he really in Ring Six against his will? Maybe he wanted to be there. Maybe he was even an evolutionist himself by now. She didn't know how she felt about all this new information but setting foot on Aquanis was indeed intriguing.

Richard's mouth hung slightly opened as his eyes darted somewhere behind her. "In theory… yes," he said after a loud exhale.

Rachel couldn't contain the soft gasp. "Really?" She didn't mean to squeal but her voice came out quite high-pitch.

"I hear a lot of excitement in your voice, Miss Watson," Kieran Bolek said from the dining table.

"Well excuse me, it's not every day you find out there's an alternative to living your whole life trapped in a steel bucket."

"Really, Miss Watson? So you wouldn't mind carrying on your shoulders the deaths of thousands of people, let alone jeopardising the first major human colonisation attempt?" The councilman finally looked up from his roller, his cold blue eyes piercing into her soul, questioning and judging her.

She stared at her feet then, chewing her bottom lip, the warmth in her cheeks no doubt making them red. "How is it even possible to detach a whole Ring?"

"It's not that easy, hence why we never gave it too much thought." Richard shook his head.

"Wait, why haven't they detached already?"

"We blew a hole in their water. Can't go anywhere without water." He choked a forced chuckle.

"So what do we do now? Are you planning on stopping them somehow?"

"What we plan doesn't concern you, little Miss," Richard replied sharply.

"Yes, Rachel. How about you let us take it from here?" Scott suggested.

"Let you take it from here? Oh no no no. I am in this as much as you are. I'll get Julian out of there either with or without you so you'd better count me in," she exclaimed and even Lee, Christoff and Alina turned with a glaring stare.

Scott sighed as his eyes bounced around the room and finally nodded with discomfort.

"You can't be serious," Richard protested, "She's just a kid."

"Trust me, knowing Rachel she won't let this go no matter what we say to her."

"She can bring nothing to the table, she…"

"Oh you'll see I am full of surprises," Rachel interrupted him.

The men exchanged a few looks among them until Kieran sliced the uneasy silence with his authoritative tone. "If Scott says it's fine then I'm good."

Richard sighed but eventually sat down at the dining table mumbling just as the main door hissed open.

"Sorry I'm a little late. I had to take care of some other stuff first," the handsome man she had seen at Administration walked in as if it were his own home. He was wearing a sleek, blue suit again, although different from the first time she'd met him. The fabric was sharper, its weave tighter and it sparkled as he moved under the bright ceiling lights.

"It's fine, we were just about to start the briefing," Richard tapped on the empty chair next to him.

"Rachel, this is Javier Rendall, deputy director of Administration," Scott got up and gestured to him, "Jav, this is Rachel…"

"Watson!" He interrupted him, "Yes, we had the pleasure of meeting already, although I wish it was under better circumstances."

"Javier here was our lead on Nightfall… until you found it that is." Scott's lips curled into a small smile but his eyes narrowed, a hint of disapproval lurking beneath the wrinkles of his raised eyebrows.

"Yeah, not thanks to your useless admins, that's for sure."

"The Admins are flooded with Icarus agents," Javier replied, bypassing her insult with a shrug.

"Javier was our man on the inside," Scott gave her a chastising look. "All the information we have about Nightfall was because of him."

"You must tell me how you managed it though..." Javier peered into her eyes while pouring himself some coffee. "How you found something so well hidden, deep into evolutionist territory that even they didn't know about." He picked up the cup and slurped a careful sip while maintaining eye contact.

"I had her debriefed when we put everyone in the infirmary," Scott answered for her. "We have more pressing matters now."

"Of course," Javier conceded, "How is your brother by the way? Has he woken up yet? Has he said anything?"

"No, I was hoping *they* would tell me." She gestured at everyone around the table as she sat opposite of Kieran Bolek.

"Well then," Richard cleared his throat after a long sigh. "Let's start with what we know already."

Rachel felt a stab of fear. Why were they moving on from Alex so quickly? "Wait, what about Alex?" She interrupted.

Richard continued, "Scotty, did you get anything from the control room?"

"No, whoever locked us out had to be there, though," Scott said, browsing through a long list on his roller.

"You mean the bitch that shoved me to the wall when I got there?" She blurted.

Scott raised his chin, his lips parted. "Aaah, that explains your concussion.

Rachel rubbed the back of her head, a faint ringing still lingering inside. Or was it her imagination?

"Losing Abeone was a heavy blow," Scot continued, "The AI has always been our first line of defence."

"Nothing we can do about it now, Scott." Richard bent over the table, balancing on his elbows and interlocking his fingers. "Abeone will take time to reboot, time we don't have. What have we told the public?"

"Our cover story is quite believable actually," Kieran answered, "I issued a statement saying there was a malfunction with the engines during the Halfway event that ended up in the containment of Ring Six."

"Are we blaming the communication jam on that as well?" Scott asked.

"Indeed we are. We are good for now but we need to act quickly before people start getting suspicious."

Rachel was getting pissed. Even with useful information they ignored her.

"Javier, do we have a statement from the Administration yet?" Richard turned to the dapper man.

Javier scrolled through his roller with his finger. "Not officially but the numbers are tallied. 18763 people across Rings One to Five."

"Which means we can finally get a full list of the evolutionists." Scott let out a nervous sigh. "Good. That leaves what, two, maybe three thousand in Ring Six?"

"More or less." Javier nodded. "Granaries, storages and livestock were all counted for, they didn't take anything before isolating themselves."

"Well, they may be delusional but at least they're honourable." Richard scoffed.

At that point, Kieran finally stood up. He seemed taller up close and scruffier than usual. His shirt was half tucked inside his pants and his blazer was wrinkled around his waist. "Our main concern now should be our two agents in Six. We have no way of knowing what Andre and Nyx are doing over there."

"They are both quite resourceful." Scott leant in, his gaze shifting between Richard and Kieran. "But they won't be able to do much without me."

"Thanks again for that," Richard sneered at her and placed his roller in the middle of the table.

"What did I do?" Rachel complained, resenting the fact that it had come out too whiny.

"If you hadn't run for the bridge, Scott would've been with them." Richard explained.

"Enough! Placing blame gets us nowhere," Scott defended her. "Show us the plan, Richard."

A blue hologram of the whole *Sagan* was projected above the roller on the table as the blonde man looked around and studied them. The three trainees had joined behind him while the two engineers were still in Scott's room. "I say we plan an infiltration here." Richard pointed at an area of the ring structure that grew bigger and took over the whole projection.

"That's the science quadrant you're showing. How do you plan... oh, I see... you're crazy," Scott said with a brief chuckle.

"What is it? Where?" Rachel leant over the table, her face almost covered by the projection.

Again, no one cared to answer her.

"That's a very risky plan, Richard," Kieran said in a cautious tone, "I'm fairly certain they will have thought of sealing all external accesses."

"You want to go outside the ship?" Rachel yelled.

"Shhhhh!" Richard put a finger in front of his mouth that wasn't enough to prevent the saliva droplets from being sprayed all over her face. "Little Miss... can you please let the adults talk for a minute?" He asked but his tone was more affirming than suggestive. "The hatches have an outside latch somewhere. I just have to find the right drawing."

"Why are you even trying to get in?" Rachel insisted despite Richard's growl. "You should be focusing on stopping them from detaching in the first place."

"They won't detach." Richard waved his hand to dismiss her suggestion.

"I thought you said..."

"The Rings are not only connected by bridges, alright? There are multiple other mechanical systems in the Core Hull that there's no way they know of, let alone release them. They're not engineers. I don't even know why I'm explaining myself to you."

"Wait... could it be?" She mumbled as she blanked out and the field trip to the Core Hull came to her mind. "Are you talking about the platforms on the top decks above the reactor? The one Lucas and James were fiddling with when everyone else was busy?"

The men all flinched and looked at her, their mouths slightly open and their eyebrows raised. Only Kieran and Javier seemed to take the news rather calmly, although the former was scanning her with his eyes, unblinking and alert.

"Are you sure about this?" Scott asked and she simply nodded. "Toz, come in here."

A tool clanged on the study's floor and the man appeared shortly after. His whole appearance was a tapestry of brown palettes. Tawny skin, bright amber eyes, bronze hair and dark umber smudges all over his face.

"Is there a chance the evolutionists know about the Ring interlocks at the Core Hull? You never told anyone, did you?"

"No, of course not," Toz shrugged.

"Rachel here claims she saw two boys messing with the interface during her field trip."

"Now that you mention it, I did see your son in the upper levels that day."

"My son? What was Julian doing up there?"

"That's what I've been trying to tell you," Rachel interjected. "We were following Lucas to find out what he knew about my brother and that's how I saw him."

"This is bad." Scott drew a long inhale. "Now that I think about it, didn't Abeone ping a warning across, something about compensating thrust?"

Richard covered his mouth with his palm, his eyes tense and unblinking "She said the Sagan was swaying, like carrying dead weight... that the problem must've been mechanical because she couldn't pinpoint the location."

"And let me guess." Rachel crossed her arms as she leant back in her chair. "Those interlocks are mechanical." She tried her hardest not to smile but there must've been a slight curl on the corner of her lip because Scott gave her a hint of a disapproving look. She had a lot offer and she wouldn't accept being treated like a child.

"Can we not re-engage the locks from Core Hull Five?" Scott suggested after an unease silence.

"No," Toz and Richard replied simultaneously but only Richard continued. "It's always the last Ring that attaches to the rest of the ship. Six to Five, Five to Four... One to shield."

"We may not have as much time as we thought then."

"That's what I said but none of you seem to take me seriously." Rachel stood up and leant on the table with both hands, feeling some of her anxiety seep away since her tendency to speak without thought had actually scored her some points this time. "Preventing the detachment should be priority."

"Why do you think they haven't sailed off in space yet, little Miss? It was me who punctured their water supply." Richard stood up as well, his taller and bulkier figure overshadowing hers.

"You've done something right, then. I'm surprised."

"Stop it!" Scott intervened. "I want to hear solutions, not squabbling."

Richard hesitantly sat back, locking eyes with her and she did the same. Another pregnant silence ensued, accompanied by glances and sighs among the people at the table. Lee, Christoff and Alina had also stopped whatever work they were doing on that wide monitor to catch up with Rachel's revelation.

"Can we not hook something to Ring Six from our end, keep it tethered?" Rachel finally spoke first.

"Little Miss..." Richard started another patronising comment but trailed off and gasped silently. "She actually gave me an idea. We can use the construction clamps."

"I told you I'm full of surprises." She quickly took the credit even though she had no idea what Richard was talking about. *She scores again.*

"Do you think they will hold?" Scott slumped back in his chair. "We're talking about technology that uses buttons and levers."

"Well, they haven't been used since the whole thing was being built so..." Kieran Bolek interrupted, "I don't see how we have an option here."

"The question is if they still work," Toz added.

"Why wouldn't they?" Richard chimed in, "That's the whole reason they are mechanical, so they wouldn't be affected by power outages or malfunctions back then," he said with confidence.

The men discussed the plan in further detail but she couldn't keep up, the terminology was foreign to her and the references made no sense. She got up to stretch her legs, walking in circles around the coffee table, her roller in hand. Julian's picture was behind red flashing letters that read 'Connection error'. She wondered when she would see him again if ever and played the imaginary scene in her head. Apart from burying her face in his chest and squeezing him tightly, she didn't really know what she would actually say to him when the time came.

A hand touched her shoulder and Scott guided her towards the corner of the living room. "Listen Rachel," he whispered, leaning in, "I know that if I told you to stay here you would follow us anyway, but this is a very dangerous operation. If there's no way to stop you from coming, at least I want to make sure you're going to be safe. That means listening to my every word and doing exactly as I say. This is not sneaking around with Julian, it's a carefully planned operation. Do you understand?"

Scott's words left her speechless as she came to the realisation of what was about to happen. This was indeed an adult operation, planned out by people who had been doing this for years.

It's not sneaking around with Julian, she repeated Scott's words in her head and simply nodded a few times.

"Good, we leave in an hour." He patted her on the back and returned to the wall monitors.

Rachel took a deep breath and headed to the kitchen for another cup of coffee when she saw Javier getting ready to leave. "Are you not coming with us?"

"I have to go check up on your brother and the rest first." He patted his blazer down after putting it on.

"Are you not working in Administration?"

"I am but I double my contribution points as a medical professional. It's what I studied after all. They don't need a medic for this anyway."

Julian had mentioned he had helped Mark after his beating from Katey but she had thought it was a first aid thing, not an actual job.

"I wish I could have done more to help," he sighed, placing a gentle hand on her shoulder.

He hadn't helped at all. In fact if he had shared everything with her she might have found Alex sooner. "You could've given me the last camera location," she blurted, not able to keep the frustration in.

"But I did tell your parents when I found out myself."

"You did?" Before bringing Alex to the infirmary, the most communication she had with her parents was when she found a day-old plate of pasta with her name on it.

"Of course. Listen, Rachel..." he gulped and licked his lips. "Be careful out there. Infiltrating Ring Six and exposing Nightfall has put a target on your back," he peered at her with his deep blue eyes before the door slid shut and he was gone.

She returned to the living room, staring at the brown swirl that had appeared on the surface of her coffee. Was she in danger? *Oh, well.* Like that had ever stopped before. She had gone through so much to get Alex, she would go through some more to get Julian.

CHAPTER 19
— JULIAN —
ENGINEERING BAY – RING 6

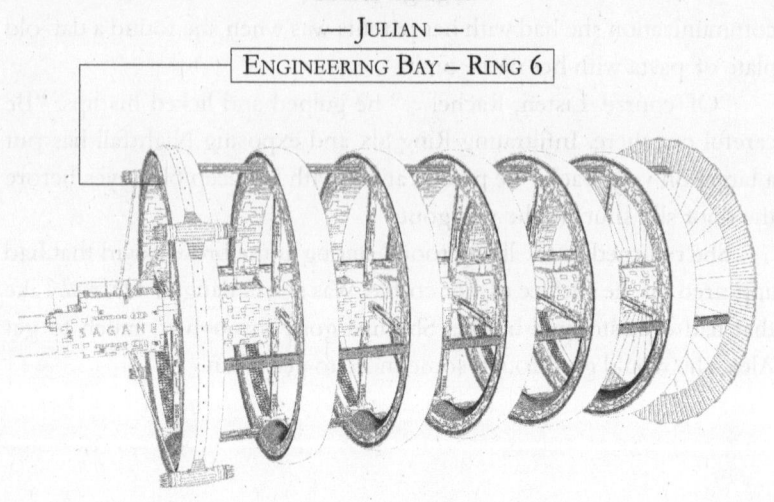

Julian dragged the tip of the long, fragile stick along the hard soil, moving it around a few times and drawing curved lines on the hard earth. He had moved from the clearing, the grass wasn't as good a canvas as rammed earth.

"Psst... kid!" The whisper made him snap out of it.

"Who's there?" He hurriedly got up and revolved around himself.

"Relax, it's us," Nyx's voice came from somewhere in front of him, her blurry figure distorting the tree behind her invisible form. She removed her helmet and her exo-suit materialised out of thin air.

"How long have you been standing there?"

"Just a minute. I had to make sure you're alone."

"Who else would I be with? I'm all alone here with these people." He kicked a pebble that ricocheted off the ground and landed on her metallic armour with an echoing clang.

The corner of her mouth twitched and she sighed. "It's alright, I'm here now. I've got you." She approached, her suit whirring as she landed her hand on his shoulder.

For a woman whom he'd briefly met a couple of days ago at Nightfall, she was weirdly casual in her tone. Probably in her late thirties—the faint creases above her cheekbones giving her away. Her thick, curly, black hair defied the centrifugal gravity, flying in all directions, creating a canopy for her shadowy eyes to hide under. The Icarus uniform she was wearing was surely not her size, dirty with red and brown stains all over and barely visible through the charcoal power armour she was in.

"We were with your father," a deep, male voice came from his right. "But we got separated before the Ring got isolated." The man in the unusual grey fedora of the twentieth century dragged his feet, rustling the leaves in his path.

"Shit... Do you at least have a plan to stop these people from detaching the Ring?" Julian asked, hoping the duo's resourcefulness didn't stop at evacuating people from secret labs.

"We had but it relied heavily on your father," Andre answered. "I was hoping you could help us instead."

"No, not a chance," Nyx said, pointing at Andre and lowering her head. "We approached to protect the kid, not to put him in danger."

"We are all alone here, it wouldn't be the worst thing to have someone who can move freely around the Ring."

"Scott would vent us," she growled.

"I can decide for myself, you know. I want to help," Julian interrupted.

"Honest, naïve and stupidly eager." Nyx looked into his eyes, her features finally softening from the permanent scowl she seemed to maintain. "You really are your father's son." She nodded slowly, exposing a tiny smirk.

"Hopefully without all his bossing," Andre chuckled.

"Great! So... what do you need me to do?" Julian asked.

"We need your access around Six. Everything is biometrically locked here," Andre explained.

"We only need you to get us into engineering. We'll do the rest," Nyx added.

"Which is?" Julian demanded for more answers. He was willing to try anything at this point.

"Destroying the repair-bot bay."

"Richard created a big enough hole in their water storage. They can't detach without fixing that first," Andre answered the question Julian had meant to ask.

He didn't know who Richard was but Nightfall had proved these people knew what they were doing. "How much time do we have?"

"It depends on how much water they've lost," Andre shrugged. "The bots have been out there all night but they only contained the leak in the morning."

"What are we waiting for then?" Julian exclaimed.

"I always liked you, kid." Nyx thumped his back and walked past him, her heavy armour flattening the grass in her path.

What do you mean 'always'? He wanted to ask but she had already moved on. He followed the woman through the greenery as her black curls swung wildly, stretching and shrinking like springs. She only turned around when she reached the entrance, holding her helmet on the side of her chest. It wasn't the spherical, standard issue, but angular with a long rectangular visor. The modular parts of her exo-suit hissed around her ankles and the shoulder pads flapped. A modern knight.

"Listen, kid." Her power armour whirred as she leant close to him. "It's us or them now. Stay behind me at all times and don't stop for anything." She picked the rifle from her back, its modules opening in succession to increase the length of the barrel and add a scope at the top. "Whenever you're ready." She beckoned towards the door panel.

He wanted to say something, show he wasn't afraid either but the words never came. He only nodded and placed his palm on the reader.

"Here, put this on your head." Nyx offered him a circular headpiece. It looked like a big bracelet and fitted on his head like a halo.

"What's this?"

"Camera deflector. Better if they can't identify who's helping us." She winked at him and rushed in the quadrant intersection.

They descended to the engineering levels below with minimum effort at hiding—barely three or four people had almost crossed paths with them but the science district was full of cover in the thick greenery that divided the laboratories on opposite sides. Nyx was leading with her rifle raised and Julian could only hope they'd stop at a level before minus eight. The image of the missing people laying there unresponsive and attached to the tubes brought a chill down his spine. They were safe now on the other side of the Ring but maybe Nightfall wasn't the only thing hidden down there.

Nyx gestured to him to come forward and he glanced at the annotation on the wall. Minus four. He forced a long exhale as he pressed his hand on the panel and the door hissed open.

"Sector six, arc one," Andre announced.

"Should be close then," Nyx jerked her head left and right at the intersection before stepping into the bulkhead. She was walking almost sideways, her knees slightly bent and the rifle propped on her shoulder.

Julian couldn't help but notice that Andre didn't have a weapon of his own nor was he in an exo-suit like his colleague. The questions had piled up, screaming inside his head while his patience was running thin.

A single shot made him jump and scrape his back against the wall. Was this really happening, weapon fire on the most peaceful ship ever built? The crackling of electricity and the clanging of metal hitting the floor echoed in the corridor. Nyx had shot a drone which now laid in pieces on the next intersection. At least it wasn't a person. Her rifle hummed again and the second drone exploded the moment it came out to investigate. She must have been using Thermal InfraRed herself, otherwise how did she know the other one was coming?

"No alarm... Good job, Nyx," Andre whispered.

"You sound surprised." Her voice was distorted through the helmet's speaker.

"Can't you hack one of these to fight on our side?" Julian asked. "You didn't seem to have a problem taking Mark's drone from him."

"This level is swarming with them. It's not that easy when their frequencies overlap."

"Stay focused," Nyx ordered, "How are we doing on time?"

"Eight minutes, twenty seconds for squadron-1 to return," Andre informed them.

"Patrol team?" Julian wondered out loud.

"The first batch of repair bots," Andre explained, "They come back to recharge before the next squadron goes out. For a couple of minutes they're all in the hangar and that's our window."

"Clear. Let's move." Nyx motioned them to follow.

They walked further into the bulkhead, stopping every few steps for Nyx to destroy the patrolling drones with deadly precision. He felt a calming sense of safety in her presence despite the hostile environment they were treading into.

"This is it," Nyx said, stopping in front of a double door. The holocircle in the middle of the frames meant he probably wouldn't have access here but he tried anyway. As expected, it buzzed and turned red.

"That's as far as you can take us. It's my turn now." Andre placed both hands inside the projection and twisted them like he was turning an imaginary valve. Lines of code appeared inside the circle and he went back to his roller.

"You've got this, right?" Nyx stepped next to him, her rifle pointing away.

Andre smirked. "All yours," he exclaimed as the disk in the middle ground loudly and the doors hissed open.

The room was small, full of projections and beeping monitors and beyond the glass wall, the repair bay was refracting the lights in silence, sealed away from the rest of the ship with a pressurisation module. It was not much different from a manufacturing facility, robotic arms were flailing about in their predetermined movements and conveyor belts were running along the length of the room on different levels.

Nyx whispered something in Andre's ear and handed him the rifle before entering the pressurisation chamber.

"Are you going in like that?" Julian asked. "You'll get decompression sickness. You need to wait for emergency pressurisation at least," he cried but the door locked behind her. "What is she doing?" He turned to Andre.

"There's not enough time." Andre pointed at the hangar shutters rolling up for squadron-1 to return, bringing with them the menacing blackness of space. "Don't worry, these exo-suits are basically a spacecraft on their own," he reassured him and focused on the main monitor, swiping through graphs and scrolling through lists until all rectangles on the screen above them turned green. "I know but there's no other option. You can come back now," he muttered, holding a finger behind his ear.

"Let's get out of here," Nyx stated, coming back to the observation room and snatching her weapon from Andre's hand.

"But nothing happened, all the repair-bots are still there," Julian pressed his finger on the glass.

"Not for long. That's why we need to run." She pulled him by the hand and pushed him out the exit. The gears of her exo-suit began to grind as she started running, its hydraulics hissing with every stride.

They made it back to the stair core but Nyx kept going. How far away would they have to go? He couldn't really run at full speed in his pyjamas and slippers. They had almost reached the ground floor when the vibration caused him to lose his footing and slip all the way to the landing below. An alarm blared immediately and the lights switched to red even though it was technically still day cycle. The ceiling tiles trembled, shifting dust and debris between the cracks.

"For your safety and security, all personnel are requested to evacuate engineering levels immediately. Hull Breach in sector six. Adjacent sectors have been sealed."

"How many explosives did you use?" Andre asked from the floor below, panting and hunched over his knees.

"I had to make sure there's nothing left." Nyx replied.

Julian scampered to the top of the stairs and got the door open. "We need to hide. This place will be crawling with Icarus people."

"They're called evolutionists by the way," Andre said.

"Although I prefer crazies," Nyx added with a faint chuckle.

"I have so many questions for when we get out of here." Julian said as he caught his breath.

"Back to the Cylidome?" Andre suggested.

"What if you guys come to my apartment?" Julian interrupted and the others shared a look, "Yeah that could work. I live alone and no one here wants to talk to me anyway."

"Hiding in plain sight. I like it." Andre seemed excited with the idea.

"Are you sure, kid?" Nyx glanced at him before bringing the scope of her rifle close to the visor of her helmet.

"Yeah, of course. Can we get out of here, please?"

"That way is clear." Nyx beckoned towards the quadrant

intersection, lowering her weapon. "I call first on the bed."

CHAPTER 20
— Rachel —
Outer Bridge – Ring 5

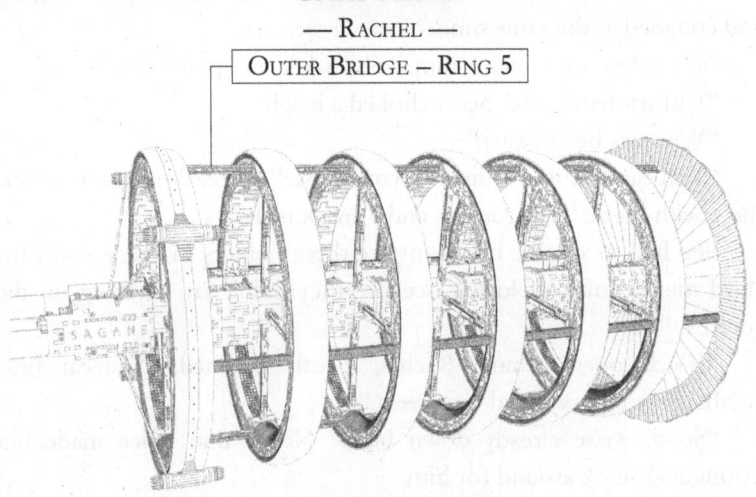

It wasn't a coincidence the quadrant intersection was empty—administration had put up holo-tape around the entrance and a projection of Kieran Bolek was lying to the frustrated citizens that the concourse was under maintenance.

"We should test the comms," Scott suggested and scratched something behind his ear before handing her a small chamfered box.

"I've never seen one of these up close," she gasped as she took the thin, transparent sticker on her fingernail to examine it. Then, carefully placing it behind her ear, she pressed on it to make sure it was nicely stuck on her skin. A deafening buzzing rang inside her head, forcing a loud scream out of her lungs. She tried covering her ears but the ringing seemed to be emanating from inside her. "Arrgh, make it stop!" She screamed as she squeezed her eyes shut.

Scott slapped her hands away from her ears and touched the sticker with his finger. It felt like a soft scratch on the skin and suddenly the pain was gone.

"Better now?" Scott smiled as she opened her tearful eyes.

"Fuck, yes!"

"Was that your first time, little Miss?" a jovial voice echoed briefly at the back of her head.

"Richard? Is that you?"

"I am honoured to be the first voice inside your head," he laughed and coughed at the same time.

"Is there a way to mute him?" She asked and pointed at her ear.

"Unfortunately no," Scott choked a laugh.

"Where is he anyway?"

"You can talk to me directly, you know?" Richard said as if he was there with them. "The rookies and I are outside."

She had to assume he meant the three trainees in space uniforms she'd met at Julian's old flat because they didn't say anything on the comms.

"It's an open channel, Rachel," Scott explained. "You can hear anything anyone says and vice versa."

"Scott, we're already down here." Noel's thin voice made her instinctively look around for him.

"Us too." Another voice added, which probably belonged to Toz.

"Almost there." The last voice was deep and hoarse. She hadn't heard it before, she assumed it was the other engineer, Mo.

"On our way to the hatch," Scott informed his team and traced the holo-circle on the bulkhead of the outer bridge. Rachel had wanted to go with Kieran—he and Noel had taken Bridge Three, the one with his latest mural. She never had a chance to see it live with all the shit that was going on. *Rachel, we talked about this*, Scott had scolded her and after a few eye rolls she was following him to Bridge Four.

There was a metal plate towards the end she had never noticed before. It was the same dark beige as the tiles around it with blotches of black and brown discolouration. Scott tapped on its corner and a screen appeared. There was a high pitch hiss and the plate popped down, swaying from the thick golden hinge. A metal ladder led to the space below, the light of the bridge barely penetrating all the way to the hidden floor beneath.

"Shine some light for me," Scott said as he placed his foot on the first rung.

She took her roller from the bun on her hair and did as she was told. The flashlight revealed big crates and abandoned equipment left there for who-knew-how-long. Dust particles were dancing on her beam of light and she covered her nose with her arm to stifle the imminent sneeze.

Scott hopped on the metal grate at the bottom of the ladder and disappeared inside the alcove. "I'm here," he stated, his voice still loud and clear as if he was next to her.

"Yes, being here is one thing, making sense of all these buttons is a whole different conversation though." Kieran sighed.

"While you guys try to figure that out, I've got to say the weather up here is great," Richard chimed in.

"Where are you exactly?" Rachel asked and gazed outside the window strip.

"Right above you, little Miss. I am slowly... making my way... to the other side," he said with brief pauses between his words.

"Are you alright?"

"So sweet of you to worry. You'd think they would have a smooth clean path for me up here."

"Can we please focus?" Toz was out of breath too. "Kieran, have you found the release lever yet?"

"I got the lever; I flicked all the right switches from your schematics but the valve won't turn. Noel, come help me out with this."

"Scott, should I come help you too?" Rachel stood at the edge of the floor hatch.

"Yes, I might need you actually."

"Ok we got the sequence," Mo said, "Let's see if this thing still works."

"Scott, it's turning," Kieran grunted.

"I can hear grinding," Noel added, "Something's happening."

"Richard, do you guys have a visual on the clamps yet?" Scott asked.

"Almost there," one of the boys replied. It sounded like Christoff from the few words they had exchanged during the briefing.

Grabbing the edge of the ladder, she tried to find the rung below her.

"We got it!" Noel cheered, "We'll go..." his sentence ended abruptly and was followed by a continuous static noise that pierced her ears and forced her to hold on tightly from the handles. The ladder started shaking as a fierce vibration coursed through the metal and into her body. The walls of the basement underneath her clanged in unison as parts of the stud wall snapped and scattered their metallic pieces on the floor. She placed her foot on the step below in a hurry and felt the cracking of the metal plate in her bone. The step was gone and so was half the ladder below her as she found herself hanging from the edge of the hatch. The vibration had subsided but was still enough to push her off the edge. She grunted to get up and shrieked when her fingers finally slipped, slamming her whole body on every single rung below her until she held onto the last one.

"What's happening? Are you okay?" Scott asked, his footsteps thundering to come check on her.

She cried as she tried to push herself back up from the upper half of the ladder. "I-I... I think so. What was that?" she said when she felt secure again, one foot on the step, the other hanging in the air like a log, the pain at her ankle so intense she considered biting her arm.

Whatever it was, it must have interfered with the radio because Scott kept repeating Kieran's and Richard's names without any response.

Rachel finally crawled up to the bridge level and leant on the window to alleviate some of the pain on her ankle.

"It sounded like Kieran and Noel figured the clamp out so they must be heading to the rendezvous point," Scott said, his voice fainter and not in her head anymore, "I'm almost done here myself, stay up there and keep trying the comms."

Her eyes darted across the empty bulkhead and she caught a glimpse of movement with the corner of her eye. Groaning as she twisted around, she took a few short breaths and held the last one inside.

Half of the bridge was gone and the other half was dangling from Ring Five. Pieces of metal and plastic flew in all directions and banged on the rest of the ship, scraping against its hull. She felt her pulse throbbing all over her body as a sudden shiver chilled the back of her neck and froze her legs. She wanted to scream but her mouth wasn't working. She followed some debris with her eyes as it hit the window and splashed against the bridge she was in. Trying to focus on the rest of the window's length, she hunched her shoulders as if the walls were closing in on her, pressuring her into a tight box. Some of the wreckage was lodged in the glazing in several parts of the bridge's window strip.

In some areas it even seemed cracked as the light refracted through the four layers of glass. Her exhale was shaky and her lips trembled. How far along was Scott with his override? She felt her legs bending inwards, barely supporting her weight, fused to the metallic floor.

"S... Sco... Scott?" she finally spoke, her lower lip still quavering from the grinding of her teeth.

"Rachel, what's happening up there? I am engaging the clamp."

"NO!" she screamed and fell on her knees above the hatch.

"What? Why?" Scott asked after coming out from the basement to where the ladder used to be.

"It's rigged. They set us up."

"What do you mean?" He grabbed the fallen part of the ladder and looked up at the hatch.

"Hull breach detected. Emergency repair measures engaged."

"Kieran? Toz? Mo?" Scott repeated again a few times and disappeared into the basement.

"We need to get out of here!" she shouted as the synthesized voice repeated its announcement over the speakers.

"Scooooott!" she screamed as loud as she could.

A thud on the glass behind her made her jump to her feet and touch her chest to make sure her heart was still beating. A man in a spacesuit was upside down banging his fist on the window strip from outside. She came close to the glass and squinted enough to make out the blonde hairs that had escaped Richard's cap. He banged on the glass one last time and pointed towards the bridge's entrance to Ring Five.

She looked down at the hatch again hoping Scott had found a way to get up and there he was, pushing a big crate under the opening. He climbed up with a groan and jumped to grab the top part of the ladder that was still there. Rachel extended her hand and pulled him up with all her strength, falling on her back right after.

"How... what... what happened?" Scott mumbled as he got on his feet and gazed at the destruction outside.

"Can we just go, please?" Rachel cried and wiped the tears from her cheeks.

Scott nodded and nudged her forward before dashing away. She followed as fast as her legs could carry her, limping every one or two steps as her ankle protested. She jolted her head to a loud cracking on the glass followed by a hiss of air that filled her whole body with shivers like thousands of needles pushing into her skin.

"Pressure destabilising. Please vacate the area immediately. Lockdown imminent."

Scott was almost at the door. He hadn't seen her falling behind. Wouldn't he have come back to help if he had? There was no countdown. She could be locked out at any moment without warning. The doors slid open on his approach and he stood under the frame to keep them open, looking back at her and waving his hand towards his chest in a hurry.

She sprinted pulling all her weight in front of her and shrieked when she felt the crack under her ankle. Tears filled her eyes as she fought to keep them open and finally gave in.

I won't make it, she sobbed as her face touched the cold floor. A loud alarm blared above her while more air hissed from the window panels behind her and suddenly she was up, floating above the metallic floor tiles. The blast doors shut with a powerful thud as the hydraulic presses sealed the bridge, putting an end to the deafening siren. She was still breathing, but her eyes were hermetically shut. She could still feel the cold tearful rivers running down her cheeks and dripping off the edges of her mouth.

"It's alright, I've got you," Scott's voice quavered as if he was about to cry too.

"You came back for me." She wiped her eyes and mouth off the salty droplets.

"I had to. Julian would've killed me," he managed to let out a brief chuckle through the snivelling.

"Can you put me down?"

"Ah, yes of course." He slowly let her on her feet but her loud groan forced his hands to instantly lift her again. "Are you sure you can walk? Maybe you twisted your ankle back there."

"No, a sprain was already there but I think running for my life made it worse... it might be broken."

"I'll carry you to the infirmary."

"No that's alright, I can walk on one leg, I just need some support. What the fuck happened back there Scott?" she asked as she tried to balance her body against his, her heart still thumping inside her chest.

"I don't know... I messed up. It's my fault Kieran... Kieran..." he never finished his sentence, looking away with a soft whimper.

"Are they really... gone?"

"You saw it yourself, there's nothing left from that bridge." He grabbed her by the waist and guided her forward.

"Who would do such a thing? You hear all these stories in history about bombs and wars, but I never thought I would actually live through one."

"Neither did I. Otherwise I would've never thought of such a plan." He covered his face with his hand to hide the tears as he stopped and balanced on his knees, wheezing.

"I-It was... it was my plan," she muttered as the realisation dawned on her.

It was her fault. She wanted so badly to be part of the mission, show the men on the table she's not the little girl they thought she was. Her chest heaved with each shuddering breath as tears spilled down her cheeks again.

So stupid... stupid and reckless.

The image of destruction replayed in her head. "I got Kieran killed... and that boy... Noel."

"It wasn't your fault, Rachel, you..."

"It was. I felt so proud of myself, thinking of tethering the bridges like I was some big shot who saved the day... and instead I only made things worse."

"Rachel, look at me." He wiped her cheek from the tears and turned her to face him. "Look at me!" He repeated when she averted her eyes in shame. "You had a general idea, nothing more. We would have come to the same conclusion anyway. I structured the mission, I dug out the schematics, I gave out the instructions, I split the teams... I sent them alone in there." His eyes darted around the floor. "We should keep moving. I need to take you to the infirmary" Scott said and nudged her towards the science district.

The infirmary in Ring Five was temporarily closed but Scott's palm had access to almost everything on the ship. Rachel hopped on one of the beds and sucked her teeth from the pain of stretching her leg. Scott tried to remove her boot as cautiously as possible and yet she shrieked at the grinding of leather on her ankle. He winced and tapped on the monitor at the foot of the bed as the robotic arms above them whirred to life. A red light swept her from head to toe and stopped above her ankle with a beep. Two more arms came down and slowly lifted her foot while wrapping it in some sort of elastic, white bandage. She allowed her head to fall back on the pillow with an exhale and closed her eyes. Her pulse was still racing inside her chest as her breathing naturally caught on to the rhythm.

"'Try to relax." Scott placed his hand above hers.

"Is everything ok with the little Miss?" Richard's voice made her head jolt.

"Richard, where have you been? Did you see what happened? Where is everyone else?" Scott turned around and touched his ear.

"Oh I saw it alright. I wouldn't have survived out there with all that debris flying around if it weren't for emergency navigation."

"Are you hurt? We're already in the infirmary, Ring Five. Can you meet us here?"

"Yes, I'll be there in ten."

She must have dozed off again on the medical bed as the knock on the door came almost right after the conversation in her head. Her foot was covered in a rigid, hexagonal lattice that weaved comfortably around her ankle and wrapped around her calf. Most of the pain had faded away but there was still a little pinch when she stood on it.

The two men were whispering and gesturing next to the wall of monitors that covered their voices in a continuous series of beeps. They embraced each other and rubbed their eyes before turning to her with forced smiles.

"How does it feel? Can you walk?" Scott was first to ask.

"I think so," she leant on the 3D printed encasement, "What were you guys talking about?"

"Nothing," Richard was fast to reply but his red eyes betrayed the truth. He had been nothing but annoying to her but there was no doubt there was a deep layer of feelings under the cold, hunky exterior.

"How long was I out?" She ran a hand through her temple and tousled her hair.

"An hour or so," Scott answered.

"Are the others ok? From the other bridges?"

"Yeah, after the explosion all teams aborted the mission like we did."

"So they can still detach at any time?"

"No, the rookies and I took care of that." Richard interjected. "We managed to clamp all bridges from the outside. Well... not all bridges." He glanced at Scott with a sigh.

"Wow, good job."

"Thanks, little Miss."

"So what do we do now? How much time did that buy us?" she asked eagerly.

"I don't know." Scott let out a puff of air. "The more pressing problem is that without Kieran to control the public, it's only a matter of time before word gets out about what's actually happening."

"Maybe that's not a bad thing," Richard sat in the swivelling chair and crossed his arms, "We've been fighting this with a tremendous handicap, maybe it's time we pulled in some more resources."

Rachel agreed but remained silent. They were fighting an uneven battle, against people who were prepared to take lives in order to win. It shouldn't have come as a surprise since their plan was to shoot off towards Epsilon Centauri and leave all the rest behind to die.

"What do you suggest?" Scott stood against the medical counter.

"Why are *we* the ones hiding?" Richard exclaimed. "Let the ship know about the evolutionists and how they are the ones who killed Kieran. At least this way his death won't be for nothing."

"You're talking revenge." Scott countered. "I don't want people to avenge his memory, Kieran wouldn't have wanted that."

"We can't play this game on our terms. Don't you see what they're prepared to do to get their way?"

"I agree we need more people on our side but I will not use Kieran's death to recruit zealots."

"Then what's your great idea? You know the clock is ticking, right? We need to act fast."

"How much time do you think we have exactly?" Rachel asked, her tiny steps finally bringing her next to them.

Richard clicked his tongue and twitched his mouth. "Hard to say. They're now bound to the *Sagan* and with who-knows-how-much water left. They're unpredictable but not stupid."

"We also have another problem," Scott started, "The engines are still on. Our data suggests we have approximately three months to start decelerating, unless we want to be eating on the windows."

"Yeah, you'll have to explain that to me, I'm not Julian, remember?" Rachel winced as she shifted her weight to the other leg again.

"It's not as bad as Scott describes it." Richard waved a dismissive hand in front of him. "The longer these engines are on though, the harder the break is going to be, meaning the centrifugal force will have to compensate massively. Otherwise the breaking force will push everyone towards the front of the ship."

Rachel couldn't visualise it in her head but nodded as if she understood. Richard was the interstellar engineer after all, there was no need to question him on physics. "But how are the evolutionists planning to slow down? Even if they detached, wouldn't they have the same issue?"

"I have a theory about that," Richard said and leant forward in his chair, "They will drive the ship into Epsilon Centauri and use the shuttles to perform reverse gravity assists between the system's gas giants."

"They will destroy the ship?" she gasped, "Why detach Six in the first place then, why not throw the whole damned thing in?"

"Well, reduced mass for starters and with the amount of gravity assists I'm assuming they want to do... it would tear it apart on the first gas giant. Too many bridges, too many weak points." She didn't know what that meant either but she let him continue. "The shuttles on the other hand are all made from a single-threaded, carbon nano-composite.

They should be able to handle it. No screws or bolts anywhere."

"Fuck, that's crazy."

"Why we call them crazies," Scott forced a chuckle.

Their rollers chimed at the same time and they all looked at each other, their eyes knowing what it meant. Rachel took the thin cylinder that was left on the medical counter and reeled it open. She had never received a notification like that before; a picture of the broken bridge covered the whole surface of the glass without any option to remove it. The headline made her eyes water again as she struggled to swallow her own saliva.

"Councilman Kieran Bolek reported dead in explosion at bridge between Rings Five and Six. With him, engineer apprentice Noel Young. Relationship between the two unknown. Authorities are looking into possible causes for the tragic losses."

"It's going to be a scandal." Richard shook his head with a sigh. "There's not even going to be time to properly send him off with the political chaos that's coming."

"I need to talk to the council." Scott jumped from his seat. "Okada will be furious she wasn't briefed on this mission. I better..."

"Why didn't the council do anything to stop all this?" Rachel interrupted.

"They did... they put *me* in charge." Scott tilted his head towards the ceiling and drew a deep inhale, his eyes closed and his lips pursed.

"Go, it's alright. I'll stay with little Miss." Richard smiled.

CHAPTER 21

— Julian —

Residential Quadrant – Ring 6

Julian sat at the bench in the ground floor plaza, his eyes wandering around the tense faces of the people who had queued up for the food kiosks. No one bothered with him anymore after his confinement was lifted. His mum had vouched her own life for his freedom—it was the bare minimum after everything she'd done.

Joining the queue at Power Snacks, he studied the humanoid waiter. Keeping Nyx and Andre hidden in his flat hadn't been that hard in the first couple of days. The only problem was sustenance. Water had been immediately rationed after the tank leak and food wasn't being manufactured at the normal rate. Nyx had suggested to him to steal some. Who would notice? The Kiosks were operated by machines.

He glanced around him to make sure no one was looking and grabbed four power bars from the basket.

"Please present your wrist to pay with contribution points," the waiter requested.

He let one of the bars drop on the floor as Nyx had instructed him and stared at the robot's humanlike eyes, feeling the beads of sweat forming on the roots of his hair. He presented his wrist over the counter with a long, shaky inhale and was relieved to see he'd paid for all four of them. Nothing escaped the unblinking cameras of the waiter.

"Move along!" The woman behind him nudged him aside.

He picked up the power bar from where it was lodged between two stone tiles and headed back to his apartment.

"Again you couldn't do it?" Nyx said when he threw their breakfast on the dining table.

"I'm sorry... it gave me that look like it was sad I wasn't going to pay. And there was another person behind me."

"Quit trying to teach the kid how to steal," Andre intervened.

"He's going to run out of points pretty soon. Especially with you asking for a second bar all the time."

"I still have a lot, don't worry." Julian explained. It wasn't a lie but he had done the maths already, at the current pace he would have to come up with an alternative in a few weeks time. Hopefully their situation wouldn't drag for that long.

"I just don't want us to be a burden on you."

"It was my idea to bring you here, remember? We'll be fine."

"Alright, kid." She shrugged and unwrapped her long, crumbly snack. "Any news about the explosion?"

"I overheard some people talking about it, they think someone tried to break in. They were boasting how they blew them away in space." He cringed and pressed his fingers inside his palm.

"I hope it wasn't our people," Andre commented.

"Is the maintenance tunnel still guarded?" Nyx asked, while munching loudly.

"Yes, they don't even allow their own people near."

"Fuck, we need a way to communicate with Scott and the others."

"My idea will work, trust me," Julian exclaimed.

"It's been four days now, if..."

"It'll work. Rachel's been here, she will know where to look."

"It's just a bit... crude," Andre said. "Don't get me wrong, I think it's brilliant but what are the chances the girl will see the little note you stuck on the window?"

"We used to do that when we were younger and didn't have rollers yet. It'll work," he repeated, trying to convince himself.

"At least the kid had an idea," Nyx tossed the empty wrapper at Andre but it swirled mid-air, landing on the table. "You're the intelligence specialist and you're sitting there eating up his contribution points." Her words caught Andre with a wide open mouth, the last bit of his power bar frozen at his fingertips before his bright, white teeth. "Just eat it." She chuckled and he didn't hesitate to do so.

"I found out about the leak while you were sleeping, didn't I?" Andre defended himself through his loud munching.

"We already knew they wouldn't be able to contain it after we destroyed their repair-bots. They're all life scientists, they have no clue about engineering." Nyx scoffed.

"Bio-engineering maybe." Andre shrugged.

"We'll just have to be careful with our showers." Julian chimed in.

"It might get a bit stinky in here," Andre laughed.

"How do you guys usually get your information?" Julian asked.

"Torture," Nyx said as she put her feet on the table.

"Tor... torture?" Julian exclaimed, noticing how Andre raised the corner of his lip, bound to burst in laughter at any moment.

"Ha ha, I'm messing with you, kid." She leant towards him so she could reach him and tousled his hair. "Andre uses tech, which we don't have here, while I like a more direct approach. Coercion, subterfuge, manipulation and if the persuasion fails then we can always blackmail."

It was hard to tell if she was still joking or not, her expressionless face providing zero hints of the truth.

"Maybe you can give me a few pointers some time," he said, acknowledging the fact that this was no longer a world of peace and fairness. "How do you do it?"

"Like now for example, I'll tell you to go see your mother and find out what she knows."

"No. Nyx..."

"Yes. Julian, it's been long enough. You can't avoid her forever."

"No, I'm not talking to her anymore."

"You have to, she's your mother. She only did what she did because she loves you."

"For her own selfish reasons!" Julian snapped, pushing himself away from the table to pace around the living room.

"Yes, horrible and misguided but.... try to think of it from her side. The ship was about to be detached, she had to make sure you were on this side."

"It wasn't her decision to make, alright?" He stopped to yell and continued his pacing.

"I know, I get it. I'm not saying you forgive her but you have to use your head, not your heart, Julian. She's our only source of information."

Julian took a moment in the silence that followed to think about it. Her argument kind of made sense but he was too furious, blood still boiling in his veins for how she had manipulated him. He knew if he talked to her again, it wouldn't end well.

The reality was that there wasn't any other option. He had to do this, the thought had crossed his mind as well but he'd never dare utter it. "Alright," he sighed, "But if she starts with her lies and excuses again, I'm out of there."

"And that's how she does it," Andre laughed out loud.

Nyx winked at him with a broad smile.

Julian huffed. "Wow, I fell for it quite easily, then."

"Not really, you riled more than some of my interrogations," Nyx got up from the dining table and tried to put an end to his aimless walk around the apartment. "Come on, kid. I didn't say anything you didn't already know." She grabbed his shoulders and stared into his eyes. "You don't have to go, no one's forcing you... but I'm sure you know it yourself it's the only option here."

"It is... unfortunately," he muttered. "I'll see you in a bit. Don't eat my bar." He pointed at it and glanced at Andre.

"You've got this kid," Nyx said just before the door closed behind him.

Julian tapped on the panel and tried to regulate his shaky breath, jerking his limbs to shake the trepidation away.

His mother came to the door, her widened eyes and vacant stare a clear sign she wasn't expecting him. "Julian?" She exclaimed, her voice barely above a whisper as her expression softened and she stepped back to let him in.

"We need to talk," Julian said firmly as he sidestepped through the threshold to avoid any physical contact.

He sat on the couch crossing his arms and legs, his eyes focusing anywhere but his mother.

"How you've been? Are you getting used to…"

"No, of course not," he snapped already, "I'm all alone here, what do you think?"

"But you're not alone, you have *me*. You did the right thing coming over." She smiled but it only ignited the flame inside him even more as her lies flooded his memory.

"I didn't come to hang around. I need answers."

"To what, monkey?" She sat opposite to him, her deep blue eyes and raised eyebrows conveying a sense of apprehension.

"Let's start with where you are with the detachment. How long before we leave everyone else behind to die?" He got straight to the point, his patience already wasted just by her presence.

"I don't know. We were sabotaged, someone blew a hole in our water supply and then destroyed the repair-bots bay. But don't worry Dr Richter has a plan already."

"Which is?" He asked, trying to conceal the smirk from being partly responsible for the delay.

"He'll cut off the power to the rest of the ship. We control the reactor. If they want to mess with us, they'll have to learn to live in the dark."

Julian shook his head and sighed. "Why am I not surprised? Everything I've heard so far from your cult is either crazy or psychopathic."

"We're not a cult. We're a group of people who believe in this mission. We're helping humanity reach a new frontier."

"Mum, you're leaving people behind to die. You're even fine with killing them early by cutting off their power."

"I was hesitant at first too, I pushed back a lot on the decision. I wanted you to see Aquanis for yourself."

"Were you always like this? How did I never see it coming? How Dad didn't?" he mumbled. She was beyond saving. There was nothing he could say that would bring her back to the right side so he thought he might as well try to get as much information from her as he could. It was the only way he could help Nyx and Andre.

"Julian..." his mum started, pursing her lips and tilting her head, "If only you could understand our vision. There's so much greatness that awaits us in Aquanis."

Greatness. Yeah, I guess there is some greatness in murder.

"Oh I can understand the vision perfectly fine, it's always been my dream to see the planet, you know that." He winced slightly. Even pretending to agree with her made him feel ill. "It's just the way you're executing it." He couldn't stop himself saying it.

"Don't be like that, monkey."

Maybe Nyx could have given him a few more pointers on manipulation because he sucked at it.

"Just... never mind," he stopped mid-sentence. His anger had faded and was now replaced by a distinct feeling of sorrow and disappointment. "So, if you cut their power they'll give you your water back? How do you see this playing out?"

"They won't have another option, you saw what happened when they tried the bridge."

"There's always an option. I only hope it's not all out war. Then all this trip would've been for nothing. Humans are doomed to repeat the never ending cycle of history."

She didn't have an answer to that or maybe she didn't want to admit she had thought about it. She played with a few strands of her ash, blonde hair and looked away. "You have a lot of him in you," she finally said.

"DON'T! Don't even start about Dad," he snapped, pointing a trembling finger at her and waiting for a few seconds to pass to make sure she wasn't going to push it. "I'd better go," he huffed and stood up.

"Come visit me, ok? I'll be here, whatever you need," she stuttered.

"Actually..." He turned around before the door. "I'm a little bit worried about contribution points. I don't think anyone here trusts me to actually contribute so I was wondering if you could help me out?"

"I will talk to Dr Richter myself and he will get you to do something. In the meantime I can't really transfer points to you but maybe... maybe I can bring you some vegetables from my hydroponics? You could make some nice soups."

"Great. That could work for now. Thanks, Mu..." he almost said it but stopped himself in time. He didn't feel like calling her that anymore, it was only a reflex, a force of habit. She wasn't the same person as the one who had raised him, or maybe she was always like that and he couldn't see it until now. She was a stranger, someone who was willing to let people suffer and die for a chance of seeing the blue planet.

CHAPTER 22
— Rachel —
Engineering Quadrant – Ring 3

The potent smell of antiseptics and disinfectants was making her nauseous as she walked through the whitewashed halls of the infirmary. The medi-bots were racing up and down paying her little notice, only to get out of her way. She looked through the small window of the door first and entered the room Alex was in. The monitors beeped in unison with their monotonous song of life support.

"Kaiden?" She exclaimed and ran to embrace him where he sat at the edge of Elizabeth Correy's bed. "I'm so glad to see you're awake."

"Hey, thanks… I wish I could say the same for my sister." He hid his lips inside his mouth as he jaw clenched.

"They'll wake up, you'll see. We got them here, they're safe now, they just need some time."

"About that… Thanks for taking care of her when that drone got me. I thought I was gone."

"We couldn't have done it without Julian's dad and his crew."

"Give yourself some credit, no one would've even found them if it wasn't for you. You're amazing, Rachel."

"Hah, thanks." She hunched her shoulders and crossed her arms with a smile. "Has anyone filled you in on what's going on with Ring Six?"

"Unfortunately, yes. That guy from Administration, Javier, was here earlier to refill their medication. Did you know he's studied psychology, biomedics and bioengineering? Three degrees, crazy."

"Yeah, he's the one taking care of them all this time."

"So Ring Six. They're still here, that's a good thing right?"

"Yeah we used the old construction clamps at the bridges, bought ourselves some time for now."

"*You* did that? Amazing was an understatement then, you're more like… like a hero or something. Uncovering mysteries, saving people, stopping the bad guys."

"Hero? Not really," she said with a shrug, glancing over to Alex's bed.

"No, I mean it. I think I…" he stopped abruptly when the switches clicked and the lights went out.

"What now?" She exhaled an annoyed breath and her heart stopped at the sight of all the medical monitors turning black.

Richard had warned them the evolutionists may resort to such measures but it was still hard to believe it. Maybe it was something else, maybe it was just a localised malfunction.

A mechanism roared under the floor followed by a deep rhythmic humming. The high pitch sound intensified and coursed through her as vibration until it reached a steady pace and then the lights came back, only they were now red as if it was the night cycle. She rushed to Alex's monitor at the foot of his bed and stared at her reflection in the black screen. Her eyes were moving left and right like a pendulum, desperate for a flicker of light. The terminals beeped one by one and her reflection was replaced by her brother's graphs once again. He was fine.

Taking her roller from the base of her ponytail, she messaged the only person who would know what was happening.

"*They cut off our power. Where are you?*" Richard replied almost instantaneously.

"Come on, let's get out of here." She beckoned towards the exit.

"Are you sure they're going to be ok?" Kaiden gestured to Alex and his sister.

"Yeah, Javier should be here soon."

She walked back through the hallways, glancing at the glowing blue light emanating from the emergency exit signs. Two women in lab coats sprinted out of a room like someone was chasing them.

"We're going to die in this shithole," the younger woman cried as she pushed her friend forward.

The science quadrant was enveloped in panicked yelps and frantic cries of distress. Some people were pacing up and down, focused on their rollers while others were making their way to the main intersection. A couple was stuck inside the lift, banging the glass for someone to come help them but their cries were inaudible. The group of scientists were the calmest of all, standing in a circle and gesturing at each other, probably discussing solutions already.

Her roller chimed and she unfolded it to see Richard's face.

"Where are you, little Miss? Are you hurt?"

"I'm fine, I was at the infirmary when it happened."

"I'll send Christoff to come get you. Stay there," he ordered, pacing around Julian's old flat while Scott and Toz argued behind him.

"I can take care of myself, I don't need an escort. We'll be there in a bit."

The residential district was a lot worse than the science quadrant. People had broken into the food kiosks, taking as many rations as they could hold in their arms. Others were fighting, threatening each other and screaming, their erratic shadows dancing in the gloomy, red ambiance. The Admins were there, trying to control the situation but with little success.

The panel buzzed green and the door creaked open. She felt a sense of pride that Scott had trusted her with access to their headquarters and she motioned Kaiden to go in.

"Little Miss, when you said you're coming back, I thought you meant Javier and you." Richard appeared in the small lobby.

"This is Kaiden, he…"

"I know who he is," he interrupted her.

"I told you I shouldn't have come." Kaiden defended himself.

"It's alright," Scott cut in, "There's no way someone who's lost a loved one to the evolutionists would be working for them."

"How are we doing?" Rachel asked, offering a mocking smile to Richard as she passed him, tapping on his belly that was coming out of his belt.

"Chaos throughout all Rings, people panicking, admin is in shambles, I'd say we're a few hours away from having the first riot ever on board the *Sagan*."

"Yeah, I was just outside," She said, glancing behind her as if she could still see the plaza.

"What's worse is that the council is thinking of appeasing their demands."

"What do they want?"

"Assistance with repairs and water of course. No surprise there." Scott scoffed, passing his roller to Lee who was waiting beside him.

"What about the clamps?"

"There's a chance they haven't noticed that yet."

"I doubt they'd blow them up though," Richard added, "An explosion like that will send them flying off in a spiral and I wouldn't bet on their navigators to correct their flight path."

"What about the AI?" Kaiden shyly interjected.

"They disabled her." Scott waved a hand, shaking his head. "Abeone would've never allowed something like this."

"Make some coffee." Richard pointed at the kitchen counter. "We'll be here for a while until the council decides how to proceed."

"Who cares what the council thinks," she almost snapped. With Kieran gone, they were just some high status, pretentious fucks. What did they know about responding to a crisis? Then again, what did she?

"Even in the most chaotic times, you need to respect the chain of command. Otherwise society crumbles," Richard said like he had rehearsed the line, "And knock that off." He pointed at her leg that was shaking up and down like a spring.

She tried to remain still but her whole body was screaming to move, to do something. She could only roll her eyes for now and join the others at the far end of the living room. Lee, Christoff and Alina were talking to two men in exosuits whom she'd barely spoken to in the last days. She struggled for their names—Josh and Faruq? They were outside the ship most of the time, monitoring Ring Six, the only people she had seen other than Nyx carrying weapons.

"Hey, nice to see you're up and kicking again." The familiar voice made her head jerk towards the study room.

"Mark! What are you doing here?" She stood up for a brief hug as their long hair intertwined.

"Julian's dad called me in. I'm working on the scenario where we have to assist the evos with their water storage."

"Uhm, no offence but are you sure you're qualified for something like that? I thought you only started working recently."

"None taken and yeah, not even close... but apparently I'm the only person from maintenance Scott trusted."

"He actually told you that?" She chuckled.

"Well, not in these exact words but that's pretty much what he meant."

"Mr Spoles, I thought I told you to get ready," Richard took his hand and handed him an open roller. "You're with Toz. Little Miss, you're with me."

"Where are we going?" She asked, jumping back on her feet.

"Engineering. I need to calibrate the generators and assess the batteries.

"Why do you need *me* then?"

"I no longer have an assistant after... you know... after the explosion."

"I was there, Richard, no need to remind me..." She sighed, the image of the outer bridge blown to pieces had embedded into her head, a sight that would probably haunt her forever.

Richard cleared his throat and looked away. "Yeah, well..."

"Pfft, okay. I'll come." She played along. The way he had asked her made it sound like he needed some company more than an actual assistant.

The panicked cries had subsided in the science quadrant and most of the people had dispersed. Only the administration officers were busy, trying to calm the remaining people down, flapping their arms wildly to convince them to stay in their queues outside the infirmary.

"How is your ankle?" Richard asked, offering a hand to support her waist.

"I think I'm limping a bit, can you tell? Tell me the truth, can you tell?"

"It's probably the cast."

"Then I do look like a weirdo. Great, now I need to hurt one of my eyes somehow and I'll be set for pirate life."

"As long as it doesn't hurt, you'll be fine, *matey*," Richard chuckled.

"Why are you being so nice?" She asked as the doors of the lift closed and they started their descent to the engineering levels. Her first impression of him wasn't the best, he was condescending and patronising, judging her every word in front of everyone on the dining table.

"What do you mean? I'm always nice."

Now it was her turn to laugh. "When I met you were a complete asshole. Wait, no. That didn't come out right."

"Well, that's the beauty of maturity, little Miss. Knowing when you're wrong and accepting it without spite."

"So you were wrong about me. You admit it!" She smiled, wishing she could have seen his face when he said that but keeping up the pace behind him was hard enough.

"The jury is still out but you've certainly proved yourself a brave… uhm, resourceful woman."

Her smile broadened. "How about we drop the *little Miss* then?"

"Nah, I think it suits you. You're small in size and *Miss* conveys a sense of independence and autonomy."

"If you say so," she replied in a mocking voice. Truth was it didn't bug her that much and she had already won her victory. She had come to like it even. Definitely better than what her dad used to call her—gingerbread. Even for that he lacked the effort.

"Come on, that's for another time. We're here." He swiped his hand on the holocircle of the huge, bulky door and took a step back.

A deep rumbling echoed in the corridor, a whirring of gears that controlled the separation of the intricate panels from their interlocking grasp. The continuous hiss of the hydraulics added to the mechanical orchestra and the vast chamber revealed itself with a rush of air that came through and flicked the strands of hair that had escaped her ponytail.

"Ladies first." Richard slightly bowed and extended his hand towards the blackness inside.

The darkness swallowed her, the dim red lights of the hallway barely reaching the metal floor tiles, casting an eerie glow across the enormous space. Her printed cast clanged with every feeble step while her other foot squeaked from the added pressure. She rubbed her nose, something was irritating her, a pungent, metallic odour.

Bleach? "What is that smell?" She finally asked.

"Ozone," Richard explained as he passed her. "Yeah, I know. It takes some getting used to it." She would've never guessed that, maybe Julian would have but he wasn't there. Who knew what Julian was doing.

The ceiling lights awakened to their presence and illuminated just how massive this section of engineering really was. The far wall was occupied by rows upon rows of towering structures that stretched to the ceiling, composed of thick metal casings that housed complex mechanical components. A series of pipes and heavy-duty cables snaked underneath the base grates and disappeared in the void below. The batteries were in the middle area, stacked neatly in rows and encased in a thick, steel frame the size of a family fridge. It must have been batteries because there was a line on the top edge of each black box, showing the full level of charge in green. Every piece of equipment was connected to each other with straight cables that seemed glued to the floor. There was no end to this room, her eyes drifted towards her tangent horizon where the machinery continued, humming in unison to keep the ship powered.

She followed Richard to the wide terminal with the long, curved screen. There were boxes and numbers that vanished when he tapped on it and were replaced by graphs.

"Yeah, that's not good," he mumbled.

"What? What is it?" She leant forward, pretending to read the information.

"We'll have to cut off some systems and divert power only to essential functions."

"What about the infirmaries? My brother is still helpless, he needs power to stay alive!" She snapped as if it was Richard's fault.

"Of course I'll keep the infirmaries. Scott is expecting riots if things don't improve somehow."

"OK, good. So what are we cutting then?"

"Anything unnecessary. Pretty much the whole recreation, some manufacturing facilities…" he trailed off as his eyes raced across the monitor. "Most of the science labs, some of the lights… we're basically in survival mode. The priority here is to keep the Rings spinning and that will drain the batteries pretty fast." He drew in a long, ramifying breath. "Here, take this and go check the batteries on this list." He handed her his roller and pointed at the far end, where the floor met the ceiling and the curvature of the Ring hid away the rest of the batteries.

She took off her long sleeve and wrapped it around her waist, making her way through the blinking lights of the metal colonnade.

"R35C12BGTX," she read the first entry on the list out loud. She had played this game before, it didn't take her more than a few seconds to realise it referred to the thirty-fifth row and twelfth column.

The acrid smell of singed circuitry and burning electronics lingered in the atmosphere, something was definitely amiss. Were they all going to die without power? Would Julian at least be safe on the other side? She inhaled deeply despite her nostrils burning from the mixture of chemicals in the air.

She finally found the first battery on her list and gasped when she noticed the scorch marks. The digital readout on the front of the unit was flashing red. How many more were damaged? There were forty-three batteries on the list. Her heart raced but she forced herself to remain calm and focused. She had a job to do and as fast as possible. She crossed off the first number and revolved around herself to find the next one.

Her tank top was stuck on her skin, smudged and smeared with black and brown stains. Sweat was dripping down her spine but she had made it all the way back to Richard. If that was what heat felt like on a planet, she'd rather stay on the *Sagan* forever. It was tiring, like all her energy had dissipated in the form of sweat.

"How many?" Richard asked with a brief glance, still occupied with the terminal.

"Thirty-six are dead. The other nine all show the same warning, a red circle with two parallel lines crossing it."

"I see," his shoulders slumped and he placed his hands at the edges of the screen, leaning over it. His blonde hair fell in front of his eyes and he let out a dragged sigh.

"That bad? Don't freak me out." Rachel handed him back the tablet but he didn't bother.

"No, I'm sorry, little Miss. It can work. We'll make it work."

"How long? The truth, Richard."

"If we can reconnect these nine back to the grid…" he tapped and swiped his fingers on the blocks in the screen. "Three months tops… and that's taking as granted people will accept to share rations."

"Fuck."

"Yeah… fuck."

PART 2

COUNTDOWN TO NO RETURN

CHAPTER 23
— JULIAN —
SCIENCE QUADRANT – RING 6

Julian jumped from his chair when the lights switched to their white cycle. Nyx was already by the window, organising her gear and powering on the systems of their makeshift control panel. It was nothing more than a few rollers and monitors hooked together but it had proved quite reliable so far.

He reached for the power bar on the table only to have his hand slapped away by Nyx. "If you can't steal them, you can't eat them," she scolded him.

He still couldn't bring himself to steal anything, even when no one was looking. He wasn't that desperate yet. They had survived on watery soups and coffee for nearly three months now, things that he could get from his mum without raising any suspicion. He hated having to rely on her but there was no alternative. A few lettuces, carrots and potatoes could sustain the three of them for quite some time with the proper rationing and that's what they'd done.

"It better be right in the exact same place when I take off the headgear. Now grab your roller and get ready," she ordered while putting on the white, shiny visor that encircled her head.

"What do they say? Is it the instructions they mentioned earlier?"

"Shhh! I'm trying to focus."

It had taken them quite some time to figure it out but at least they had a way of communicating with the other side, crude as it may have been. His idea had worked. They were lucky his place was on that side of the Ring looking over the front of the *Sagan*, otherwise Rachel wouldn't even have bothered looking. A week had passed before Nyx saw the message Rachel had left on the window of their safe house in Ring Five. The first communications were very badly timed, sometimes taking the whole day just to exchange a few words. They had agreed on a specific time since then, every light cycle change meant there was a new piece of paper taped to the window of the opposite Ring. Julian still hadn't tried the visor himself—he had managed to focus his gaze on the opposite window without getting too dizzy from the spin of the Rings but extending his vision and trying to find the right spot was a whole other level for him.

"It's time and location. Quickly, write it down," she yelled at him. "2300r R6SQH04 EVA in," Nyx enunciated every letter and number.

"Eleven o'clock, relative time, Ring Six science quadrant, section H-04. What's the last bit?"

Nyx let out a sinister laugh. "You don't want to know, kid." The woman rarely smiled let alone laugh but when she did, it was quite loud. "Go wake up Andre. We need to start getting ready."

Julian frowned and went to his bedroom. Was Eva someone they knew? He nudged Andre on the shoulder and tried to avert his eyes from the saliva that was dripping out of his mouth and onto his chest. The big man gulped and licked his lips before half opening his eyes.

"Is it time already?" he complained with a yawn.

"Nyx told me to wake you up. My dad wrote us instructions, something about someone called Eva."

Andre's chuckle was muffled by the pillow and he coughed as he sat up. "E-V-A, kid... as in Extra Vehicular Activity."

"Is that what I think it is?"

"Don't worry, you won't have to go anywhere, they're probably bringing someone in, maybe even your father himself."

Was his dad really coming in Six? He smirked at the thought of wrapping his arms around him and hearing about what had happened on the other side all this time. The communications had always been very short and precise, never including any personal news. The way

Andre talked about things reminded him a lot of his dad, the passion and excitement in his eyes when bringing up subjects that had nothing to do with their situation. From history to socio-political doctrines, he could talk for hours and hours just like his dad. Nyx would always scoff and roll her eyes but she too would do the same from time to time only for war tactics and weapon systems. He had gotten used to both of them in the last few months, kind of like a new family in his isolated nightmare.

He left Andre alone to change and returned to the living room where Nyx was staring at a projection of the ship on the big monitor. She was leaning against the table twisting strands of her wild hair into braids.

"You could have told me E-V-A means going out in space," he complained.

"Shit, he told you already? I wanted to see the look on your face. Don't worry about it, it's followed by *in* which means infiltration. They'll probably bring in a team. That's why they need us to be there, to guide them to safety on their arrival. Or maybe open the bridges for a bigger force to come in."

"So it has come to this after all. Humanity's craving for violence wins again."

"Alright, little Scott." Nyx smiled and tousled his hair.

"Do you think he's coming too?"

"I hope so kid. I'll tell you what, if you weren't here to talk about your science and history all the time I might have missed the old bastard."

"The kid is right though." Andre joined them and went straight for the coffee pot. "It's hard to believe we've come so far away into the cosmos only to act like pre-space humans."

"We were doing fine until they decided to detach from the rest of the *Sagan*," Nyx countered.

"Do you think they can still do that, after the council gave them the water they wanted?"

Nyx clicked her tongue and shrugged. "It's probably why Scott is bringing in a team."

"What is Scott's plan exactly?" Andre sat at the dining table.

"Some action finally," Nyx sighed and waved her hands at the monitor, zooming out to a 3D representation of the whole ship. "They plan to enter here, at the science quadrant, which means we'll have to sneak our way past the intersection guards."

"Don't these hatches need a maintenance pin to be overridden?" Andre stood beside her inhaling the vapours from his coffee at hand.

"They probably have one. I'm sure Scott knows that, he wouldn't have chosen that entry point if he didn't."

"It's a good plan," Andre exclaimed. "Lightly guarded, clear path to our HQ and I'm sure no one expects a breach there. They're too busy monitoring the bridges."

Julian bit the skin around his thumb. "I just dont know if we should trust my mum. She told me everyone should stay home tonight but not *why*."

"All the more reason why Scott should bring in a team before they do whatever it is they're planning," Andre argued and Julian agreed. If anything, it would make their task easier with less evos around.

"So, what is our play here?" Julian asked, "I go first as always, distract the guard and you come in and take him out?"

"Kid's a natural," Nyx winked at him and sank into the couch in the middle of the room.

"Then I guess I'm on containment duty again," Andre huffed.

"We each have our strengths. I'm the muscle, you're the computer systems guy and the kid's the decoy."

"Heeey," Julian protested a little whinier than he wanted. "If it wasn't for me you wouldn't even be able to get into the science quadrant. Are you forgetting I am the reason you have access around the Ring?"

"Ok, sorry. He's also the palm reader," Nyx stated quite seriously but her eyes smiled and the corner of her lips twitched upwards.

"That's not better."

"I am joking, kid. You know how much I value your help all these months. If it wasn't for you I wouldn't even have this bad boy here." She placed the pistol on the coffee table and turned it on.

The cracking noises sounded like stones being crushed inside it, followed by a faint humming that progressively became louder and louder until it reached a final boom. He had gone through a lot of trouble to print just the one pistol and even then Nyx hadn't been satisfied, expecting at least a kinetic rifle like her old one. He had argued the HALASER pistol was a better investment as it wasn't dependent on ammunition, which was why she wasn't using her own rifle anymore. He had spent all night alone in the engineering lab, waiting for the printer to produce and assemble the pieces and then had sneaked his way around the science levels above for the power capacitors. The evolutionists must have found out at some point because his second try to print another one was met with biometric locks on all manufacturing facilities. He hadn't liked the idea of making weapons but Nyx had convinced him it was a necessary means of protection. The presence of guns on every guard's hip had made him uneasy, always having to look behind his back as his outsider status remained unchanged.

Nyx hid her pistol in the holster that encircled her right thigh and put on her brown, leather jacket that apparently predated the ship's launch. It was a shame her exo-suit had run out of power only a week ago, they could've really used its stealth mode. "Don't bite your nails!" she slapped his hand away from his mouth.

Andre grabbed his grey fedora from the table and squeezed his big, bald head inside while staring at Julian. "Do we need to go through the mission brief one last time maybe?" he asked while pressing the camera deflector halo through the hat.

"No, I'm good. I know what I'm doing, don't worry about me," Julian tried to reassure both Andre and himself.

He went out first to scout ahead. A calm silence permeated in the residential quadrant so late in the red light cycle but they stuck to their usual mission plan—Nyx and Andre would use the vents to the stair core like he'd done with Mark and Rachel when they discovered Nightfall and Julian would take the route through the plaza to open the door from the outside.

Nyx gave him an approving nod and stayed with Andre under the pilotis while Julian went in the quadrant intersection.

The two guards were having a conversation by the outer bridge blast door—they had counted on them being together, otherwise the plan wouldn't work. The hissing of the door made them turn and wave a hand to Julian as they approached him.

"Mr. Walker, again with your night walks?" the older man with the short, sideways fringe beckoned him.

"You know me... no friends, no girlfriend, what else is there to do?"

"You won't find either at this time of night."

"Come on guys, I thought the whole difference between us and the rest of the *Sagan* is that we don't have ridiculous rules or curfew. Why all this questioning?"

"You're a flight risk, Julian," the blonde boy clicked his tongue. He was around the same age as him but much taller.

"What flight risk? I stopped caring a long time ago. What are you so afraid I'm going to do, open the door for an infiltration team to come sweep the place while everyone is asleep?" he chuckled and walked past them pointing at the bridge's heavy door. He had to force their attention to the outer bridge somehow so Andre and Nyx could slip inside.

"Even *we* can't open that one. It's biometrically locked to Dr. Richter only."

"Don't tell him that, how daft are you?" the older man nudged the boy's arm.

"As I said, I don't care..." Julian trailed off as Nyx and Andre sneaked behind them into the concourse. "Are you guys not bored standing here all night? Don't you have families or better things to do?" Julian leant against the window strip of the outer wall.

"That's Dr. Richter's orders. We have to protect the Ring at all costs," the blonde boy pressed his boot on the floor.

"I'm just saying, you could be in Recreation chatting up a girl, dancing, singing. I love singing." He prepared the groundwork, glancing at his partners who were now almost behind the two guards. "I don't waaaaaaaant to be the reasoooooooon," he almost yelled, his voice definitely not cut out for singing.

The guards cringed and covered their ears but didn't get the chance to comment on his awful performance. Four arms tightened around their necks and after a few seconds they were both on the floor unconscious.

"Good job, kid," Nyx patted him on his back.

"I don't know about them, I personally think your voice was mesmerising." Andre chuckled and moved to the window with a cautious look.

Julian drew a sharp breath like someone had just punched him in the gut. Seeing someone outside the ship wasn't an everyday occurrence. The sharp features of the astronaut's face were barely lit as his visor touched the outer layer of the glass, revealing some of his bright, blonde hairs that had escaped his snoopy cap and were flailing above the wrinkles of his forehead. He gave them a thumbs up and slowly pointed towards the science quadrant.

"Is that a friendly?" Julian asked nervously.

"Yes, that's Richard Lahtinen. He's part of our team," Andre reassured him. "They're making their way to science E-V-A. I counted six."

"Come on kid, show us your magic hand," Nyx stabilised her gun on the palm of her free hand and crouched next to the door.

Julian pressed on the reader and entered the silent quadrant bathed in dim red. There was no movement at first but he managed to get a glimpse of two guards walking along the balustrades of the upper levels. The curvature of the quadrant made it impossible to know if there were more beyond the tangent horizon.

He crooked a finger to the others and soon they were under the pilotis, briskly walking towards the stair core.

Nyx made a fist and kept it close to her head as she scanned the floors opposite and above them. Julian knew the gesture meant he was supposed to stop and just observe. Nyx had spent countless hours teaching him all the different silent commands for their night missions, shouting at him when he'd get an answer wrong.

Her fist turned into an open palm towards her face and she waved it back and forth. She pointed at Julian and drew an imaginary rectangle in the air. He knew that sign as well. It was the usual order he would receive during these missions.

Open the door... always opening a door.

Andre nodded and crossed his fingers—the sign of good luck—as he headed downstairs while Julian led Nyx up the stair core, following the map on his open roller for guidance. He was panting by the time he reached the sixth level and pressed his back against the wall for a breather before going into the hallway. The science wing looked awfully eerie at night, the bright, polished and reflective surfaces of the morning cycle becoming a nightmarish tapestry of scarlet shapes, drenched in the gloomy red of the night cycle.

"Hey you! You shouldn't be here!" The loud voice startled him so much he hopped off his feet.

The voice belonged to a short man with spiky, black hair, dressed in the blue, Icarus uniform. He had appeared at the intersection out of nowhere and was already aiming his rifle at him.

There was no reason for him to shoot but despite the reassuring thought, his heart was about to poke a hole in his chest. He lifted his arms high and tried to steal a glance at his teammate, although his peripheral vision could only gather so much. Nyx was standing against the wall gesturing to him to join her.

"Present your wrist for scanning." The guard moved cautiously as the humming of his rifle powering up echoed on the dented walls.

Julian exchanged a quick look between Nyx and the enemy and with a sudden move he jumped behind the wall extrusion.

"HEY! Come back! Possible hostile on level six, E19. Requesting backup." The man came in running, a mistake Nyx took advantage of as she grabbed him and almost like dancing, she spun him around and threw him to the opposite wall with a force that shook the panels. The guard flopped on the floor and Nyx made sure he was completely out when the heel of her gun landed on his forehead.

Julian glanced at the camera on the ceiling, the red dot was still blinking, meaning Andre was still down in engineering. He tapped on the top of his head to make sure the infrared deflector was still pointing forward and adjusted it to fit firmly through his hair.

"What do we do now?" he asked.

"There's no aborting this mission. We can't leave them outside waiting. We carry on," Nyx said, her black eyes steady and unblinking, her resolve unwavering. "Stay behind me kid, I won't let anything happen to you." She was the one leading this time, her knees half bent, her steps cautious and her pistol steadily balanced inside her hands.

They hadn't even reached the next intersection when part of the wall next to him shattered with a loud thud, sending pieces of wallboard all over his face. He had instinctively ducked but not in time to prevent the splinters piercing his cheek. He winced and tightened his jaw. The second shot hit the opposite wall and he ducked again as he slid in the temporary safety of the intersection. Nyx pulled him further inside and crouched out of the wall. Her weapon hummed rapidly and she hid behind the extrusion again.

"Clear," she announced with a slight smirk.

"But... you never even fired."

"That's a HALASER you printed, Julian. It's not fancy but it does the job."

"But there was no beam!" He replied confused as he rubbed his face where the debris had hit him.

"I thought you knew your science, kid," she chuckled. "Come on, you can do your homework later." She pulled him beside her further into the perpendicular hallway.

Julian didn't have time to think back to the laser course in his virtual reality. His body was dragged forward by Nyx's firm hand on his collar.

Their sprint didn't last long. A large man, almost double his size, jumped them from the next junction, grabbing Nyx's arm and causing Julian to stumble as she released his collar to defend herself. The man pounded her arm to the wall until her gun finally dropped. He positioned his leg between hers and tried to trip her down. Julian kicked him above his calves like Nyx had shown him for bringing down bigger opponents but the brute barely flinched. Nyx growled and pushed free from his tight grasp. She went for the gun but as she kneeled on the floor, their enemy kicked her from behind. Her body splayed on the wall sending the pistol spinning to knock Julian's feet. He locked eyes with him, two black holes ready to devour anything that came too close. His skin was not overly affected by the red light, dark and matt, almost like a silhouette against a fiery background.

Julian held his breath as his opponent charged at him. Did he have enough time to grab the gun? Even if he did, was he going to shoot? He reached for it but never got the chance to point it. His enemy smacked it out of his hands, a slap so violent it numbed his skin and sent a stinging pain up his arms. The man gripped Julian from the neck and lifted him off the floor to his eye level with one arm. His nostrils flared wide and the stench of his breath made Julian cringe in disgust. It was the same man who had threatened him back in the Halfway event, a menacing walking tower.

"I knew we shouldn't trust a deviant like you," he threatened in his deep voice.

"Put him down, you piece of shit!" Nyx sidekicked his knee but the man stood still. He threw Julian to the wall and turned his attention back to the immediate threat. Julian coughed, the wind knocked out of him and tried to get on his feet, wheezing for new breaths.

He glanced up to see Nyx on the offensive, a few quick punches in his stomach and an uppercut that must have dislocated his jaw. Her movements were fast and agile like a choreographed dance where the outcome was pain instead of fun. She somehow climbed under his waist and onto his back wrapping her legs around his chest and her arms around his neck. He lost his balance for a second and moved backwards pushing Nyx to the wall. The boards crumbled from the force as he tried to squish her between his back and the wall. Julian scanned the room for the gun. He stifled a groan and sucked his teeth to contain the pain as he rushed to grab the pistol.

The man roared and with a final push Nyx released her grasp and fell on the floor, the red lights amplifying the dark, red liquid dripping out her nose. He kneeled above her, ready to snuff the life out of her as his broad arms squeezed her neck. She tapped her hand to the floor and her legs jerked uncontrollably.

Julian had the pistol in his hand, aiming but trembling. His lungs cried for a breath but his throat was shut. His finger hugged the trigger and he squinted, aiming for the arm or shoulder, he couldn't see the light beam. He drew a shaky inhale and pulled it. The weapon powered up rapidly and a red dot in the man's back disintegrated shirt and skin. In an instant he was down on the floor beside Nyx. The pistol dropped from his hands and his body collapsed, balancing only on his palms on the cold, metallic floor.

"Thank you kid." Nyx tried to find her voice but it came out raspy.

"I owe you one." She coughed, holding her chest.

He looked up to make sure Nyx was ok and that's when he saw it. The scorching hole in the man's chest that brought him to the uncomfortable realisation. He had killed him, taken away his life, his potential, his dreams, his thoughts, his very existence.

"I...I-I killed him."

Nyx grabbed his shoulder and pulled him up. She took a breath, ready to say something but only sighed. "Look at me. You saved me. You took a life, yes... but allowed me to keep mine." she pulled him inside her arms and softly kissed his forehead. "I'll always love you for that."

Her words, while comforting, did little to diminish his guilt. He couldn't think about it now, he had to keep going but all he could see was the lifeless eyes of the man staring motionless into the void.

"Come on, we've got to go," Nyx picked up the gun and snapped to the intersection where a set of footsteps were rhythmically approaching. "I'm not taking any more chances," she said and pointed the gun at the edge of the wall.

She only missed by a few inches as she averted her aim last second. Andre just stood there with widened eyes and his hands in the air, one of them holding his fedora.

"Shit! I could have killed you, you idiot!" Nyx whispered loudly and let out a sigh.

"How would I know you're here? What are you even doing here? I thought you'd be at the airlock by now," he complained and studied the dead body with his eyes.

"We had a... complication... but it's been dealt with now. Come on kid, time to go."

Julian stood back on his feet and checked his roller. "It's this way." He pointed to the end of the hallway, glancing back at the dead body.

That intersection only had three branches which meant they were at the outermost part of the quadrant, the only barrier between them and space, a few layers of reinforced hull. A blue arrow was glowing on the wall annotated with the phrase "Towards H04 E-V-A Hall"

"Look out!" Nyx pulled him aside as two more shots shattered parts of the wall.

"They're still on us. I think we should abort," Andre suggested.

"But my dad is…"

"There's no point locking ourselves in a room while an army is waiting for us outside." Andre insisted.

"I don't think we have an option. RUN!" Nyx pushed them both forward as two more guards appeared from the other corridor.

Julian felt his back exposed, naked and fragile. If these ballistic weapons could make the walls crumble like that, there was no telling what a bullet would do to his body. The seared hole in the man he had killed flashed before his eyes. Was it instant for him? Maybe he deserved the same fate.

Their enemy had a clear shot and the next turn was quite far away. The short bursts came like cannon fire but the hits were nowhere near him. He glanced back at Nyx and both his feet and heart stopped working. She was still at the intersection leaning in and out of the small extrusion, returning the fire with her small pistol.

"What are you doing? COME ON!" He screamed.

"I'm returning the favour kid." She smiled while taking cover behind the splintered edge of the wall. "GO! RUN!"

The last shot flew past him and he ducked again. The repeating fire coming from the perpendicular corridor had almost stripped away the first layer of the wall where the annotation used to be. A grey gas hissed from within it and the synthesised computer voice immediately came on the speakers with more bad news.

"Warning, oxygen flow disrupted...
rerouting... rerouting...
Ventilation will now be shut down in sections G23, G24 and H1
Please evacuate these areas immediately
Lockdown imminent."

"Julian, don't think, just come!" Andre waved his hand back and forth towards his chest.

"We can't just leave her!" He wished Andre would come and drag him, take the choice away from him—he would welcome it this time. His feet were stuck on the floor, unwilling to go either forward or backwards. He could only stare at her as she mouthed the word 'Go' with a nod.

"I can't leave you," he cried, his fists clenched as he realised just how powerless he truly was.

Nyx sprinted towards him, blindly firing her weapon behind her. The laser was visible this time as it passed through the smoke cloud that had accumulated at the intersection. She grabbed his hand and dragged him with her.

His feet vibrated with every step as the blast doors kept coming down on the rest of the corridors in quick succession. Andre was waiting for them with his arm extended while the alarm blared in bright blue above the junction.

He felt a sudden push at his back and he was down, face first on the floor as the door came crashing down behind him.

Andre helped him up, the only other person in the empty hallway as Julian revolved around himself.

"Where is Nyx?"

"She's a stubborn old gal, son. She stayed back to buy us some time. Let's not waste it."

"But they'll kill her in there."

"Eeh, I don't know. You know how tough she is. Trust me, she's been through worse."

"Worse than *this*?" Julian pushed his brows together. She really was a badass but even if she could somehow manage to survive the evos, there was also the lockdown that would suffocate her.

"Do you think the infiltration team will have weapons too? We need to come back and help her."

"If Richard managed to convince your father, then probably yeah. Come on now, let's move on."

Julian noticed the H04 stencil on the wall. They were close now. The E-V-A prep hall was easy to distinguish in its red surroundings, its blue light above the doors shining like a beacon.

The inside looked like it hadn't been used in a long time or maybe it was just regularly kept neat and tidy. Spacesuits were hanging from a continuous rack on the sides which was interrupted by cupboards that stretched from floor to ceiling. In the middle, a stretched oval bench split the room in two identical halves and united towards the airlock where six exosuits laid still, like metal guardians ready to be awakened.

"Do you think she's ok?" Julian asked after they had put on their main suits.

"Don't worry about Nyx. What you should worry about is if the crazies found some way around her," Andre reassured him again and pointed at the door.

Julian leant out of the frame and scanned the hallways. The sight of the two armed guards walking side by side with their weapons propped on their shoulders filled his head with doubts. Had they gone past her or through her?

"Shit!" he whispered and pressed his hand on the reader until a red lock icon appeared on the screen. "Two evos coming our way, maybe more behind them."

"We need to find something to block the door."

"Block the door? How are we going to get the team out?"

"We won't. It's us who are going out."

Julian's heart must have stopped for a second and it seemed he had forgotten how to breathe.

One in, one out, in… and out, his whole body trembled and shivered.

"JULIAN!" Andre waved a hand in front of him. "Wake up, son."

"The-th-there's no way I'm going out… there." He shook his head repeatedly.

"Help me move these cupboards first, then you can have your panic attack."

Julian followed Andre's order but his mind was back at the first time he had gone out the ship. Even with Rachel's support, he hadn't moved an inch past the airlock. And that was a supposedly safe, school exercise not running along the outside of the Ring untethered. He felt naked again, vulnerable and small. He glanced at his thumb and wiped the blood from its edge inside his suit's pocket. How long had he been biting it?

"Ugh, it won't budge," Andre groaned.

The door clanged with a thud followed by a repeated pounding.

"We know you're in there. Open the door and I promise you won't get hurt." The shout from the other side was muffled and distorted.

Julian ran to the door and kneeled in front of the reader.

"No, what are you doing? Don't open it!" Andre tried to stop him.

"I'm just buying us some more time." He placed his finger under the plastic encasement as Mark had done in what seemed a very long time ago and tapped twice.

The reader split in four pieces for each side, revealing the cabling inside. Mark had used his pin to unlock the control room door but he needed to do the opposite this time. He grabbed the cables and disconnected them with a swift pull.

"I'm impressed," Andre cocked his head. "Now keep it up and get in the exosuit."

Julian let out a strong puff of air as he came to the realisation that there was no other option. His last hope was that his dad was already outside waiting for him and ready to help him across to safety.

The metallic humanoid armour enveloped him. It whirred and hissed as it locked around his body. He felt very light, like he had suddenly lost fifty pounds of weight; walking forward only required the minimum effort from his muscles.

The inner door of the airlock hissed and the valve turned upside down.

In and out... in and out... in and out, the counting in his head couldn't keep up with the rapid rhythm of his shaky breaths.

"Emergency pressurisation initialised."

The screen on the opposite wall turned on after the computer announcement and presented them with the countdown.

Four minutes... just four minutes and... black space... emptiness... spinning... in the middle of nowhere...

"Do you think Nyx made it out ok?" he asked in his shaky voice, trying to distract himself.

"I told you, she can take care of herself, just like we can. Don't worry, everything is going to be ok."

"Andre, there's got to be another way. I can't go outside. I can't do it." His eyes welled up, frustrating him for not being able to wipe the cold droplets from running down his cheeks.

"Julian? Andre, is that you?" The familiar voice echoed inside his helmet like a liberating war cry.

"Dad?" He repeated a few times, banging the side of his helmet to make sure it was working.

The only reply came from the preparation hall as a small woman squeezed through the half broken door, spitting her incomprehensive threats and pointing at them.

"Sit down, they can't get in here." Andre extended his hand to stop him from getting up.

He only wanted to see how many there were, although what difference would it make now? He glanced at the ticking clock and buckled up again, scratching his fingers inside his clammy palms under the glove. The thud made him flinch. They had broken in and were trying to pry the door open. Then a brief stop and a burst of shots that reverberated through the metal hull.

"Scott, we're under heavy fire, we need to evacuate."

"We... change... plan," his dad's voice was breaking up but at least now he was sure he was out there, waiting for him.

He took one long, deep inhale as he glanced at the clock that was counting down its last minute. He exchanged a glance between the astronaut waiting outside in the empty, cold space and the frantic scowls of the evolutionists trying to break in from the other side. He could feel his pulse beside his nails, the need to bite them causing his thumb to rub ineffectively at his fingers, the fabric too thick to satisfy. He glanced at the clock again as every passing second felt like an eternity.

CHAPTER 24
— Rachel —
E.V.A – Outer space

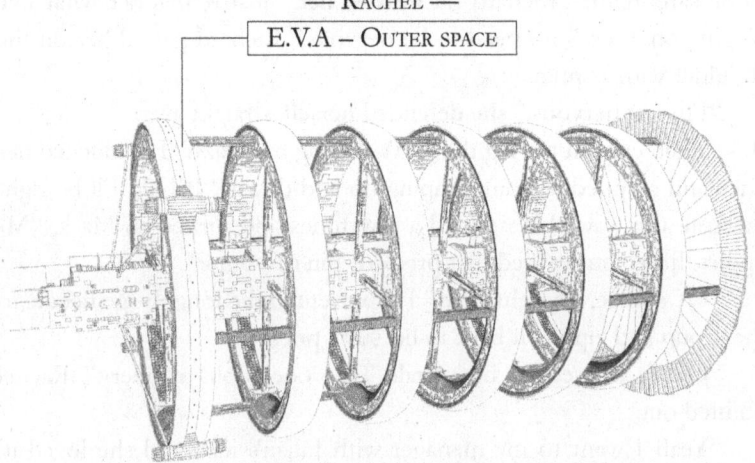

Her helmet hissed as it locked behind her neck. She had expected pure oxygen to smell a bit differently but apart from the tickling inside her nose, it felt the same as the air she was used to.

"Now don't forget what we talked about," Richard started again, "Proper enunciation is very important. What were the words?"

"This a quiz?" Mark scoffed, "Clean helmet, emergency navigation."

'I am not that worried about you, you've had your hours outside the ship, same as Lee and Christoff. Rachel on the other hand hasn't been out much. I need to make sure you can take care of yourselves if something happens."

There it is.

No matter how many times she had proved her usefulness to the group, it still felt like they were babysitting her. Fixing the batteries, coming up with the idea that had enabled them to communicate with Ring Six, picking up Kieran's role to control the narrative to the public, what else did they want? The last one was not entirely true, unless of course spreading gossip about the evolutionists at school counted for guiding the information feed.

She didn't share any of her thoughts. She had to control her breathing to calm down her racing pulse and let the pure oxygen fill her body. She would see him in a few hours.

"Come on now, don't give me that look. You know I only want you to be safe, right?" Richard sat next to her. "Just remember what I've taught you, there's no need to be nervous," Richard patted her on the shoulder with a smile.

"I'm not nervous," she defended herself straight away.

"Then explain the leg thing, it's driving me crazy." He touched her knee and stopped it from jumping up and down. "It's ok, I'll be right there all the way." He nodded a few times and turned to Mark, "Mr Spoles, have you secured that precious pin of yours?"

"Of course, it's right here." He presented the long, beige needle to the group and zipped it back in his suit's pocket.

"Didn't it used to be metal? This one looks rubbery," Rachel pointed out.

"Yeah I went to my manager with Julian's idea and she loved it. Don't tell him."

"Ok, I think we're good with oxygen," Scott said with authority and stepped into the indentation on the wall where the exoskeleton was.

She took one last, deep breath and disconnected the tube from the back of her suit. The body armour was waiting for her with its spine and thorax open like a carcass after an animal feast. Most of its surfaces were made from a honeycomb lattice that cleverly hid the hydraulics and electronic systems under its protective plating. She stepped inside and brought it to life as it whirred and hissed to embrace her whole body.

"All hear me ok?" Richard's voice rang inside her head. "One, two, one, two."

"Good copy," Scott was first to verify the comms were working and the rest of the team followed. "This is it everyone. Let's go save our future."

The hatch slid open allowing the menacing darkness of space to creep inside the pressurisation module. It was fortunate she was last in the line they had formed so Richard couldn't comment on the hesitation in her steps. She had done a few EVAs in the last couple of months but Richard had always made her wear a tether. She felt exposed this time. Every step had to be carefully placed so that the magnetic boots could detach and re-engage. It was a weird feeling walking outside the hatch and then continuing along the outer wall. A different reality where the laws of physics didn't apply and she could walk from the floor to the wall, to the ceiling and vice versa.

The outer bridge was still dangling from the edge of Ring Five, a broken reminder of the lengths the evolutionists were prepared to go to remain in control of the engines.

They had chosen the bridge of the science quadrant this time. It meant a smaller journey outside the ship and a low profile entry point. It was also a safer route than going from outside the Ring through the shuttles. Richard had suggested it but Scott was sure the boarding bridges would be sealed. The shortest path would've been through Core Hull Five but the evos had completely barricaded all doors from their side. Rachel had suggested blasting them open but Richard had been particularly scared of debris finding its way to the spinning mechanism. It could potentially cause a chain reaction and tear the whole *Sagan* apart.

"Be careful on the jump," Richard cautioned them when they reached the end of the bridge as he hopped above the window of the concourse inside. "Wait, don't jump yet," he ordered while gesturing to someone inside.

Was it Julian and the other team? Who else could it be? She moved forward and leant over the edge with the correct footing before hurtling towards the hull of Ring Six. Passing by the window of the quadrant intersection, she saw no one inside other than the two bodies lying on the floor.

"Get your weapons ready, we might run into trouble on the way in," Richard said while grunting to walk faster along the hull.

She tapped above the trigger of the pistol, holstered at the side of her leg and took a long shaky breath. The fact that there were now guns on board the ship seemed surreal. Scott had been against it since the beginning but Richard was right, they had to play on the same terms. Even so, there was some pleasure in firing the blue kinetic rounds at the fake practice target. Richard had taught her how to shoot but she wasn't sure she was ready to fire at a real person. Were the others? Kaiden had said multiple times he couldn't wait to get his revenge on all those responsible for his sister's state. Christoff always kept to himself, only talking to her when he had to, his thoughts were a mystery but the adults seemed to trust him. Mark had objected to an all-out war since the beginning but now that their time was up, he had come to terms with it.

"So much for stealth," Lee said.

"We knew this was a possibility," Scott replied. "Stay focused."

"The hatch should be close," Mark remarked.

Her eyes scanned the dark expanse for the pressurisation module. They had kept the headlights off so as not to attract attention and the hull was barely visible, blending seamlessly into the inky blackness that surrounded them. Only the exterior lights guided their way, thousands as they may have been, they glowed as bright as the stars behind them, casting eerie shadows on the intricate design of the outer hull.

She followed her team, grunting from the effort it took to even walk until she landed on something soft and squishy. It was a stray cable, clad in its matte black insulation and perfectly camouflaged against the hull. Her magboot failed on the rubbery surface but at the same time she had let the other foot go. She slowly drifted away, floating in nothingness as she frantically flailed her hands for something to grab on. Her heart raced and as she spun around herself in weightlessness, she saw a pointy rod coming out of the ship—an antenna. Gritting her teeth, she stretched out her arm until her fingers touched the thin cylinder and she was safe again. So many drills and simulations with Richard and now was the time to fuck up. Thankfully, no one had noticed and she focused back on her team that had progressed further towards the middle of the Ring's width.

I can do this!

Richard stopped in front of the airlock and Mark moved next to him to investigate.

"She... care... worry," the unknown voice inside her head was breaking up.

"Who said that?" She asked, leaning forward to focus.

"Got to be... way... can't...outside," this time she recognized the second voice. She hadn't heard it in a long time but it was definitely him.

"Julian? Andre is that you?" Scott exclaimed.

"We... vy fire... need... evacuate."

"Did he say they're under fire?" Rachel felt a sudden pulsing inside her chest.

"We need to change the plan," Scott said and turned to look beyond Rachel behind them.

"We need to help them!" She protested.

"Not possible anymore, little Miss. I see them, they are going through emergency pressurisation. We can't go in anymore." Richard had pressed his visor against the circular window of the hatch.

The static continued but it was too inconsistent to make sense.

"So what do we do? Are we really going back?" Mark asked moving away from the door panel he had almost unlocked.

"Yes, you, Christoff and Rachel start backtracking to the outer bridge," Scott ordered.

"Shouldn't we..."

"Rachel, don't start!" Scott didn't give her a chance to finish her sentence even though she only wanted to question why not all of them together.

She only nodded and twisted her body around. She had learned to follow his lead in the last few months but this time it was harder, Julian was right there on the other side of the airlock. She would have to trust in the fact that she was leaving him in the hands of his own father.

"Where is Nyx?" Scott asked inside her head.

They had come out. She glanced behind to find the two exo-suits already walking along the exterior of the Ring.

"She stayed behind to make sure we have time for emergency pressurisation," the deep older voice sounded like Andre.

"Why, what happened?" Scott asked as the man passed him.

"We were discovered on our way in. Some sections were isolated, quite a mess actually."

"There was... th-there was some... some shooting involved," Julian stuttered.

Rachel could only imagine what it must have been like for him being outside the ship. It felt like someone had punched her in the stomach, sealing her breath inside. Her whole body was urging her to fly to him and squeeze his suit but Scott must've seen her stopping and gestured her to move on. Her vision blurred and she felt the cold tears pooling inside her eyelids. She shook her head but the watery blob remained.

"Clean Helmet," she enunciated softly hoping their conversation would mask her command.

A hiss above her head sucked the moisture from her skin, clearing her vision but drying her eyes so much, she could feel her eyeballs.

"We'll find some other way to get in. The important thing is that you're ok and we're all together again," Scott squeezed Julian in through the shoulder pad of the exo-suit.

"Can we save this beautiful reunion for the debriefing?" Richard interjected.

Rachel reached the jump point and stopped when she caught a glimpse of movement inside the concourse. There were at least four people near the blast door fiddling with the controls. She moved behind one of the extruded plates to hide from the woman that had pressed her face against the window, eyes scanning the blackness outside.

"Uhm, guys we need to pick up the pace, fast," she said leaning out of her cover.

"R-Rachel?" Julian stammered.

"Now is not the time for reunions, people," Richard implored, "What is it, little Miss?"

"There are people inside the intersection. They're doing something to the door."

"Shit, let's hurry up," Scott was already out of breath.

"You'll have to run for it. Come on, I've got you." Mark had already jumped and opened his arms to receive her.

Running in the magboots was actually easier than walking, each step almost like a little hop. Their suits bumped and she locked her feet to the ground once again.

"Start moving back to Ring Five," Scott's yell made her ears twitch.

The rest of the group was almost there, running as if they were moving in slow motion until they reached the edge.

"Ok, you next," Scott said after Richard hopped on the bridge with ease.

"Oh, no, no, no, there's no way," Julian mumbled.

"Come on son, I'm right behind you."

"No, Dad, I can't." The crack in his voice made her stop and turn around. She had to go back for him.

"Where are you going? Go back to Five," Richard said when she approached.

"You go! I got this. *We* got this, right Julian?" she stood at the edge and finally saw him.

His lips had parted—he was probably breathing from the mouth, not able to control his panic attack. Her throat felt heavy again, her eyes and nostrils burning.

No, I can't cry again. Not now.

"In… and out," she said, waving her hands up and down in a steady rhythm.

There was a twitch on his lip like he had tried to smile, bringing the lump back inside her throat.

"Come on, grab my hand. I know you can do this." She smiled and extended her hand. "Just look at me," she said when she saw the fear in his face, the way his brows had curled.

"Uhuh," his voice trembled, "What if I'm left behind when I let go, Rach?"

"You won't, there's inertia," Richard explained.

"Yeah, you see? Science!" Rachel almost hung from the ledge, extending her arm as far as she could. "Just imagine you're in the VR chair. Soon you'll take off the visor and we'll be back in the HUB, but first you have to finish this level with me."

Julian hid his lips inside his mouth and narrowed his eyes with determination. Bending his knees, he pressed a button on his arm and hurtled himself towards her.

Their fingertips touched and she secured him with her other hand, grunting as her body twisted from his velocity.

She groaned as she tried to pull him back and felt a sudden thump at her back stretching her spine as she was pushed away from the bridge. Her soles felt the vibration first which then coursed throughout her body despite the protection of her suit. Everything was spinning. There was no up or down, no right or left, only a swirling haze of bright trails of lights and debris as her body spun uncontrollably in the empty space.

Fuck, fuck, fuck!

She tightened her grip on Julian's hand and pulled him in, wrapping her legs around his waist to keep him there. It was harder than she thought as if he was trying to push himself away.

"Rach?" He called out for her when their visors touched, his voice faint and barely audible was not coming through the comms. His eyes were squeezed shut and his jaw clenched. He was having his worst fear realised.

Giving up wasn't an option. She just needed to orient herself. How far had they gone and how fast?

"Emergency navigation!" she ordered, feeling the light tug of something being released from the back of her suit.

"Emergency navigation activated"

The female voice inside her helmet reassured her for a brief moment. Another tug on her back—the tension of a tether reaching its maximum length and the spinning stopped.

She took a sharp, deep breath when she realised they had gone over the outer rim shield and shivered in the thought of being left behind in the cold, empty space.

The force of hitting the exterior plates of the engine was sudden and painful, but she managed to lock her boots on the extruded metal panels. She fought to keep Julian next to her, but he was slipping away like he was trying to get away from her.

And that's when she saw it. A jet of air hissing from behind his back where his compressed oxygen had cracked. The jet was enough to propel him in the opposite direction of the hole but she held on to his hand with all her remaining strength. She clenched her teeth and screamed as she pulled him close to her and tapped on the icon on his arm that engaged his magboots.

His eyes were closed and his head tilted freely inside his helmet. A sharp pain pierced her heart as the unimaginable crossed her mind.

"JULIAN!" she shrieked, grabbing his shoulders and pushing their visors together. She tapped on the sides of his helmet a few times shaking his head inside until his eyes opened and he gasped for air.

"Are you ok?" she cried as every muscle on her body trembled.

She saw his mouth moving but no sound reached her. Then their visors touched and she could hear his echo somehow. "I- I think so... where are we?"

"Literally on one of the ARK engines. Might be a good thing the Halfway event didn't go as planned after all, if they were in reverse, we'd be burnt to a crisp by now."

"If they were reversed we wouldn't be in this situation in the first place."

"Fair enough. How much oxygen have you got? Your canister is cracked."

"What?" his eyes widened and his nostrils flared widely, "15%... 14% now."

"Fuck... Richard showed me once... Fuck! There is supposed to be some emergency tape here somewhere," she patted herself down until she felt a bulge on her side.

"Where's my dad? He was right next to me."

She couldn't think of an answer, a comforting one at least, she just took out the small green roll and stuck a few pieces over the hole.

"Don't worry about that now. Let's get ourselves somewhere safe first. Navigation got me tethered somewhere, let's follow the rope... but we'll have to jump to the outer shield."

"Yeah, no way I'm doing that."

"Julian, come on! It's a small jump and we're secured." She shook the tether to make sure it was hooked on her suit. Think of it like this, you'll be standing upside down under the floor of a low level flat."

"Oh, that's comforting," he jerked his head left and right, the glass of his visor squeaking upon hers.

"Do you want to live? You'll have to jump!" She snapped at his unwillingness to cooperate for his own good.

"I don't think I'll make it anyway, it's 13% now."

"I went through way too much to have you dying on me! Now, come on... we won't go anywhere else other than where the rope is." She grabbed his hand and offered a reassuring nod before taking the leap.

The drift was slow and steady as they followed the tether to the edge of the Ring's rim. She engaged her magboots again and glanced behind to the enormous structure towering above them. She was sure no one had ever seen one of the engines so close. Its cylindrical shape came out on the sides like a fat man's belly and extended its enormous steel arms to the shield that was protecting it from micro-asteroids. Where was the bright, yellow tail though? The engines had stopped, all of them sitting there silently like sleeping giants. Only two were visible from where she stood but there was no beam from the others. Richard had told them that would happen if the evolutionists were ever to detach, the start of the realignment procedure.

Fuck!

She turned to Julian and their visors touched again as he squeezed his fingers under her shoulder pads.

"8%," he cried, the panic clear in his wide, blue eyes.

Fuck! She had a way bigger problem to worry about. Ring Six being possibly detached seemed like a minor inconvenience compared to losing Julian. The thought made every single hair on her body jitter. The truth was she didn't know where she was going, just following the tether. Even if they could find a hatch in time, they wouldn't be able to open it without Mark's pin. She just had to keep going though.

She climbed under the edge of the shield trying not to be taken back by the elegance of the synchronous dance the *Sagan*'s Rings were performing.

Julian gripped her hand and held her in place. "I'm going to throw up," he gurgled, his voice back inside her head once again.

"Comms are back? Richard? Scott?" She yelled inside her helmet.

"No one can hear you. There's still so much static," He groaned, probably trying to keep himself from vomiting.

"Fuck! Try to take small breaths. Remember what I always told you and just fixate on a single point. No spinning, just a straight line, focus on the straight line, Julian."

He gurgled again but couldn't stop the orange vile from filling the inside of his helmet.

"Fuck, say the phrase 'clean helmet'," she closed her eyes as her own mechanism sucked the air in front of her.

Julian repeated her words and bent on his knees. She leant over him to help him up and that's when she saw it.

It wasn't an explosion that had knocked them off the bridge, not like the one that had killed Kieran and Noel at least. The remaining three bridges had sustained some damage but they were still there. The problem was they were not connected to Ring Six anymore.

The evolutionists had detached.

Julian hadn't noticed yet and that was the last thing he needed. She had to get him to safety first. That was all that mattered.

"Come on, I see the end of the hook over there at the shuttle." She pulled him on his feet. "Wait, the shuttles!"

"What makes you think they won't be locked?"

"My suit can open the door in an emergency. Come on, grab my hand. Isn't there a way to fucking reel me in the hook?"

Her question activated the mechanism at her back and pulled her towards the end of the tether.

"Deactivate your boots!" She screamed at him while fighting to not let his hand go.

Julian hesitated for a second but the little oxygen that was left in his suit must have given him a push to let go of the surface.

"Rach, it says oxygen levels critical. Argh, make that warning stop ringing inside my ears," he shrieked.

"Soon Julian, almost there."

The whirring stopped and Rachel found herself in front of a big hook that was attached to a handle on the side of the shuttle's airlock.

"Emergency navigation completed. Opening shuttle door,"

"Yes! Did you hear that? My suit can get us in! Julian?" She twisted her body and noticed his calm, motionless face, "No, no, no, no, no, no, don't do this to me, we made it. Look, the door is open. Julian, wake up!" she cried and shook his shoulders to find there was no resistance. Her eyes burned again and her throat clenched like someone was choking her.

"No, Julian, PLEASE!" The tears pooled around her eyes again blocking her vision, "Clean... helmet," she snivelled and unlocked his magboots.

"Emergency pressurisation."

"Clean helm... clean... cl..." her throat couldn't produce any more words, only a loud cry coming out from deep within her chest.

She looked at the countdown on the wall and clicked the sides of her own helmet—Julian wouldn't survive five minutes. She inhaled as much oxygen as her lungs could carry and threw it on the ground—a bad move as it turned out. Her lungs burnt almost immediately and she felt her saliva boiling. She was burning from the inside out. She locked the helmet back on and fell back against the wall, her eyes closed and the world around her spinning. Richard had trained her on it but CPR was out of the question. She cursed herself for never paying attention to any of the science courses. A vague memory came to mind about decompression sickness but with Julian on the brink of death, she never thought it through.

Groaning to get up, she scampered to the other side of the pressurisation module until she found the green cross and banged her fist on its metal casing. Everything was blurry and she must have been drifting in and out of consciousness as the clock ticked down faster than normal every time she glanced at it. Shooting pains ran throughout her body, her muscles felt stiff and her joints numb. She blinked, her eyes bulging out, about to explode, and finally tapped on the word she could never pronounce—defibrillator.

The spider-like medi-bot descended from the ceiling above her and scanned its surroundings, attaching a tube at Julian's oxygen compartment and two thick wires through his exo-suit.

She shut her eyes and fell back on the wall with a thud.

She could only wait now.

CHAPTER 25

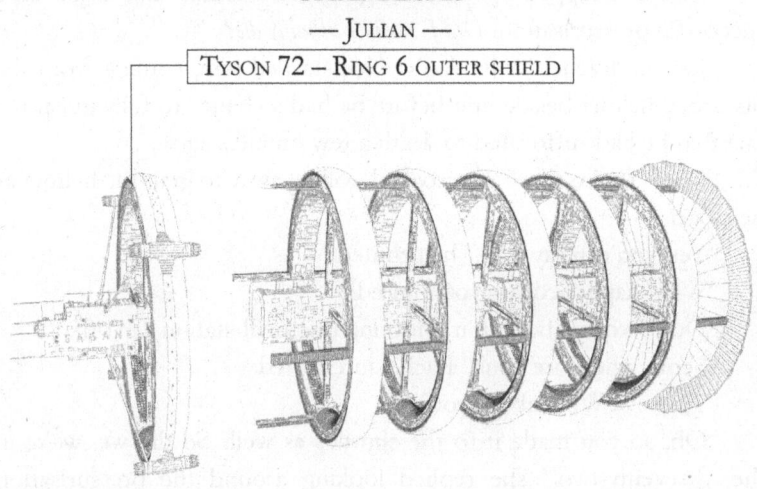

— Julian —

Tyson 72 – Ring 6 outer shield

The alarm snapped him back to existence on a prolonged gasp which dried his throat, forcing a continuous cough that strained his lungs. A blurry silhouette towered over him, partially blocking the blinding light above him. His sense of taste was the first to come back, the stale, damp smell of the airlock.

"It's alright, I'm here," Rachel's face came into focus as she softly caressed his arm up and down.

His eyes darted around the room and then focused back at her. How he had missed those green irises.

She smiled but didn't utter a word, just kept looking at him. There was no need for words anyway, nothing could possibly describe that pulsing feeling inside his chest accurately. He sat up and pulled her to him so that her head could rest on his chest, comfortably under his chin as he squeezed her tight.

"I missed you so much," she snivelled.

"I missed you too, Rach... I missed you too." He let out a cathartic exhale, the aroma of pine trees seeping in from her hair, bringing him back home where he was comfortable and safe, where he could close his eyes for a second and breathe.

"I can't believe... I-I thought you were gone." Rachel sniffed, her arms tightening around his waist.

His eyes snapped open, landing on the monitor that displayed a successful pressurisation. *Did I... did I actually die?*

"Julian... Rachel?" His dad's voice startled him, coming from the discarded helmet beside him before he had a chance to fully grasp the fact that he had suffocated to death a few minutes ago.

"Dad? You're alive!" he croaked, rolling away to grab the helmet as he stood.

"Yes, you can say that," he grunted.

"What happened, are you injured?"

"Don't worry about it, it's nothing the medi-station can't fix."

"Scott, where are you?" Rachel interjected.

"*Tyson-78*. What about you?"

"Oh, so you made it to the shuttles as well? So did we, we're in the... seventy-two," she replied looking around the pressurisation module for the number.

"I am so glad you're both ok. Now get off the comms and stay put. I'll get myself patched up and make my way to you."

"What about the others?" Rachel asked, kneeling next to the helmet.

"I honestly don't know."

"Scott... they detached it." she uttered hesitantly, her words driving a sharp pain in Julian's chest. He had kept his eyes shut when the force pushed him in space and after that it was hard to concentrate on anything else other than the percentage of his oxygen.

"I know... but we still have time. It won't be easy for them to realign manually without Abeone."

"Richard said a day, even without the AI" she countered, her voice reaching a higher pitch.

"It'll have to do. Now maintain radio silence until I get there. There should be some long lasting food and water at the back."

"When is that going to be? Dad? Dad? I guess he went offline," Julian huffed, flopping on the bench behind him with a thud. He balanced his elbows on his knees and ran both hands through his sweaty face.

"Here, have some water." She offered a metal, grey canister as if she had produced it out of thin air.

He didn't ask where she'd found it, only twisted the cap and poured the tepid liquid down his throat.

"Don't worry about him, he's going to be fine. He's Scott Walker," Rachel continued when Julian leant back, finally refreshed.

"I guess you did spend a lot of time with him all these months, huh? Did he give you a hard time?"

"Nah, he was always very kind and understanding and he actually did save my life back when the first bridge exploded."

"You were there when it happened?" He stood up, running a hand through his greasy hair that was falling in front of his eyes.

"It was our first mission, to attach the construction clamps. Why do you think the evos didn't detach sooner?"

"Because we destroyed their repair-bots?"

Rachel smiled, tilting her head. "We have a lot of catching up to do. Let's find some food first." She stepped in the wall cavity where the exosuit whirred open and attached itself to the wall next to the others of its kind.

"Should we not keep these on? How long do you think until my dad gets here?"

"It'll probably be a few hours. *Tyson-78* is on the other side of the agricultural quadrant so it'll take him some time. Plus, who knows how long he'll stay in the medi-station."

"How-how do you know all this?"

"It was in the briefing. We studied the shuttles because Richard wanted to use them as access to Ring Six. Apparently your dad was right as always, it seems the boarding bridges are retracted and sealed just as he thought."

Julian wanted to comment on her avid knowledge but the words never came to him. She reminded him a little bit of Nyx, only younger and smaller. Nyx... was she even alive at that point?

"Did they really detach? You saw it?"

"With my own eyes... Not much we can do, Julian. Scott... I mean your dad said to wait here and you need time to recover."

"And since when do you follow orders?"

"Since Richard taught me how to use this." She presented a pistol and gave it a few twirls with her finger, before locking it in place between the grip and her palm.

Julian couldn't contain the smirk. It was like watching a ginger version of Nyx playing with her blade. Nyx would've also given it a kiss though.

"What are you smiling about? I'm serious."

"Nothing, it's just weird seeing you after all these months like this," he admitted, gesturing to her with a wave of his hand. "It seems I missed a lot."

"Let's get something to eat and we'll talk." She rubbed her stomach above the space uniform, pressing her lips together.

Julian disengaged his exosuit and joined her at the back where she was already rifling through the various cupboards. The interior of the shuttle was a lot different than the rest of the *Sagan*. There were no pipes, no wires, no metal panels, only a continuous light grey stream of thin lines that joined and curved together to form the long oval tube of the inside. Even the panels and cupboards seemed to be part of the ship, a holistic architectural amalgamation of that grey material like a thread weaving through a piece of fabric.

"Catch!" Rachel forced his reflexes.

The power bar almost slipped from his hands but he caught it on the second try. It was crispy and bland, a tasteless containment of energy he had to consume to satisfy his growling stomach.

"So tell me… what did I miss all these months?" Rachel cringed after the first bite.

"Not too much, nothing super exciting."

"Nothing exciting? How about living with the two top operatives on the ship? Or your mum turning out to be an evolutionist? Or finally getting together with your biggest crush?"

"We didn't get together." He shook his head dismissively. "It turns out she was only leading me on to keep me in Ring Six before the lockdown," he said as the memory of that day played inside his head.

"Oh, bummer…"

"It wasn't actually. If anything, I think it made me see her for who she truly was, a short-sighted pawn playing her idle part in a chess game with no winners."

Rachel giggled and snorted.

"What?" he asked, not able to see what was funny about his answer.

"Oh, I missed you, my weirdo." She laughed again and hugged him tightly. "Tell me, is that game also happening on an endless chessboard with no boundaries, a constant reminder of the futility of their efforts?" she chuckled.

"You know what? That's actually amazing, YES! You just came up with that now?"

"Of course. What, do you think you're the only smart ass around here?"

"No, I didn't mean..."

"I'm joking." She ran her fingers up and down his arm, tilting her head.

"What about you? Did you ever find out who was responsible for Nightfall?"

"No, not yet. They're all still in coma so no new leads... which is weird because Javier said there's nothing wrong with them, I don't understand why none of them have woken up."

"At least they're alive."

"Yeah, I guess," she sighed, "But let's not talk about Alex please. Tell me about Nyx. Is she as badass as the guys describe her?"

"Oh yeah, we did quite a few missions together. I think you'd like her... I just hope you get the chance to meet her. She... she stayed behind to buy us time for the pressurisation. I hope she made it somehow..." Julian walked towards the bridge of the shuttle where four chairs were spaced evenly around their silent panels.

He hadn't realised it before, but there was no glass at the front. How were people supposed to navigate these things without seeing where they're going? Those grey lines were everywhere, enveloping the whole structure like a cocoon, or were they the structure itself?

"Weird ship, huh?" Rachel interrupted his observations.

"Andre mentioned it at some point... that they're made out of a single-threaded carbon nano-composite but I didn't expect it to look like that."

"Well, that's why their plan relies heavily on the shuttles." Rachel moved in front of him, "I have to ask you... how come you didn't join them? I would expect you to be thrilled to finally set foot on Aquanis."

"I was in the beginning. When I found out, first thing I did was to message you but Lydia's dad took my roller. Then they told me the plan was to detach the whole Ring and leave all of you behind, so yeah... wasn't really willing to sacrifice everyone else for a chance to see a planet."

"But you still stayed."

"I didn't stay." He said when he'd finished chewing the last bit of his bar and sat in the command chair on the left. "I ran... as fast as I could but my mother caught me just before the bridge."

Rachel chuckled. "That's so funny. Your dad tackled me while inside the bridge to keep me from getting into Six."

"Wait, so you're the reason he stayed behind?"

"Why am I the reason? He could have let me pass and we would all be in Six since the beginning. Maybe we would have even resolved this crisis by now."

"What were you even doing on that bridge?"

"You messaged me you were still in Six and that they were locking it down."

"And you thought you'd come rescue me somehow?"

She slightly nodded and turned to touch the terminal on the other side.

"How would you have even found me? They'd taken my roller by that point."

"I wasn't thinking, okay? I had just found Alex, I couldn't bear the thought of losing you too."

"You could have put your life in danger, Rach. These people here, they don't mess around," he said in a much more scolding tone than he'd intended and got back on his feet.

She had turned her back to him, idly drawing circles on the dusty screen of the panel with her finger.

"You still don't get it, do you?" She said softly, her voice a little louder than a whisper.

"What?" He asked but she only sighed, "Rach, what?"

"Julian..." She started, taking a deep breath, her shoulders stretching, and letting it all out shakily before continuing, "You know what, fuck it," she exclaimed and turned to face him, balancing on the edge of the terminal and leaning slightly forward. "We may die at some other explosion, or we could be shot out of nowhere, or suffocate in space so I'm just going to say it…" She licked her lips and met his eyes. "I'm in love with you."

Julian felt an unexpected warmth spreading across his chest, the vulnerability in her voice and the sincerity in her eyes numbing his body as his throat tightened. He had suspected that she might have wanted more of their relationship, but love him?

"Always have been," she continued, blinking a couple of times, the water in her eyelids refracting the bright light of the shuttle, making her eyes sparkle. "So I don't care about the risks, I don't care if we're going to reach that fucking planet and I certainly don't care about some delusional crazies with guns, as long as I am with you. And even if you don't feel the same, I will still try to keep you safe. Why do you think I came along on this mission, to enjoy Richard's nagging on a beautiful night outside the ship?"

The words in his head were jumbled and no sentence could be formed. It actually did make sense the more he thought about it. She had always been there for him as he had been for her. How had he not seen it all this time? He contained the frustrated growl inside, feeling an urge to hit himself on the head.

Her pupils had covered most of the green in her eyes as she stood there staring at him, her eyebrows raised and her red lips slightly apart, waiting for him to say something.

He had focused on everything he couldn't have other than the one thing that was right there all along. Did anything else even matter at that point? She was right there in front of him, having risked her life multiple times for him, having saved him from staying behind in the darkness of space and even bringing him back to life. The last thought creeped inside his head and made his spine tingle.

He had died but had he ever really lived before?

His chest constricted and he felt like he was suffocating again but this time it wasn't panic that made his heart thump inside his chest. It was her—the eyes he'd always thought beautiful, the cute upward turn of her nose, her meticulously neatened eyebrows and plump lips, all suddenly like magnets drawing him in. She loved him.

He breached the distance between them and grabbed her hands, their fingers intertwining as he met her eyes again. The warmth of her breath caressed his skin, shaky and heavy, its cadence irregular. She didn't look away this time, her eyes locked with his as they danced from left to right uncontrollably. His gaze fell to her lips as he stroked her hair, tucking the loose strands behind her ear.

"I love you too Rach," he whispered, a huge load relieved from his chest as he leant in.

Their lips touched and he was no longer aware of his surroundings, no longer concerned with what lay ahead. Strands of her hair grazed his face and tickled him while he felt her fingers slowly sliding up his chest and interlocking behind his neck.

"I can't believe I'm kissing you," she said softly and pulled him harder towards her.

"Why haven't we been doing this all this time?"

"Shhh… no thinking, just kiss me." She let out a soft moan while her fingers slid down to the zipper at his collarbone.

She exposed his shoulders and pulled his uniform down, leaving his upper body naked against her. Was he supposed to do the same? Where was this going? Her fingernails pierced his back and her warm lips pressed against his neck as a tingle coursed through his whole body. She was right, this wasn't the time to think, he couldn't think, only go along with wherever the moment would take him. He located her zipper and pulled it down, revealing the black, strapless bra that deprived their bodies from fully uniting. He was expecting her to pull back but she dragged the rest of his uniform down, leaving him with nothing but his underwear.

Is this really happening?

His head snapped to the airlock when the alarm blared and his whole body shivered at the thought of his dad catching him half naked with Rachel. He shouldn't have been able to arrive so quickly though so who was it? He hastily put his uniform back on with a glance at Rachel who was doing the same.

"That can't be Scott. Who the fuck knows we're here? She huffed and swiftly tied her hair in a loose bun on top of her head.

He scanned the interior of the shuttle for anything that could be used as a weapon, although he wasn't really sure what he was even looking for.

He approached the airlock and stared at the flashing letters on the long panel above the blast door.

"Boarding platform raised"

"Uhmmm...Rach? I never thought I'd use these words in real life but... we've got company."

He felt naked and exposed, only this time he was wearing all his clothes.

"Fuck... fuck! Do you have a gun?"

"No. It wasn't that easy to print anything back in Six. I barely managed to get one for Nyx. Even if I had one, I'm not sure I could use one again."

"Again?" She snapped with widened eyes. "When did you..."

"Now is not the time for that. Maybe we can turn on the systems, see if we can lock the hatch from here?"

"Do you know how to do that?"

"No but how hard could it be?" he said and turned on the main panel at the front.

The interior of the shuttle lit up with monitors and panels as a deep male voice informed him systems were online.

"Why doesn't this ship have any fucking furniture? We need to block this door somehow," Rachel cried and kicked one of the cupboards.

The wide touchscreen in the middle displayed numbers and graphs next to an outline of the ship. There were some buttons but he didn't know what their function was even though they were written in plain English. He tapped on the only one he was familiar with—cameras—and turned around at the beeping sound. The walls of the shuttle had opened windows to the space outside, although the grey material was still there.

He held his breath and shivered as the bridge clanged on the outer wall of the shuttle and sent a series of faint vibrations through the floor. Rachel peeked through the small window of the internal hatch and immediately crouched against it.

"Fuck, fuck, fuck!" Her voice strained as she looked at him in shock. She was clutching her small pistol, hands shaking close to her chest.

"Behind the chairs!" He motioned her to come over to his position.

She hopped and sprinted to him with her back hunched and her head lowered. "Exosuits... four of them," she said as Julian wrapped his arm around her.

"Give me the gun." He extended his open palm in front of her.

"Fuck no!" She protested and kept it away from his reach.

"Rach, you don't know what it feels like..." he tried to keep his voice calm as the unmoving, lifeless eyes of the man he'd killed flashed in his mind, "I can't let you find out. Give me the gun... please?" He peered into her eyes, uncaring if it sounded like begging.

He had to protect her any way he could, from herself as well as the people who were about to breach the shuttle door.

"I hope you can aim as good as me," she handed him the pistol and nodded.

"I can aim just fine. Now go hide inside that cupboard." He pointed at the other end of the shuttle. "And don't let them see you."

"Fuck no! There's no way I'm leaving you alone here."

"There's no..."

"NO! Forget it, whatever happens to you, happens to me."

"Aaargh, you're so stubborn," he growled and with a long inhale he softly caressed her face. "Listen, you already saved my life, and I don't just mean back at the airlock. Let me do the same for you, I will never forgive myself if I don't."

"I'd rather die than live the rest of my life without you. Now give me back my gun."

"I can't do that. I'm not going to let you carry the death of a person on your shoulders. Trust me, it will haunt you forever."

"What would you know about..." she trailed off as her expression froze at his nod.

Had he scared her? Her eyes had widened even more than usual but she didn't move a single muscle on her face, only stayed there scanning him.

"Trust me, I know what I'm doing Rach." He pulled her inside his chest and kissed her hair.

"I hope you're right." She threw her hands around his neck and kissed him.

"Now go! GO!"

She hugged the wall and slid to the end of the shuttle without any further protest. She grunted as she tried to squeeze herself inside one of the cupboards but finally the door closed.

His finger hugged the trigger as the clock ticked silently above the door. His heart was thundering inside his chest like an ARK thruster, three drummings for every tick. Could he really take another life? If it was four of them, he and Rachel could only come out alive if he could kill all of them. He really didn't want to pull the trigger. What a horrible thing to strip someone of his existence.

In and out... in and out.

The door hissed and his pistol recoiled. A blue disk was thrown in the middle of the shuttle, spinning and swirling its light around its core as fast as an electron around its nucleus. It beeped faster and faster while Julian aimed his gun at it. Was it a grenade? No, they wouldn't risk detonating explosives in such a small space, that was crazy. Its beeping reached its climax and a bright flash blinded him.

CHAPTER 26
— Rachel —

RESIDENTIAL QUADRANT LOWER LEVELS – RING 6

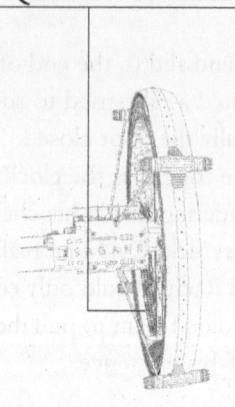

Every breath was shorter and sharper than the previous one while she tried to remain still, curled like a ball. Hugging her knees, she pressed them against her chest. There had only been one shot, followed by silence. Had they killed him and left? She felt cold streams run along her cheeks and tickle her ears as they pooled inside her lobes. She shivered and her chest spasmed, pushing her knees away.

"Clear!" The loud male voice came from inside the shuttle.

"Help me grab him. We need to take him back to TC," another man said.

"Why not just put a bullet in his head?" The third voice belonged to a woman, abrasive and oddly familiar. It had been a few months since she'd last heard her in the theatre but it must've been her. "We detached, who cares now?"

"No, he will want to question him."

He was alive! That was good news at least.

"I don't think he would've done the same with us," the woman replied.

"Just do as you're told, Katey!"

So it *was* her.

The boarding party kept talking but their voices were distorted now.

Rachel rolled out of the cabinet and ran to the airlock where the two men in the rear had balanced Julian between their shoulders, leaving his feet to drag freely along the bridge that connected the shuttle to the Ring. She scanned the room behind her for her gun but they must've taken it. The exosuit was the only alternative—she wasn't taking any chances this time, no more hiding, no more subtlety.

Running inside the ship was a lot easier. Seeing where her next step would land was invaluable apparently as the power armour almost carried her legs with a slight hop at every stride. The helmet was not necessary for breathing but the infrared vision was quite helpful in keeping up with the enemy team even though it was Julian's yellow silhouette she was really following. They had come out on the ground floor of the recreation quadrant and stopped at the intersection concourse.

"You didn't get the other guy?" The guard stepped aside for them to pass.

"No, I heard they escorted him to Ring Five. Apparently there was an extraction team in place."

"Dr Richter is furious. He'll be out for blood for whoever is responsible. I'd wager communication teams." The guard walked alongside them.

"You think someone from the silent teams over there betrayed us?"

Scott had suggested on many occasions there were evolutionists left behind to keep tabs on things but they had never been able to flush anyone out.

The door shut in front of her but she could still see the faint colours surrounding their bodies. She tapped on the screen on her right wrist and swiped her finger until a lightning icon appeared. The electric current arced and linked to the panel and she winced away from the crackling sound and the smoke that vanished as suddenly as it had appeared. The holocircle disappeared and the frames hissed apart but the door was still almost shut. It barely required any effort for her mechanically assisted arms to pry it open but her position was made now, the intersection guard was coming to investigate.

The guard didn't get a chance to utter a word. She punched him right in the face the moment he got in and sent him flying to the other end of the frame.

Dragging his body inside the recreation quadrant, she stripped him of his gun. Now, she had to hurry to the other side of the concourse before they could hide Julian away in the residential blocks.

Bypassing the next door, she hopped inside, her eyes searching for other threats. The enemy team was past her tangent horizon but their heat signatures faintly flickered where the lifts would be.

The only evidence that someone had been at the plaza was the number on the lift that indicated the last floor it had stopped. Where was everyone? Wasn't this their glorious moment after detaching from the rest of the ship? She was expecting celebrations, not the dead silence of a gloomy quadrant.

She didn't give it a second thought, it worked in her favour for now. The lower levels weren't that different from the upper ones, two residential blocks on opposite sides of the quadrant's length and connected with sky bridges at multiple levels. Yet a weird feeling came over her when she climbed down the stairs to find herself at the top floor of the lower residential. The plaza and food kiosks were above her grey ceiling while below her, a twenty storey drop.

She saw the evolutionists coming out of a flat on the opposite blocks, two floors below and she dashed back to the stair core. By the time she made it down there, the lift was going up again, a lonely yellow silhouette left behind. Her infrared switched to visible light and the HUD on her visor zoomed to the person on the other side of the sky bridge.

Ares, Lucas' wingman in mischief. A few years ago they were running laps together and now he was guarding the love of her life in a prison. There was no time to reflect on how times had changed, if she was to free Julian somehow it had to be now. She swiped her finger on the side of her pistol until a music note appeared with a diagonal line crossing over it. Was she going to shoot him? Was there even an alternative?

Jumping out of the balustrade, she was almost relieved to see Ares entering the flat next to the one he was guarding. That was her window.

"What is the little dragon doing so far away from her lair?" The male voice startled her and she turned around, gun in her hands.

"Wow, steady...ok, ok." Lucas raised his arms in the air.

"Tell me, why every fucking time some shit happens, you are always around?"

"Hey, I was only coming to see Ares. I don't know what you're talking about."

"They captured Julian. Your buddy is standing guard."

"And let me guess, you're here to free him. The girl who saved everyone." His cocky sneer was intolerable to look at.

"How about the girl holding a gun?" she flicked the pistol and squeezed it tighter.

"You don't have what it takes to pull the trigger."

"I'm behind enemy lines, alone and running out of options. You really want to take me up on that bet?"

His smug, scornful expression faded. Maybe he did have some brain cells still capable of producing actual thoughts.

"So... where do we go from here? You shoot me, you let me go, what's happening?"

"First, you tell me what *really* happened to Alex. Then take your pal and leave so I can take Julian out of here." She opened her thin, rectangular visor. It was better to keep her voice quiet than relying on the helmet's speakers.

"Pfft, again with Alex. Your stupid brother wouldn't be where he is if he had listened to me."

"What does that mean?"

"Our recruitment branch flagged him as a possible candidate so I started talking to him, yeah? He was miserable, thinking of venting himself so I sat down with him one day after therapy and showed him Icarus. He was excited at first but then he wanted to tell Priya, who wasn't cleared." He paused as he sat at the edge of the balustrade, his eyes darting away from her. His enormous chest heaved and he ran his hands through the shaved sides of his hair, interlocking them behind his neck. "Anyway..." he continued, a strain in his voice she had never heard before. "We're in a clearing and the head of operations tells me some higher up gave the order to take him out."

"Who gave that order?"

"I don't know, but high enough in the chain to scare the guy. So he did what he always does with these kinds of orders, he put Alex to sleep."

"So, you admit it? You knew what was going to happen to him?" Her weapon kept slipping inside her trembling hands but the target was big enough.

"Alex was actually lucky there was a machine ready at Nightfall. Priya on the other hand…" he trailed off, his gaze dropping to the floor.

"*Lucky*?" She enunciated the word so loudly it barely sounded as it should. "That operations lead, what's his name?"

"Oh, no way I'm telling you that. You'll have to shoot me."

"What's his name, Lucas?" The pistol hummed as it powered up, her heart racing from what she was about to do.

"Look, if I tell you they'll kill me anyway so you might as well pull that trigger."

Her chest tightened and her throat closed as she unwillingly applied pressure on the trigger. "Lucas…" She warned him, squeezing her eyes to let go of the tears pooling inside.

The boy shook his head and with a sudden movement reached out to disarm her. The pistol beeped to a climax and the recoil pushed her back.

"Are you crazy?" Lucas cried as he jumped in place, his eyes finally filled with the fear she craved to see in them.

"Next one will be between your eyes," she threatened. Her hand must have moved last second, otherwise there was no way she would've missed.

"These people are my family, alright? I won't turn on them."

"Fuck sake Lucas. These people have been using you since you were born, only keeping you around to monitor their experiment."

His grimace of disbelief had a hint of sarcasm but she eventually sighed and lowered her weapon.

"I don't know how to tell you this, but you're merely a product of eugenics… gene editing before you were even born. Hey, look at that, I did know how to tell you after all."

His arrogant scoff was followed by an infuriating, brief chuckle. "Nah, you're lying… you're lying to get me distracted and run away."

"I'm the one with the gun, remember?" she waved the pistol

in front of her. "And it's not just you, many others had their genes tempered with by your precious little cult."

"It's not a cult, they're..."

"Stop defending them! I saw the logs myself. That Kerzinov of yours, do you know what goes into those nano-injections?"

Lucas furrowed his brows. Maybe she was getting through to him. She took his silence as a sign to stay on the offensive. "Inhibitors for the side effects of the gene edits. The endless hunger, the anger management issues, the..."

"I *am* always angry!"

"Exactly. They created you Lucas. Made you exactly what they wanted you to be, a brute, a soldier... a pawn," she spat the last insult.

Lucas gazed at his feet with no response. Her words must have had an impact on him, however slightly.

"Now, Julian. I need you to get your friend, who by the way is also bio-enhanced, and get the hell out of here."

"Ares is... also an experiment?"

Rachel sighed and nodded. This was taking way longer than the time she had available.

"Why would I even help you? Even if what you're saying is true, it doesn't change anything."

"Because I have a gun pointed at you which I will use on both you and Ares to get to Julian. I'm giving you an option to walk away with a bit of dignity for once."

"You're a ruthless woman, Rachel Watson, proper dragon. Going through all this trouble to get who, Julian?" He pursed his lips in a cringe and shook his shoulders.

"I love him, alright? And he loves me. But what would you even know about love? You were created to carry out attack orders, you wouldn't even understand complex emotions." She rebuked him.

"Even if I *was* created as you say, I'm still me, I can think and feel and..."

"Then prove it. The best option for you here is to take Ares and go." She flicked her gun to the right as a gesture for him to start moving—and surprisingly, he did.

He glanced behind him a few times but Rachel was fast to hold her gun up high.

"No funny business. You get him and leave. I can see you." She tapped on the visor as it came down to seal her helmet, replacing his big burly body with a yellow-red figure.

Lucas knocked on the door a few times until Ares appeared, his hands full with power bars and water canisters. It didn't take him long to convince Ares to leave—all it took apparently was their weird handshake and a promise to return the favour.

"Quite the performance," Rachel said with a slow clap when the lift took Ares to the upper levels. "Only problem is that you're still here."

"I'll help you get Walker out of here."

Rachel laughed sarcastically as she cautiously approached him. "Why would I ever trust you?"

"I got Ares out of here, didn't I?"

"Yeah, that's not even close to being enough."

"Look, despite what you may think, I do wish things were different. If I'd told you all this stuff back when Alex went in Nightfall, maybe we wouldn't be in this situation. Maybe Priya would still be alive."

"Are these words seriously coming out of your mouth? Where is the Lucas I know with all his mocking and condescension?" Her mechanical arms whirred as she crossed them in front of her chest.

"What you should ask yourself is how you plan to get out of here after you get Walker," he remarked as he pressed his palm on the door panel. "Ladies first." He showed her in.

"So you can lock me in as well?" She raised her gun on him.

Lucas rolled his eyes as he went in, turning on the lights with a wave as he got past the kitchen.

"What is this, where is everyone?"

"What did you expect, actual cells? Each prisoner has their own room." He tapped on the door at the end to reveal the bedroom, clad in darkness.

Julian was lying in the bed with his hands hanging from the edge of the mattress and his body splayed.

"Julian!" she called out to him and rushed around the bed to where his head was, flat on the dirty sheet without even a pillow.

She removed her helmet completely and whispered his name again close to his ear. His head jerked and he rubbed his face in the sheet.

"Wake up you little deviant," Lucas sneered.

"Ra-Rachel?" He half opened his eyes and her heart fluttered.

"I'm here, I've got you." She ran her fingers through his face and into his hair.

"What happened? Are we... Are we home?"

"Come on, let me help you up."

He sat upright and scanned the room around him until he saw Lucas standing at the door. "What is he doing here?"

"He is saving your ass." Lucas snapped.

"Seriously?" Julian turned to her with a puzzled look.

"It's a long story. Come on, the sooner we leave here the better."

"Where's my food you imbeciles?" The female voice was distorted behind one of the other bedrooms.

"Nyx?" Julian muttered and ran to the living room, squeezing past Lucas' broad shoulders.

"I guess you want me to free her as well?" Lucas tilted his head with an eye roll.

"Well, duh!"

The woman kept banging on the door until she was finally free, her fist still close to her face, ready for another thump. Her hair was even wilder than Rachel remembered, her eyes swollen and red were barely able to focus on the people in front of her as she leant against the frame.

"I can't believe you're alive. When you stayed behind I thought... I thought I'd lost you." Julian threw himself in her arms and squeezed her tightly.

"After I took down everything they threw at me they resorted to cheap countermeasures, smoke screens and stun disks." Her posture suddenly corrected itself when she realised who had freed her from her confinement and she rushed out shoving Lucas like a battering ram. She wasn't a small woman—even slightly taller and bulkier than Julian—but pushing Lucas like that required a lot of strength. "Why is Bjorgen here?"

"He's helping us," Rachel answered first.

Nyx glanced at Julian's uncomfortable nod and turned back to Rachel. "How can you trust this guy?"

"I don't really but he did free you both so he's on my good side... for now."

Nyx eyed both her and Lucas from top to bottom and focused on the gun at her hip. "Nice gun you've got there. May I see it?"

Rachel hesitated at first but this was Nyx Sincroft. The guys back at HQ had always said the best about her.

"Kinetic!" Nyx pressed the button on the side to expose the clip, "You've used it already?" She asked and Julian jerked his head to look at her, his eyes wide and disappointed.

"A warning shot... thankfully for Lucas, he listened to reason for once in his life."

"Smart boy." She brought it close and took a whiff of the barrel.

Rachel couldn't stop the snorting chuckle in time. It came like a reflex to the sight of the grown woman sniffing the weapon.

"Thanks," Nyx said as she shut the clip back in its socket with a loud click.

"No, no, no, you're not taking my gun." Her laughter quickly turned into a growl.

"Rach, trust me, she knows what she's doing."

"Doesn't matter. I gave you my gun once and look what happened."

"How many people have you killed, girl?"

"I'm really close to my first right now." She snapped at her with the disarming move Richard had shown her but Nyx was quicker, more experienced.

"Nice try but I'm keeping it."

Rachel bared her teeth with a shrill yelp and punched the stud wall, tearing a hole and leaving debris to gush out like a waterfall. "I'm sick and tired of everyone treating me like a little girl."

"You're in an exosuit, why do you need the pistol?" Nyx insisted, unfazed by her outburst.

Rachel gritted her teeth and her jaw tightened. She wanted to scream but only took a deep breath from her nose, shakily letting it out slowly from her half opened lips as Richard had taught her for moments like this.

"Look what you did to the wall," Nyx continued, "You're *wearing* a weapon!"

Rachel extended her arms in front of her and stared at the modular, metal plates that enveloped her knuckles under the fabric of the uniform's gloves. No scratch, no pain from the impact. The memory of sending the guard flying flooded her mind. She hadn't checked if he was okay, she didn't have time. In fact she couldn't even remember his face, only the pistol that she hastily stole from his floppy body. If that was the damage she could deliver to solid wall, then it was quite possible human bones wouldn't fare better. She took another long breath and cursed Richard for only teaching her how smart this thing was. She knew how to bypass systems, switch between different visual wavelengths, smoke and flight systems, first aid... all defensive and protective.

"Let's get out of here," she muttered under her breath.

"How?" Julian asked, turning to Nyx. "They've already detached the Ring."

"Yes, how?" Nyx repeated, raising the pistol to point it at Lucas. His eyes widened and he raised his hands in the air in reflex. "You know I'll do it," Nyx continued sidestepping to come between Lucas and Julian. "Kids, get out! You don't want to be here for what follows."

"Steady, woman. I've helped you out so far, haven't I?" Lucas defended himself.

"Then talk!" Nyx ordered.

"I don't know, shuttles? No, too far away. Maintenance tunnels under the outer bridge... no, they're not connected anymore. Only real option is to jump the distance now while the Ring is still close."

"We're not jumping anywhere!" Julian protested. "Why do we need to go back anyway? We need to stay here and stop the realignment."

"Julian, we can't on our own." Rachel shook her head.

"You know I'm always up for a fight, kid" Nyx only tilted her head, maintaining her unbroken gaze to her interrogation subject. "But we're three here and they're three thousand. The longer we stay, the more chances we'll get caught again."

Julian drew a heavy breath. Rachel was sure he knew it was the right choice, it was the jump that scared him and despite how much she wanted to caress his beautifully chiselled cheekbones and tell him everything would be okay, their time was running out. "How long before you fire up the engines again?" She turned to Lucas.

"What am I a scientist?" Lucas scoffed and dry coughed when Nyx's pistol hummed. "I don't know, alright? A few hours, maybe a day?"

"Not good enough, Luke." Rachel clicked her tongue, taking a step in front of Nyx.

"Look, all I know is that the sleeper agents are coming back tomorrow at 1700, so probably after that."

"Which shuttle?" She pressed on.

"I really don't know."

Nyx's grip tightened around the pistol but Rachel raised a hand in front of its trajectory. "Then I want the names of these agents."

"No, I've said enough already."

"Lucas... Do we really have to do this dance again? Apparently I don't need a weapon this time." She cocked her head, smashing her fist in her palm and caught Nyx's smirky grimace with the corner of her eye.

"I don't even know all of them. Some are very high ranking." Lucas took a step back against the wall.

"Julian, give him your roller." She beckoned him to come forward. The exosuit was delicate but not flexible enough to grab her own inside the uniform.

"Don't break this one too, please," Julian said, extending his arm at full length to hand Lucas the device.

Lucas scoffed but took it in his hands, tapping hesitantly at the portraits of people. "There." He tossed the roller to Julian like a disk and fixed his widened eyes back at Rachel. "I never gave you this information."

"I never even saw you." She nodded.

"Let's go then." Nyx lowered her pistol and nudged Julian towards the door.

"Wait!" Lucas pleaded. "One last thing... you need to punch me."

"Gladly, but why?" Rachel smiled.

"When they find out you've escaped they'll ask questions. Better to say I couldn't beat an exo-suit."

"What if I kill you?"

"You said it yourself, I'm bio-enhanced. I can take it."

"Alright then." She didn't need much persuasion, it was a dream come true; punch Lucas right in his arrogant face.

"Oh and one last piece of advice… run a drug check on Alex."

"A drug check? Why would Alex…"

"Just do it woman! Now punch me."

The metal plates covering her knuckles clanged as she rubbed them together in preparation for the hit. All her combat training with Richard would finally prove useful. She lowered her right shoulder and dug her back foot in the ground as the mechanism whirred and she delivered two fast hits, one on his chest and one on his face, forcing him on the floor with a loud groan.

"Very… good, little dragon," Lucas muttered, sucking his teeth before rolling on his back and resting his body on the floor.

CHAPTER 27
— JULIAN —
RESIDENTIAL QUADRANT - RING 4

Julian stood at the edge of the platform outside the observatory module, the vast expanse of space stretching out before him, an endless sea of darkness dotted with the distant flickers of stars. His palms grew clammy inside his gloves as he peered at the enormity of the *Sagan* pulling away. How could he propel himself through such emptiness? The thought of being untethered, drifting freely in space sent shivers down his spine. The trajectory of the jump was highlighted in a dotted, yellow line through his visor but pointing at nothing. He had to jump towards it and hope he'd land on the outer bridge after the Ring's revolution.

In... and out... in and out.

"I'll be with you the whole way," Rachel's soft voice rang inside his head as she touched his hand, their fingers interlocking through the metal plates of their exo-suits.

"I know you've got this, kid," Nyx encouraged him while Julian clenched his jaw and tightened his fists.

He would give anything to be able to bite his nails, all of them one by one. He imagined doing it as he chewed on his lips instead.

"T-minus twenty seconds," Nyx announced. "There are people counting on us, let's not keep them waiting."

Nyx was right. He couldn't let fear dictate his actions, not when lives depended on that leap of faith. He touched his chest over the metal armour, feeling sick again.

T-minus ten seconds, he glanced at the notification from his visor as he bent his knees in preparation.

"Three... two... one... JUMP!" Nyx ordered.

He pushed off with all his might, his body hurtling through the vacuum of space with his eyes half opened, suit thrusters engaged and vibrating his back.

"Nyx?" He cried when he saw her slowly passing him, the yellow trail of her thruster making her look like a slow moving photon.

"You're doing fine, kid. I'll prepare for the landing."

"I'm still here with you," Rachel said. Her voice was calm and soft; surprisingly helpful in making the anxiety that clawed his mind manageable.

The outer bridges of Ring Five rotated in front of him, the yellow flightpath on his visor shifting and recalculating constantly.

It was actually quite cool how inertia and the laws of physics worked, so many forces at play in that moment and all of them predictable to the last millisecond.

His visor beeped as the flightpath flashed with the proximity warning.

"Hold on tight!" Nyx said, grabbing the rail of the bridge. "Engage magboots!" She was so graceful in her movements, she must have done things like this a thousand times.

Julian crashed on the platform and hurriedly reached for the protruding rails before bouncing away from their safety. Finally on solid ground. The jump had taken one minute and twelve seconds but it had felt like eternity. He got on his feet and turned around, staring back at Ring Six shrinking in the distance. His dad was still there, alone.

"He's going to be fine," Rachel said as if she had read his mind. "He's Scott Walker after all. He can do anything, just like you." She smiled and bumped her visor on his.

Yes, his dad could take care of himself but the fact did nothing to alleviate the guilt in his chest.

"Well done, both of you. Now let's keep going." Nyx opened the hatch and one by one they entered Ring Five, one step closer to home.

"For your safety and security, all citizens are advised to stay in the designated safe zones until further notice. Rationing of power and supplies is in effect. Please remain calm as we're doing everything in our power to resolve the situation...

For your safety and security..."

The synthesized voice repeated the message in a loop as they entered the residential quadrant of Ring Four. The once peaceful and quiet neighbourhood he remembered had transformed into a surreal scene of chaos and despair. His legs froze and a pulse radiated from his chest all over his body. He had noticed the limited lighting on his way there but didn't think twice about it; it was expected after all as the ship was basically running on fumes. There were no lights at all in this part of the ship, only the blue emergency sirens flickered like enraged quasars, casting their eerie shadows on the nightmarish tableau of insanity that had greeted him home. The air reverberated with anguished cries and overlapping voices that blended together in a cacophony of fear and frustration.

"Let's keep moving," Nyx said but belayed her own order, her gaze fixated on the sight in front of them, her dark eyes shimmering with the bright blue reflection of the crazed lights.

His head snapped to the beam of light that appeared out of nowhere beside him. Rachel had put her helmet back on, her face hidden behind the intense illumination of the suit's guide lights.

Julian wished she had never turned them on. Maybe in the darkness he wouldn't have noticed the motionless bodies scattered around the ground floor, or the streams of blood glistening in the light like rivers of jewels. He winced at the macabre sight of disfigured bodies and crashed bones as the knot in his stomach tightened and he felt sick again. He covered his mouth with his hand and looked up at the sky bridges. Had they committed suicide or pushed over the ledges?

Nyx nudged him forward. Luckily the exo-suit did most of the work to get his legs moving as they were almost numb, trembling inside the little wiggle room that the armour's encasement allowed. They walked through the middle strip, the grass flattened on either side by the stampede of people running past them in all directions, their faces etched with fear and panic.

"It's a lot worse than last time," Rachel remarked.

"Last time we were still one ship. How can we even help them?" Julian asked, his mind on overdrive for a possible solution.

"We can't..." Nyx replied straight away. "Not right now. Only thing we can do is focus on our mission."

Julian drew a deep breath but his lungs cried for more air. There was no end to the madness, even the plaza was decimated as people had broken in the kiosks, hurriedly grabbing as many supplies as they could carry. The primal survival instinct had taken over as the boundaries of morality and civility seemed dissolved, replaced by a ruthless scramble for resources.

They headed for the lifts and up to his old flat. It was weird Rachel had access to it and he didn't.

"Little Miss!" The blonde man he'd seen gesturing from outside the ship during their first attempt to escape Ring Six exclaimed and ran to Rachel, pulling her in his embrace before she even had a chance to get out of her exo-suit. "I'm so glad you're ok."

"I'm here too, you useless engineer," Nyx offered a fist bump, a greeting she and Andre were using frequently during their time at Ring Six.

His old apartment looked like a base of operations—not a home anymore and crowded with strangers. He scanned their faces just as Nyx voiced what he was thinking. "I see you got yourself a small army here," she said before raiding the fridge for food.

"Mark!" He exclaimed when he saw him, running and throwing his arms around his taller friend.

"Ouch, easy," Mark groaned but returned the embrace, "I missed you too, buddy." He said after the hug had lasted for more than what was probably necessary.

"I like the new look," Julian commented on his shorter hair, now barely reaching his shoulders.

For a brief moment everything was back to normal, he was in his old flat with Mark and Rachel, pondering if he should suggest a quick round of Dragon Quest. Unfortunately it was out of the question with Ring Six pulling further and further away from them by the minute.

"Come on, we need to talk to Javier," Rachel interjected and nudged him towards the man in the blue suit.

Julian had only seen him in that therapy session and while treating Mark's wounds after saving him from Katey. Rachel on the other hand seemed comfortable around him, he was the person taking care of her brother after all.

"You want to do this *now*?" Javier asked when Rachel requested the drug test Lucas had recommended—he might have been a pain in the ass all his life but his suggestion was not so far-fetched. It had been three months already, at least one of them should have shown some improvement.

"Yes, while we were in Six, we found out that leftover evolutionists might be keeping them in a coma on purpose," Rachel answered sternly. There was no denying her when she had that look on her face—brows pushed together and wide eyes waiting, full of conviction.

"No one has messed with the stuff I'm giving them, just life support, no hard substances," Javier countered.

"We won't know for sure until you run the tests," Rachel was fast with the reply. "No stone unturned."

Javier reluctantly gave in to Rachel's insistence raising his hands in the air with a shrug. Rachel even urged him to leave for the infirmary right away and he did, exchanging a few silent words with Richard first.

They got out of the exosuits and Julian patted himself down, unable to get his shirt unstuck from his chest under the space uniform. He'd give anything for a shower and fresh clothes. Rachel didn't seem to mind, she was already at the dining table, talking to a young group of people.

They were around Julian's age but their faces were completely new to him apart from Kaiden Correy. Two of the others were in space uniforms, their names taped on the top left of their chests—Lee and Christoff. He was about to go look for Nyx, who had disappeared in the surprising gathering at his old home, when he saw a face he'd never expected to see there.

Liam never saw the hug coming and groaned from Julian's force. "Hey, welcome back." He smiled.

"Thanks, I'd like to say it's good to be back but...."

"The ship's haemorrhaging power and we're hours away from imminent death?"

"Yeah... that," Julian chuckled nervously. He was miserable the last three months in Ring Six but it couldn't compare to the chaos and death that had befallen the rest of the *Sagan* on his return. He shook his head, twitching the corner of his mouth.

"Was *he* there?" Liam asked with a raised eyebrow.

"Yeah but we avoided each other every time I saw him. He actually saved me from a beating on my first day." It felt like years ago when James had escorted him to the Cylidome. If he hadn't, Julian would've probably never met Nyx and Andre there. Maybe he'd still be stuck in Six, waiting for the inevitable start of the engines to signal the point of no return. "What are you doing here?" He finally asked after shaking the last thought away.

"Rachel didn't tell you, huh? I guess I'm not priority news... but yeah, I am part of your dad's group, I've been training with Richard and her all this time."

"When did that happen?"

"I don't know, few months ago? When word got out that this cult had taken over Ring Six, people panicked. Some even wanted to willingly join them on the other side."

"Really? If only they knew the whole truth."

"The council made a public statement about this but it only made things worse. It divided everyone."

"Hopefully we can put an end to this madness soon," He replied as Nyx's shouting drowned the last part of his optimistic sentence.

"Shut up! No! We're doing this!" Nyx came out of the study with red cheeks and an unforgiving scowl. Her hair was so wild, flailing up in the air that Julian tapped his foot on the floor to make sure there was still gravity.

"Ok people, listen up!" Her commanding voice brought a satisfying end to overlapping chatters. "We've only got one chance at this and we need to execute it perfectly. All captures at the same time. We can't risk having them alert each other."

"Remember!" Andre paused for a second, sparing a glance at his colleague, "Subdue only. Nothing lethal."

"I'm sending out your personal targets," Nyx continued with an eye roll, "Once you've stunned them, call in the medi-bot. Andre has programmed them to bring them back here instead of the infirmary when they identify them. Everybody clear?"

The synchronous beeping of rollers sparked another round of indistinct chatter.

Nyx approached Julian and brought a roller in front him while wrapping her arm around his shoulders.

"How about this guy here, Kevin Zhao?" The picture of the man filled the screen. His hair was white, bleached most likely and his eyes small and narrow. "He's at the Knowledge Hub here on Ring Four."

Julian nodded, hiding his lips inside his mouth.

"I know you're not a fan of violence but this is us or them. It's survival Julian." She pivoted in front of him, putting her hands on both his shoulders and looked deep into his eyes. "Containing these people and invading Ring Six is our last chance. It has to be this way."

"I've got it."

"I know you do, kid." She tapped him at the back and finally replaced that frown with a smile.

"Seems like we're in different parts of the ship." Rachel leant over his chest for a glimpse of his roller. "Be careful, ok?" She warmed his cheek with her palm.

"You too." Julian grazed her loose hair behind her ear and leant in to kiss her.

A dry cough ruined their moment. Richard had crossed his arms in front of them. "I don't mean to interrupt whatever this is but we're kind of on the clock here."

Rachel hid her lips inside her mouth and took a step back, her cheeks flushed with a rosy red colour.

"Be careful out there, little Miss. Nyx has given you a nasty target. Remember what I taught you," Richard said, taking her into his embrace.

Rachel rested her head in his chest, her eyes closed and her small arms joined around the man's back. "I can take care of myself, Richard."

"I know you can." He kissed her on the forehead and disappeared at the back of the living room.

The Hub hadn't changed much since his isolation at Ring Six. His boots squeaked on the polished acrylic tiles, the air felt light and crisp and the curved lights on the ceiling continued the same static dance he remembered them performing along the elliptical glass pods. There were barely any people, a surprising contrast to its past vibrancy. He wasn't going to book a VRA but he approached the circular counter in the middle anyway, running his fingers along its polished, white plastic.

This plan didn't feel right. Surely there was another way to resolve all this. *It's us or them, it's survival*, he recalled Nyx's words as his grip on the pistol tightened inside its holster, firm but trembling. The black eyes of the man whose life he had taken away flashed before his eyes, the horrible deed weighing him down as if the gravity had increased. This time was different, this time he was on the offensive. Kevin Zhao was defenceless, completely still in one of the virtual armchairs.

Julian hesitantly approached, slowly revealing his taser and his target flinched as if he knew what was coming.

How long had it been since he was last here? It seemed such a long time ago, when life was simpler and his only worry was which of the millions of beaches he would visit. No matter how complicated his reality was now, it was surely better than any virtual place on a forgotten planet. Rachel was his girlfriend. He was going to spend the rest of his life with her and it didn't matter if it was on some seaside on Earth or an underwater habitat on Aquanis or even the *Sagan*. It felt odd and at the same time relieving that he didn't care anymore, as long as he was with her. But first he would have to make sure the ship survived and the first step towards that goal was to point the gun to the man with the bleached hair in front of him.

Julian pulled the trigger and Kevin Zhao barely grunted as his muscles spasmed and his hands fell on the sides of the armchair. He tapped on his roller for medical assistance and soon enough a medi-bot was there, hovering a few inches above the ground. It unfolded a modular, expanding panel from its insides, waiting for the body to be placed on its long, flat bed.

"Patient is Matthew Yang, born male, age twenty-eight. Assessing injury."

"Wait, what did you say his name was?" Julian leant against the bed so much the bot's frame scraped the floor.

"Patient is unconscious. Proceeding to the nearest infirmary."

"No, not the infirmary you stupid robot!" He tried to push the hovering bed but it barely budged.

He looked around in panic but no one was even there to notice his immoral act. His heart started racing again as the bed floated away.

The medi-bot kept moving forward, leaving the Hub and continuing through the empty hallways until it entered the internal lift. Julian called Nyx and then Rachel but neither of them picked up. He tried a message instead, staring at the unconscious body on the moving bed.

"I must've hit the wrong person. Medi-bot is taking him to the infirmary."

Holding his roller with the picture of Kevin Zhao in front of him, he studied the features of the mysterious person. Unless he had a twin brother, that was definitely the right guy. But then again, the bot had mentioned a different surname. He followed it to the quadrant intersection and into the science district all the while glancing at the curious looks of passers-by. The bot didn't make it any easier, screaming at everyone that this was a medical emergency while prompting them to get out of its way. His forehead and neck felt hot. His t-shirt was stuck on his chest and his back tickled him as the beads of sweat trickled down his spine.

"Is he ok?" A young woman with thin, circular glasses approached him while opening her white lab coat to reveal a stethoscope. "Let me take a look."

"It's nothing, he... h-he just fainted," he blurted, moving between the bed and the woman to block her vision.

"I can't just let a patient like that go." Her persistence annoyed him. He had only tased him.

She tapped on the front of the bed and put it at a halt.

I wish I knew about that function earlier. A blue screen appeared above the man's head, displaying numbers and graphs that seemed to catch the doctor's interest. Julian looked around him at the people that had now stopped to observe the scene. He tried to hide his face but they had now formed an irregular circle around him.

"He's not breathing!" She tapped a few times on the screen and the bed started accelerating as fast as a drone.

The siren blared deep inside his ear drums and made him flinch but he followed the Doppler effect to its destination through the double glass doors of the infirmary. Had he killed another person, possibly an innocent one this time? His chest pumped and decompressed to the same rapid rhythm of the siren.

Once inside the emergency room, the woman attached some cabled stickers to the ribs and chest of the unconscious man and turned to the monitor next to her. Julian stood at a distance and nibbled on his thumbnail. The monitor beeped and the man arched his spine with a long gasp. He was alive, Julian could finally breathe as well. The doctor helped him to sit up and pointed a light at his eyes. The difficult part was over but now the questions would begin. He switched hands and bit his other thumbnail.

"Where... huh?" Matthew Yang could barely get the words out through his rapid, shallow breathing. "I...I-I can't... b-breathe!"

"Quick, find the cupboard that says benzodiazepines!" she ordered him.

"Benzo-what?"

"Benzo-dia-ze-pines!" she yelled.

Julian rushed to the end of the room and studied the little screens on each of the cupboards until he found the long, difficult word he was looking for.

"It's all empty!"

"How can it be empty? Are you sure it's the right one?" the doctor cried from beside the bed, frantically pulling cables and tapping on different devices.

"Yeah, benzo-diazepines. There's nothing here." Julian leant inside the shelves to make sure his eyes weren't deceiving him.

The door that connected the emergency room to the rest of the infirmary busted open and Javier marched in, glass of water in one hand and two white pills on the other.

"I've got it from here, Anna. You're off the clock anyway."

"He's having a..."

"It's ok, I've got it. Here, take this." He offered the pills and water to Matthew Yang.

The woman stayed for a few seconds and stood up when Matthew's breathing returned to normal. "Right," she sighed, "I am going to go then, leaving you in the capable hands of Dr Rendall."

"Go get some rest, An. You deserve it," Javier said with a smile.

"What's the point? They left us behind to die." She took off her circular glasses and folded them inside the pocket of her lab coat. "Oh, do you know you're out of benzodiazepines?" She remarked before the door.

"What are benzodines for?" Julian asked, certain he was pronouncing it wrong while he checked the other drawers for the elusive meds.

"They can treat a range of conditions from anxiety and panic attacks to induced comas for intracranial swelling and chronic seizures; the list goes on. We mainly use them as sedatives though."

The doctor left and Julian turned back to the medical station where Javier had leant in and was examining Matthew's ear up close. Was someone using these drugs to keep Alex and the others in a coma? The doctor had said it herself, induced coma, and all of them were gone.

"Hey Javier, did you have a chance to run those drug tests? Any benzo-diaze-pines?" He asked, hoping for some answers.

"As I expected, nothing out of the ordinary."

"Any chance they could be untraceable? All these drugs are gone, I can't find a single canister that's not completely empty."

"People eat these pills like candy, especially these last few months." Javier threw a dismissive hand while staring at the monitor beside the bed. "Don't forget we live in a place where the number one health issue is depression."

Julian licked his lips and pondered on that thought for a moment. "Still... how can there be none left?"

"Because this is not Earth. It takes time to manufacture something and the resources are very limited."

Julian paused again to reassemble his thoughts. There was some validity in Javier's argument but it seemed too fast, too easy an answer. If there was one thing science had taught him all these years was to only trust the evidence.

"Can I see the results as well?"

"You don't trust me?" Javier pulled back, his brows curled and his eyes narrowed—offended.

"No, I'm just curious about their vitals," he lied. Something was amiss. "No muscle atrophy, no weight loss, no brain damage..." Julian stopped his waffling when he caught Javier studying him. "I like science, what can I do?" He blurted.

"You're so much like your father," Javier said with a brief smile before placing another pillow behind Matthew's head. "This way... after you." He opened the door and beckoned him to go through.

Julian went first into the empty hallway until Javier passed in front of him and opened the door to a small room filled with monitors and storage spaces.

"It's that terminal in the middle." Javier pointed at the back of the room to the long, curved screen. "Can you even understand this stuff?"

"Some of it... probably." He shrugged. The truth was none of it but he had to at least try.

There were no patient names. Shouldn't there have been a list with the blood work of each individual? He tapped on the keyboard for the search function and typed Alex's full name. The screen went dark as it loaded the information and that's when he saw the reflection that made his heart stop and the hairs of his body rise like sunflowers yearning for the morning sun.

Javier was holding a syringe above his shoulders, the pointy end facing down towards Julian's back. He slid and turned, trying to block the injection from puncturing his body. The syringe flew from Javier's hands and landed on a shelf, droplets of yellow liquid flowing on its plastic, smooth surface.

"What the fuck are you..." Julian didn't have time to finish his sentence as he got shoved to the wall of monitors.

The glass behind him shattered and the pain transferred from his back all over his body. Javier made a move for the syringe. Julian groaned and gritted his teeth but managed to get there in time, pushing Javier with all his momentum until they both fell on the ground. What was happening? No, there was no time to think, not when he had to dodge punches.

Javier pulled him from his shirt and rolled him over to the side. This time the fist met his face and pushed it further into the floor. Julian kneed him in the stomach just before Javier could lock his legs and crawled away. He glanced at the shelf, where the syringe was supposed to be. It had dropped on the floor, its contents swooshing inside the casing. He caught Javier charging towards him with the corner of his eye but was too late to defend. His relentless enemy crushed on his ribs, head first and spun him around, throwing him to the other side of the room. Julian crossed his arms around his chest and groaned loudly. His eyes closed on their own but he blinked back to reality.

He hurried back on his feet and put some distance between Javier and the syringe. He patted himself down and took his taser out but Javier charged again, forcing a tight grapple around Julian's waist. The weapon swirled to the other side of the room and disappeared under the bottom shelves. Julian banged on his attacker's head with both hands, joined together like a hammer. His wrists started hurting from the impacts on Javier's bones but he'd rather break his hands than surrender to this maniac. He felt the grasp around his waist weakening and finally pushed him away, but not before Javier could trip him on the ground again. They both stood up at the same time panting like some crazed animals, the only difference between them, the syringe in Javier's hand. The fight was reset but he still had some strength left.

"I'm sorry, Julian, this wasn't how I wanted this to go down," Javier said, empty words that didn't justify his actions.

The door slammed open behind him and Richard came to a sudden halt. Rachel was behind him, outside the threshold but Julian didn't dare take his eyes away from Javier's hand again.

"What is going on here? Julian, what is this?" Richard demanded.

"This guy lured me in here to stab me with who-knows-what poison is in there."

Javier's eyes jumped between Julian and his new allies but he said nothing. He only kept stealing glances at the door behind them.

"Javier, explain yourself!" Richard raised his voice.

"I know this seems bad but trust me, I'm trying to do the right thing here."

"You were trying to jab me with that thing, you lunatic!" Julian exclaimed, pointing at the syringe. "He's the one who put them all in comas," he cried as the final piece of the puzzle brought up all the previous clues and memories in his head, coalescing them to the man in front of him.

"No, no, no, there's no way. He's on *our* team." Richard sounded as shocked as Julian.

"I *am* on your team," Javier insisted, his body swaying to the rhythms of adrenaline. If I hadn't put these kids to sleep, they'd be dead now. All of them!"

"The operations lead…" Rachel slowly walked in, "You're the one who created Nightfall." Her voice was threatening. Her eyes had narrowed and her lips slightly parted, revealing her gritted teeth.

"Listen to me, I saved these kids! The others wanted to kill them, labelling them as liabilities. If I hadn't done what I did, your brother would be somewhere in the empty space behind us like many others already. At least now he is still alive. I saved him!"

"You-y-y-you SAVED HIM?" her mouth stretched wide as she yelled the question. Her eyes almost bulged out, the previously beautiful tapestry of green and yellow now replaced by two dilated circles of blackness. Her breathing was loud and shaky, her chest expanding to accommodate her deep inhales. She reached for the holster under her belt and raised the gun with trembling hands.

"Wha-what are you doing there, little Miss?" Richard extended his hands but didn't get closer to her.

"What I waited a long time to do."

"Rach, that's kinetic." Julian turned to her, making sure Javier was still in his peripheral vision.

"I'm fully aware of that, Julian," she said as the pistol powered up progressively.

"You can't do that, little Miss. Don't pull that trigger."

"I don't care!" She yelled. "That fucking piece of shit deserves it!"

"Javier, put the syringe down please," Richard ordered and Javier obeyed. "There, you wouldn't kill a defenceless man, would you?"

"Rach, please don't do this," Julian implored.

"He took Alex from me... and he was about to take... to take you too." Her voice broke and she wiped her tears with her upper arms, not losing sight of her target.

"Rach, listen to me." He cautiously placed one foot in front of the other. "It's over. We got him. We'll take Alex off the drugs and he'll be back to normal. And as for me, I'm still right here."

"He doesn't deserve to live!" She squeezed her eyes shut for the tears to escape the flooded pools on her eyelids.

"Rach, killing someone changes something deep within you. You don't want to be that person." He took one more step closer with his open arm extended. "Trust me, I wish I could take mine back. Give me the gun and I'll give you my taser. You can electrocute him all you want."

She didn't reply, only stared at the man responsible for her misery. Her hands were shaking but her grip on the pistol was firm.

A shadowy figure breached the light of the room so fast Julian barely got a glimpse of him. He only heard Richard's thundering cry as the reflective blade slashed the side of his neck and he fell on his knees, the knife dropping with him to bounce on the floor with a resounding clang.

Rachel didn't have time to turn to his cry, the man tackled her to the floor but not before her pistol fired. Julian looked around him trying to understand what had just happened and how he was the only one still standing. He lunged, shoving the man away from Rachel as he spared a brief glance at Richard who had curled into a ball on the ground, blood squirting from his neck to stain the white panels with rivers of crimson red.

He turned to the enemy—Matthew Yang—landing a solid kick to the man's stomach, once, twice, thrice while Rachel rushed to Richard's side. He couldn't stop kicking. Even as he felt Matthew's ribs snap, something had taken over him, had him pressing the heel of his boot down on the man's face. He heard another crack but kept on with the assault until his opponent's body stopped moving and his hands fell limp next to him. He revolved around himself, his vision blurred and he started feeling his arms and legs again as if he had lost control of their movements for a minute.

So much blood.

Javier was down on all fours groaning but still alive. He coughed repeatedly and tried to cover his mouth. The red droplets escaped through his fingers and joined the existing blood lake in front of him with a ripple. He was no longer a threat.

Julian sat on his knees beside Rachel. She had her hands pressed on top of each other, pushing down on Richard's neck with stretched arms.

"You're fine, everything's going to be fine," she reassured him, the trembling in her voice betraying her shocked state.

Julian stared at the scalpel on the floor, a red thick slime covering its sharp edge and glanced behind him. The only doctor who could have helped was fighting for his own life. He peered at the shelves and grabbed a bandage case above him. He didn't know what to do but he had to do something.

"Little Miss..." Richard wheezed.

"Don't strain your voice. We're going to fix you up, right Julian?"

"Uhuh." Julian nodded, his mind blank, unable to find words.

"Listen to me." Richard gasped for air. "I know I've been hard on you sometimes..."

"Yeah you've been a pain in the ass." She smiled through her sniffing and grabbed the end of the bandage.

Richard tried to laugh but he coughed instead, gurgling on the blood that had already filled his mouth. "I only ever wanted to make you stronger than you already are. A brave, courageous woman. I-I'm so proud of who you've become in the past months." He smiled and grazed her face with his trembling fingers, painting her cheeks with streaks of red. "You... are... you're the daughter I always wished I had."

His arm dropped beside him and his head tilted, his empty eyes gazing into nothing.

"Richard? Richard? Don't do this to me, you old fool." She grabbed him by his orange uniform and shook him repeatedly, hitting him with both hands on the chest—the force of actual punches. She let out a shriek and dug her head under his neck. Her face was covered in blood, dripping from her hair but apparently she didn't care. She sobbed, although it sounded more like screaming than crying. Her whole body trembled, her once vibrant posture shattered as she curled in Richard's chest.

Julian felt the lump in his throat growing heavier, unable to swallow what little saliva was left in his dry mouth. He wanted to hold her, offer some form of comfort but he knew no words or gestures could mend the depth of her sorrow.

"I-I... I only wanted..." Javier started with a cough.

"You shut the fuck up!" Julian turned to him and kicked him in the face, sending him into the pool of his own blood on the floor.

He grabbed his pistol from where it had rolled under the storage unit and pulled the trigger twice, one for Javier, one for Matthew.

CHAPTER 28
— Rachel —
Flat 14D - Ring 4

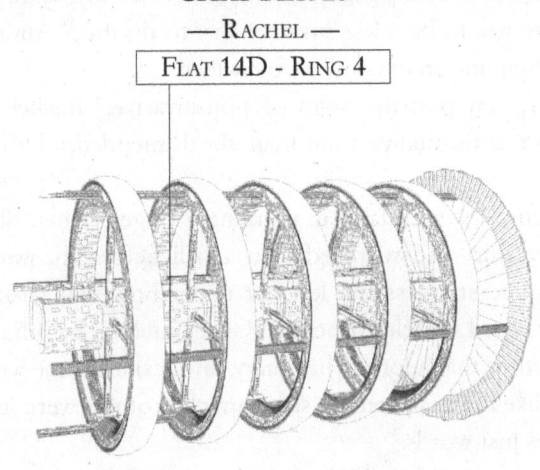

"Nyx, that's enough!" Andre's loud voice made Rachel avert her eyes from staring at the empty wall. She hadn't slept all night but her eyes were still open somehow, tired and heavy from all the tears that had dried on her face.

Nyx had been torturing the captives for a couple of hours now. No one had agreed in the beginning but as the point of no return was only hours away, many of them had finally sided with her. Not that it made any difference, she had started the interrogations straight after Richard's death. Rachel had wanted to get in there with her but Andre hadn't let her. She wanted them to suffer, make them feel the same pain they had inflicted upon her. Especially Mathew Yang—she was barely holding herself from latching forward and twisting his helpless little neck as he sat there, his back against the wall, silent.

Nyx came out of the main bedroom slamming the door behind her and pulling the curls from her hair that had almost turned into coils. She gestured to Andre to follow her into the study and Rachel finally stood up from her chair to join them.

"Did you confirm Lucas' data?" She asked, her fist still clenched and her breaths short and shallow.

"This one had the right time but different shuttle number." Nyx tossed the flat piece of silicon on Scott's table that was now stained with streaks of blood, pooling in the grooves of the wood.

"There has to be a less invasive way to do this," Andre protested while maintaining an uncomfortable wince.

"We're way past the point of non-invasive," Rachel replied in a much more authoritative tone than she'd intended. She barely knew Andre.

"Exactly," Nyx exclaimed, pointing a finger at her. She removed her sweaty shirt and wrinkled it in a ball before throwing it at the armchair. The strapless bra left her upper body half naked and her incredibly toned muscles exposed. Rachel couldn't help but notice the various tattoos that adorned her shiny, tawny skin. Some were cool and colourful like the snake on her sternum while others were simple and in some cases just words.

"We have a problem," Julian announced and everyone turned to the doorless frame where he and Mark had appeared.

Nyx didn't seem bothered by their presence as she calmly took her time putting on her new shirt.

"What is it this time?" Andre was the first one to ask after an exasperated inhale.

"We were going through Richard's algorithms…" Julian walked in and lowered his voice while glancing behind him.

Rachel didn't give him a chance to continue as she snuck in his chest for a quick hug. She needed it, she needed him after Richard's death and couldn't care if the others would think less of her for expressing her feelings in the middle of another bad news revelation. Julian had been doing important work with Mark all the time Nyx was interrogating the sleeper agents but that didn't mean she had to abstain from the closeness and comfort his embrace offered. She felt vulnerable as the first tears ran down her cheeks and she stifled the whimper, wiping her face on Julian's shirt before turning around to face Nyx and Andre.

"I loved Richard too, kid." Nyx placed a hand on her shoulder. Referring to him in the past tense twisted the knife that was already lodged in her chest since his death. "I've known him for as long as I know myself…" she paused as her mouth twitched to the side with a difficult breath. "I know it's hard to hear but we'll have to mourn him later. If we let it consume us, there will be no one to mourn *us*."

"It's not what Richard would've wanted," Andre added.

Julian was biting his nails again, probably uncomfortable with her outburst but he remained silent, his eyes darting around the room. Was she overthinking this? Everyone was agitated, maybe it was a response to the news he was about to share.

"Yeah, I'm sorry," she said softly and cleared her throat from the tight invisible grip."

"Nothing to be sorry about, Rach." Julian squeezed her in one last time and took out his roller. "Richard was a great man... and he's going to help us even now. He was tracking Ring Six since it detached, which is now 430,000 miles away."

"That's a lot, right?" Rachel blurted before realising how stupid that made her sound. In her defence, she never had to think about numbers above a kilometre or so which was each Ring's radius.

"That's double the distance of Earth to its moon," Julian explained, his avid scientific knowledge bringing a smirk on her face despite her embarrassment.

"The real question lies in the angle of the vector," Andre chimed in, "Is this 430,000 miles in front of us?"

"Thankfully, no," Mark said, "There's no heat signature and they've disabled Abeone so they're realigning manually with micro-thrusters. If anything they're slightly behind."

The main flat door slammed with force and the heavy footsteps quickly reached the room they were all in.

"It's crazy out there," Lee exclaimed, flicking his usual fringe away from his eyes. His shirt was sweaty under the armpits and the sleeves of his black jumper were rolled up to his elbows.

Alina was right behind him, trying to catch her breath against the doorless frame while running both hands through her black hair, wiping the sweat away in her palms.

"What happened?" Christoff joined them with a hand on Lee's shoulder who was still panting.

"They... they're taking the shuttles!"

"Who?" Rachel asked as her stomach clenched and a sharp, cold tingle rushed across her skin. "We caught all of them... right?" She wondered with furrowed brows, the sense of betrayal crawling up her spine. Had Lucas missed some names on his list?

"Not the evos... people!" Alina cried.

She felt relieved, only to realise a second later the gravity of Alina's words.

"Five Tysons left already," Lee continued, "They're going to beg the evos to let them in Six."

"How are they piloting them? Not many other than me know how to," Nyx remarked.

"They're desperate," Rachel whispered under her breath. They knew they were going to die anyway so they did everything in their power to save their families, she justified them in her head. She was lucky to have the inside information from Scott's group, it had never crossed her mind how scared the rest of the population might have been all this time, especially now that death was imminent.

"What is the council doing about all this? How can they let everyone run rampant, suicides, murders, looting?" Julian asked the room.

"The council is holed up in their headquarters," Christoff replied, "Who knows what escape plan they have."

"No, we are the *Sagan*'s last and only hope," Nyx said.

The conversation came to an abrupt end when a continuous beeping blared from the living room.

"R-Ri.... Rich...R-Richard?" The familiar voice was breaking up.

Andre squeezed through the young people in the room almost shoving Christoff on his way out as he rushed to the wall of screens.

"Scott? Scotty? Is that you?" He yelled at the monitor.

Julian glanced at her and they both ran to the living room trying to find Scott's face among the monitors.

Everyone else followed apart from Nyx who had sat in the worn, swivelling chair, twisting the curls of her thick hair into locks.

"Andre? I'm glad to hear your voice," Scott exclaimed from the speakers, but there was no visual.

"Dad! Are you alright?" Julian jumped in but Andre shushed him with a finger in front of his mouth.

"I'm fine, son. Listen, I don't know how much time I have before they notice I'm skipping one frequency of the jamming sequence. I managed to tamper with a communication station here in the upper science floors, but once they realise what I've done, they'll come for me. I've disabled the proximity sensors along the rim so next time you try to come over here, use the camo function and no one will see you coming. Can… can you still hear me?"

"Yes, Scott, we're coming in under the guise of the sleeper shuttle," Andre said.

"So you will actually board? What platform? I'll wait for you there."

"We… we don't know yet."

The silence that followed meant that either the connection was lost or that Scott had taken the news badly.

"Dad?" Julian shouted at the monitors.

"I'm here…. listen, I'll lay low and hide down at engineering by the bioplastics plant. They don't use these printers. Come get me and we can take over their control room."

"Sounds like a plan, Scotty," Andre replied, a hint of a smile forming on the corner of his lip. "Until then, stay safe."

There was no answer this time. The white noise continued until Nyx joined them in the living room. "I guess they found him."

"This changes the mission then," Julian said, "We need to rescue my dad."

"Your dad can take care of himself even better than me, kid. Don't worry about him."

"No, but we do have to get to him first," Rachel interjected. "If there's a chance we can have Scott handling the control room, that will work massively in our favour. No offence Andre, I'm sure you know what you're doing but Scott is… Scott."

"No offence taken. It's true, I'd feel much better having him with me down there."

"First we need to verify which shuttle and what time." Nyx unsheathed her blade from her thigh and twirled it between her fingers. Rachel used to do the same with her pistol, spin it inside her palm and catch it at the right time so her finger would hug the trigger. It seemed a lot scarier with a blade though.

"Has Javier woken up?" Rachel asked, the pistol trick reminding her how she had shot him. It was an accident really but she didn't feel bad about it. Right now she was more disappointed than scared that the bullet had missed his heart by a few inches. "We can't waste any more time with the rest of them here," she suggested, the adrenaline starting to course through her veins as she imagined doing the interrogation herself. He was still unconscious in the next door flat. That's what Kaiden had told her anyway, she hadn't been able to check on him on her own. She knew she would snap the moment she saw him, but maybe this time some physical pain was what they needed to get the right information. She wondered if she would be able to stop herself, her whole body screaming to push her forward and twist their necks, both his and Matthew Yang's. Even thinking about the latter brought a bitter taste in her mouth and she cringed, refraining from spitting right there in front of everyone.

"I know that look," Nyx said, her eyes already focused on her when Rachel turned to the sound of her voice. "You're not going in there… but don't worry, I'll make sure he suffers appropriately." She flipped the blade in the air and grabbed it with a swoop, pointing it downwards as she passed through Christoff and Lee.

No one protested. They all knew it had to be done.

⚛

The repetitive thuds on the common wall between the flats came to a stop. There hadn't been any muffled shrieks or distant cries in a while as everyone sat around waiting for Nyx to come back. Only Rachel was pacing in a circle around the coffee table, stealing glances at the tied captives lined up against the outer wall of the living room. There was something burning inside her, an angst to find out what Nyx had done with Javier and a question she wanted answered—*why?* Not that anyone could give her that even if they were willing. Andre had stuck a little sticker on the side of their necks much like a comms device, only this was supposed to prevent them from talking.

She stopped her frantic walk and stared at Julian who was sitting by the dining table, one hand on his roller and the other on his lips, mercilessly chewed around the fingertips. He ran his free hand through his thick hair and blew a puff of air, rubbing his neck with an inaudible groan. Neither of them had slept since their failed infiltration or showered or eaten for that matter. He turned to her and their eyes met as if she had telepathically called him. His eyes were red and droopy but he offered a smile with a slight nod. *Everything will be ok, we have each other*, she imagined him saying.

The door panel beeped and her attention turned to the entrance. Everyone stood up and cleared a path as Nyx came through, uncaring for who was in front of her on her way to the study. Rachel beckoned Julian to follow and squeezed through Alina and Lee to get to the other side of the apartment.

The boys were in there already, Mark, Christoff, Lee and Kaiden all talking over each other, trying to explain something to the older engineer, Toz. Nyx flopped down the armchair and stretched her legs, running both hands from cheeks to neck, smudging the streaks of dried blood all over her face. No one asked but it was clear they were all hanging from her lips, silent and still like statues.

Julian kneeled next to her, offering his bottle of water which she took without hesitation and gulped to the last drop.

"1700, *Tyson-32*," Nyx finally said.

"That's only three hours from now!" Andre barged in.

"Give me a second and let's gear up."

"We can't just go in force and hope for the best," Julian protested, getting back on his feet, "We need a plan."

"I'll go find your father in the control room, the rest of you..." Andre started.

"We'll overrun their Core Hull," Nyx finished his sentence.

"You want to take everyone and lock yourselves in a weightless cylinder?" Rachel argued. "That's a suicide mission."

"Desperate times..." Toz said, trailing off.

"Desperate times don't call for stupid measures," she insisted despite Toz' scowl at her rudeness.

Scott was in Ring Six and Richard was gone, none of these people trusted her and she didn't have another three months to prove her worth. If there was a better plan in her head, she had to put it on the table.

"We need the Core Hull." Nyx got up with a dismissive tone and tapped on the roller on Scott's desk. A projection of Ring Six came up, zoomed at the middle cylinder that supported the ring structure.

"I didn't say we didn't, but we can't hold this position for long." She pointed at the connection between the inner bridges and the Core Hull. "Four points of entry, minimal cover inside, how long will you be able to hold out?"

"We only need to last until we attach back to the *Sagan*," Andre argued.

"You won't. What I'm proposing is a diversion," she said and manipulated the projection to focus on the residential quadrant while glancing at the eyes that were suddenly focused on her.

Toz was scratching his chin, Nyx had slightly raised an eyebrow and Andre had leant in Scott's old leather chair. She had their attention.

She took advantage of the silence and carried on with explaining her plan. "Split into two teams, the main force takes control of the resi here, we draw everyone out and a specialised team can sneak in the engine section."

Someone had to talk now because that was it, that was all she had. The details could be worked out later. If she improvised that too she would risk sounding stupid.

"What if the evos don't buy it?" Nyx leant with both hands on the desk, her curly, upward ringlets covering a big portion of the projection.

"We'll be in exo-suits and weapons. They'll definitely get everyone there."

Nyx nodded, her eyes still fixed on the design of the quadrant. A good sign. If Nyx was on board the rest would surely follow.

"Do you hear what you're saying?" Julian interjected, "You want to deliberately have all the evolutionists come after you?"

Julian had caught on faster than anyone else there. He knew her better than everyone of course, he was always there inside her head like a permanent comms device, listening to her every thought. She wanted to take the team to the residential district herself.

"It may be risky but we'll be in our suits," she assured him, not believing it fully herself.

"No, absolutely not! They'll eventually get you cornered and kill you."

"If we don't do this mission right, we're all dead anyway!"

"I like your plan," Nyx interrupted their first fight.

"No, Nyx, you can't let her do that," Julian cried. It was sweet he was so worried about her but she had to do this.

"You know the stakes, kid. Unfortunately, she's right."

"What about you guys? You're fine with that?" Julian turned to the boys and Alina who were watching idly all this time.

"I'm in," Kaiden was the first to agree, albeit for the wrong reasons probably. His hatred for the evos had become unhinged in the last weeks, eager to get the opportunity for payback. He was more of a liability in her team than an asset but she took it, as long as it would get the others going too.

Alina, Christoff and Lee nodded at the same time.

"Count me in too," Mark said with a grin and stood from the comfy armchair he'd stolen from Nyx when she had approached the projection. That boy was too enthusiastic about everything even when it was about heading towards certain death.

"No, you're the best thing we have after Richard," Nyx countered, "You, Toz, Julian and I are going to the engines.

"My man J and I, together again!" Mark wrapped his arm around Julian's shoulder, shaking him back and forth.

"I suggest you take this seriously, you're carrying twenty thousand lives on your shoulders." Nyx was quick to chastise him.

"You can count on me Nee."

"NYX!" She enunciated. "The x is not silent."

"Right, my b."

Nyx rolled her eyes and flicked her black ringlets away from her eyes. "Stick to your relative encrypted channel. You should only contact the other group in an emergency," she continued as if the previous conversation had never happened.

"Come on people, pack your things. We're leaving in sixty minutes," Andre ordered.

The group quickly disbanded, the only one left was Liam who was leaning against the doorless opening of the study. Their eyes met and without saying anything he came close and enveloped her in his embrace.

"I heard about what happened, I know how much Richard meant to you."

"I... I haven't really had the time to process it. I still expect him to show up from some corner and say something like *why are you not getting ready, little Miss?*" She deepened her voice to sound like him, covering up the snuffle with a brief chuckle.

Liam rubbed her back and pulled away. "I'm here for you if you want to talk or something, you know that, right?"

She had heard the same sentence repeated with different words and order a few times already but Liam seemed truly sincere. "I know... thanks," she said softly with a slight nod.

"I'm coming with you to Ring Six."

"Good. It's about time we ended this."

CHAPTER 29
— Julian —

Agricultural Quadrant - Ring 6

His helmet beeped again from where it was attached at the back of his exosuit, prompting him to check the little screen on his wrist.

Hundred and twenty-eight, his heart rate was displayed in big numbers. It had gone up since the last alert which was no surprise. They hadn't enabled the exterior cameras but he knew they were in the middle of nowhere. He was born and raised in space but this was different, the shuttle was somewhere between the *Sagan* and Ring Six, completely alone and exposed. If Nyx miscalculated their flight path, that would be a very short, one way trip. He bit around the nail of his ring finger. It was the only one that wasn't numb and bearing flesh.

"Nyx said we should be there in a few minutes." Rachel sat next to him, holding her rifle from its long barrel and spinning it on its axis against the floor.

It was a strange sight seeing her like this, all powerful in her exosuit, trained and ready for combat but at the same time the young girl he grew up with was still somewhere in there, using a dangerous weapon as a spinner.

"Rach..." he started, his eyes darting across the shuttle to make sure no one was in earshot. The words were on his lips but not easy to utter with so many people around. He had been thinking about what he was going to say since they'd gotten in the shuttle. After the docking to

Ring Six, their teams would split and there was no guarantee they would ever see each other again. Everything had to go right and if history had taught him anything, usually nothing does. "I wanted to say thank you," he whispered, lingering at her beautiful, green eyes shimmering in the dim light of the spacecraft.

"For what?"

"For saving me."

"You saved me in *Tyson-72*, I saved you later. That's how we do it, we've got each other's backs."

"No... I meant for saving *me* in general. I was miserable, unwilling to face reality but with you... I feel like life is good... like it's actually worth living and it doesn't matter where we are."

"Even here in the middle of space?" She raised an eyebrow but her whole face was lit up with a smile.

"As long as we're together." He leant in to kiss her but their chest plates clanged before their lips could touch and they both let out an uncomfortable chuckle.

"It's a shame we had to go through all this to finally work out our feelings. If only you had picked up on all the hints I kept giving you," she said jokingly, but her tone couldn't conceal a sense of disappointment.

"What hints? There were no hints," he countered even though he had picked up on a few irregular behaviours.

"There were plenty, Julian, come on. Have you forgotten the picnic in Cylidome Three? I literally jumped on you."

"I did pick up on that." He grinned. "I... I just didn't want to ruin our friendship, we've known each other since we were born, I was scared."

"Come on, lovebirds, we're here," Nyx interrupted, "Helmets on! Toz, bring us in."

Julian took a deep breath and checked his pulse again. *Eighty two*, he exhaled.

Everyone squeezed inside the pressurisation module which was clearly not meant for so many people, especially in thick, metal plated exo-suits. The bright lights around the circular hatch flickered in a steady rhythm, coming closer and closer as Toz performed the final docking manoeuvre. He couldn't see much from the little, round window of their crowded module but it seemed they had matched the speed and angle of Ring Six.

"This is it, everyone," Nyx started, her voice filled with passion as her rifle hummed. "If you doubt yourselves for a second, thousands of lives will be lost. Let's go take our ship back!"

The pressurisation module filled with cheers and exclaims. Julian looked at Rachel as the thud reverberated through the hatch and the vibration coursed through him.

"I love you," she mouthed as the mechanism ground and the door hissed open.

Nyx was the first to come out, no hesitation in her short bursts. The guards never stood a chance—they were waiting for sleeper agents to return and instead they were faced with a killing machine.

"Team A, follow me. Channel with Team B is closed from now on," Nyx's voice echoed inside his helmet and soon two lines were formed, heading in different directions at the end of the boarding platform.

Julian was following his column closely as they navigated through the lower levels of the agricultural quadrant, silent but gripping his pistol tight. He didn't have the time to meet most of his team, he barely remembered all their names apart from Faruq and Dimitri with whom he had exchanged a few words back in the *Sagan*. They were twenty-three in total, including himself; a good force, granted they were all armed and in exo-suits.

Nyx raised her fist next to her ear and they all stopped and spread out in front of the shut blast door.

"They've isolated sections of the ship," Toz pointed out.

Julian stopped next to Mark and balanced on his knees. They were running in a steady pace for the past ten minutes but he wasn't even panting, the armour had been doing most of the work for him.

Mark kneeled in front of the panel and a blue spark connected his fingertips with it. The crackling sound was followed by smoke and the door buzzed half open.

Julian followed him through, his exo-suit whirring with a persistent grinding as he tried to squeeze through the narrow opening into what seemed to be an active hydroponics farm.

The earthy, spicy odour brought back memories of his childhood as they walked through the long tables that housed the many different vegetables, each under a uniquely coloured light. The trickling of water under the floor tiles gave the illusion there was a small waterfall nearby. He stopped for a second and leant on the edge of the long tray to observe the little, green, round fruits coming out of a thick stem. They felt rubbery to touch but the bushy leaves around them were smooth and soft.

His eyes focused away from the plant in front of him and he peered through to the end of the artificial farm where a woman was standing in front of a wall monitor. Her hair was golden bright in its light and she was wearing a white lab coat that stretched all the way to her ankles. His heart pounded but he sidestepped carefully until he reached Nyx. He brought two fingers in front of his eyes and pointed at the direction of the woman. Nyx raised her fist at the height of her head and waved forward. Her knees were bent, her rifle steadily resting on her shoulder and she cautiously moved through the vegetable trays without the slightest bit of sound. She gestured to the others to go around and beckoned him to follow her.

The woman's face became clearer as he approached, blurry but recognisable in the reflection of the screen.

"Mum?" The word slipped out of his mouth before he realised he'd said it.

His mother shrieked and jumped in shock, pushing her back against the wall of monitors. "Monkey?" She squinted, lowering her head. "What are you doing here? They said you left before detachment," she exclaimed after exchanging a few worried glances between Nyx and himself.

Julian released his helmet, letting it lock in its slot behind his back. "We're here to put an end to this."

"What end, what are you talking about? I'm so glad you're back, I thought I lost you. Come here," she said and took a step forward with open arms before the humming from Nyx's rifle forced her to a halt.

"Don't start with your theatrics. We're going to bring Six back to the *Sagan*."

"Again with this, I thought you had let it go already."

"Of course not, why would you think that? But what am I saying?" He scoffed. "That would require you to know your son at the basic level."

"Julian..." Nyx cautioned him.

"It's ok, we'll be on our way in a minute," He didn't let her finish.

Mark and Toz converged to their location followed by the rest of the team, their weapons in hand but not aiming yet.

"I see you have a whole team with you. Mark, I'm disappointed to see you here as well. You're older, you should have advised my son against this madness."

"It was actually Rachel who got me involved in the first place," Mark replied with some hesitation.

"I can think for myself," Julian sputtered. "You can't stop me this time."

"I never tried to stop you, monkey."

"Enough with the monkey!" He completely snapped, his shout echoing around the grand span of the hydroponics.

"All I did was try to show you a better way," his mother said as she put her hand in the coat's pocket.

"Don't even think about it, Freddie," Nyx threatened again but his mother slowly pulled out her roller anyway.

"Don't do it Mum!" He took out his pistol and pointed it at her.

"Is that how brainwashed you are that you would hold a gun against your own mother?"

"Almost as brainwashed as you when you held your own son a prisoner against his will, you selfish, narcissistic..."

"Bitch," Nyx completed what he wanted to say.

"Don't you dare judge me, Sincroft. What do you even know about raising a child?"

"You know less about me, Freddie than you do your own son." Nyx shook her head.

"I know you removed your name from the birth list the first chance you got. At least you had some self-awareness, you knew how incapable you were of it."

"I only did that because Scott wanted a kid. He was pushing thirty and would've missed out. You wouldn't even have Julian if it wasn't for me."

"Is that your desperate attempt to turn my son against me?" His mother scoffed.

"It's the truth. I did what I did to bump him up on the list. A young woman takes off her name, an older couple can have a kid, you know how it works."

"Good choice apparently," his mother muttered bitterly.

"How can you say that?" Julian protested, "Who says that? Who do you think has taken care of me all this time?"

"But she didn't raise you, I did. How can you trust this woman more than me?"

"This has nothing to do with trust. I may know nothing about raising kids but I'm sure I would never force my son into any situation unwillingly, especially twice if you press that button now."

"You will find soon enough that there are times you know better than letting your child make a terrible mistake they will later regret."

"Dad always said mistakes are good, and I agree. There's no other way to learn anything. This is not one of those times though. At least my choice today means my conscience will be clear."

"I'm sorry you feel this way but as I'm clearly the only adult here I have to make the right choice. For all of us." She tapped on the screen and the alarm blared with a deafening ringing.

He covered his ears as his mother fell to the ground. Had Nyx taken the shot? He glanced behind him with his jaw clenched and his teeth locked. She was still holding the rifle on her shoulder, completely unfazed by the siren.

"What did you do?" He screamed.

"Don't worry, I only tased her. Did you think I'd really kill your mother?"

"I don't know... what do we do now? We can't just leave her here."

Nyx put her helmet back on and knocked on its outer shell with her fist.

"Good idea," he said and did the same. The alarm was finally muffled and he sighed in relief.

"We stick to the plan," Nyx's voice was inside his head once again. "Freddie will be fine here but we definitely won't be if we linger."

"What if she's hurt?"

"We need to get to the core lift," Mark joined the radio conversation, "I hate to say it J, but she did pull the alarm on us."

"Let's go, kid." Nyx picked up the pace while still walking slightly sideways with her knees bent.

He stared at his mother lying on the floor, a peaceful expression painted on her face as her chest rhythmically grew in and out. Something inside him was pushing him to kneel beside her, to make sure she was okay but he hesitated to move. He only stole a last glance of her and let out a long sigh as he dashed forward to catch up with the team.

The bright blue sirens spun their beams of light like neutron stars, distorting the red hues of the dimly lit corridor. Shades of violet streaked through the walls like a deranged rave party, one where he had taken some hallucinogenic drug he couldn't pronounce. Then again, running in an exo-suit, gun in hand and attempting an infiltration in a separated Ring would have required drugs to imagine a few months back.

He followed Toz and Faruq up the stair core glancing at the numbers decreasing with each floor. The suit whirred with every step and lent him its hydraulic strength to climb faster and effortlessly until they reached the ground floor.

"Infrared," Nyx ordered, kicking the door and rushing out.

Her rifle hummed again and he saw the yellow shape falling on the ground, flattening the grass around it. They had come out near the exit of the Cylidome where he had first met Nyx and Andre. He glanced behind him at the nightmarish version of the forest in infrared and a chill tingled his neck. Tall, black spikes towered over an intricate web of grey foliage. Branches extended like deformed crawling creatures trying to reach each other by blending with the darkness at their roots.

"Mark, the door," Julian said when they reached the quadrant intersection, relieved to not be on door duty for once.

His visor touched the wall but there wasn't much he could tell about the other side. Red and yellow pipes blocked the thick wall that divided the Cylidome with the quadrant intersection.

The panel chimed and the door slid open as a round splashed on the frame and splintered the plastic cover.

"Combat mode," Julian exclaimed instinctively and the HUD on his visor changed again, tracking his team with a green triangle above their heads.

"These crazies are shooting to kill," Nyx said as she kneeled next to Mark. She leant out and fired a few rapid bursts that were returned before she even had a chance to hide her face behind the threshold.

Julian stole a brief glance at the atrium only for his visor to identify the three hostiles with a red circle above them. "Light or gas?" He asked.

"Fuck' em, try both!" Dimitri said.

He extended his arm out of the frame, waiting for the panel on his suit to turn green and fired twice, wincing at the recoil.

Nyx sprinted out, firing as she moved until she disappeared into the smoke cloud.

"Clear," she said and Julian switched back to infrared, running all the way to the other side where the entrance to the residential quadrant was. There wasn't time to think about the yellow bodies on the floor, he had to make sure no more would appear.

"Spoles, Toz, door!" Nyx ordered and they both kneeled side by side in front of the core lift door.

Julian tried to find a pattern in the colours behind the door he was responsible to guard. Any hint of yellow movement or shape would mean more trouble. He held his pistol to his chest and glanced at the monitor on his arm.

Hundred and thirty-five bpm.

"We're in," Mark announced.

"No one's coming, my side." Julian verified one last time and stuck two round devices on each side of the door's frame. The electric trap would buy them some extra time in case more evolutionists came after them.

They strapped themselves in the big lift and Toz pressed the red button. Last time he was here was on the school field day. Everyone had told him he wouldn't get another chance to see the Core Hull unless he became an interstellar scientist or a physicist or something. There was always a sliver of hope inside him that comforted the notion he would visit it again but the scenario always involved him being in a white lab coat not an exo-suit and a pistol.

"We've done well so far," Nyx said, her eyes scanning them one by one, "Don't lose focus. Neutralise any resistance, and retake navigational controls."

"What about our exit strategy?" Julian asked and Nyx looked away. "We were supposed to sneak in here, not have an army waiting for us on the way back."

"Yes, how do you reckon we're going to get out?" Toz leant forward.

"We're not." Nyx stared blankly at the wall opposite of her.

"So, this is a suicide mission then," Mark said what Julian had gathered already.

"We will do what needs to be done and hold off for as long as possible." Nyx was stern, her voice sharper than her blade.

"You can't be serious!" Faruq raised his voice.

"She's right," Julian agreed and used the silence that ensued to formulate his thoughts into a sentence. "If these engines fire again, if we don't do this now, the whole *Sagan* will be gone... lost... adrift forever in the emptiness of space."

"Well said, kid." Nyx gave him an approving nod.

"My man J Walker and his depressing poetry, exclusively tonight on the *Sagan*'s special," Mark snickered but with little humour—a puff of air through the nose and half a smile was all he got as a response.

"We'll take on anything they throw at us," Nyx said. "Even with the alarm, we caught them by surprise."

The lift screeched to a stop and the doors opened to the catwalk that connected Core Hulls Five and Six.

"Wait here," Mark said when he unbuckled. "Scanning for traps."

Weapons clicked and hummed as the team got up and prepared themselves.

"It's clear," Mark exclaimed rushing back to the lift, his magboots shaking the metal grating.

Julian followed the team on the suspended bridge as the colossal pistons whirred and hissed to maintain the Ring's centrifugal force. The access to Core Hull Five—thousands of miles away now—was completely destroyed, the metal melted and fused to become part of the wall. No wonder no one had been able to infiltrate Six from there.

He picked up the pace, gun in hand, and rushed towards the end of catwalk where Mark and Toz were trying to bypass the massive circular hatch. The fate of their travelling world would depend on how the next part would go.

CHAPTER 30

— Rachel —

Quadrant Intersection - Ring 6

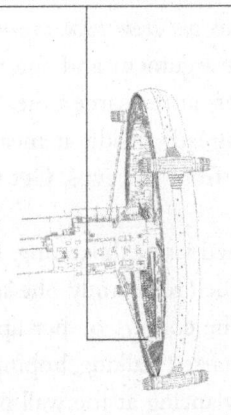

Rachel led her team along the edge of the Cylidome, next to the beginning of the glass lattice that spanned the entire arch to the other side. Usually the exterior lights from the rest of the ship would find a way to invade the secluded forest of each Ring but here, the menacing darkness of space had crept in, basking the spiky trees in an eerie silence. She had to get Andre to the control room first which was in the opposite direction of the residential district and she had to do it fast, before Julian's team would reach the Core Hull.

"Engine ignition in thirty minutes. Please remain inside and fasten your seatbelts."

The announcement made them all stop and focus on the invisible speakers above them. She had never heard an actual person talking on the intercom, it felt primitive to not have the AI do it. Then again they had killed it the first chance they had, Abeone would have never allowed for any of this to happen.

"The odds are in our favour," Liam said in a playful tone.

"Did you not hear what he just said?" Christoff countered immediately.

"Yeah, that's not good news," Lee added.

"We have to pick up the pace," Alina said in her thin voice.

"Stop it!" Rachel ordered. She couldn't allow confusion and doubt to take over her team. She glanced at Andre who gave her an approving nod, his eyes telling her to *put them back in line*. Kaiden and Lee were about to get into another argument and she moved in between them slapping both their helmets at the same time. "We don't have time for bickering. If everyone's already inside, it means we have our job cut out for us, less resistance from the evos. Get it together, we're not on a school trip!"

The silence that ensued was exhilarating, her command respected and her order accepted, albeit reluctantly. She suppressed the smirk that was threatening to raise the corners of her lips. "Let's move on." She finally waved a hand and started walking, hoping everyone would follow. "Enable TIR," she said, glancing at the wall on her left, searching for any shadows behind her. They were coming, she was leading her own team, the realisation dawned on her as a sense of responsibility and excitement filled her body with adrenaline.

They crossed the last part of the forest through the grass to get to the centre of the quadrant's width, where the huge bulk-door to the intersection was. Andre rushed to the panel but before he could even start the bypass of the red holo-circle, the doors slid open and three guards came running. They must have been sprinting already as they were as shocked to see her as she was. The one who came first, a young man with brown hair and grey eyes, couldn't stop himself in time and bumped into her, tackling her back as she lost her balance. Weapons hummed and bursts were fired, the smell of burnt plastic and scrapped metal potent enough to infiltrate her helmet.

The man's cheek was pressed against her visor and his crooked teeth squeaked against the glass. After realising what had just happened, she pushed him over and punched him into unconsciousness. One hit was all it took as the metal around her gloves clanged on his cheekbones and she heard a crack, her eyes widening at the haunting sound. She kneeled over him and checked his vitals. He was wheezing loudly but the rest of his body was unresponsive. He was still alive and she didn't waste any more time above him when there were more bodies around her.

Alina was down with her back against the dent of the wall, panting with difficulty. The metal plates that covered her chest and shoulders had been peeled off and smoke was still swirling around the black holes near her collar. The other guard was laying close to her with his face on the floor, a small river of blood coursing through the grout of the tiles.

"I killed him," Kaiden said, almost boasting about it.

The smile on his face sent shudders down her spine as if an instinct had taken over inside her. It felt like fear but she wasn't afraid, only shocked at the ease with which her teammate had used lethal force.

There was no time to process this now. "You think you can walk?" she asked, putting her hand on Alina's shoulder.

"Uhuh, the suit took the brunt of it."

She helped her up and snapped to the sound of the siren that suddenly blared, reverberating inside her helmet.

"Was that us?" Christoff asked and they all exchanged a few looks among themselves, their blank stares and raised eyebrows betraying their panic.

Had she failed everyone already? Richard would have been disappointed.

"Take his comms," Andre kneeled in front of one of the guards and pointed at the man she had knocked out.

Good idea. She wouldn't have thought of it herself in a million years. She peeled the transparent sticker with her nail and stuck it under her ear after removing her helmet. The pandemonium of overlapping voices was distorted but deafening enough to make her squirm.

"Intercept... Core Hull... protect Dr Richter at all...all units..." She stripped the comm and flicked it away. She couldn't bear it anymore but it was enough to figure out what had happened. Julian's team was made. Her heart fluttered as she looked at Andre who had probably come to the same realisation.

"You should go," Andre groaned while getting up on his feet.

"What's going on?" Lee interjected.

"Evos are diverging to the Core Hull. Are you sure you'll be fine on your own?" She asked, hoping Andre would be able to take care of himself. He was a tech guy, not like Nyx.

"Don't worry about me. I'll be alright," he assured her and turned towards the science quadrant. "This is where we part ways, Miss Watson. Good luck." He beckoned them and disappeared in the curvature of the Ring.

"Should we go help Mark and Julian?" Liam broke the silence.

She was playing scenarios in her head, each of them somehow ending in Julian's death and her spine shivering.

"Fuck Julian, we should…"

"Shut the fuck up, Kaiden!" She spat as her legs felt weak, unable to hold the weight of the decision she had to make.

Her chest burned and her pulse throbbed under her ears. Julian was in trouble, why was she even thinking about it? She took a deep, shaky breath and her eyes darted across the faces of her team members. Thousands of innocent people were counting on her doing the right thing. *You know what you have to do, little Miss,* she heard Richard's voice inside her head. He was right but that didn't prevent the tears pooling under her eyelids. She turned around, hiding her vulnerability from her team—they couldn't see her like this.

"Rach?" Liam pressed and she let out a shaky exhale.

"No, we need to divert their forces to us. Our mission is to control the resi and funnel them in there." She couldn't believe she was choosing the option that would leave Julian pinned down in a dead end. He was with Nyx, she would be able to take care of him; from what little time she had spent with her, she seemed like a ruthless hurricane in battle.

Her gaze lingered on Liam, he wasn't as well trained as the others but she knew she could rely on him to follow her lead. Kaiden was a wildcard, consumed by rage for everything that had happened to him and his sister. He had already been reckless killing that guard but she couldn't dwell on it now. Lee and Christoff were trained soldiers despite their young age, she was confident they would be able to hold their own in what was to come. And then there were Alina, Josh and Tommy. Alina was around her age but she barely knew her. They hadn't talked much but she had supposedly done more reconnaissance missions than her. The men were a lot older than her, even though Rachel could sense the fear radiating from their eyes.

She locked her helmet back with a hiss and raised her rifle to her chest as the weapon hummed in a high pitch frequency. "Let's go take our ship back!"

The team nodded, everyone's eyes fixed upon her with a steely determination.

She led them back the same way they had come, keeping a steady pace on her jog as the exosuits whirred like a war machine trampling everything in its path.

"Enable combat mode!" She ordered when she reached the quadrant intersection between the agricultural and residential quadrants. She kept her infrared though, blurry and distorted as it may have been through the thick walls, she could definitely distinguish the silhouettes behind it. "Take positions. Liam, door on my mark." She kneeled in front of the door and made sure she had a clear path to the thermal targets, glancing at the side of her rifle to make sure the electric rounds were enabled. "Three, two, one... mark!"

The electrical current sizzled at the panel and the holo-circle crackled, disappearing in thin air as the bulkhead slid open. The weapons roared to life, unleashing a swift and deadly assault, dropping evolutionists on the floor before they even had a chance to realise what was happening. Their fire was focused on the group that was gathered outside the lift to the internal bridge, an easy target even for an inexperienced shot like Alina.

The returning fire came with a vengeance, bullets whizzing through the air and splashing on the door frame and the grass behind them. Rachel's heart pounded and she scampered behind the wall. "Cover! Suppressing fire!" She yelled, trying to read the myriad of data displayed on her visor. The enemy was too spread out for stun disks or shock grenades. The only way in there was precise aiming.

She glanced at the smoke coming out of Lee's armour but he was still standing, leaning out of the wall's indentation to fire his short bursts like nothing had happened. The scent of ozone and burning circuits hung heavy in the air already. Her finger hugged the trigger and with a swift motion she pivoted out of the already chipped cover of the wall, her eyes searching for the red circles on her visor. Time seemed to slow down as her vision narrowed and her mechanical arms adjusted her aim, each short burst finding its target.

The enemy fire stopped for a second and she leant out to assess the situation. There weren't that many left but she caught the immediate threat with the corner of her eye, the stun disks sliding on the floor and stopping right after the intersection where her team was.

"Sun shades!" She screamed and a second visor rolled down from her helmet, engulfing her in an impenetrable darkness. She had never used this before, there was no star anywhere near the ship when she'd go out for training but Richard had told her about its purpose.

The disks whirled to their climax, releasing their bright light in all directions but her team was still standing. *It worked!* Alina and Tommy had looked away, probably unable to find the command on their visor but at least they weren't incapacitated.

"Take them down, we need to push forward from this position," Rachel ordered and the team came out of cover like a choreographed dancing move, releasing a barrage of shots that echoed in the open atrium of the intersection.

Something burst open with a loud hiss, followed by a rhythmic, plashing patter. The infrared imaging shifted from bright reds and yellows to calmer hues of blue and she exposed herself to see the sprinkler system dousing everything in water. The evolutionists scurried around for cover behind... no, the visor was playing tricks on her; behind a pile of bodies. They had used the stun disks to regroup and form a barricade made out of their fellow fallen comrades.

Her HUD was as confused as her, unable to find targets in this grotesque amalgamation of bodies. Christoff and Liam leant out of cover but quickly returned behind the wall without firing.

"What is that?" Liam asked, his eyes widened and locked on her for answers.

"What do we do now?" Lee chimed in with another question for her.

She had to control this area, it was critical to the plan but how could she bypass the human shield without lethal rounds?

"Switch to ballistic and bury them in the floor," Kaiden suggested.

"Kaiden, I swear..." she trailed off without saying the series of insults out loud. She had to remain calm for her team, to lead by example. "We're not them, we won't use lethal force unless absolutely necessary," she said although she didn't fully believe it herself. There was a little flame inside her that urged her to show no compassion, no mercy for these people because they had shown none for Richard. He wouldn't have wanted that, he didn't even let her kill Javier. It required almost all her focus to contain that flame, she knew very well there was no going back if it was ever ignited.

Bullets ricocheted off the wall and the echoes of rapid fire filled the ship once again as her team instinctively stepped out to respond. Rachel focused on the patch of heavy blue that had amassed on the floor near the evolutionists and she tilted her head for a clearer view outside the Thermal InfraRed overlay. Their twisted plan of using their own people as shields would be their undoing—they had piled them up near the grate, where water was pooling under them, unable to flow properly into the drainage pipes.

She clicked the safety on her neck and her helmet hissed. Neither TIR nor combat mode would help her here. She kneeled out of the frame and brought the scope to her right eye, aiming for the body of water behind them as she pulled the trigger.

The round splashed on the water, the discharge travelling through the ripples to form white and blue arcs that instantly connected to the enemy in a chain reaction. They all shrieked as their bodies convulsed uncontrollably, the surge of electric energy coursing through them, illuminating their contorted features in a nightmarish glow. They all crumpled to the floor like withered leaves, the spark of vitality within them extinguished. What had she done?

"Wow, well done, boss," Kaiden commented on her terrible idea.

"Move in. Fan out," she ordered locking back her helmet and step by step they advanced.

Rachel scanned her surroundings for any remaining threat, her visor displaying a collection of the new data around her. The tension had eased but her body still felt stiff as she approached the evolutionists, laying on top of each other, all drenched in water. The sudden silence was unnerving, only the light drizzle of the sprinklers continued, bombarding their metal armours with a distinct clanging and metallic echoes. The visor identified the bodies and checked for vitals, the loading bar taking an eternity to calculate. They were all alive. She let out the breath she didn't know she was holding in, fogging up the inside of her helmet. She had won the first battle but the mission was far from over.

"Everyone alright? Any injuries?" She turned to her team, her gaze landing at Liam. His jaw was set tight and his brows furrowed as he nodded, a palpable sense of determination in his eyes that she needed to see to reassure herself she could keep doing this.

"All good," Christoff and Lee said at the same time and the others followed with the confirmation.

"Secure the area, detain the evos," she commanded. They had seized one of the quadrant intersections but there were three more that could lead the enemy to Julian. The thought crossed her mind again, taking that lift and defending Julian at the Core Hull but she shook it off with another order. "Alina, Lee and Tommy stay here and cover our backs. Use the traps we brought with us and maintain TIR imaging." She gave Lee a glance, hoping she was leaving the right people behind.

"Don't worry, we've got this, don't we Alina?" Lee assured her.

Rachel gave him an approving nod, trying to convey with her steady stare what she couldn't say on the comms without crushing their confidence. *Take care of them, hold this position at all costs.*

"The rest of you, wedge formation on my point," she instructed and her teammates quickly formed the line around her.

"Round two," Liam said as they neared the double door of the residential district.

"We must've already drawn their attention back there," Rachel remarked, "We'll have to cause an even bigger ruckus in there to draw them back in."

"Looking forward to it." Kaiden was scarily eager for the next stage.

"Be mindful of civilians," she implored them. "Not everyone in there is an idealistic, selfish motherfucker."

"What happens when we take control and all the evos come rushing in to defend it?" Christoff asked the question she was dreading.

"We maintain control!" She answered sharply, raising her rifle in front of her visor.

CHAPTER 31
— Julian —
Core Hull - Ring 6

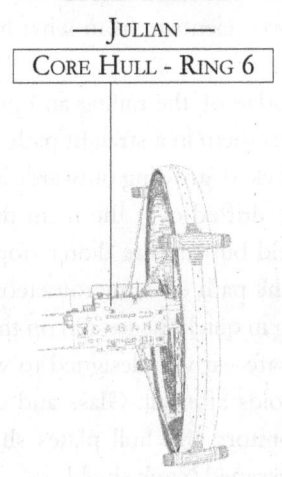

The circular blast door split in half, its mechanism grinding as the interlocking pieces detached and hid inside the cavity. Shades of purple and pink bled into the catwalk, reminding him of the last time he was here and the overwhelming feeling of being in the nuclear reactor's presence.

"Stop where you are!" One of the guards shouted as he raised his pistol from the platform. There were two in total on the top deck, standing by the monitors of the far wall.

He had expected a bigger force defending the engines. Maybe there were others lurking in the other levels or maybe luck had finally smiled at him.

Nyx disposed them quickly at the head of the column and gave the order for the team to split. Seven of them were to stay at the top decks and the rest of them to continue to the main platform in the middle of the Hull's length.

They used the exo-suit's thrusters to fly from outside the circular deck, almost like Rachel had done during their field trip when she was following Lucas. Julian had opted for the ladders back then but there was no time to waste now. The team floated in a single line and as they got closer to the bright pink light of the fusion reactor, Nyx held a fist in the air with one hand and waved the other one forward. The team split again. Only Nyx and Julian were to be left on this level.

Two guards and two scientists from what his HUD could inform him.

Nyx grabbed the edge of the railing and pushed herself forward, hurtling herself towards them in a straight path.

Her exosuit arm clicked, growing outwards in an instant to become a full body shield. She drifted over the main deck, keeping her body curled behind the shield but the fire didn't stop. It sounded like they were suddenly inside the path of a micrometeor shower, the constant bombardment clanging in quick succession on the square metallic piece that was keeping her safe—it was designed to withstand the potential energy of micro-asteroids after all. Glass and debris floated freely in every direction as monitors and hull plates shattered and splintered from the rounds that escaped Nyx's shield.

Nyx came to a stop half way through the distance and she was now pushed backwards. All that kinetic energy must have negated her thrust completely. The two thrusters above her waist glowed blue and she pressed on, charging like a crazed bull.

"Don't shoot in here! Are you crazy?" The woman in the white coat was screaming and the firing stopped. Her short, blonde hair had become a spiked afro in zero g.

Julian gazed at the reckless destruction around him; monitors were shattered, walls had constellations of black holes embedded in them and loose cables zapped electricity at their ends.

"Input systems failure.
The ship's energy distribution will divert to critical areas"

The female voice on the speakers issued the warning with a hint of threat.

The lights flickered and then they were out completely. Only the emergency exit signs kept their vivid blue colour. Only the area around the elliptical reactor in the centre was illuminated, the product of the controlled fusion still bright and pink.

"TIR!" Nyx ordered but Julian had already enabled the Thermal InfraRed overlay, following the yellow signatures that appeared like little planets in front of the bright, menacing light of the fusion chamber, their artificial sun.

He engaged his mag boots and locked himself on the inner shell of the hull, away from the decking.. Vibrations coursed through his feet as if something was moving underneath him in the parts of the ship that were covered.

He had to take the shot. This would be the only chance he would get before lights were back on and his position completely exposed. He swiped his finger on the side of his pistol as fast as flicking through the pages of an old paper book until the electric bullet appeared, a shell with a lightning inside. Hovering his aim around the hostile figures, he felt his arms moving on their own, adjusting—weapon and exosuit were connected, following the orders of his eyes on the HUD. His arms moved again after the first shot, guiding his aim and he fired the second round.

The evolutionists stretched their arms and spines backwards with a cry as their weapons floated away from them.

"I said no more guns!" The woman cried again. Her silhouette was more red than it was yellow. "Are you people out of your mind?"

"Nice shot, kid," Nyx commented and Julian ran to her while she was already dragging the guards along, tying their arms behind their back to the railing. The lights came back on with a loud rumbling and the whole hull started whirring and hissing again.

Julian removed his helmet. Maybe his visor was foggy or his eyes were playing a trick on him, otherwise he'd have to accept she was one of them. "Ms Carter? Is that you?"

His physics teacher hid her lips inside her mouth and tilted her head. "Oh, Julian… what are you doing here my sweet boy?" Her tone carried a sense of sorrow.

"I could ask you the same thing. You're a cosmitist, how can you buy into all this?"

"It's precisely because of my expertise in the cosmic sciences that I am here. The numbers don't lie Julian, I did most of the calculations myself."

"And did you factor in the thousands of lives you're sacrificing in your equation?" He spat.

"History is full of sacrifices for the greater good," Ms Carter defended in a hollow statement.

"Don't lecture me on history, it's not your field," Julian replied sharply.

"Julian, you're making a terrible mistake here," she insisted, taking a feeble step and glancing at the monitor behind her.

"No, I think you're about to make a mistake by pressing whatever is flashing there," he said as he raised his gun on her.

His former teacher froze and stared at him with a blank, stoic look. "What happened to you, Julian?" She shook her head in disappointment but Julian saw her foot sliding further back.

He sighed and swallowed with difficulty "Don't make me do this," he threatened through gritted teeth as Nyx twisted her body and raised her rifle as well.

"You don't understand, Julian. What we're doing here... that was the original plan of the *Sagan* when it set out from Earth. If you'd let me explain..."

"Step away from the monitor and I'm all ears."

Ms Carter exchanged a look between Julian and Nyx's rifle, finally letting out a pained exhale and coming forward. Nyx launched herself towards her, grabbing his old teacher and quickly locking her arms behind her back.

"Nyx, we have a problem," the voice came from the helmet at his back, followed by a series of short bursts from the upper decks.

"What is it, Dimi?" Nyx asked, growling as she detained Ms Carter.

"This thing... it doesn't die!" More weapons fired and more shrieks followed.

"Faruq, all ok down there?" Nyx asked.

"Yes, area is secured. I'll go help Dimitri."

"Good, I'll be there in a second."

"Do you really think people would have signed up if the journey took almost three hundred years?" Ms Carter groaned from Nyx's force. "It's always meant to be a three generations trip. It was the council who forced the halfway event."

"Hah, no... you're just making this up." Julian shook his head. "That's why it's called generation ship, because multiple generations were supposed to live and die here."

"That's what cosmic scientists wanted you to believe," she countered as Nyx dragged her to the edge of the rails. "The records show there was a big debate while the ship was being built. Cosmitists believed the ship couldn't handle the stresses of high G deceleration so they wanted a longer trip, completely disregarding the effects of growing up knowing your destiny is to die in space. *We* had warned them, people wouldn't fare well psychologically and we were right. I'm sure you can attest to that."

Her last argument had struck a chord. All his life, he had cursed the fact he was born in a floating prison. Who would have willingly wanted a life like that? "We?" He asked, narrowing his eyes.

"Life scientists. Psychologists, biologists, anatomists, neuroscientists, and every field that has to do with a person's wellbeing. We all agreed that the trip should be made within the maximum lifespan, a hundred and sixty years."

"That's the maximum?" he scoffed, "Who lives that long?"

"Don't listen to her," Nyx interjected, "She's full of lies, all of them are." She tripped Ms Carter to the floor and attached her handcuffs to the rail.

"I'm telling you the truth, your mind is just too small to comprehend it, Miss Sincroft." His teacher jerked her body, trying to free herself from Nyx's tight grip, "If the cosmic scientists, your precious council, hadn't banned every technological advancement our species has made, we'd even be able to live past two hundred."

"And they could then make the trip from Earth to Aquanis in just one lifetime?" Julian's curiosity had peaked.

"That was the original plan. And they would have achieved it if they weren't sent back to Earth by force."

Tyson-7. It wasn't possible she was telling the truth, she had to be making all that up.

His mind drifted to the inscription Rachel had found in the Cylidome, *we were sent back but our voices still live here.* Were these the first life scientists Ms Carter was talking about?

"Don't let her get in your head, kid!" Nyx snapped him out of it. "Whatever the original plan was, I'm sure it didn't involve killing thousands of innocent people to achieve it." She shoved the teacher on the floor, her head banging on the metallic, hollow tiles with a thud.

"You won't get away with this, Sincroft," Ms Carter groaned and squeezed her eyes shut, seemingly trying to contain the pain.

"Watch me!" Nyx didn't even turn to face her. She engaged her thrusters again and slowly ascended towards the upper deck. Faruq and the rest of the team appeared on Julian's deck but continued further up, following Nyx.

"She has no chance against him," Ms Carter whispered with a whimper, only she wasn't crying, she was laughing—a sinister chuckle that intensified as she got herself up and rested her back against the vertical rail.

"Against who?" Julian demanded, raising his pistol with both hands to the deck above him.

There were more shots fired and he leant out of the railing to get a better view of what was happening above him. Debris was flying everywhere and the finer particles had amassed together to form clouds of shimmering dust, fluctuating slightly like an amoeba in the absence of gravity.

A thud shook the whole structure and he saw the back of an exosuit being pushed at the rails, bending them as they creaked against the invisible force. The metal finally snapped with a shrill echo and Nyx was sent flying away in the empty space, spinning backwards until she crashed on the outer wall and her body bounced back, her thrusters fuming to get her reoriented.

Julian glanced at Ms Carter who seemed to be enjoying the view and his attention suddenly turned to the scientist sliding down the ladder from the floor above. His lab coat was full of holes, burnt around the edges that funnelled in smoke, trailing behind him like an ethereal shadow. A black liquid had dried around the hip pockets, smeared all the way to the neck line where his chest was exposed, a reflective, silvery material that looked like an exosuit.

"I've worked too hard to watch it all fall apart by some ignorant fools," Dr Richter spat, his piercing blue eyes locked with Julian's. He marched towards him, his stride determined and unstoppable despite the weapon Julian was aiming at him.

"Albert, no! Julian was just lied to," Ms Carter cried, "He can be convinced."

The scientist stopped for a quick glance at his colleague and scoffed. "I'm not taking any chances. Not this close to ignition."

Julian's helmet swivelled over his head to a hissing lock as his palms grew clammy and his pistol kept slipping inside his grip despite the exosuit's supporting knuckles. His heart must have stopped as his breath was caught in his throat. He pulled the trigger and the round splashed on Dr Richter's chest, the blue arcs of electricity stretching away from his body to connect to the ladder instead. The current emitted a glow as it sizzled on the round metal bars and dissipated with a crackle. He pulled again repeatedly, each shot faring worse than the previous until the doctor breached the distance and grabbed him from the neck. He felt his body stretched as the magnetic pull of his boots loosened and his feet finally detached from the floor. The metal plate around his collar bent and cracked, the exosuit's protection around his neck failing and he groaned, trying to free himself from the grip that threatened to end his life. He caught Nyx with the corner of his eye, hurtling through the void at full thrust, grabbing the doctor by the waist and using her momentum to throw him to the nuclear reactor. She tapped on her arm and kneeled in front of him, her hand extended for the linear, flaming plume to burst out of a module above her knuckles. Dr Richter turned away, presenting his back for cover as the lab coat disintegrated in seconds and a red glow enveloped him. There was no scream or cry, only an uneasy silence and the petrified form of the doctor.

Richter growled, a menacing grin on his face as though he had enjoyed being burnt alive.

The flame had subsided but a residual glow lingered, a palette of fiery red and yellow radiance, its incandescence across the seams of his power armour impossible. Julian narrowed his eyes and took a step forward.

No, it wasn't an exosuit under his burnt lab coat, it was... his own body, naked and smooth, all made from some kind of alloy. The ultimate integration of man and machine. Was there anything organic left inside him? Anything below his neck was metallic, glowing red for having sustained the flame that would melt the hardest metals.

He slapped Nyx with the back of his hand and she hit the floor, head first as the helmet warped and the visor shattered. She didn't even try to get up. Julian's stomach clenched and his chest contracted, sending a piercing pain through his heart while he waited for her eyes to twitch and open again.

"You know, none of this would've happened if your father had done his job right," Dr Richter turned his focus back at Julian.

"What does my dad have to do with all this?" His throat had closed and the words came out dry and raspy as his eyelids pooled with tears.

"An archivist that doesn't know his own history," he scoffed.

"W-What do you mean?"

"I won't waste my breath explaining something to a dead man." He launched himself towards him.

Julian shuddered, his mind going into overdrive as his eyes settled on the bright pink light seeping out the window of the fusion chamber. Maybe fire was weak, but plasma was supposed to be millions of degrees. He engaged his thrusters and swooped to the side to avoid Richter's charge, almost losing his balance at the landing.

"Mark, Toz, are you there?" he asked, hoping at least one of the engineers was still conscious—still alive.

"A little busy here, J," Mark was panting inside Julian's helmet.

"Are you losing ground up there?" Toz added. "Where is Nyx, we need more time down here."

"I need you to open the fusion chamber," Julian exclaimed, running to gain some distance from the crazed scientist.

"What?" Both of them protested but only Toz continued, "That's extremely dangerous, Julian."

"Just do it!" He cried as Richter closed in and kicked him off his feet.

"Where is Nyx?" Toz insisted.

"Fucking do it, Toz!" Julian grunted, shoving his pursuer away.

"I see your friends are trying to mess with my engines," Richter stopped and glanced at the bottom decks, turning away towards the edge of the platform.

The door behind Julian hissed open, drawing his attention for a brief glance, revealing the small antechamber to the fusion reactor.

"Manual tether," he enunciated and swayed his head to bring Richter's body at the centre of his visor.

His chest recoiled at the ejection of the hook that pierced Richter's metallic back and held him in place before he was able to jump away from the railings. Thermal, electrical and kinetic methods had all been futile, but the sharp, graphene-tipped spear had penetrated. Maybe the alloy his body was made of was weaker when heated. He wished he could do the fast maths in his head but he settled for the hypothesis.

He backpedalled to the antechamber and braced his feet against the frame as the tether started reeling in, dragging Richter across the floor. He flicked the red cover on the terminal and pressed the button with his fist.

"Authorisation required"

He growled at the monitor and the synthesised voice, searching for the input. A circle had appeared on the screen, tagged with an annotation.

Biometric lock and the icon of an eye.

He locked Richter's hand behind his back the way Nyx had shown him and pushed him close to the screen. The doctor growled, regaining his strength after the injury but not fast enough to prevent the circle from turning green. Julian smashed the button and then Richter's head on the terminal as the blast door hissed with a low rumbling.

"Nuclear fusion chamber environment breached.
Emergency shutdown protocols initiated.
Venting core."

The circle of plasma hovering around the toroid shape of the reactor fluctuated and disappeared as smoke filled the chamber. The sight distracted him and he never saw the punch coming. His helmet buckled and he crashed on the terminal behind him. Richter was quick and agile for his age, then again his body was an exosuit by itself, even better maybe.

"Shutdown complete.
Please, ensure you're wearing all necessary
gear to proceed with chamber maintenance."

The blast door hissed open and their eyes locked, circling each other like hunter and prey, although who was which was hard to say.

"It's a shame it has come to this," Richter started, a sinister smile curling upon his lips. "Such potential... wasted," he spat, his furrowed brows exuding a sense of superiority that made even his slightest of movements seem calculated and deliberate.

"At least it's mine to waste," he replied, correcting his stance to match his opponent's posture.

"We could have built a whole new world on Aquanis, Julian. If only you could see my vision. Water domes, spaceports, beautiful plazas and landscapes..."

"All on the shoulders of twenty thousand innocent souls," Julian snapped, trying for a grapple but Richter slipped away, launching a flurry of precise counter attacks, pushing Julian closer and closer to the fusion chamber.

Julian parried and dodged a few but the attacks were endless, Richter didn't stop as if he had an endless supply of energy. His visor filled with an array of mechanical warnings but he paid no attention to them, he was determined to fight until his exosuit was a piece of scrap metal.

He finally managed to push back, but the crazed scientist charged again. Julian swayed to the left milliseconds before the impact and used the momentum to drive him head first to the frame of the blast door. Panic took over him—his dodging manoeuvre had placed him inside the toroidal metal tiles of the nuclear chamber. Richter groaned, shaking his head—the only part of him that was still human—and Julian found the opportunity to drag him in and send him to the centre column with a loud clang. The rhythmic hiss of vented steam shrouded the room in a hazy mist and he removed his helmet, casting it aside—the warnings had piled up, distracting him from what he needed to do.

A form appeared through the thick cloud of water droplets and he raised his hands to defend himself. Their arms locked in a brutal contest of strength and will as his muscles strained to push his attacker back into the core.

"I always knew you were a liability, Walker, but your mother insisted."

"On this, we can agree." Julian gritted his teeth and screamed to summon any remaining strength left within him.

He slipped his hands under Richter's arms and flicked them upwards, giving him the opportunity to strike free. He kept on screaming with every punch that landed on Richter's face until the doctor finally gave in, his eyes darting around the room, their vitality extinguished.

Julian gave a final shove and Richter flopped at the bottom of the column. He rushed back to the antechamber and hastily locked the blast door behind him as a mix of relief and exhaustion washed over him. The cooling jets continued their ghostly dance, shrouding the fusion chamber in an ghostly ambiance.

Silence.

He leant against the terminal, his breath ragged and his ears drumming as he allowed himself to shut his eyes for a brief moment. The thud at the blast door snapped him back and his gaze fell on Richter's eyes, now desperate and afraid. The computer beeped and he jerked back to his feet, staring at the message that had taken over the whole screen.

Re-engage nuclear fusion core? Y/N

He could end everything with the press of a button but his hand wasn't willing.

"Don't do it, Julian!" Richter's voice was barely audible, muffled and distorted through the blast door.

For all the misery and despair Richter was responsible for, it wasn't Julian's choice to make. He offered a last glance at the scientist and ran back to the main platform.

He kneeled next to Nyx who was still on the floor and removed her helmet. She was still alive but unresponsive no matter how much Julian shook her head around.

"Come on, wake up, Nyx. I need you," he muttered, taking her helmet and putting it on.

"Mark, Toz, are you still there?"

"Julian! What's going on up there?" Mark cried.

"Long story. How are you guys doing?"

"We have seven minutes until engine ignition. We've been waiting for Nyx's orders," Toz screamed inside his head.

"Nyx is down. Alive but badly hurt."

"Fuck!" Mark exclaimed. "You have three lifts coming your way, J. Retreat down here immediately!"

"Will do. Mark, lock the nuclear reactor," he ordered and rushed to the bulkhead at the top deck, placing two stun traps at each side of the circular door. He did the same for the other two catwalks, finally returning to Nyx and sliding his arms under her to lift her up.

She weighed nothing in zero G but it still took effort to climb to the lower levels with a grown woman in his arms.

He checked his arm panel while drifting downwards to make sure the traps were armed and his eye stayed at the number that displayed his heartbeat. *Hundred and fifty-four.*

The icons of the traps lit up with a yellow overlay and he heard the shrieks echoing throughout the Core Hull.

The magboots pulled him to the ground and he saw Mark and Toz in front of two wide terminals, frantically waving their hands, shifting through the information on the transparent monitors.

"What do we do?" Julian asked as he approached, placing Nyx softly on the floor. "Even if we prevent the engines from firing, there's no way out of here. I stopped some of them but…"

"We defend this position at all costs," Toz said, panting to catch his breath. "Hopefully Rachel will secure the residential quad and they'll have to fall back."

"What if they don't?" Julian voiced the question in his head. From what he'd seen so far, these people were not very empathetic, maybe they were willing to leave all the civilians defenceless in order to retake the Core Hull.

"Then we take as many as we can with us," Mark replied.

Julian remained silent, drawing in a long inhale.

Rachel's team should've already been engaged in the resi by now, what was the harm in opening the channel? Both teams were exposed, this was no longer a covert operation, it was a battle for survival.

He tapped on Rachel's portrait on his arm and cleared his throat. "Rach? Are you okay down there?"

Mark and Toz snapped at him in shock but they must have come to the same realisation because they said nothing to stop him and returned to their terminals.

"J-Julian?" Rachel said in disbelief. "I thought…"

"No time for caution anymore," He interrupted her. "Have you secured resi yet?"

"No… not yet," she grunted. It sounded like she was running, the gunfire in the background making his heart jump inside his chest. "We're actually pinned down."

He didn't know what to say. He couldn't help her. He couldn't even help himself. His chest felt cold and hollow, his shoulders slumped and his determination slowly dissipating.

"Engine cut off!" Mark cheered.

"What's the point, we've only postponed the inevitable," Toz sighed.

"Did you take control of the Core Hull?" Rachel asked, a hint of desperation in her voice as she panted loudly.

"No… we got Richter but now we're cornered. We won't last long, just the three of us."

Julian stared at the monitors, unable to form thoughts, let alone formulate any more sentences. The decks above him clanged and he raised his gaze to the boots that had landed on the floor above them. He counted fourteen yellow shapes but who knew how many more were following behind.

"Rach…"

"I know, Julian. I love you too."

His muscles were numb, barely holding the pistol in his hand. Needles prickled his spine and his vision blurred as a hand touched his shoulder and his whole body jerked.

"We've got this, kid," Nyx groaned, giving him a side glance and a slight curl on her lip. "But I'll need my helmet."

Julian felt the muscles on his face stretching wide as he appeased Nyx's order, a tiny flame of hope reigniting inside him. "I'm glad you're okay."

"Thanks for not leaving me up there, kid," Nyx tousled his hair over his cap.

"I would never leave you," Julian replied, a knot in his throat making the words come out in a higher pitch.

"Now back to the terminals." She beckoned him towards the engineers. "Stay in cover. Mark, how long to navigate this thing back to the *Sagan*?"

"Pfft, even without the threat of imminent death it would probably take me hours if not days," Mark scoffed.

"Start then. Worst case we buy the others some more time. Toz, come on, let's lay everything we have on them."

"I'm not going to stay back and watch. I can fight," Julian protested, "I beat Richter myself!"

"And you were wearing a helmet." Nyx gave him a scowl he knew too well. It was not up for debate.

Nyx opened up her shield, Toz took cover behind the main column and Julian hid behind the terminal with Mark, his pistol aiming at the opening above them for an opportunity. The first three evolutionists never saw what hit them, their blood forming floating droplets around them as their momentum carried them to the floor. Nyx and Toz were using kinetic rounds but when Julian hovered his finger above the little menu on his pistol his hand froze, unable to swipe to the lethal setting.

"Toz, cover the flank," Nyx ordered and the old engineer scurried to where Julian was.

There were three or four ladders connecting each deck but the space outside the railings of each platform was exposed like scaffolding around a skyscraper of the old world. The evolutionists split, their magboots clanging in different directions above them, as they pressed on with the assault. Julian ducked under the base of the terminal as shots flew past him and blindly returned the fire.

Toz shrieked when two enemies snuck behind him and emptied their weapons on his exosuit. He remained still, his eyes widened, staring at nothing as the metal exoskeleton enveloping him was now inert.

Nyx pivoted behind her, the rifle steady in her arms and took them down, one shot for each. Julian winced and faced away. It was one thing to see someone die, a whole different story witnessing a hole above their eyes, blood and brain dripping out in an ethereal trail. His mouth filled with saliva in preparation for the bile piling under his throat and he placed a hand in front of his mouth, gagging.

"Mark, get Toz out of there," Nyx ordered even though Mark had already left his post to get him.

The blinking message at the opposite screen caught Julian's attention as he crawled to get to it and snuck a peek under the crossfire.

Enable AI navigational control? Y/N

The AI could take care of things on its own, maybe even get them back to the *Sagan* in a shorter time. They wouldn't last until then, he knew that but it was the only option, the only hope for someone else to carry on with their plan. He tapped on the *yes* circle twice for the verification and all screens turned to black. Had he fucked up?

> "I'll now take over the flight path to Aquanis.
> 2.23 light seconds delay in internal processing.
> Investigating discrepancy."

It was strange to hear Abeone talking again—he had almost missed the warm, melodic voice of the AI during his time in the isolated Ring, her balanced resonance carrying a comforting sense of safety.

The firing stopped and a pregnant silence swept the lower decks of the Core Hull. The smell of burnt metal hung heavy in the air and a bitter taste lingered on his tongue.

"What have you done?" Mark cried. "Abeone is unpredictable right now with all the chaos that's been going on."

A short burst made him jump and he turned to the direction it had come from. Nyx was unaffected by the turn of events as expected, using the evo's surprise to her advantage.

> "Core Hull Six is detached from the processing
> unit by a distance of 2.23 light seconds.
> Water storage modules missing. Immediate action
> is required. Survival of the ship is my top priority.
> Calculating new flight path to the *Sagan*.

Reattachment possible within acceptable risk.
Please, brace for high G manoeuvre."

"Fuck!" Mark screamed louder than Julian had ever heard him before, dragging Toz behind the terminals as fast as he could, grunting with every pull.

An invisible force shoved him forward. The mag-boots kept him attached to the metal decking but his head smashed on the intricate surface of the terminal. He squeezed his forehead with his palm, trying to contain the pain, his eyes shut as he sucked his teeth in. He brought his hand forward and drew a sharp breath at the sight of blood dripping down the lines of his palm. If that was the force exerted on the Core Hull, he didn't even want to imagine how hard the ring structure was hit.

What have I done?

CHAPTER 32
— Rachel —

Residential Quadrant - Ring 6

The blocks were teeming with people and an inconsistent chatter echoed through the wide middle strip. Some were yawning and stretching like they had just woken up, others were looking around confused and the ones from the first few flats seemed very interested in the team of exo-suits that had just disrupted their moment of glory.

"Christoff, Kaiden, move ahead and scout the plaza. Josh and Liam, you're with me," she ordered as they delved deeper into the open strip, following the neatly trimmed path between the grassy sections.

She cleared her throat and swallowed before engaging the speakers of her helmet to their max volume.

"People of Ring Six. For your own safety, please return to your homes and stay inside. The Ring has now been taken over."

The crowd at the balustrades booed her and even threw objects but seemed contained for now. Grey rectangles kept popping on her visor, scanning their faces and turning green in the absence of weaponry. Some of them had their rollers however, recording her every move. Maybe that was a good thing though. If they were sharing what was going on in resi, that would draw all of the evolutionists in there.

"How do you suppose we contain all these people?" Liam asked.

"We don't need to. They are harmless for now," Rachel replied, hoping her statement was true.

"Are you sure about that, love?" Liam pointed at Christoff and Kaiden where the Ring curved and the ceiling united with the floor.

A group of men had reached the ground floor and were menacingly heading towards her vanguard.

"Go back to your homes, or we'll have to use force," She yelled through the speaker, hoping her threat would serve as adequate intimidation.

Christoff and Kaiden both raised their guns and stood back to back as they quickly got surrounded.

"Fuck!" She muttered under her breath and ran towards her team as the plaza filled her tangent horizon.

"I zapped two guys, Rach!" Alina cheered inside her helmet. "But there are more coming... and some people have come downstairs behind you and they're staring at me."

Rachel glanced over her shoulder where the residential entrance had almost disappeared inside the Ring's curvature.

"Go back to Alina," she ordered Liam and beckoned him towards the quadrant intersection they had come through. "Fuck this, switch to combat mode. Only electric bul..."

The shot was fired before she could finish her sentence and a young blonde boy fell on the floor in front of Kaiden.

Fuck, I really hope that wasn't kinetic, she tried to reassure herself, otherwise the situation would turn very ugly very soon.

A unanimous gasp resounded in the residential district, followed by shrieks. The crowd on the ground was unpredictable as some of them held their gaped mouths, others rushed to the boy and others squeezed their fists in an anger that was about to explode.

A shot came out of her line of sight and burned a patch of grass, sending plants and soil everywhere.

Kaiden and Christoff ran for the columns that supported the residential blocks above them, shoving any evolutionist on their way.

She was almost there now, close enough to see the glistening red colour that had painted the grass around the boy. Kaiden had killed another one.

"Use the crazies as human shields like they did," Kaiden yelled.

"No! Leave the civilians out of it! What's wrong with you?" She screamed even louder than him as she reached the centre of the plaza

"We can't afford being nice here."

"I said NO! That's an order, Kaiden!"

"We'll definitely die if we don't defend ourselves."

"Christoff, smoke the way to the recreation quad. They're not wearing exo-suits to see through it. Use the infrared."

"Got it," Christoff extended his arm and launched two canisters over the people that were now running away screaming.

"Kaiden, you're wearing the engineering suit. Tasers, close combat. Neutralise the mob."

"I still think…"

"Shut it and follow the fucking order! No casualties!"

"Rach, we're surrounded here." Liam sounded out of breath. "I took down some guys that went for my gun but they've closed us in."

"Barricade the way to the Cylidome, create a bottleneck."

"You've got it. Come on Alina, get up."

The lights flickered and the people on the balustrades bursted in screams and cries again. Kaiden rushed into the crowd with his hydraulics whirring loudly as he zapped everyone around him with electric currents that arced away from his exosuit. That was her chance to squeeze through and end up on the other side where the smoke had created a thick cloud, climbing rapidly all the way to the steel lattice at the top.

Three jittery, yellow silhouettes were cautiously moving through the smoke but she could see them clearly behind her visor. She bent one knee and rested the other flat on the grass while raising her rifle. Her shoulder barely felt the recoil through her suit and one after the other, they all fell on the ground trembling as their bodies arched uncontrollably from the electricity.

The lights came on again and completely went out, leaving only a series of black lines under the balustrades. She disabled the infrared and squinted for her eyes to adjust to the blue exit arrows that had replaced the black lines. Was that Julian's doing? If they had completed their mission, Nyx would've opened the channel again. She was tempted to do it herself, but if her train of thought was wrong, she would certainly give away their position.

"Kaiden and Christoff, report," she ordered when even her infrared vision couldn't distinguish what had happened behind her among the sea of yellow and red shapes.

"All under control, boss," Kaiden's tone was sarcastic but she didn't have the time now to address his insubordination.

"Liam?"

"We're at a standstill with some evos here but most of them dispersed when the lights went out."

"Was that us?" Christoff joined the circus of voices in her head.

"I don't know." She sighed while standing up. Her chest wanted to come out of the exo-suit, there was not enough space to breathe.

"What do we do now?" Lee asked.

"We keep this area hot and occupied. Don't forget our job is to give as much time as we can to Julian's team."

"It's kind of quiet now," Christoff said, "I think we scared them."

"Or they're regrouping," Liam offered a reason that made more sense in her head.

"It's the calm before the storm," Kaiden added.

"Everyone, regroup at the plaza," she ordered and joined Kaiden and Christoff in dragging the unconscious people inside the inactive food kiosks.

The lifeless body of the blonde boy was still laying on the grass a few feet away. At least his eyes were closed, she could pretend he was tased like the rest of them. She focused on Kaiden's portrait at the corner of her visor's HUD and coughed a couple of times to get his attention.

"I don't want to have to repeat myself, if you use lethal rounds again, I'll put you down myself."

The silence on her radio was infuriating. She glanced at him as he was pushing an unconscious woman to a corner with his foot.

"I just didn't have time to switch. He basically charged at me." Kaiden's voice was calm and steady as if he had taken the time to practice the excuse.

The lights flickered once again and changed to their bright white setting, skipping the orange colours of the early evening hours.

"MURDERERS!" someone yelled from the balustrades and was quickly joined by an incoherent mixture of threats and curses, the irony of their wording probably not clear to them.

Her visor kept beeping as it scanned their faces. She swept every floor all the way to her tangent horizon where her helmet finally locked on the twenty-two red rectangles.

"Take cover at the kiosks. We hold this position no matter what," she said and leant outside the colourful tent of the Spicy Foods canteen.

The fire exchange was ineffective as her team returned the shots almost blindly, only coming out of cover for a few seconds before more ballistic rounds splintered the previously smooth surfaces of the kiosks.

She stood still for a minute and waited for the sound their rifles made when they recharged. She slid out on the tiled path, her visor fast enough to lock on two of them and she repeatedly pulled the trigger. She hit them both, their weapons dropping flat on the gras and their bodies following like chopped trees.

The second try was a miss as the electric bullet splashed on the thick column that supported the apartment blocks, barely leaving a mark.

A shriek inside her helmet made her heart flutter and she scoured the plaza for her teammates.

"They're... behind us too," Liam grunted and sucked his teeth as he limped his way inside the small kitchen of the Sweet Delights next to the idle robot waiter.

"Are you okay?" She asked, her heart still screaming to get out of her power armour.

"Just a scratch... I think they hit the mechanism on the hip connection though. I can't move my leg."

"You can't take off the suit now. Stay there and don't come out," she said and swapped combat mode for infrared, feeling vulnerable already without the aim assist. "Four on the left colonnade, five on the right. Cover our flanks guys."

"We're getting surrounded," Christoff said what she had feared already.

Debris was ejected everywhere and all she could hear on the comms was the rasped breathing of her teammates as they ran and changed positions behind the structures that weren't already decimated.

"R-Rach? Are you okay down there?" Julian's voice startled her, averting her gaze from the threatening silhouettes as her eyes darted around the chaos and she focused on the conversation in her head.

"J-Julian?" she muttered in disbelief. If he had opened the channel did that mean their mission was successful? "I thought..."

"No time for caution anymore," He interrupted her. "Have you secured resi yet?"

"No... not yet," she grunted, strafing away from the splinters ejected from the barrage on the wall that was protecting her. She changed position, crouching the whole time until she was behind the storage space of the food kiosk. "We're actually pinned down. Did you take control of the Core Hull?" she asked, resting her back against the storage cabinets. She needed a break, just a few seconds to breathe.

"No..."Julian sighed. "We got Richter but now we're cornered. We won't last long, just the three of us." His voice was filled with sorrow and anguish. He hadn't opened the channel because the mission was successful but because they had all failed. This was goodbye.

The lump in her throat felt heavy and she blinked to spill the tears aside. She muted herself from everyone before the snivelling started and her body contracted inside her armour.

"Clean... helmet," she said, her voice shaking as her lips quavered.

"Rach..." Julian paused, probably fighting for his life as well.

"I know, Julian, I love you too," She said, trying to keep her voice from cracking again.

There was no response this time. Would things have been different if she had gone to him in the first place? She would never know now. Everything had turned to shit but she wouldn't go down crying, especially when her team was still out there fighting. She drew a deep breath, letting it out with a strong huff as she got back on her feet, her rifle ready and humming. They were outnumbered and surrounded, the only option she had was a crazy one but she was willing to try it.

She stepped out of the Spicy Foods canteen and enabled the megaphone to make sure she was heard over all the firing. She walked to the middle of the plaza, bullets whizzing over her as her armour took the brunt of the ones that hit her. "Dr Richter is captured... it's over. Drop your weapons and surrender peacefully."

Surprisingly the shooting stopped, albeit for Kaiden taking advantage of the opportunity to drop another evolutionist.

"Hold your fire!" Rachel growled. "There's no need for more bloodshed."

"Liar!" The masculine voice came from the main enemy group that had come from the recreation quad.

"Liar!" The crowd at the balustrades yelled in unison like a choir.

"Check your comms, our team has your leader. Drop your weapons and no harm will come to him," she carried on with her bluff and switched to her team's channel. "Lock your targets. Alina and Lee, prepare stun disks."

"Do we really have Richter?" Christoff asked.

"That's irrelevant right now. Do as I said."

There was commotion among the evolutionist teams, they were probably trying to verify her claim, gesturing at each other, their weapons still clutched in their arms.

"Let them kill him, he deserves it." A familiar voice rose above the others and her visor zoomed in to investigate, the data coming up as it focused.

Name: Lucas Bjorgen
Age: 19u
Contribution Points: 430

"Luke, what are you talking about, brother?" Ares appeared in the open, shifting through his teammates to reach his equally large friend.

"He experimented on us, both you and me and who knows how many others."

"Whoever told you that, they're lying. They just wanted to turn you against us, against your own people."

"I have proof, Ares. I know what this piece of shit has done. We're better off without him."

"They don't have him anyway, they're bluffing. Our team just secured the Core Hull."

If Ares was telling the truth, the mission had failed, she would never see Julian again. "Julian?" She tried the comms but there was no answer. She swallowed with difficulty as her finger hugged the trigger. "Open fire on my mark, no holding back," she ordered, tapping the rifle's menu with her thumb until the rocket icon appeared, the ballistic rounds. If this was the end, she'd take everyone down with her.

She aimed for the ground where most of them were gathered, determined to start counting when an invisible force pushed her sideways and sent her flying through the crumbling wall of the Power Snacks kiosk. Her visor shattered, showering her with pieces of glass that tumbled further inside her uniform.

"Is everyone alright?" She asked, the inactive exosuit weighing down on her as she strained to move her muscles.

"What kind of weapon was that?" Christoff asked, his voice no longer in her head but coming from somewhere beside her.

She couldn't move her left arm and her legs felt numb as she limped to get to Christoff. She offered the other hand and gritted her teeth trying to lift him up, the borrowed strength of her exosuit now gone.

Christoff's visor retracted back in the helmet and he wiped the river of blood that was rushing down his forehead "I've got Rachel," he said, patting himself down to clear the debris.

"What was that?" Alina's voice came from Christoff' helmet.

"I don't know," Rachel muttered and shook her head, climbing out of the rubble that used to house her delicious power bars.

She stumbled and cursed as she fell on her knees, only to witness such a horrific sight, a grotesque transformation of the landscape in front of her that made her heart stop.

The bodies were everywhere. Blood was flowing through the grout of the tiled path like an ancient ritual Scott had shown her once. The grassy paths were stained with shining, crimson red on their tips, bent and distorted from the weight of the blood pooling on them. Overlapping cries and shrieks and wails resounded in the whole quadrant as she remained there, her legs fused to the solid ground beneath her, unable to move any of her muscles. The long window strip under the apartment blocks was blocked by the silent husks of the people who were just a minute ago firing upon them.

She looked up at the never ending nightmare where people were hanging from the sky bridges and balustrades trying to crawl their way back to safety.

"What is... this?" Liam helped her up. He had come out of his exosuit as well, his eyes widened and his features frozen as he slowly revolved around himself.

She had to say something, she was their leader after all. She needed to reassure her team and keep them from falling apart but the words inside her head couldn't be arranged in a way that would form a sentence—one that would make sense at least. She saw Lee clutching his stomach outside the metal plates of his suit, falling on his knees and then throwing his helmet away seconds before emptying his stomach next to the table outside Sweet Delights. She gagged and instinctively tried to cover her mouth, the sour stench filling her throat making everything worse and she pinched her nose shut. She felt an excess of saliva accumulating in her mouth and she knew the acid was not far behind. The air felt wet and heavy, the foul smell almost like an old rusty pipe in the maintenance tunnels as she wiped her lips on the sleeve of her uniform.

"Give me your helmet," she ordered Kaiden who had just arrived at the scene, the corner of his mouth tipped as if he was enjoying the view.

Kaiden complied and she held it upside down, like a big microphone, "Julian? Was that the engines?"

"Fuck," Lee and Josh exclaimed at the same time.

"We lost then?" Alina's voice cracked.

No one answered. The silence was excruciating, only interrupted by the cries of the people still fighting for their lives. She opened the channel to everyone from their original strike force and repeated the question.

"Rachel, this is Mark. No, this was Abeone's doing, she's taking us back to the *Sagan*."

She let out the breath she was holding in, a cathartic exhale as her team cheered around her, hugging and raising their fists in the air.

"That's it? We did it?" Christoff exclaimed.

"We fucking did it!" Kaiden cheered.

"Yeah... we did," Rachel said, taking a step forward. "But at what cost?" She muttered as her eyes darted around the sea of lifeless bodies.

"Where is Julian? He's not answering his comms."

"We're still fighting here, Miss Watson," Nyx's voice was as calm as ever. "Have you secured the resi?"

"There's nothing to secure... we're the only ones standing."

CHAPTER 33
— Julian —

> Core Hull - Ring 6

The crossfire started again with an increased intensity as more boots clanged on the upper decks. *It's us or them*, he heard Nyx's voice in his head although she had climbed one floor up, too busy with her rampage to say anything.

"Watch out!" Mark cautioned him and fired his pistol above Julian's head. The evolutionist on the railings floated away from the force of the bullets, leaving a scattered trail of blood behind him.

Another shot came from nowhere, ricocheting between the terminal and Mark's armour with an ear splitting echo; everything was louder without a helmet. Julian instinctively faced away and scampered behind the short edge of the terminal. Leaning out, he returned the fire but his aim was terrible at that distance, especially without the help of the exosuit to guide his arms.

"Mark, look away!" he implored while detaching the stun disk from the metal arm of his spacesuit. He had to manually enable it and time his throw right for it to be effective. There was also the element of the necessary downward force to keep it from bouncing off in the absence of gravity. *Three... twoo... one...*

The disk spun on the floor, grinding on the metal decking as friction produced sparks that followed its path. He never saw them falling, he didn't know when to open his eyes but there they were, two of them behind the main column, their bodies leaning towards the floor, anchored by their magboots. How many were still left?

He heard Nyx screaming, a warcry of bloodlust and he finally stood up on his feet to scout the platform.

"Oh, J... why did you do this?" Mark mumbled, focused back on the transparent screens in front of him.

"It was the last resort, it would've all been for nothing if I hadn't," he defended himself.

"Well, I can't lock her out now. I don't know how the evos did it in the first place."

"Why would you want to? Abeone is taking us back."

"You heard her, J. The ship's survival is priority. She doesn't care about us. What if she does another high G turn like that? Did you think about the rest of the people on the Ring before pressing that button?"

"What do you mean?"

"You saw what happened here in near-zero G with that manoeuvre, what do you think happened in the rest of the Ring?"

"I didn't know, I thought the AI would make things go faster," he cried with a raised voice, his eyes darting around the deck, his surroundings out of focus and blurry as a shiver passed through the hairs of his skin. Was he responsible for the deaths of who-knew-how-many innocent civilians? He was trying to save everyone on the *Sagan*, the thought never crossed his mind that there were innocents on this Ring as well. Kids, spouses who maybe weren't part of the Icarus movement, people like him that were trapped here against their wishes; he had doomed them all.

"Yeah, ok," Mark said, snapping him out of his spiral.

He hadn't said anything out loud, had he?

"Nyx says what's done is done and that she needs me up there," Mark continued.

"What are we going to do with Toz?" Julian asked, kneeling in front of the old engineer. His eyes were closed and his features calm.

"His vitals are fine, just unconscious," Mark explained.

"What about..."

"Rachel is fine as well, I talked to her. Stay here and protect Toz."

"I can fight too! I won't sit back and watch you get killed."

"I'm sorry, J… Nyx's orders."

"Well, I don't care. I'm coming up there."

Mark's nostrils flared and his mouth twitched to the side but he eventually nodded. He jumped up the opening only grabbing the last rung of the ladder to find his footing on the floor above.

Julian followed into the bullet storm, an endless ricochet of kinetic rounds and debris scattered in all directions.

"Surrender your weapons," a man shouted from the floors above. "You're cornered and outnumbered. If you don't comply, your only way out is in body bags."

"I was about to say the same thing to you," Julian blurted.

"I thought I told you to stay at the terminals," Nyx snapped at him while taking cover behind a long desk as her rifle hummed progressively to recharge.

"It's us or them, Nyx." He hit her with her own words. "I won't be the last one to die alone."

"You won't die at all, son," his dad's voice came with a barrage of fire that rained down with percussive impact.

His chest sent a pulse throughout his body and he looked up with a grin, trying to find his dad's figure through the perforated metal tiles. The assault was brief and effective, the evolutionists hadn't realised their rear was breached until it was already too late.

Julian climbed to the next levels, trying to avert his gaze from the swaying bodies, still magnetically attached to the floor. Their limp forms danced with an eerie grace as their disarrayed limbs floated freely, arms up and fingers splayed as if reaching for something beyond their grasp.

"Dad," he exclaimed, running towards him and embracing him with such force that almost pushed him away.

"Easy with that exosuit, Julian," his father grunted. He wasn't wearing power armour so the hug must have been difficult to withstand. "You don't know how happy I am to see you, son." He smiled widely, placing both hands on Julian's cheeks.

The last time he had seen him was right before the Ring's separation. He was too preoccupied with being outside the ship and the jump that almost cost him his life to remember anything clearly.

He dug his head in his father's neck and closed his eyes. There was a pungent smell coming off his hairy skin but he let it all in, a sense of safety and security enveloping him like a second armour.

"All clear," Andre's voice made him look up at the nuclear fusion reactor.

"I've got Richter! I locked him in there," he pointed behind his father.

His dad glanced at the chamber and returned to him with a grin, clicking his tongue as his lips parted. "I'm so proud of you, son." He caressed his cheek again.

Tears formed on Julian's eyelids and his throat felt sore as if he was trying to swallow a rock, a sense of validation and accomplishment washing over him.

"Yeah but I also enabled the AI." He blurted, pursing his lips, ready to negate his dad's words.

"Julian, the weight of responsibility can be heavy when we make tough choices." His father placed one hand on his shoulder pad and peered into his eyes, raising his glasses up his nose with the other. "Enabling Abeone was a decision born out of the need to save lives back at the *Sagan*, yet the loss of civilians here is a profound burden to bear, I know. You feel guilty but that's the price of acknowledging the pain caused… the first step of living with the consequences of your actions. The only thing you can do now is use that pain to fuel your determination to prevent more tragedies."

"Did I really kill a lot of people?" He asked, his legs suddenly unable to support his weight.

"Rachel said it's a bloodbath," Mark interjected.

"Mark, you're not helping," Nyx growled.

"What? He'll find out soon enough," Mark countered, "I'm sorry, J."

"I-I…I didn't…" Julian stuttered, suddenly feeling like he was carrying a boulder on his shoulders. He drew a long, shaky breath, his lungs screaming for more air. "I-I thought the AI would give a warning at least."

"The ship comes first," Andre said with a sigh. "It's a good thing the core lift is on rails otherwise we'd be soup on the walls.

"That's because you made it like that," Ms Carter spat from the railing she was still tied to. "The whole lot of you, arrogant cosmic fucks. Everything's about the ship."

"Said the woman who was willing to sacrifice thousands for her own selfish reasons," his dad snapped at her.

"We wouldn't have to if you hadn't sent the original team of the *Sagan* away. Brilliant scientists who valued life more than anything."

"You speak as if we were the ones that did that, putting so many at risk for something our forefathers did a hundred years ago... *presumably*. We only have your word for it."

"You're the archivist, don't you have access to the repository?"

His father hid his lips inside his mouth and cocked his head with no answer.

"Surely the person responsible for recording everything that happens on the ship should have access to that, don't you think?" Ms Carter offered a mocking smile and a sinister chuckle as if she was enjoying the dialogue despite being tied down.

"Enough out of you," Nyx intervened and stuck a transparent device on Ms Carter's neck, right above her collarbone.

His former teacher moved her mouth but no sound was produced. She scowled, her nostrils flaring wide as she bared her teeth and shook her shackles with a strong huff.

"Come on, let's get you out of here," Nyx said, placing a hand at Julian's back. "You need a new helmet."

"There should be emergency equipment over there." Andre pointed at a series of long cabinets around the outer walls of the cylindrical hull. "Oh... what the hell happened here?" He asked when he realised the storages were either empty or completely shattered.

"They pissed me off," Nyx replied, raising her rifle in front of her for another recharge.

CHAPTER 34
— Rachel —
Science Quadrant - Ring 5

The bright, white lights flickered in the distance, not fuzzy stars some light years away but manmade. They were closing in on the *Sagan*. Her team was lined up against the window strip under the apartment blocks, their faces pressed against the first layer of glass which was full of dirty handprints and the foggy condensation of their breaths.

Her back felt itchy and she tried to wriggle her body inside the exosuit, the fabric of the uniform providing little satisfaction against the smooth metal armour. She could have showered if she really wanted, Scott had left apartment 5C open for them. The threat hadn't completely gone away though, there were still evolutionist groups out there in the other quadrants, lurking in the shadows for the opportune moment. Everyone else was locked inside their homes, who knew for how long. *Until we reattach at least*, was all Scott had told her.

She glanced over her shoulder to the sound of metal footsteps and followed Julian with her eyes until he joined her by the window. He sighed, staring at the endless blackness and rested his hands on his hips. It was probably eating him from within but he didn't say anything. The bots had cleaned up everything before he arrived at the resi but the metallic scent still lingered. There were still some faint, red streaks on the balustrades and the grass was still stained with dried up blood that had created a layer on top of the soil. He didn't want to talk about it, she had asked him quite a few times already. If killing one person was already too heavy of a load to bear, she couldn't imagine how this felt. The only thing she could do now was distract him.

She licked her lips and leant against the window with a forced smile. "You don't get dizzy anymore, do you?"

"Huh?" he said, startled. He was in his own world again, not the best place to be at the moment, especially for an overthinker like him.

"From the spinning… you don't get disoriented."

"The *Sagan* is still quite far away, so not really. It gets me when all the Rings spin together… when the ship stands in the spotlight on a stage shrouded in darkness."

Rachel tried to contain herself but her chest spasmed and the laugh came out with a snort. "Come here, my weirdo." She wrapped her arm around his waist and leant against his shoulder plate.

She gazed outside at the glimmering lights coming closer and closer, normality finally within her grasp. Julian must have been doing the same as he stood there like a statue, his cold metal armour making the side of her face numb.

"Soon, we can put all this behind us," she broke the silence with the words that kept repeating inside her head.

"I don't think I ever will." Julian drew a loud breath, letting out a shaky exhale as his exosuit vibrated from containing his shivering body.

She took a long breath and chewed the inside of her bottom lip, the pain from seeing him like this too harrowing.

"I understand you don't want to talk about what happened but Julian, it's me… I'm not saying now but whenever you feel like you want to talk…"

"I will, Rach. It's just still all too fresh."

They stood like that in silence until the AI's announcement made everyone turn towards the plaza.

> "Docking sequence initiated.
> Brace for final approach."

"Rachel, gather your team and get ready at the outer bridge." Scott's voice came from the helmet at her back. "Make sure we're clear for docking."

"Come on, kid. I'll meet you at the rendezvous point." Nyx said through Julian's radio.

"Good luck," Julian said, his deep blue eyes glistening in the lights of the morning cycle like the oceans they would never see.

"Everything's going to be fine," she said and stepped on her toes for a kiss, their bulky power armours becoming an annoying obstacle in their brief moment.

Their lips parted as soon as they had touched but they both lingered, his intoxicating scent drawing her in again. She traced her fingertips around the contours of his face and their exosuits clanged as she leant in again. Their mouths moved in sync and their breaths intertwined as he softly grazed her hair behind her ear and her whole body tingled.

Julian pulled back and cleared his throat, that goofy smile she loved so much finally returning on his face.

"Bye," he whispered and turned away as his helmet pivoted from his back to lock over his face.

She shook her limbs to let go of the goose bumps and unholstered her pistol as her team gathered around her. Liam was pretending to look around the plaza and Christoff was whistling in a funny tune. Alina was still at the window and Kaiden was further away, sitting on a bench with his brows furrowed and his jaw clenched. Next to him, Lee had slumped over his legs, elbows balanced on his knees and pistol swaying from his index finger.

"Are you ready to go back home?" She asked over the comms when her helmet hissed on the exoskeleton that enveloped her.

"It's about fucking time," Liam exclaimed.

⚛

The sealed bulkhead of the outer bridge came into view, the colossal ship and its five Rings looming behind it. Only the external lights were sparkling in the distance, the edges of the Rings blending in the darkness of space around them as if a blackout had occurred in their time away. Scott had been in communication with the council the moment they had taken over Ring Six and the jamming was disabled.

They had assured him everything was under control and power from the batteries was distributed evenly to last as much as possible. That was what Scott had told her at least. Her only concern was the infirmaries, she didn't care if people had spent a few days in darkness, she had been through way worse for all of them. Alex was helpless though, dependent on the reliability of the life support systems.

Her loud exhale fogged her visor as a faint rumble resonated under her feet, vibrating with a low frequency as the metal tiles creaked. She glanced twice behind her at the quadrant intersection, one quick look at the residential entrance and another for the agricultural. Scott had locked everything from the control room and Alina had placed more stun traps around the doors just in case.

Her body swayed front and back but her boots kept her in place, the lateral forces meant micro thrusters were engaged. They were entering the last stage of docking. Neither Mark nor Toz would've done this manually without the AI, an argument she had used to ease Julian's pain but without success. She had been focusing so much on making him feel better that she hadn't really spent time processing the image of chaos herself. It was locked away in some corner at the back of her head, the bodies, the blood, the silence, all making her skin crawl just by bringing it up even for a second.

The whole atrium croaked and shuddered as a muffled thud echoed through the hull of the ship. She could feel the metal grinding and mechanisms whirring behind the blast door, the growling of machinery under her feet that shook her armour.

"Docking complete. Please stand by."

The blast door hissed after Abeone's announcement and the interlocking mechanism rotated counter clockwise, retreating back inside the outer wall, the usual sliding door of the *Sagan*'s bulkheads free at last. She approached the small horizontal window on the left panel and peered into the bridge, her gaze landing on the hatch on the floor. It seemed like an eternity ago, her first mission with Scott's group. She could have died back then if it wasn't for Julian's dad and she could have died a hundred times after that but she was still standing, Ring Six secured and attached back to the *Sagan*, her own team standing in line behind her.

"Scott, all good down there? Anything shady?" She asked over the comms.

"I've locked down everything. If there are evolutionists left, they're locked in somewhere."

"I'm going in then," she said and changed the channel specifically to her team. "Admins will be here shortly. You know what to do."

"Do we really have to escort them around?" Kaiden complained, fast to question her order.

"Unless you don't want the unlimited contribution points for life, you'll do it," she spat and Kaiden remained silent.

Rachel stepped onto the bridge, five hundred metres to go until she was home. Particles danced in the soft rays of the ceiling spotlights and her eyes darted to the cracked glass on her right, a reminder of the explosion that had cost Kieran and Noel their lives. A shudder ran up her spine and she picked up the pace, the silence and emptiness of the bridge making her uncomfortable.

The door on the other side slid open before she was even close. Dozens, possibly hundreds of faces waiting, cramped on top of each other for a better view—a better view of her? They all broke out in cheers and applause when she went through the threshold and she stood still, unsure if she should smile or wave or carry on with her task. Almost everyone had their rollers out to record her entrance, even the admins that were supposed to go into Ring Six to collect the evolutionists.

Rachel removed her helmet and raised her fist in the air with a grin, consumed by the exhilarating feeling of acceptance and praise. "Renovations are officially finished," she exclaimed and the crowd went mad, cheering and jumping like their favourite musician had appeared on stage.

She beckoned the leader of the admin team towards the outer bridge behind her and started making her way towards the agricultural quadrant as people grazed her exosuit while opening a path for her.

Three young boys stopped her for a picture and some older folk were even crying, thanking her and kissing her armour.

She finally made it out from the sea of people as the crowd thinned out towards the end of the quadrant intersection. The lights had returned to the rest of the *Sagan*, but the Cylidome was still drenched in a gloomy darkness. Most of the trees had completely shed their leafy shells and were now exposed, skeletal silhouettes that towered above her like massive thorns. Was it the absence of light during all these months? She would ask Julian on their next picnic. Maybe now that everything was over she could actually enjoy it.

The science quadrant was quiet, the lights of the infirmary still glowing in their usual blue and white. There was still a trail of teenagers following her. It was cool when she'd first arrived but she was going to see Alex now, she needed her privacy. She stopped by the armoury first, only admins were allowed in there and even if her new fans could get through it, there was the specialised arsenal after that. Only Scott's group had access there, personally granted by councilman Opoku.

She slipped inside and relieved herself from the exosuit that had become an extension of her limbs. It was the first time since they had boarded the shuttle to Ring Six that her body felt so free, the cool air penetrating the shirt that had stuck on her skin. The odour was quite pungent and she wrinkled her nose as she immediately took it off and looked for a replacement in the nearby cabinets.

She used the internal hallways to get to the infirmary and headed straight to Alex's room. There was a new bed on the other side of the wall, opposite to where the fifteen comatose patients remained. The man that occupied it looked familiar but his face was so heavily bruised it was hard to tell who was concealed behind all the black patches and deformed skin.

She checked the monitor at the foot of the bed and let out a brief chuckle. "You got what you deserved after all," she muttered as she studied the man's features.

You put so many kids in comas that in the end you had a taste of your own poison.

Nyx must have beaten him quite hard for that information of the shuttle. This was no longer Javier Rendall but a misshapen husk of the madman.

A faint mutter broke the monotonous beeping of the life support and she jumped around against Javier's bed. It was followed by a soft groan and her whole body shivered. Her eyes searched for the origin of the sound and she caught a glimpse of movement under Alex's sheet.

"Alex?" She rushed to her brother's side and knelt in front of the bed.

Alex's lips parted for a second and a low rumbling sound came out, a word almost too faint to make sense.

Rachel stroked his unattended, overgrown hair away from his forehead and repeated his name, leaning over him as his eyelashes twitched and he finally opened his eyes.

"You know I hate that," he said, rubbing his eyes.

"Alex!" She squealed, diving under his chin, her whole chest shaking. He was alive, talking and moving! "How are you feeling?" She asked, pulling back and he only bobbed his head around. "I knew you'd come back to me."

"Way sooner than I'd hoped though." His lips curled and his eyes darted somewhere behind her.

"What's that supposed to mean?" She pushed her brows together at the unexpected reply.

Maybe the meds had messed with his head. All this time in a coma could've had an adverse effect on him, but then again everyone had verified there was no brain damage, no memory loss, no significant reduction in mass.

"Well, we're still in space, aren't we?"

She nodded, studying him. What was wrong with him?

"Then it was all a lie, wasn't it?" Alex huffed, staring blankly at the ceiling.

You're scaring me, Alex, stop it.

"What was? Alex, talk to me!" She implored him but her brother remained silent. "You seem disappointed… I thought you'd be grateful you even woke up after everything Javier did to you."

His eyes lit up and slowly moved towards her again. "Y-You know? About J-Javier?"

"Yeah, I found out about everything. I never stopped looking for you. He's right there… in a coma as well but for different reasons.

One of my associates beat him up real good. I only wish I had done it myself."

Alex sat up and stole a glance to the bed at the opposite side of the room. "No, no, no..." he cried, "They didn't tell me it was Javier."

"Alex, what are you talking about?"

"I woke up after you left." His gaze fell back on her with a sigh. "Or at least that's what they told me." He grabbed the water bottle from beside his bed and gulped what was left inside.

It suddenly made sense. He was talking and moving normally—not what she'd expect from someone waking up from a coma. On the other hand, he seemed rather sad about Javier, no sane person would do that.

"Alex, you do realise Javier is the reason you've spent the last four months in this bed," she said, more like a question than a statement.

"He said that was necessary for the deep sleep."

"You *knew*?" She felt her eyes twitching from how wide she had unwillingly opened them.

"Yes, I knew. They were going to vent me if I didn't. Javier saved me."

"What are you talking about?" She stood up and crossed her fingers behind her neck as her heart raced and her whole body shivered.

"It doesn't matter now." He looked away again. "I hear you stopped Icarus."

"Yes, we did. Everything is fine."

"How is spending the rest of our shitty lives on this shitty ship *fine*? They were our only salvation."

"What salvation, you moron?" she screamed at him, "You just said they were going to vent you."

"Only because I wanted to tell Priya and Julian about it. Javier hid me away. He said I'd be safe if they thought I was dead and I could wake up at Aquanis."

Her lips parted but no words came out. She drew a shaky breath instead and paced up and down between Alex and Elizabeth's beds. "You told Julian?"

"I told no one. Lucas tried to convince them I could still be trusted but it was too late so I had to choose between death and sleep."

"Bjorgen?" She stood still for a second. That motherfucker was telling the truth after all.

"Yeah, he's in our physics class."

"You said you wanted to tell Priya and Julian about Icarus, why not me, Alex?"

"Because you don't know how it feels, Rach," Alex raised his voice, coughing, his back shaking the whole headboard. "Our life here never bothered you. Always happy, socialising, partying, joking around, never phased by the fact that our whole world fits in a few kilometres around a ring structure."

The bottom part of her jaw trembled and she pursed her lips, but she managed to hold the tears back, holding her breath in. *I went through tons of shit to get you and this is the thank you I get?* She didn't dare utter it, only swallowed with difficulty, happy that he was fully awake and forming full sentences.

"I-I... I couldn't do it anymore," Alex continued over her silence, "This ship... this forsaken piece of junk... it was just a better option than living like this forever."

"And you didn't stop for a second to think that you'd be leaving everyone else behind to die, including me?"

"What are you talking about? Icarus was supposed to keep the engines on to get us all to Epsilon Centauri faster."

"They detached Ring Six, Alex. We just got it back to the *Sagan*."

His widened eyes and slightly open mouth meant they hadn't told him the full story. Or he was playing dumb to save her feelings but she wanted to believe the former. Either way, there was nothing else to say. It was all over now. Maybe if he had more time to recover and was aware of the whole story, he would see things differently.

She shook her head, pacing around his bed. She had pictured this moment a thousand times in her head but it always played out as the big sister saving her lost brother. Alex didn't want to be saved, he had gone in Nightfall willingly. The realisation scared her more than the secret lab of nightmares itself.

"You haven' told Mum about any of this, right?" she asked. "Have they come to see you?"

The loud scoff was expected. "Mum has," he said, licking his lips and looking at his crossed hands on his lap. Of course their dad wouldn't bother. "You're not going to tell them about all this, are you?"

"What are big sisters for?" She said, trying hard to form a smile. No matter what had transpired in the last months, he was still her little brother—alive and well. All their disagreements could be worked out in screaming matches later.

"Rach, can you bring me some power bar or something? This goo soup they're giving me here is shit."

"Sure." She smiled again, this time effortlessly. "It's nice to have you back."

"Love you too, sis."

CHAPTER 35
— Julian —
Science Quadrant - Ring 2

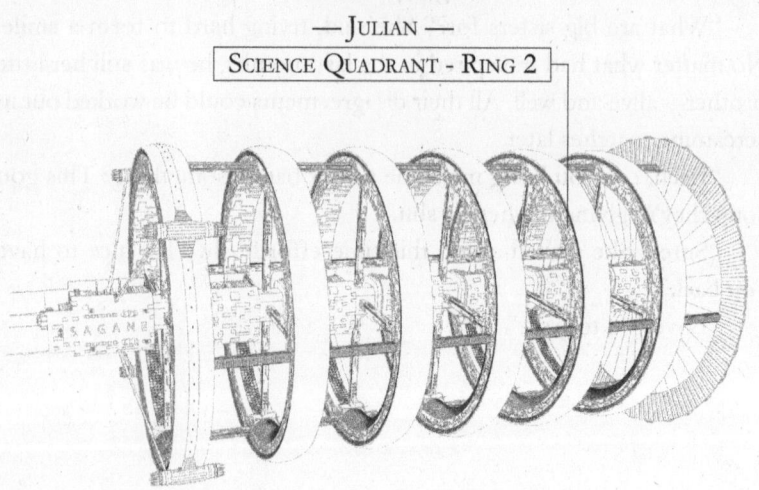

The grand hall was larger and shinier than he remembered. There were no decorations but the geodesic dome was a magnificent architectural masterpiece even without any adornments. He had missed the chance to see it in its glory during the Halfway event, he was stuck in Ring Six and unknowingly caught in the chaos that followed its isolation. The man responsible for all of it was now sitting in the middle of the circular stage, surrounded by council members who were there to pass judgement on his actions.

He spotted Rachel's ginger ponytail and weaved his way through the crowd to reach her. Mark and Liam were standing on either side of her and he squeezed through to give her a kiss before asking how the trial was going.

"Di Natale has been questioning him for the past half hour," Liam said and stretched his back with a relieved groan.

"Yeah but Richter keeps deflecting," Rachel added, "I don't understand why they can't use an inhibitor, loosen him up so he spills everything."

"Human rights, Rach," Mark replied, "Although I think he's more machine than he is human, maybe it wouldn't even work on him."

"You know he still has some organs," Julian commented, "When I had him locked in the reactor he peed in a corner."

"Where did he pee from? He doesn't have a thingy," Liam chuckled.

"Some kind of hole? I don't know... and I don't *want* to know."

"Is he really a hundred and twenty-seven years old?" Mark asked. "He looks surprisingly good for an old man."

"He's a walking bio-enhancement, what do you expect?" Julian scoffed.

"Still can't believe you beat him all by yourself," Liam said with a soft chuckle, "You sure it wasn't Nyx?"

"No, it was all him," Rachel threw her arms around his neck and pressed her soft lips on his cheek.

Julian felt his face burning up as Mark and Liam's gaze remained upon him, wide grins decorating both their faces.

"Trust me, I wish it was Nyx," Julian admitted. "They want me to get on stage for an award or something and do a little speech."

"Hero of the *Sagan*." Mark extended his arms above his head as if he was holding a virtual title on his palms.

"Not even close. A hero doesn't kill innocent people."

"You didn't kill anyone!" Rachel snapped and softly punched him on the arm.

Everyone had told him the same but he couldn't bring himself to let go of the guilt that was weighing him down. It was the AI they had said and that he couldn't have known. It was only partially true. If he had more time to think about it, he would've reached to the conclusion that Abeone would prioritise the ship. It was reckless, a decision that he knew would haunt him forever.

"You saved everyone," Rachel continued. "All these people here would be dead by now if it wasn't for you. Stop beating yourself up over it."

She had a point but that didn't mean he could shake it off just like that. Four nights had passed since the attachment of Ring Six and the nightmares hadn't stopped. The screams of anguish and agony were tormenting his dreams even though he hadn't actually heard them.

"Just get on stage and accept your award, J. You deserve it. Richter would've killed us all." Mark patted him on the back.

"I don't know... I might not even be here when they announce it."

"Scott agreed to check it out?" Rachel's eyes widened as she tilted her head, grabbing his arm to make him turn towards her.

"Yeah, we're going in now, while the council is occupied here."

"Where? Just the two of you?" Liam leant in, lowering his voice and glancing cautiously around him.

"The repository," Julian whispered as they all huddled in. "I don't trust this council any more than I did the evolutionists. Look at them, all peppy and smug now but when people needed them they hid away in their headquarters and did nothing."

"I'm sure people won't forget that," Liam said, glancing at the stage. "Everyone is happy to even be alive now but when it all goes back to normal, I think there'll be a shift in power."

"I should hope so, "Rachel agreed. "Look at Okada in her fancy new dress. She's done nothing apart from giving us authorisation to print weapons and yet she acts like she's the one who saved everyone."

Erin Okada approached the accused in the centre of the stage, holding her long dress that was almost trailing on the floor. Her pitch black hair was tied in a bun on top of her head as always, the two long sticks that were holding it together protruding high above it.

"Dr Albert Richter, would you care to enlighten us with the events that led to the isolation and detachment of Ring Six?"

"Surely, my dear Erin. I was born only a few months after the *Sagan* started its engines. The first child to take residence aboard its magnificent halls. I still remember the Earth through my window, I must have been three or four. It looked like nothing more than a bright star among the countless others but we were still inside the solar system back then and going remarkably slow, telescopes could still see our old blue marble."

"Objection! Irrelevant!" Ms Okada cried and revolved around herself, her dress flying in a spiral like a ballerina.

"Sustained." The deep male baritone of councilman Opoku echoed throughout the hall. "Need I remind you that this is a trial on your condemned actions on attempted murder of thousands of lives by the detachment of Ring Six?"

The audience murmured, spitting threats, and accusations at Richter while calling him all sorts of names. The scientist seemed unfazed by all of it, way too calm for someone who was on trial, almost indifferent to its verdict or the chaos he was causing as a slight grin formed on his wrinkly face.

"I only did what our forefathers sent us out here to do," Richter said, his mechanical arms resting idle on his legs and his back straightened, not too different from an android waiter at the food plaza.

The crowd broke in whispers and silent nudges, the indistinct chatter piling up with intensity. The overlapping conversations rapidly united in a single background noise until Councilman Opoku demanded silence, drowning all other voices under his own.

"Is this your strategy, rile these good people up with your twisted words?" Erin Okada stood in front of Dr Richter with a scowl.

"It's about time they knew the true reason for this journey they are unwillingly part of, don't you think?"

"You are responsible for almost bringing that journey to a short-lived end," Ms Okada pressed on, twirling her wavy purple dress as she stepped away from the centre stage and towards the rest of the council members. "I don't know what the point of this is, we know he committed his crimes, the evidence is all over the place."

Julian's pocket buzzed and he slid his roller out, hunching over it so no one could see his dad's message.

"There are procedures we must adhere to, even for him," councilman Opoku said in an authoritative tone while Julian slowly backed away through the crowd and writhed his way towards the exit.

He found his dad waiting at the quadrant intersection and they briskly walked from the recreation quadrant of Ring Three to the science quadrant of Ring Two. Their talks had almost become mission briefings the last few days. His dad had brought up his mother a few times but Julian stopped him every time, the pain in his chest from her betrayal still fresh.

His father led him to the upper floors and through the wide corridors like he knew exactly where he was going until he reached a transparent partition. The space inside was vast and open with only a few pieces of furniture, its purpose engraved on the glass in a huge font—*Council Headquarters*.

"How are we getting in?" Julian asked while his father placed his open roller in front of the revolving door's panel.

"Lucky for us I still have Kieran's palm print," he exclaimed when it chimed with a green light. "And even luckier that they never disabled it."

"Isn't that illegal?"

"Highly. I could have my contribution points zeroed for this. Come, this way." He swooped through the glass panels of the revolving door and into the other side where he manipulated the panel to lock down the doors.

Julian followed his father closely as he climbed over the turnstiles and hopped up the steps that led to the main chamber. He had only seen this place in pictures and it was as breath-taking as he had always imagined it to be. There were little trees every few feet and on both sides of the room like a natural colonnade. It led to an oval table at the end which was probably made from one single piece of oak, large and heavy with its bark still preserved on its thick side. The opposite end of the room featured a wall of monitors, now black and silent. In front of them, six black tiles broke the continuity of the grey polished, concrete floor. He furrowed his brows when he realised it was indeed concrete he was standing on, solid and soundless to step on in comparison to the usual metal panels across the rest of the ship.

His father knelt above one of the tiles with his roller and jumped back when it hissed and disappeared below. A mechanism roared below him and a pedestal protruded from the hole left behind, stopping at the height of his waist and culminating in a bronze pyramid at the top. The base was made of extruded cells arranged on a hexagonal grid with a tiny light at the centre of each cell that varied in colour. Some were blue, others were red or white but all together were enough to illuminate the column underneath the base of the pyramid.

"Is this the repository?" Julian asked while studying the weird piece of technology before him.

"Part of it. One of six." He beckoned towards the other tiles.

"You seem excited," he chuckled, "When was the last time you were here?"

"I've never seen it opening!" His dad said with a broad smile, the enthusiasm painted across his stretched cheekbones.

"But you're the archivist."

"Think of it as a time capsule that is supposed to be protected at all costs. It carries the whole Earth in it."

"It seems awfully small for that."

"Well, there are six of them and they're immensely compressed."

"Are you sure we won't get in trouble for opening it?"

"Oh we're in *a lot* of trouble already, but the pursuit of truth and knowledge accepts no cowards, my son."

Julian sighed uncomfortably but at the same time felt quite proud of his dad. Fearless and inquisitive about everything in life he was, the best example any kid would be lucky to have.

"What do you think we'll find here?" He asked as he got closer to the pedestal.

"Everything that happens on the *Sagan* is streamed directly here. This is the backup of backups. If they're hiding something, it's going to be here. Everything is preserved, nothing can be deleted."

The four faces of the little pyramid turned into a translucent, illuminated blue and a holographic panel appeared above its apex, mirroring the shape and size of the pyramid itself. His father placed both his index fingers on two opposite sides, swiping and twisting them to guide the overwhelming information on the panel.

"Is there no keyboard? It might be faster," Julian asked, trying to understand how his dad was shifting through the countless folders hovering in front of them.

"I'm trying my best, son. I've never used it before either."

"There! Stop! No, go back!" Julian cried when he saw the surname 'Richter' in the early-years logs.

It was a video of a man in his forties who didn't look anything like the Dr Richter he knew. He had dark brown eyes matching the colour of his thick, wavy hair and his complexion was rough as if he was working the mines of Ganymede. He was holding a baby in his arms and pointing outside the window at the still visible back then Earth. "A hundred and sixty years left for Aquanis. I definitely won't make it, even with my new heart and cell repair but you will. We're doing this for you," the man said and stroked the few hairs on his baby's head.

The log changed and it was now the same man, but in his living room trying to help his baby crawl while talking to his wife on his roller. "The engineers are making their move and the cosmitists are backing them. We can't hide forever. They'll eventually find us."

The video stopped and his father went back to a screen of endless lines, scrolling down while his eyes scanned for the right clue.

"Do you think that was Dr Richter's father? Why did you stop it?" Julian asked.

"I'm going through the database of first passengers on board," he replied and took a break to quickly push his glasses up his nose bridge. "There, Klaus and Irina Richter. Firstborn son, Albert Jonas Richter, born thirteen of the sixth, twenty-one thirteen."

"So, he really was the first baby on the *Sagan*!" Julian exclaimed as his roller beeped in his pocket.

They know someone infiltrated their HQ. Get out of there fast."

He didn't reply to Rachel, only reeled in his roller and turned to his dad again. "They know we're here."

"We have less time than I thought," his dad raised his glasses up again.

"Did you find anything else?"

"No, nothing. Neither Klaus nor Irina exist in my own database," his dad let out a long frustrated exhale and put his own roller back in his pocket.

"Could it be they really left on *Tyson-7*?" Julian suggested, his heart racing as everything started to make sense.

"*Tyson-7*! Of course, why didn't I think of that?" His dad's eyes glimmered in the reflection of the hologram. "Wait, how do you know about that?"

"It's how we found Nightfall. The passcode was the date it was expelled from the *Sagan*."

"That's quite smart, son." His father chuckled, giving him a brief glance. "I never thought about it twice, I guess I presumed some people just didn't want to be part of this expedition, it sounded normal back then, they were still close to Jupiter at the time."

"Are you suggesting they locked them all in that shuttle and sent them to Ganymede before they could expose them?"

"We're in uncharted waters here, son, anything is possible."

"What about the children though? They must have been too young to remember anything anyway."

"My thoughts exactly. The question remains though, who are *they*?"

"Early form of council?"

"Then why did it take them another forty-something years to officially assemble the council?"

"I don't know Dad... you're the archivist."

"Exactly! I'm the archivist, I should know..." he paused in the middle of his sentence and scratched his nose. "You know there was an old Earth saying *history is written by the victors*. It might be that the history I found and put together all these years was forged by the winners... the council."

"Are we really saying that the council squashed the original plan for their benefit?"

"No... no, no, Kieran would have said something. I knew him all my life, he wasn't that type of person."

"Maybe he didn't know either. Would it be crazy to assume that the higher ups manipulated him like everyone else?"

"I'd like to believe that. Then again, council members are supposed to be equal."

"As far as *you* know."

"Hmmm... the question remains, why did they do it?"

"I don't want to say it but maybe there's some truth in that cosmic—life sciences feud about the duration of the journey? Are there any more logs from Klaus Richter?"

His father put his hands back on the pyramid's sides and brought up a new video of Klaus Richter running in the hallways, holding his son by the hand while his wife was following behind them.

"Daddy, why are we running?"

Klaus didn't answer and glanced over his shoulder.

"They found us," Irina cried.

Klaus stopped abruptly and turned into what looked like a

manufacturing facility. "Listen Albie," he said as he left the roller on the floor, the camera pointing at the pipes and ducts hanging from the ceiling. "I need you to do me a favour, can you do that for daddy?"

"Uhuh," the child nodded.

"Can you make me a nice hand extension? You know which one it is on the panel?"

"Yeah, like the one we did for throwing the ball?" little Albert cheered.

"Yeah, make one in any colour you want and we can play catch in the forest."

"Klaus!" Irina entered the video frame, placing her hand on his shoulder and replacing him in front of their child.

"I love you so much my boy." Her voice cracked as she kissed him on the forehead and brought him to her chest.

"Irina, they're coming!" Klaus picked up the roller and dragged her out. He stood in front of the door for a second, tears running freely on his cheeks.

"Mummy needs to go but Mr Carter will come pick you up, ok my boy?"

Klaus locked the valve of the entrance while snivelling and wiping his nose with his arm. "We can't be found here... it will lead them to him."

"I-I... I can't leave him there alone. He's our little boy, Klaus," Irina sobbed.

"It's the only way to save him, baby. Come on, before they see us." He took her arm and started running as the camera flailed uncontrollably.

The log changed and it was Irina Richter talking on the video this time. "Albie, you might not understand what I'm talking about when you see this but you need to trust mummy and daddy and never forget what we fought for. Don't talk to anyone apart from Mr Carter, ok? He's going to take good care of you."

"Irina!" Klaus yelled from behind her and she looked away from the screen, her lips pursed and her eyelids overflowed with tears.

"I love you so much." She turned back to the camera as her voice cracked. "Mummy will always be with you... even when she's not around."

"Irina!"

She tried to stifle the sob that was visibly coming as she put her lips on the camera and everything went black.

"What the fuck did we just watch?" Julian placed his hands behind his neck and scratched the back of his head.

"I'm so stumped I'll even let your swearing slide."

"Dad, do you think they killed Dr Richter's parents?"

"We have to find that shuttle's manifest," his dad said and went back to the pyramid controls. "There it is! *Tyson-7*!"

"Seventy-six entries?" Julian exclaimed. "That's a lot of people."

"Here, Klaus Richter, Irina Richter. They were on it."

"Colin and Eve Carter. Are these the ones the Richters were supposed to leave their kid with? They're here too."

"That would mean Albert grew up completely alone."

"So they did send them away. What a horrible thing to do, leaving all these children orphaned. Wait... Dad, did you see this?"

"Mayer? It could be the same surname, a coincidence, it doesn't mean it's..."

"Mum?"

"No... no, I would have known if she was in it from the beginning."

"Would you, Dad? Maybe that's the reason she was interested in you in the first place, to keep tabs on what the archivist is archiving." Even the thought made him feel sick but it wasn't that far-fetched. She had proved to be a master of manipulation after all.

"That's enough, Julian!" His dad shouted as they both turned to the explosion that came from the lobby.

Julian ran to the steps and leant out to find the revolving door in pieces and three men shifting through debris, the lasers of their rifles penetrating the thick smoke of fire and ashes.

He felt naked without his exosuit, he had gotten used to the protection it offered.

"Dad! What do we do?" He whispered as he dashed back to the pedestal.

His father had knelt in front of it, rushing to complete some sort of transfer to his roller from the hexagonal cells.

"Put your hands in the air and step away from the panel!" One of the invaders barked the order.

"OK, OK." His dad lifted his hands in the air, letting the roller fall down on the floor.

"Dad?"

"Just do as they say. We'll be alright."

"You are arrested for conspiracy and treason against the *Sagan* authorities."

"Treason, seriously?" Julian sputtered.

"Face the wall and put your hands behind your backs."

Julian hesitated and glanced at his dad until he felt a thud on his back and a sharp pain that forced him on his knees. His cheek squished against the cold rough wall and suddenly his wrists were tied together.

"We got them, ma'am," one of them said as their footsteps retreated. "Should we capture or terminate?"

"Terminate?" Julian cried and turned his head back only to wince away from the blinding laser right on his eyes.

"Are the repositories online?" The voice came from their radio. It sounded a lot like Erin Okada but it was muffled and distorted.

"One of the pedestals is operating as we speak, yes," the same guard replied.

"Terminate." The order was sharp and shot a pain inside Julian's chest as his spine shivered and his muscles felt stiff and useless.

"Dad?" He looked at him again, hoping he had some divine plan that could get them out of this.

His father only winked with half a smile. Did he really have a plan? The thought didn't reassure him for long as the weapons hummed behind him as they powered up.

Three rapid bursts were fired and Julian squeezed his eyes shut. He could feel his heart screaming inside him and his pulse vibrating along every vein in his body but he was still alive.

Wait, the laser rifles don't produce a sound when they fire.

"You didn't have to wait until the last second," his dad said as he stood up against the wall.

"I just got here," Nyx's voice came with a cathartic relief.

"In that case, I should have been way more scared," his dad chuckled and presented his hands to Nyx to remove the cuffs.

"It's so good to see you," Julian ran to her and dove inside her arms.

He took a deep breath and released it slowly and shakily from his mouth as he felt the warmth of her exposed skin between her collarbones.

"I've got you, kid," she said and tousled his hair.

"We need to tell everyone what we found here," Julian exclaimed as he pulled back to unfold his roller.

"The trial is almost finished. They'll announce him guilty on all charges."

"Is Andre down there?" his dad asked, returning back to the pedestal.

"No, he's still on damage control at Ring Six."

"That's not good, we need to present all this data in the grand hall for everyone to see."

"Send it to Rachel," Julian chimed in, "Mark's with her, he'll know how to hook it up."

CHAPTER 36
— Rachel —
The Grand Hall - Ring 3

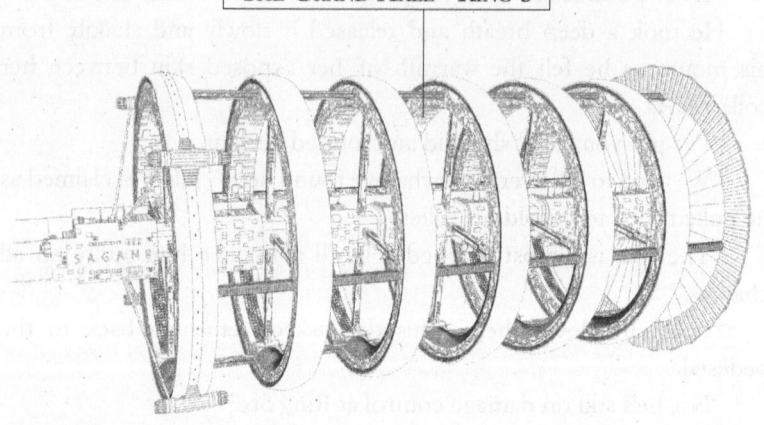

The audience was getting restless, most of them were standing now, arms either crossed in front of their chests or locked on their hips. The overlapping shouts were inconsistent but she could make out a few insults directed both towards Richter and Okada.

"The people have a right to know what you took away from them," Dr Richter said, "You and your scheming little council, it is because of people like you we had to leave Earth in the first place. So hungry for power and control…"

"You dare speak of *control*?" The council woman yelled so loudly Rachel instinctively winced from the microphone's echo.

"They should have given us some popcorn at the door," Mark said, locking hands behind his neck and leaning back in his chair.

"Yeah, it's more like a reality drama now," Liam chuckled.

Rachel tried for a smile but her muscles barely moved. She reeled her roller open again, staring at the empty blue screen, waiting. What was Julian still doing there? The council had surely dispatched admins to go safeguard their headquarters by now. It was very likely Julian wasn't even carrying a gun either, he had vowed never to touch one again.

"Let's take a break so everyone can recollect themselves and get back to it with a fresh pair of eyes," councilman Opoku snapped her out of it.

Erin Okada flailed her hands in the air, clearly annoyed and climbed down the steps from the stage.

Her roller finally chimed but the notification was quite different from what she'd expected. "Database Transfer, 1%?" She muttered and the boys turned to check on her. "Scott is sending us something!"

"Yeah, I got a message too," Mark exclaimed, "He says to hook it up on the apex holo and wait for further instructions."

"Whatever they're sending, it must be important." Rachel studied the area around them for snooping eyes and looked up where the geodesic dome was culminating in a single point.

"I kind of feel left out now," Liam sat back in his chair, pursing his lips and pretending to be sad. "I'm here too, I can help."

"Then get up. Go find the others. I think I saw Christoff with his parents and Lee should be wherever you see a shortage of drinks. Alina..."

"I think Alina's still in her flat. She hasn't come out since we returned."

"Maybe leave her out of it, yeah," she agreed. Alina hadn't dealt with the bloodshed in Ring Six as easily as the others. In all fairness Rachel hadn't dealt with it at all, she'd rather process it at her own time when everything was finished. Alex needed her more than ever to come back to the world, he couldn't see her spiralling and she knew she would if she allowed herself to think about it. "Message the rest and come find us at..." She trailed off, revolving around herself to find the console. "Mark, how do they set the holos up?"

"This way." Mark grabbed her arm and shifted through the crowd. "It's that raised platform over there." He pointed at the cantilever deck above them, flicking his hair back with a jerk of his head.

"How do we get up there?" She studied the extended platform, clad in glass and illuminated in a dim red light in contrast to the bright white of the grand hall.

"That door there," Mark exclaimed. "I might be able to convince the guards that I need to do some repairs."

"No time for that." She lifted up her dress and unholstered the pistol she had tied around her thigh.

"So you just carry one of these with you at all times now?" Mark asked, lifting the corner of his lip for a sarcastic grin.

"Kind of," she replied with a shrug, trying to muffle the weapon's humming inside her dress.

She approached the guard on the right, glancing behind her for any witnesses, the pistol concealed under her palm. She noticed how his eyes stopped at her hands and his brows furrowed. He moved his finger behind his ear but Rachel didn't give him a chance to speak. The second shot was seconds behind, her aim precise even without scope. Mark rushed to hold the guard upright, his fingers hidden inside his sleeves as he tried to avoid contact. She tried to do the same for the other man, needles prickling along her scalp as loose strands of hair stood up, trying to escape her tightly tied bun. She grabbed him from the chest pockets of his uniform and guided him towards the door panel, pressing his hand against it until it turned green. She wrapped his arm around her and took him inside, shoving him to the floor with a grunt before her knees bent inwards.

These fucking heels every time.

"You're a wild woman, Rachel," Mark exclaimed with a brief laugh while locking the door behind them.

"You just realised that?" She teased him, throwing her heels next to the unconscious guard.

The seven flights of stairs wound her up and she stood at the landing, panting. "I hope... you can get... the door because I'm not going back down there to drag that guard."

Mark kneeled in front of the panel and did his thing while she took position behind him, her pistol ready, balanced on her palm. The door slid back inside the wall and the gun recoiled inside her hands. The poor woman that was managing the booth was quite old but she could feel bad about tasing her later. Mark replaced her in the control chair as Rachel dragged her wrinkly body outside the room.

"Do you know how to work this equipment?" She asked, looking around the countless monitors, live feeds, buttons, graphs and switches, all illuminated with a variety of colours that shone bright in the faint, dark red of the ceiling lights.

"Yeah, I've got this," Mark claimed but that's what he always said, regardless of if he actually knew how to do it. She studied him for a second as he flicked through the different panels with ease, pivoting with his swivel chair to the monitors around him.

Her roller chimed again and her brows furrowed at Julian's message. He was back at the grand hall, asking her how she was doing with her part of the job. Her eyes focused on the main HUD, which was covering the whole area of the glass facing the interior of the dome, transparent information running along its edges.

"Find, Julian Walker," she enunciated and red circles popped on the glass, swirling around like bees until one of them flashed green and zoomed in on Julian's face. "Is the transfer complete?" She asked as Erin Okada took to the stage once again.

Mark produced a bar on the bottom left corner of the HUD showing the progress still going, almost halfway through and returned to the terminal in front of him.

Rachel took a deep breath, munching on the inside of her lip and tapping her bare foot on the cold floor. Whatever Scott and Julian had sent, they had to project it before the trial ended or before they were caught.

"Thank you for your patience tonight," Okada started, "We thought it'd be good to take a break from this man's trial and take a moment to commend the person responsible for his capture. You know of course who I'm talking about, please welcome on stage, Mr Julian Walker!"

The crowd cheered beneath her and a smile formed on Rachel's face.

"Spotlights please?" Okada ordered, looking up at the control booth.

"Fuck, that's us right?" Mark jumped from his chair and searched the controls on the panel. "Fuck, I wasn't ready for spotlights."

"Uhm... Spotlights on the selected person?" She cried, flailing her hands in ignorance and a beam of light landed on Julian, his black hair shimmering with streaks of a reflective glow.

Scott held his son's arm until the steps and whispered something in his ear. Julian nodded and looked around him as if he was trying to find someone in the crowd. Was it her? She glanced at the progression of the transfer and back at her boyfriend shyly climbing on stage. His steps were small and indecisive, stopping and starting again as Okada guided him to where he should stand. The applause slowly dissipated to an absolute silence but Julian didn't speak. His eyes darted across the huge dome, his lips slightly parted and he raised a hand on his forehead to hide from the blinding spotlight. His thumb was twitching, scratching around the nail of his index finger and then against his trousers.

Don't bite it, Julian.

He raised his hand but stopped just before his chin as if he had heard her.

"Mr Walker, in appreciation of your efforts and determination to bring this madman to an end, the council hereby awards you with this commemorative pin of the *Sagan*." Erin Okada seemed quite aggressive in the way she stabbed the pin on Julian's chest, almost shoving him back. "The unlimited contribution points generously offered to you on behalf of the council is the least we can do to appreciate your massive contribution to uniting the *Sagan*."

"I only united the structural parts of the *Sagan*, Ms Okada," Julian finally started, his eyes fixated upon the councilwoman with an intense scowl. "I have failed to unite its people though." His voice trembled and his right leg was twitching back and forth.

Erin Okada stepped aside and Julian stood still, his eyes wide open and his brows raised as he licked his lips and cleared his throat.

"There is still division, I can see it right here before me, the selfish gene still persists even billions of miles away from Earth. A need to get our way, a craving for power even when there are no villas or luxurious lifestyle to tempt us on this forsaken, floating world..."

The crowd agreed, nodding like marionettes attached on the same string. Julian had such a way with words. Rachel had always found it silly and funny but here, now, he sounded like he belonged, like a revered scientist.

The HUD flashed a warning with a blaring alarm and her breath was caught inside her lungs. "Projectile weapons detected?" She exclaimed as she traced the highlighted red patches on the glass. The HUD zoomed in on the man and woman holding pistols on their sides, hidden among the sea of people. No one would notice as they moved their way through and closer to the stage, clear intent on their focused gaze. Her pulse was throbbing inside her ear and her heart seemed like it was going to be dislocated from its own beating. Was Julian their target? "Fuck, fuck, fuck, fuck, fuck... FUCK!"

The roller almost slipped from her hands as she got it open to call her team on the ground. "Highlight Liam Evans, Christoff Jansen and Lee McKinley," she enunciated and three more annotations appeared on the overlay.

"It's almost inconceivable what we've been through the last few months," Julian continued, completely unaware of the threat. He was on a roll now without stutters and fidgeting. "I'm still having a hard time realising what has happened. We had to print weapons, isolated ourselves from each other, schemed against each other... killed each other."

"Because of him!" Someone shouted from the crowd, pointing at Richter still sitting in his chair at the centre of the stage. The scientist was staring at Julian with a sinister grin on his face as if he was about to burst into manic laughter.

"Yes... and no," Julian answered, biting his lip and shaking his head as the audience started an inconsistent questioning.

She would've too if she didn't know Julian that well, his words were formulated in his head minutes before he'd utter them. She glanced at the transfer, almost complete now. Why was it taking so long, how much data had Scott sent them?

"Rach?" Liam's voice came from the roller in her hand. The other two boys had joined in but there was too much background noise to hear anything. She cursed that she'd chosen not to bring comms devices to the trial, coordinating through the rollers was impossible.

"Liam, there's a man on your right, brown, short hair, black vest, beige pants. You need to take him down, he's about to shoot someone," she cried, staring at the highlighted silhouette shifting through the crowd. "Christoff, you're close to a woman, she's literally twenty feet in front of you. Black hair, afro, yellow dress ankle length, light brown jacket on top. Detain her immediately, no questions asked."

Her heart was pounding and she leant on the terminal, her face almost touching the overlaid projection on the booth's glass.

"While Richter's actions are truly condemned," Julian was still talking, "And yes I do agree he should be convicted for his crimes, we should focus more on the underlying problem here, the real reason we got into this mess in the first place. Science shouldn't take sides, it should be guiding us to a single, irrefutable truth, a truth our esteemed council has hidden from us." Julian gestured to the row of chairs the council members were sitting in as the crowd gasped and the noisy chatter started again.

"Mr Walker, there's no need for such accusations…" Erin Okada paused for a second and her lips started moving again, only her voice was inaudible now.

The assassins shoved the people in front of them. They were in a hurry. They wouldn't let Julian finish. Her throat felt heavy and her jaw trembled as her lungs screamed for a full breath.

"Liam! Christoff!"

"I see her," Christoff exclaimed, his figure picking up the pace on Rachel's HUD.

"It's not an accusation but simply the truth," Julian said, "Isn't that why you gave the order to have me and my father killed?"

"What?" Rachel gasped, same as most of the audience. She had to buy her team more time, the woman Christoff was chasing had raised her pistol, aiming. "Spotlight on the highlighted people," she blurted and beams of light came from all directions to bask the assassins as well as her team in light.

The woman got startled and tried to hide the weapon inside her jacket but everyone around her saw it. Shrieks and cries echoed throughout the dome and the woman looked around her, probably weighing her options. She took out the gun again, revolving around herself, pushing everyone away as if the weapon had produced an invisible force field of fear. Christoff jumped at her from her blind spot, tackling her to the ground and securing the gun. Liam did the same but not before the man's pistol went off, sending everyone away in panic.

"These are the lengths they're willing to go to silence me," Julian raised his voice above the cacophony of chaos.

"Traitors!" Someone yelled.

"How do we know these hired guns weren't meant for me and the rest of the council?" Okada spat, swirling her dress in a fury to get close to Julian. "A scheme of yours to overthrow the council."

"You seem quite aggressive for a woman who only a few minutes ago commended me with the highest of praise." Julian said as if nothing had happened. How was he *that* calm?

Okada stood still, the flaring of her nostrils visible even from the control booth. "Truth is, we only have your word to believe for the capture of Dr Richter."

"Yes, the truth is bitter for people who don't want to accept it," Julian replied in a sharp tone.

"It's done," Mark exclaimed, bringing up a new overlaying panel on the screen.

The amount of data was immense but Scott had tagged a few folders already, probably the ones they wanted to share with the rest of the ship. The files consisted of videos, logs, documents, images, graphical data, the list went on and on.

"Did he say which one to play first?" Mark asked, shifting through the information as he opened and closed different types of files, flooding the screen with overlapping windows.

"How about that one? The manifest of *Tyson-7*," Rachel suggested, the only name in there that made sense to her.

"Let's all calm down for a second here," Councilman Opoku intervened in his deep baritone. "Mr Walker, if you have nothing relevant to say about Albert Richter's trial or his capture, I suggest you kindly get off the stage so we can continue."

"No… not this time," Julian shook his head, his unblinking eyes emanating a resolve that made Rachel's hairs rise.

A blue panel appeared from the apex of the dome, unveiling the names on board *Tyson-7* as it stretched and stopped above the stage. It was the first time Rachel was seeing this too and she narrowed her eyes to make out the letters.

"Here's what the council has been keeping from us all this time," Julian announced as Erin Okada looked up, bringing her hand in front of her mouth. "Richter, Carter, Yau, Thompson, Bjorgen… the people that were sent away on our missing shuttle back in year three."

The whole dome went silent and Dr Richter finally let out the hysterical laugh he was holding in all this time behind that provocative grin. "Aah, vindication," he exclaimed, his loud exhale sounding like a soft gust of wind through the speakers.

"Just because they ruined your life, it doesn't give you the right to ruin everyone else's," Julian snapped as the hologram morphed into a document Mark had found in Scott's files showing the original journey timeline of the *Sagan*.

"You're sharing the evidence yourself. The trip was supposed to take around a hundred and sixty years but they got rid of all of us before we could challenge them." Richter's tone carried a bitter resentment as if he was tasting the world's most disgusting poison just by uttering these words.

"No, you fucked up, the council fucked up and the people who were born on this forsaken remnant of humanity's hope for colonisation are the ones who paid the price."

"Yeah!" The cheer was unanimous among the crowd.

Rachel leant above the terminal, resting her head inside her palms, staring speechless at the man she loved. He was in the zone.

"A hundred and twenty-eight relative years away from Earth with no way of knowing what's happening back there. We are the pioneers of our species, the first explorers in this unprecedented frontier and we squandered it all for the right to sit on a throne that doesn't exist… over personal differences and reckless science that was taken for granted." Julian was on a roll now, moving up and down the stage, his pacing steady and his posture straight and confident as the audience remained still in silence, captivated by his words. "I remember a 3D mural I saw a while ago by Kieran Bolek. It read *United we stand* and had six interlocking rings on a fist. I'm not one for art but it stuck with me. When will our species ever learn to cooperate? Why do we always have to go through anguish and misery for it to happen?"

"You can't cooperate with the evolutionists, Mr Walker," Okada interrupted him.

"Shut up, let him talk," a few voices were heard from the crowd and Julian allowed a small smirk to decorate his face.

"That's what *you* think… and the same goes for them. What about the rest of us and our right to decide for ourselves? Has scientocracy become so totalitarian that we've forgotten about democracy?"

"The science dictated that the ship wouldn't handle the stresses. Their plan was bad from the beginning. It required..."

"That's not how science works." Julian didn't let her finish. "It's ever changing, constantly reviewed and partially accepted until a better hypothesis comes along. For three hundred years we believed Newton's laws to be irrefutable, only to get a deeper understanding of how the universe actually works when Einstein came along."

"Our plan would've worked," Richter found the opportunity to chime in. "We had extensive data on the trip's course."

"No, you did it for your own selfish, narcissistic agenda. You call yourself a life scientist, yet you were willing to sacrifice so many lives for your own aspirations."

"What life is there to live on this ship, Julian? We're constantly producing antidepressants because everyone is miserable, surviving mostly on gooey sludges of food, trapped in a cycle of exhausting repetition. You can't deny you've felt it yourself already. I saved as many as I could and offered them an escape out of this prison, a vision and a hope to look forward to."

"You're right... I always thought I was unlucky for having been born here, I always struggled with finding a purpose... but I recently came to the realisation that trying to find the meaning of life is futile. It doesn't hide behind some accomplishment or reaching some far away planet, or filling up a bucket list. You could be looking all your life and yet find no meaning to it. It shouldn't hurt to be alive. It should be celebrated. I would trade days of exploring new biomes for only a few seconds with the person I love. I would rather spend an hour with her in the Cylidome than a lifetime alone on Aquanis. We create meaning ourselves."

Rachel wiped the cold tears from the corner of her eyes. She wanted to rush down there, climb on stage and kiss him, nestle inside his embrace and rest her head comfortably under his chin. Julian looked at the control booth, smiling, even though he probably couldn't see her through the myriads of data overlaid on the glass. She felt a smile broaden across her own face and a warm feeling pulsated within her.

Some couples in the audience turned to kiss each other and the majority of people nodded in silence.

"My man, J, has a way with words, doesn't he?" Mark commented, leaning back in his chair and placing his feet on the terminal.

"Mr Walker," councilman Opoku started, "Since you seem to know everything, what would your great suggestion be?"

"The choice has been taken away from us, both by you and the evolutionists." Julian pointed at everyone on stage. "I say it's time to decide our future for ourselves, get all the scientists together and vote. What was it called back then, dad?" He searched for Scott at the steps of the stage. "A referendum!"

The grand hall filled with cheers and overlapping exclamations as Julian stood there, in the centre of it all, looking around him with that beautiful smile of his.

※

Rachel opened the door for Alex and motioned him to go inside. Her mum ran to him, squeezing him in her arms while her dad stood at the back against the kitchen counter.

"Did they finally clear him?" Her mum glanced at her.

"Yeah, fit to join society once again." Rachel patted her brother at the back with a grin.

Alex sighed and moved to the living room after a brief hug with their dad. He sat on the couch and crossed his arms, his eyes darting around their apartment. "I had hoped I'd wake up somewhere with windows."

"No more of that talk," her mother scolded him straight away, "These people used you and threw you away like trash."

"Let him be, Mum. He needs time to adjust," Rachel defended him, flopping on the puffy cushion next to him. Alex had been through a lot, attacking him would only make things worse.

"What happened to the rest of Icarus?" Alex lowered his voice and leant towards her.

"All confined to the lower resi of Ring Six for now."

"So it's definite then, we're not reaching Aquanis any time soon." Alex's eyes dropped to his feet and his lips pursed.

"One of the options on the ballot will be to shorten the trip but I don't know how exactly or by how many years. Julian explains it best. Come with us and you can ask him yourself."

"No thanks, I think I'll hang around here for a while."

"Ok, stay safe. Don't piss off Mum," she whispered and gave him a quick kiss on the cheek before he could protest.

The plaza in Ring Four was teeming with people, most of human-driven jobs had been halted, giving everyone an excuse to linger a bit longer around the food kiosks. Rachel was just glad she wasn't coming here with another trolley packed with boxes. Julian had moved back with his dad completely, although she wouldn't have minded an empty house now that they were officially together. He was always dodging the question when asked but Rachel knew it was because of his mother being confined on the lower levels more than Ring Six reminding him of everything that had happened there.

She spotted Scott first, recognising him from his glasses and next to him, Julian was slurping a bowl of a tasty looking soup.

"I see you're enjoying your unlimited contribution points," she gave him a kiss while his mouth was still full and sat opposite to them.

None of them said anything, only glanced at her with tense jaws and twitching lips.

"What? What now?" She asked, lifting herself slightly off the seat, expecting a secret to be whispered.

Scott pushed his glasses up his nose bridge and let out a difficult exhale. "It's Freddie... I found more data on the repository showing her involvement in Icarus since she was a child. There are some communication logs I don't dare see for myself."

"Can we not talk about her again?" Julian snapped, spitting droplets of the earthy broth as he spoke.

"Julian, she says what we had was true and I believe her."

"Dad, how can you say that when she literally left you to die?" Julian's spoon fumbled on his fingers and dropped on the floor with a clang.

"Maybe we should talk about something else then?" Rachel intervened, seeing as Julian was getting very agitated. "Have the scientists come to an agreement yet about accelerating forward? Alex was asking."

"Yeah, and I think it'll be the winning vote, or at least that's what the preliminary data shows." Scott replied.

"Of course it'll win." Julian drowned a burp behind his fist as he paused. "It's the middle ground between cosmitists and evolutionists. The ship has a high chance of survival, granted we solve some cold metal fusion issues and babies who are born now will maybe get to step on Aquanis."

"I'm sure the evos are not too happy about it." Rachel remarked.

"Well they can't do anything about it anyway from their cells."

Scott clicked his tongue and his lips parted, ready to scold Julian for his attitude but didn't utter a word.

"J, the committee is looking for you for that interview you promised." Mark appeared out of nowhere, a half-eaten power bar in his hand as he sat down next to his friend.

"Not again. What more do they want from me?" Julian stretched his arms with a stifled yawn.

"You're their hero now!" Mark dug his fingers in Julian's shoulder and squeezed, shaking him back and forth.

"Oh no, here they come," Rachel said when she caught the admin uniforms with the corner of her eye. "Come on, let's bail." She rushed around the table and pulled his arm.

Julian didn't protest, only asked where they were going as she held on to his hand, guiding him away from the residential district. No one saw them entering the Cylidome and she finally slowed down, taking the flattened path towards the middle of the overgrown flora. It was the least of their problems a few months ago to tend to their garden so everything had grown tall and wild.

"I think we lost them, where are you taking me?" Julian asked through a brief chuckle.

"Where no one can find us." She glanced at him with a smile.

She peered through the tall pine trees in the distance and let go of his hand to run towards the patch of grass that was shining bright in the absence of towering shadows.

She stood in the light and closed her eyes, letting the intricate aromas flood her nostrils.

"Oh, I see what you're doing," Julian said as he walked by her towards the centre of the clearing.

"You do, don't you," she playfully mocked his tone and grabbed his arm, pulling him down as she sat on the crunchy leaves and laid back on the soft soil.

"It seems like forever ago we were here, looking for clues about Alex's disappearance," Julian said, staring at the steel lattice above them.

"Remember you came up with that stupid idea for a picnic?"

"Hey, I was trying to distract you. I didn't know how to handle the whole situation."

"I know…" She turned to him, staring at his deep blue eyes glistening in the light. "You were there for me from start to end." Her mind traced back to everything that had happened, all the obstacles and near death experiences, all the actual deaths of people she cared about and the ones she didn't even know. "You asked me back then where I would want to live if I was born on Earth, do you remember what I said?"

"Yeah, the suburbs of a vibrant city," he rolled to the side to meet her eyes.

"I'm very glad I was born here and not on Earth. I wouldn't have met you there."

"You know, I always spent so much time in VR, visiting places, thinking about Aquanis and hating my existence on this ship but now… I'd never trade it for anything, as long as I have you."

Rachel leant over him and their lips touched, their warm breaths becoming one. She wiggled inside his embrace and they both looked up at the bright stars in the vast distance, their light piercing through the darkness from millions of miles away to grant them this moment, just the two of them on a ship in the middle of nowhere.

EPILOGUE
—Julian—
Aquanis Orbit

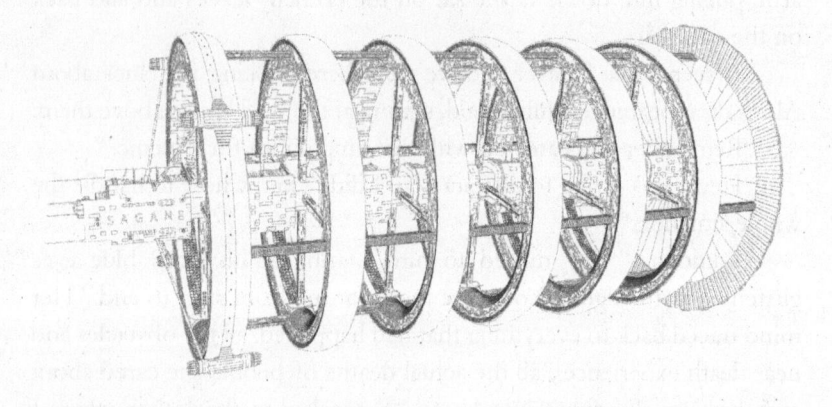

Julian laid still on the comfortable bed in the far wing of the infirmary, his frail body barely able to move. The gentle hum of machinery and life support filled the air with white noise that allowed his mind to drift and his eyes to focus once again on the view outside the window, at the majestic blue marble floating in the emptiness that surrounded it.

Aquanis, the name was fitting after all, for its vast oceans dominated the view, stretching as far as the eye could see. The dark blue waters reflected the distant sunlight, creating a glowing atmosphere like a halo enveloping the planet. Small landmasses and islands dotted the ocean, shrouded in a haze of clouds, their lush greenery and unique terrain concealed beneath the veiling mist. Its pale companion, Odoiporos, was rising behind the planet, partially shrouded in shadow, its sunny side filled with craters that could be seen even from the geosynchronous orbit the *Sagan* was occupying. It had come as a surprise to everyone to find out their new home had two moons. Odoiporos had only presented itself on Julian's telescopes when they entered the heliopause of the new system. He had objected to the name but it was supposed to be an honour—having a celestial body named after him. It meant *he who walks forever* in the long forgotten Greek language of the world they had left behind, a play on the literal interpretation of his last name. Similar in size as Earth's Luna but three quarters of the distance away, scientists were already debating the effects it would have on Aquanis—a tide powerhouse. If that wasn't enough to stir the waters of the massive oceans, the second moon, Skotos, was there to assist. Almost half the size of Odoiporos, its orbit was twice as fast around Aquanis, in a farther orbit. The numbers suggested it wouldn't be visible with the naked eye from the planet's surface, hence the name 'darkness'.

Two hundred and fifteen relative years after its first engine ignition, the *Sagan* had finally made it in one piece, old and croaky at every junction much like Julian himself. Another chapter in the human story was about to start, one that needed neither the ship nor him. He let out a soft sigh, fogging up the mask that was supplying him with oxygen and slowly turned to the sound of the door buzzing.

Rachel came in first, followed by their grandson who timidly leant out of the frame before stepping inside. Rachel sat in the chair by the bed and stroked Julian's hair with a smile, the creases around her lips stretching to unite with the wrinkles on her cheeks like an intricate mountain range.

"Hi grandpa," Sol said in his cheery voice with a slight bow of his head and a shy wave.

It was obvious the boy had come to say goodbye, they all had already. The medi-bot had given him a few more weeks of life and even though they had offered him the possibility to bend the rules and print synthetic organs, he had declined to become a machine.

He took off the mask despite Rachel's protest and breathed in the stale air of the room, narrowing his eyes to adjust from the darkness of space out his window to the luminosity of the bright spotlights.

"You can go, it's ok," he told Rachel, his voice a little more than a croaky whisper as he tried to clear his dry throat.

Rachel nodded and leant over with difficulty to kiss him on the forehead, the warmth of her cracked lips rejuvenating the life left inside him.

"I'll be in the lobby." She limped her way to the foot of the bed and caressed Sol's face before leaving the room.

His grandson bit his lips, his mouth twitching and his eyes darting around the room, anywhere other than Julian as he sat in the chair by the window and leant forward, elbows balanced on his knees. His brows had been furrowed since he had walked in, probably uncomfortable with the experience of seeing someone in his final days.

"You know…" Julian paused for a cough that shook his whole body. "When I was your age I wouldn't even dare look outside the window."

"Really?" Sol finally turned to face him and quickly diverted his gaze outside.

"Yeah, the spinning… it used to give me massive headaches."

"But you can look now, right?"

"Yeah. A lot of things in life seem impossible at first when you're young but given time, effort and proper support there's nothing you can't overcome."

"Grandpa…" the boy started, pursing his lips and meeting his eyes. "Why don't you want the cybernetic parts? You could come with us on the shuttle. Dad says we might even reach the atmosphere."

"I'm fine with having seen it from here. It's up to your generation now to explore it and make it your home," he paused to clear his throat with a cough. "Besides, a hundred and four years is more than enough."

"Are you really not sad that you travelled all this way and… and you won't see it?"

If he didn't feel another cough coming he would've laughed. Kids had no filter, they would say exactly what was in their heads.

"Sol, I'll tell you something to remember from your grandpa, alright? Some people were born in mediaeval times on Earth fighting to survive, others during the space revolution but never went to space, others were born on Ganymede and never left the mines… I lived my whole life in the middle of nowhere and you will soon live yours on a lush, new planet. If you're waiting for an external factor to make your life interesting, you're going to miss the opportunity to create something interesting and unique yourself."

Sol tilted his head, probably trying to process Julian's long sentence. "Does exploring Aquanis count as an external factor? Because I can't wait to do that."

"Yes, it does. What I mean though is that even though you'll live through the age of exploration, it's your kids that will build the first cities and your grandkids will probably expand to metropolis and their kids will expand to take over the whole system.

Sol stared at him quizzically, uneasy silence following as a series of planets and cities ran through Julian's mind like a video on high speed where every second represented a century. Buildings climbed to the sky in quick succession and hundreds of suns rose and set while the wind carried the clouds over an endless horizon. He saw spaceships much like his own flying across the vastness of space and reaching other planets. New cities grew, each one with their own unique architecture style, an infinite palette of colours and shapes.

He didn't want to scare the kid but at twelve years old, he was old enough to hear it and Julian's time was running out anyway.

"I see," Sol muttered, his lips parting to continue but only producing a sigh instead.

"All I'm saying is life is in the present, now. If you focus too much on the future, you'll forget to actually live."

The door buzzed but the doctor remained at the frame. "Your parents are asking for you," she announced and extended a hand to Sol.

"I'm coming," the boy replied with a nod and approached Julian's bed as the door shut with a thud. He was careful not to step or push any of the tubes that were keeping Julian alive and nested his head under Julian's chin. "I love you, grandpa." There was a crack in his voice but he didn't cry. Brave kid.

"I love you too, Sol." Julian whispered and softly tousled the boy's hair, shifting downwards to caress his back.

His grandson headed for the door and Julian was alone again. He pondered on whether he wished he was young again like Sol, able to explore every nook of Aquanis, every cave and underwater biome, dip his feet in the sand and watch the sun rise, letting the rays pierce the clouds and warm his face. It had once been his dream when he was his age. He remembered himself obsessing over the fact that he was born on the *Sagan* right at the middle of the trip, spending all his time in virtual reality to experience the planet his great grandparents had left behind. He almost expected that bitter feeling to resurface just by thinking about it but it never came. He smiled and took a deep breath, drifting to the side of the pillow to stare out the window again.

The blue planet was spinning on its tilted axis ever so slightly, streaks of clouds performing their tireless ethereal dance orchestrated by the Coriolis force. The moons had moved further away as they followed their orbit around the ocean world, a cosmic ballet that would continue for millennia to come. The clouds on the southern hemisphere parted and for a second he thought he saw a green light flickering on the surface—or could it have been an aurora? There were so many mysteries waiting down there for Sol's generation to solve.

He closed his eyes, the view etched in his mind but swiftly replaced by the faces of his loved ones, moments of laughter and intimacy succeeding one another as a profound sense of gratitude swept through him. His own journey had come to an end but he found solace in the life he had lived. For without him and everyone else who'd fought beside him, there wouldn't be a generation left to witness the grandeur of Aquanis.

It was their turn now.

ACKNOWLEDGEMENT

I don't remember the exact moment I had the idea for this book but I'm sure it derived from something Neil De Grasse Tyson had said in one of his podcasts. *My personal* astrophysicist helped me every step of the way without even knowing it and it would be a terrible oversight if he didn't occupy the first place in my acknowledgements. You might have already noticed the dedication at the beginning or the name of the shuttles throughout the story. Dr Tyson not only sparked my curiosity for science but also offered me a new worldview, a cosmic perspective. When I first started writing this book, it was a well-kept secret in fear of ridicule. The only person that knew of my aspiration to become an author was my wife. Emile (the Lithuanian name for Emily) has been there since the beginning, since I shared my very first thoughts about the plot back in our flat in Elephant & Castle. The sheer patience of the woman still astounds me, sitting there and listening to all my twists and plot holes with genuine interest. I am confident I wouldn't have even gotten half way through the first draft if it wasn't for her.

A massive thanks to Serran Aziz-Benstead, for without my critique partner and her immense help with prose and plot, this would have been a complete mess. I am very lucky to have met her when I was still in the first draft.

A special thanks to my editor Anna Schechter (and the overarching editor Max Gorlov), who urged me to raise the stakes and urgency in the plot and helped me get from a mediocre first draft to an interesting manuscript.

Lastly, I owe thanks to all my Alpha and Beta readers whose feedback made me see problems I hadn't spotted before and opened new avenues for improvement.

ABOUT THE AUTHOR

Ilias Siametis studied architecture but ended up becoming a construction planner. When the work day ends he is a father of twins and after bedtime he finally becomes a writer. A big science nerd, he's in love with the stars and the future. In the rare case he has some free time, he designs and 3D prints all sorts of things, reminiscing the time he used to play games instead. He lives in London, UK.

Instagram: isiametiswrites
TikTok: iliassiametiswrites

Milton Keynes UK
Ingram Content Group UK Ltd.
UKHW042249030424
440589UK00004B/221